IR

D0374898

UNWELCOME TO WISE ACRES. HERE THERE BE GRAMMONSTERS.

ALSO BY DALE E. BASYE

DALE E. BASYE

ILLUSTRATIONS BY **BOB DOB**

RANDOM HOUSE  NEW YORK

WiSE ACRES

THE SEVENTH CiRCLE OF
~ HECK ~

Text copyright © 2013 by Dale E. Basye
Jacket art and interior illustrations copyright © 2013 by Bob Dob

Visit us on the Web! randomhouse.com/kids

Educators and librarians, for a variety of teaching tools, visit us at
RHTeachersLibrarians.com

wherethebadkidsgo.com

Library of Congress Cataloging-in-Publication Data
Basye, Dale E.
Wise Acres : the seventh circle of Heck / by Dale E. Basye ;
illustrations by Bob Dob. —1st ed.
p. cm.
Summary: "Milton and Marlo Fauster are sent to Wise Acres,
the circle of Heck for kids who sass back, where the new vice principal,
Lewis Carroll, has them debate in a War of the Words broadcast throughout the
underworld, with a reward of heaven for the winner and the ultimate punishment,
the real h-e-double-hockey-sticks, for the loser." —Provided by publisher
ISBN 978-0-307-98185-1 (trade : alk. paper) —
ISBN 978-0-307-98186-8 (lib. bdg. : alk. paper) — ISBN 978-0-307-98187-5 (ebook)
[1. Brothers and sisters—Fiction. 2. Behavior—Fiction. 3. Future life—Fiction.
4. Reformatories—Fiction. 5. Schools—Fiction. 6. Humorous stories.]
I. Dob, Bob, ill. II. Title.
PZ7.B2938Wi 2013 [Fic]—dc23 2012037195

Printed in the United States of America

10 9 8 7 6 5 4 3 2 1

First Edition

COMEDIAN GROUCHO MARX ONCE SAID, "OUTSIDE OF A DOG,
A BOOK IS MAN'S BEST FRIEND. INSIDE OF A DOG,
IT'S TOO DARK TO READ." SO I CAN THINK OF NO BETTER
DEDICATION FOR A BOOK ABOUT BOOKS AND READING AND
LANGUAGE THAN MY LATE DOG SIMON CORN KERNEL HAPPY
TAILS BASYE, OR SIMON FOR SHORT. (ACTUALLY, AS A
HEIGHT-CHALLENGED JACK RUSSELL TERROR/TERRIER,
EVERYTHING ABOUT SIMON WAS SHORT.) I IMAGINE HIM NOW IN
THE FURAFTER, A CANINE ON CLOUD NINE, GAMBOLING ABOUT ON
THE REALLY BIG FARM UPSTAIRS, EITHER CHASING SQUIRRELS OR
SOMEHOW CONVINCING THE MORE GULLIBLE DOGS TO DO IT
FOR HIM. AFTER ALL, EVERY DOG HAS HIS DAY,
AND NOW SIMON HAS AN ETERNITY OF THEM. LUCKY DOG!

★ CONTENTS ★

WISE ACRES

THE SEVENTH CIRCLE OF
~ HECK ~

FOREWORD

As many believe, there is a place above and a place below. But there are also places in between. Some not quite awfully perfect and others not quite perfectly awful.

One of these places is crowded with kids with sharp tongues that cut deep, kids who sass back with a vengeance, kids who—if served a bowl of alphabet soup—don't merely see lunch but see an opportunity to deeply offend.

Even just talking about Wise Acres—the seventh (or sixth, depending) of Heck's sinister circles—is enough to get one's verbal hackles up.

Sticks and stones may break your bones, but down here, words hurt far, far more. Especially when wielded by those with a cool and cruel demeanor (and in Heck, demeanor you are, the better).

You tart-tongued tykes out there are likely grumbling as to why being "sassy" is even a bad thing to begin with. Well, it depends on who you ask. To your parents, teachers, and most any authority figure, sassiness is soundly in the "bad" column. To your friends, it's probably endlessly amusing—that is, until your sassy tongue is trained upon them, then maybe, um, not so much.

Imagine, if you will (or even if you won't, just shut your eyes and play along), a battlefield of barbs where every spiteful soldier, dug deep in their trenchant trenches, prays they never run out of ammunition. A combative zone where no one has the right to remain silent, and anything and everything you say can and will be taken out of context, garbled, spat back, and used against you in a court of finding flaw.

The mysterious Powers That Be (and any of its associated or subsidiary enterprises, including but not limited to the Powers That Be Evil) have stitched this and countless other subjective realities together into a sprawling quilt of space and time.

Some of these quantum patches may not even seem like places. But they are all around you and go by many names. Some feel like eternity. And some of them actually are eternity, at least for a little while. Think all of this sounds foolish? Well, I know you are but what am I?!

1 · TO GRAMMAR'S HOUSE WE GO

ELEVEN-YEAR-OLD MILTON FAUSTER and his thirteen-year-old sister, Marlo, were not so different from your average children making a grudging trek to their first day at a new school. Only instead of having been dropped off by distracted parents on their way to work, Milton and Marlo had been dragged kicking and screaming out of a stagecoach by decomposing demons and thrown roughly to the unhallowed ground. Instead of carrying backpacks stuffed with new notebooks and sharpened pencils, Milton cradled his pet ferret, Lucky, in a filthy kerchief while Marlo sulked along holding nothing but a grudge against the snarled web of supremely sucky events that conspired against her. And instead of making their way to a new school wearing the latest fall fashions,

3

Milton and Marlo were headed for Wise Acres—the circle of Heck for kids who sass back—dressed in shabby hand-me-downs splotched with dried blood.

Oh, and there was the whole "being stone-cold dead way before your time" thing, too.

The sleek black stagecoach, drawn by two hideous, snorting Night Mares, sped away behind the Fauster children in a tight crescent, its wooden wheels slicing across the rumpled, reddish-brown hills. The freakish whinnies of the festering horses faded away into nothing.

The only sound Milton and Marlo made as they trudged along was the crinkle of footfalls. The rolling hills seemed to be coated with a vast carpet of paper so ancient that it shredded beneath the Fausters' filthy boots. It was as if their shoes were having a secret conversation composed of dry crumples and scrunches.

A wind picked up, whipping itself into a squall. Milton coughed at the gagging, sickly sweet stench. His face and arms were speckled with dark, pricking droplets of what looked like ink. Milton glanced over at his sister. Marlo was slogging through the shredded paper just behind him, her head hung low and brooding.

Marlo sighed softly to herself and rubbed her red-rimmed eyes, wiping away a tear that left a smudge of black ink-rain on her cheek. Being dead was starting to get her down. Even her first kiss had been tainted by the fact that the boy on the other side of those perfect, pouty lips had been a fallen hit-angel who was simply using her to find Milton and slit his throat with a gleaming razor-feather.

"Oww!" Milton cried out, touching his now-bleeding cheek. He pulled out what looked like a big splinter. A few hundred feet away was a gnarled grove of nasty-looking trees. Angry blasts of wind sheared swarms of needles from the trees and sent them whizzing into the air like clouds of tiny wooden daggers.

"Seriously, li'l *bother*," Marlo said with a croak, her voice craggy from lack of use, "how much can a splinter possibly— *Oww!*"

Marlo yanked a small needle, sort of like a pine needle, from her forearm. After examining it, though, she discovered it was really a tiny, tightly rolled parchment. Marlo unrolled it and squinted at the itsy-bitsy letters formed in the pulpy, leaflike paper:

What are yew looking at?!

Milton glanced over Marlo's shoulder at the note, then surveyed the grove of sinister trees up ahead. The trees sported ropes of mottled, flaking bark coiling up their trunks.

"They spelled 'you' wrong," Marlo said.

"No, they didn't . . . or *it* didn't," Milton said, pointing to a nearby tree. "It's like a weird hybrid of a sycamore and a yew tree."

"Must be a *Syca-Yew*," Marlo said as she crumpled up

the parchment and tossed it at the tree. "Well, I'm sick of you, *too,* you dumb tree!"

Milton squinted through his broken Coke-bottle glasses at another clump of spindly trees covered with furrowed bark and sharp, pink-purple leaves. A gust of wind rustled the leaves, causing them to wag mockingly and—if the irritating hiss was any indication—*jeer.*

"I'm going to say, considering we're near Wise Acres, that those are a form of *Sass*afras," Milton said.

Marlo plunked down on the shredded-paper ground. "Where *is* Wise Acres anyway?" she groused, taking off her boots and massaging her aching feet. "Maybe it disappeared, too . . . just like Precocia did."

Milton sat cross-legged beside his sister.

So many unbelievable things had happened to him and Marlo since their untimely passing. Yet their latest exploits in Precocia—the circle of Heck for kids who grow up too fast—were their most unbelievable, in that not only did Precocia no longer exist, but also apparently it had never existed in the first place.

Precocia's vice principals, Napoléon and Cleopatra, had wanted to plug up the Fountain of Youth, effectively terminating childhood, making Heck—where the souls of the darned toil for all eternity or until they turn eighteen, whichever comes first—obsolete. To save childhood, Milton and Marlo had altered reality: thwarting Napoléon and Cleopatra's plot by eliminating Precocia altogether.

Milton sighed and stared up at the smudgy orange-purple sky, which looked like a bruise in the final stages of fading, and untied his kerchief pouch. Lucky, Milton's pet ferret, spilled out of the filthy rag like fuzzy white milk, pooling on the ground to yawn and stretch. Milton scratched his pet just underneath the chin. Lucky pressed into his master's touch, hoping to squeeze out every drop of sensation from the boy's just-made-for-scritching fingers before curling up and falling back asleep on Milton's lap.

"That was it?" Milton said with a smile. "That was your big day and now it's back to bed?"

A gust of wind sent another swarm of Syca-Yew needles into the air.

"Oww! *Fluffernutter!*" Marlo squealed as she sat up and picked a needle from her forehead. She unrolled the parchment leaf.

You fell out of the ugly tree and hit every branch on the way down. And I should know!

Marlo tore up the leaf in disgust. She cast it into the reeking wind. "This already blows and we're not even *there* yet!" she complained.

ZOT!!

With an explosive clap of thunder, a huge, shaggy *something* suddenly appeared a dozen yards away from Milton and Marlo. Something with big, bad eyes. And big, bad ears. And big, bad teeth. Something that looked a heck of a lot like a big, bad wolf.

"Okay, maybe the rude needlely trees weren't so bad," Marlo whispered.

The seven-foot-tall beast stood upright on its muscular haunches, looking every inch the savage monster. Its pupils "ticked" along the rims of its wide yellow eyes like the hands of a nightmarish clock. Its coarse gray fur was matted with blood. The only element detracting from the creature's untamed ferocity was the half-eaten briefcase it clutched with its razor-sharp claws.

Milton's throat was so tight and dry with fear that swallowing felt like trying to drown an inflatable pool toy.

The creature growled softly as it sniffed the air with its foam-flecked muzzle.

Lucky stirred on Milton's lap, awoken by the sudden blast of overpowering predator musk. Milton tried to clamp his ferret's jaws shut with his fingers, but he was too late. Lucky hissed and spat at the wolf-beast with a ferret's foolish fury.

The creature spun about on its massive back paws. Milton and Marlo huddled together in a petrified ball. The wolf-beast reared back, snarling, as if to pounce, then stopped short as it sniffed at Lucky.

"We've . . . g-gotta run," Milton croaked as he contorted his paralyzed lips to form words. "Now's our chance."

Marlo nodded weakly and the two of them sprang off the ground and toward the grove. The Fausters weaved past the prickly Sassafras trees that hissed and whistled at them in the sulfurous breeze. Milton could hear the wolf-beast trotting behind them. Faster and faster. Huffing and puffing and gearing up to blow them down.

"Keep . . . going," Milton panted, taking his sister's sweaty hand. "It's . . . closing in."

Marlo flopped along in her untied boots. A gust of wind pelted them with a shower of Syca-Yew splinters.

"Oww!" Marlo grunted as she and Milton tripped through the tangle of roots and low-lying branches. "It's irritating . . . like being . . . *needled*."

Their clothes ripped and torn, the Fausters cleared the grove. Milton and Marlo could finally see the gates of Wise Acres a few hundred feet ahead of them, crowning the top of the knoll like a towering tiara of gnarled black metal.

The wind shrieked beyond the small hill, chilling Milton's blood. Branches snapped behind him and his sister.

"AHROOOOOOO WOO WOOOahhhhh!" howled the wolf-beast as it drew nearer.

"I think I just peed a bit," Marlo muttered as she cast a wary glance behind her. "Hopefully that will make me taste bad."

The trees shuddered in an oncoming rush of thrashing violence. Milton and Marlo could see the dark, shaggy shape of the creature lumbering toward them through the splintering trees.

"Run!" Milton shouted.

He and his sister scaled the steep hill, earning every labored footfall. The gates of Wise Acres were now less than a hundred feet away.

The wolf-beast parted the Syca-Yews as if they were a spindly wooden curtain. It glared furiously at Milton and Marlo, its pinpricked pupils ticking along the rims of its burning yellow eyes like a time bomb. It bounded toward them, pulverizing the trees behind it with a thump of its savage haunches.

"We can't . . . make it . . . in time," Milton gasped.

Marlo turned with a sudden surge of indignant rage. "Who's afraid of you, you big, bad ugly wolf?!" she roared.

Startled, the creature skidded to a halt.

"Well, *we* are," Marlo continued. "You can probably smell that. But we're not going to just stand here and let you eat us! Not by the hair on my chinny chin chin that I probably should have plucked before I died!"

The wolf-beast squinted its glowing yellow-green eyes at Marlo, momentarily appraising her as a potential threat before letting loose a keening howl.

"*AHROOOOOOO WOO WOOOahhhhh!*"

"Nice try," Milton muttered as he clutched his sister's hand.

"I have a feeling this ain't gonna be pretty," Marlo whispered.

Isn't *going to be pretty,* Milton corrected in his head as the creature bared its long, yellow fangs and pounced.

2 · BIRDS OF A FEATHER MOCK TOGETHER

THE BLOOD–SPATTERED WOLF–BEAST lunged at Milton and Marlo. Yet suddenly, as if tugged back by an invisible leash, it stopped short. Milton peeked through his fingers. The creature rose onto its haunches and stared off into space, flickering back and forth. It was as if it were straddling two dimensions, its weight shifting from one reality to another.

Milton looked in the direction of the beast's startled gaze but could see nothing. The creature seemed to sputter on and off like a dying flashlight before it was engulfed by a large shadow. It dropped its mauled briefcase to the ground before covering its gruesome head and cowering. Whimpering like a scolded Chihuahua pup, the wolf-beast abruptly . . .

ZOT!!

. . . disappeared into thin air.

The wind whistled its unnerving tune. After a few fearful seconds, Milton and Marlo disentangled themselves and rose to their feet. Marlo dusted off her filthy dress.

"I must have scarified it," she said.

The half-eaten briefcase twitched on the ground. Something inside its battered, brown-leather shell rustled and scratched. The fur on Lucky's fuzzy white back stiffened.

Milton cautiously approached the case.

"What could possibly be in a wolf's briefcase?" he said as he knelt in front of it.

Marlo shrugged. "Lunch, maybe? Three little pigs in a blanket?"

Milton shook his head as he carefully opened the gash in the leather case.

"It seemed pretty hungry for something packing a—"

Something white and fuzzy darted out of the briefcase.

"Lucky?"

A pink-eyed ferret scrambled onto the shredded-paper ground. It sniffed the air with a twitch of its wet nose. Lucky—identical to the strange new animal in every way—crept toward the other ferret cautiously and took deep snoutfuls of the intruder's musk. The two ferrets hissed heartily at each other before attacking in a flurry of gnashing teeth and scrabbling claws.

Milton and Marlo pried the furious animals apart, their forearms paying the price in the form of countless oozing ferret scratches. Milton studied the squirming ferret in Marlo's arms.

"This will sound crazy—"

"As most sentences beginning with 'this will sound crazy' generally do . . ."

"—but I think *both* of them are Lucky."

"What? But how?"

Milton shook his head as he knelt down and felt around inside the torn leather briefcase.

"I don't know," Milton muttered. "Maybe something in here will help explain. . . ."

He pulled out a torn three-by-five-inch index card. Milton puzzled over the gibberish written upon it.

hewhaY

"Hewhay?" Marlo asked, looking over her brother's shoulder. "What does that mean?"

"No clue," he said with a shrug. Milton tucked the torn card into his pants pocket.

Milton turned to face the gates of Wise Acres (a circle that, before—in another version of the afterlife—had been called Lipptor). Gnarled white-yellow sticks and rough gray stones were lashed against the rusted rails with what looked like used typewriter ribbon. The sticks—which resembled broken bones—formed hundreds of Xs along the warped, weather-beaten wrought-iron fence encircling the top of the hill, with the knobbly rocks filling in the gaps.

Milton wiped the smears off his glasses with his thumb. He squinted at the gate. The iron rails were actually old typewriter parts welded together into motley lumps: cylinders pockmarked with thousands of hammered characters, type bars twisted into braids, and carriage-return levers forced into little bows. Miles of worn typewriter ribbon were woven around the iron bars so that they looked like dreary, neglected Maypoles.

"How do you think we get in?" Marlo asked. "There's so much junk here, I can't even find the—"

The two Luckys hissed in unison. The Fausters could hear frantic scratching, followed by a quick meow and a pungent blast of manure.

Twenty feet away was a patch of pink grit. A gray-striped tabby cat with a leather pouch grinned a wide, vaguely guilty smirk and scampered away through the bars. Milton and Marlo bounded after it. Something was written on the pink, tongue-shaped plot of gravel.

UNWELCOM TOO WIZE AKERZ, read the message, spelled out in fresh cat poo.

Marlo tried to wave the acrid stench away. "Ugh . . . that's one smart cat, but his spelling *stinks*." She scanned the tangle of bars. "How do you think we get— Wait, what's this? A doorbell?"

Marlo jabbed a raspberry-colored button inset in one of the wrought-iron rails. A long black tongue, protruding from two black lips, waggled back at Marlo, spraying her with spit.

PPPTHHPTHPFFTHPPPT!!!

Marlo scowled and wiped the slobber from her face. "I can already tell I'm going to hate this place. . . ."

The wind kicked up. It blew a spray of black ink droplets from behind the gates while sending the Sassafras grove into another bout of rustling jeers.

Milton gulped. "Whatever we do, we should try to get inside," he said, casting a wary glance at the darkening sky. "Before we meet any more wolves."

Milton noticed a pair of metal hands welded above the black lips that had given his sister a wet Bronx cheer. They were attached to a pair of cast-iron faces that thumbed their noses at the Fausters. Milton grabbed one of the hands.

"Pull," he said, gesturing to the other hand with his head.

Marlo wrapped her pale Goth fingers around the large, black metal hand and heaved herself backward. After a couple of full-body tugs, Milton and Marlo jerked open the heavy iron gate and wedged themselves through the gap.

Concealed inside the contorted fence of sticks,

stones, and corroded iron bars were large, rounded stone plates—twenty-six of them—each with a letter of the alphabet carved into the smooth rock. Rushing rivers of ink gushed around the stone circles, sloshing against them with sporadic explosions of pitch-black spray.

The lettered plates were arranged like the keys of a massive typewriter in three rows—Z to M, A to L, and Q to P—leading up to a crescent-shaped trench filled with long iron sledgehammers. Perched atop the hill's peak was a massive black drum, its sleek head facing the Fausters as they crept inside the enclosure. The gate squealed closed behind them, shutting with a thunderous clang. Directly in front of them was a large, heavy-duty turnstile, like the kind one might find at an amusement park, only the *last* thing the Fausters were presently feeling was *amused*.

Sprouting from opposite sides of the compound were huge hand-shaped trees. Their thick "thumb" limbs were tucked into deep shafts in the sides of the hill where the rivers of ink issued forth. The trees made it seem as if the hill itself were a giant, obnoxious kid, mocking all who entered. Their pale gray leaves twitched nervously.

"The leaves are weird," Milton murmured as he strained to bring them into sharper focus through his cracked lenses.

"Those aren't leaves," Marlo said as she tentatively stepped toward them for a better look. "They're—"

Marlo had inadvertently passed through the turnstile. It clicked forebodingly behind her. The hill trembled beneath their feet and a piercing whistle rent the air. The trees' "leaves" began to screech.

"—*birds,*" Marlo said.

The pale gray birds flew from the branches in great feathery clouds, leaving the trees suddenly, almost embarrassingly, denuded. They came at the Fausters like a squadron of jet fighters.

"They're coming right for us!" Marlo squealed.

"They're coming right for us!" the birds screeched back in mocking unison.

"Mockingbirds," Milton said as the flocks descended.

A ferocious squawking storm of beaks and claws tore at their clothes. Marlo screamed as she tried to bat them away. The birds mimicked her cry as they swept into the sky, circling, building momentum for another attack. Milton pressed himself against the turnstile, yet it wouldn't budge.

"What do we do?" Marlo yelped.

"What do we do?!"

"The stones," Milton said. "I think I know what we have to do."

The dark, screeching clots of mockingbirds rushed back down toward the Fausters. Marlo, her cheeks scratched and bleeding, gazed fearfully at the sky.

"What? Throw them? You know, like killing two birds with one stone?"

"No . . . I think we have to spell our names," Milton replied. "The turnstile only allows one kid at a time, so maybe we have to type our names using the steps to somehow get inside."

The mockingbirds spilled down from the sky like feathered bombs.

"Cover your eyes!" Milton yelled.

"Cover your eyes!" the birds screeched as they attacked the Fausters.

Milton and Marlo dove to the ground, covering their heads as the birds pecked and tore at their backs. The flock of angry birds flew past, pooling together into a dark gray cloud.

Marlo rose shakily to her feet.

"Okay, Brainiac, this better work, or else there's gonna be an all-night noogie dance party busting moves on your head," she said, brandishing a row of pointy knuckles.

The mockingbirds swarmed together in swooshing, swirling eddies, gathering deadly speed before darting down from the sky in cruel formation.

"Hurry!" Milton yelled.

"Hurry!" the birds jeered.

Marlo tore across the shredded-paper ground.

She hopped onto the circular stone marked "M." One of the iron sledgehammers nestled in the trench slammed into the side of the huge black drum.

"*M!*" the drum boomed, leaving a large "M" imprinted in its quivering skin.

The mockingbirds rushed past the Fausters in a vicious, pecking surge. Marlo clouted herself in the head as a bird, trapped in her unruly blue hair, jabbed at her scalp with its pointy beak.

"Run to the 'A'!" Milton yelled, pointing to the stone step.

"*Run to the 'A'!*" the birds screeched.

Marlo hopped down from the stone circle as the birds streaked up to the sky. She sprinted along the next row of steps, sloshing along in the shallow gush of ink. Marlo dove onto the last stone. It clicked, sending another sledgehammer pounding into the drum.

"*A!*" boomed the drum on top of the hill.

Marlo bounded off the step and, with a few skips up the slope, hurled herself against the next stone.

"*R!*"

The mockingbirds coiled together like a great plumed serpent about to strike.

Marlo wiped away the sweat dripping down into her stinging eyes. She stared down the row of large stone typewriter keys. The next letter was at the very end of the second row. She hopped down from the step and ran for all she was worth.

"Here I am," she panted to herself. "Just a girl . . . darned for all eternity . . . going straight to—"

"*L!*" the drum thundered as Marlo rolled across the round "L" step.

She lay there, gasping for breath, the cool stone slab leeching away the sting from the wounds on her back.

"Hurry!" Milton yelled from behind the turnstile. "Just one more!"

"*Just one more!*" mocked the birds as they dive-bombed Marlo, plunging down—beaks-first—from the sky.

Marlo screamed and spun in tight circles, frantically waving her arms in the air as she sloshed across the coursing stream of ink and flopped down, face-first on the final stone letter.

"*O!*"

The enormous drum rattled, with the name MARLO fading away to nothing into its vibrating skin. It rotated until it faced the dark pink-purple sky. The mockingbirds alighted upon the large hand-shaped trees, resuming their original perches along the finger branches.

The drumhead popped open, revealing a spiral metal staircase that led deep down into the hill. Marlo rolled off the "O" stone and clambered toward the drum opening. She eyed the mockingbirds carefully as she approached.

Marlo stepped inside the stairwell.

"Catch you on the flip side, Diet Squirt."

Milton nodded as the drumhead closed over Marlo.

The enormous black drum rotated back to its original position. Milton took a deep breath and pushed hard against the turnstile. This time, it opened.

The hill quivered and shook. The piercing whistle sounded and the mockingbirds exploded into sudden, furious flight.

Milton ran for the nearby "M" stone and quickly scrambled on top of it. A sledgehammer pounded the drum.

"*M!*" it boomed, leaving behind a dripping black "M," barely visible against the drum's taut black skin.

The mockingbirds whipped themselves into a squawking cyclone above. Milton bounded across the slope, sloshing through the cascading rivers of ink, and spelled his name as quickly as his legs would allow.

Just as the birds rained down upon him like feathered death, Milton slid onto the "N" step.

"*N!*" the drum boomed.

The name MILTON disappeared into the skin of the black drum as it rotated atop the hill. The drumhead popped open, granting access to the secret stairwell.

"Thanks, Marlo," Milton mumbled sarcastically. "No, really, you go on ahead . . . don't wait up. I'll be fine. . . ."

Milton lay on the cool stone slab.

Another circle, full of bitter teachers and miserable kids. Why bother? Marlo and I did something huge. We somehow undid something in the logical framework of Heck, a realm ruled by rules. But what use was it all? We're still here. Heck is still in business. . . .

A pulsing whistle screamed in the distance. Milton sighed and rose wearily to his feet.

No rest for the unjustly-accused-of-being-wicked . . .

He staggered toward the drum and cautiously stepped inside.

The drumhead sealed shut over Milton's head as he stumbled down the turret staircase in the dark. The air was heavy with a stale tang that tickled Milton's sinuses. There was also a sharp undercurrent of . . . *burning.*

Wise Acres, Milton thought with trepidation. *Where the sassy kids go.* He forced his stiff lips into a confident smirk.

"Sticks and stones may break my bones, but words can never hurt me," he mumbled just before tripping on a step. *"Right?!"*

3 · LiViNG iN A TAUNTED HOUSE

"HAVE A NICE trip, Li'l Bro Pipsqueak?" Marlo said as Milton, crumpled on the ground, rose slowly to his feet.

Marlo was loitering by a post at the end of the spiral stairs where a demonized parrot roosted.

"Brock! Li'l Bro Pipsqueak!" squawked the mangy, sparsely feathered parrot, its evil eyes gleaming cold green fire. Marlo swatted the creature away.

"Hey, only *I* get to say stuff like that to my lame nerdy brother!" she yelled.

"Thanks?" Milton said as the parrot's black-and-blue feathers fluttered to the floor like plumed confetti in an irritating-bird parade.

Milton squinted out past an arched Gothic doorway that led into Wise Acres. It was a dirty, poorly lit dump, from what Milton could make out. Ragged halls branched out from beyond the stairwell. The halls resembled rambling tunnels twisting through a mountain of compressed paper, with stray pages flapping in the stale breeze.

Both Luckys suddenly reared back—cradled in the arms of a Fauster—and hissed matching blasts of anchovy breath.

Two roly-poly demons with long snouts and perky, pointy ears waddled toward them. It was as if some mad scientist had surgically installed a hyphen between a pig and a kangaroo, making a "pig-aroo." The creatures were so cute that Marlo's knees turned instantly to tapioca pudding. She squatted to the ground.

"Awwww," she cooed, holding her arms out for an embrace. "Just *look* at you two adorable—"

Long snakelike tongues shot out of the demons' mouths and coiled around Milton's and Marlo's ankles.

"Aaaaaaaarrrrrdvaaaarrrrksssss!" Milton screamed as he and his sister were dragged by their ankles. The demons' sticky tongues coiled tightly as the demons toddled backward along the corridor.

Wise Acres—as best as Milton could see as he skidded across layers of dust and crumbling debris—was a meandering, subterranean burrow. With all of the trash and broken bric-a-brac, it looked like hordes of hoarders had hoarded their hoards here.

Pages from torn-up old library books that people

had written in (something that irritated Milton to no end) and old instruction manuals for outdated technology (*VCRs for Dummies* . . . *How to Install Your Dial-Up Modem* . . .) were strewn along the corridor. Milton reached out for the wall. A piece of it tore off in his hand.

It's like someone dug out shafts in a book mine, Milton thought as he bounced up and down on his back.

An electronic news ticker was installed along the peeling, pale-yellow walls. It displayed a gush of intensely uninteresting "news" streaming past in a blur of bright green digital characters.

Just got home. Totally BORED!! Going to microwave some broccoli. Yummm! . . . Hey! Hey! What's up? Nothing much. How bout u? Same here . . . An idea for a blog occurred to me about how I write my blogs. So I decided to blog about it . . . u comin 2nite?! lol yeah b/c u r drivin me—thx!!!!! :) . . .

The aardvark demons untied their tongues and sent the Fausters tumbling down into a tumbledown tearoom. Milton and Marlo lay on the cracked, mold-green linoleum floor—filthy and panting—surrounded by gawking, sneering children sitting stiffly on mismatched lawn furniture.

Milton scanned the diverse group of faces. Though vastly different, the faces themselves were all arranged in the same way: in cold, carefully crafted formations of contempt.

Marlo trembled beside her brother. For some reason, none of the other circles of Heck had struck her in quite this way. There, most of the kids were too busy being persecuted by Principal Bubb, power-hungry vice principals, and assorted other demonic entities to actually turn on one another. But not here—Marlo could instantly tell. In Wise Acres, it was clearly every kid for him- or herself.

The long moment crested like a wave. A malicious glimmer ignited the cold glares of the children, passing from one to the other like a match, until suddenly . . .

"MWUAHAHAHAHAHA!!!!"

The room detonated with mocking jeers. The walls shoved the laughter back and forth, like a bunch of bullies throwing around a foreign-exchange student. The laughter was sharp and cruel, the children's mouths smiling but their eyes glittering like frozen beetles.

Milton rose off the filthy floor, ignoring the hoots, hollers, and finger-pointing. He helped Marlo to her feet.

"This doesn't bother you, does it?" Marlo said to her brother. "All of the laughing."

Milton shrugged. "I'm used to it," he said, pushing up his glasses. "When you're in the Chess Club, Knowledge Bowl, Science Olympiad, and the Junior United Nations, you develop a pretty thick skin to ridicule."

Marlo gazed at her brother with, while not quite awe, at least something in awe's overflow parking lot.

"Not me," Marlo replied, smoothing out her shabby, hopelessly wrinkled dress. "I'm not used to being on this side of Laugh-at-You Avenue. But just you wait: I'm about to give them all a piece of my—"

A shapely woman in a flowing white robe appeared suddenly at Marlo's side. She stuck a flat piece of blue wood on Marlo's tongue.

"Wait, what are you—" Milton asked just before the woman wedged a piece of wood into his mouth.

The beautiful, barefoot woman, her dark curly hair piled up on top of her head, grinned at the Fausters. Milton squinted at the woman's beaming untarnished smile and felt himself disappear inside, but in a good way. Marlo rolled her eyes at her besotted brother.

"I am the goddess Peitho," the lovely woman said. "And welcome to the Audaci-Tea House! You're just in time for Vice Principal Carroll's latest story!"

Marlo stuck out her tongue. It felt numb, heavy, and—in a weird way—kind of sad.

"Wha give?" she mumbled.

"Tongue depressors," the lovely woman replied. "The new vice principal prefers a speechless audience. He's only been here a week, so he doesn't realize yet that it takes more than a Novocain-soaked stick to tamp down *these* tart tongues! Excuse me . . ."

An odd-looking man was sitting in the corner of the

café. He wore a Victorian waistcoat and checked his pocket watch with the obsessive incessancy of a teenage girl checking her cell phone.

"Thice Pinthibal Cawoll?" Milton mumbled with his clinically depressed tongue. "*The* Lewith Cawoll?"

"Whothz he?" Marlo asked.

"He wote *Alith in Wonderland.*"

Milton found it odd that Principal Bubb would suddenly switch vice principals right before he and his sister arrived in Wise Acres. The principal was a time-less creature set in her wicked ways, not one to go out on a *whim* and make hasty changes. She was obviously up to something downright despicable. But what?

Vice Principal Carroll was seated before a nest of fringed pillows, lounging on a small rosewood love seat carved with delicate leaves and bunches of grapes. One by one, the other children left their lawn chairs and sat down on the pillows. Milton watched the vice principal daintily sip a cup of tea. The man seemed fragile and fussy, like some quaint porcelain figurine set upon a grandmother's mantelpiece.

"Ch-children," Vice Principal Carroll said with a slight stammer as he beckoned Milton and Marlo for-ward. "Come c-closer . . . the t-time has come to t-talk of many things: of shoes and ships and sealing wax . . . of cabbages and kings . . ."

Milton and Marlo sat down on a pair of unoccupied

pillows at the edge of the vice principal's story-time solar system.

A mousy little girl with stringy brown curls, old granny glasses, and a pinched expression (as if sucking on an invisible lemon) looked back at the Fausters.

"Nice entrance," the girl said with a smirk, fighting to enunciate despite her depressed tongue.

She held out her tiny white hand. Milton held out his hand in kind, yet the girl ignored it and proceeded to pet one of the Luckys, who was poking out of Milton's filthy shirt.

"Ferrets . . . cool," the girl said. "My name is Pansy Cornett."

"I'm Milton," Milton said, chewing on his tongue as if to give the sluggish piece of meat in his mouth CPR. "This is my sister, Marlo."

"Where are you from?" Pansy asked.

"Kansas."

Pansy snorted. "You know what you call a smart, attractive person in Kansas?"

"No, what?" Milton replied.

"A *tourist* . . ."

Vice Principal Carroll removed several pages from his waistcoat pocket before glancing fearfully at the children as if they were a mob of kinderghosts who had suddenly materialized before him.

"W-well then, I would like to read a poem I wrote

just this morning," he said as he spread out the papers on his knee. "It's called 'Molly Coddles Codswallop'!"

Molly coddles codswallop
With cake and party favors.
Her rocking horses gallop
At words with strange new flavors.
These playful verbal dollops
Dance on her tongue to savor.

A pair of talking shoes,
Molly crayons to her feet,
In color-blinded hues,
They giggle down the street.
A lobster grows confused,
"What a shame I cannot speak!"

The children stared at one another, sitting atop their pillows.

"That made no sense whatsoever," a serious-looking boy with a knitted brow said.

"Like the part where the lobster said he couldn't talk," a pretty girl with burgundy-streaked bangs and too much lip gloss added. "I mean, how could he tell us that?"

Vice Principal Carroll pinched the bridge of his nose, just between his sunken eyes. "*It's a p-poem,* Mr. Babcock and Miss Youngblood. About n-not being about anything."

"*I know what your poem is about,*" the boy, Mr.

Babcock, said with a smirk before looking down at his watch. "About half-past interesting . . ."

The children chuckled, their tongues recovering from their brief depression.

"Seriously," the boy added. "*I* could write a poem better than that."

Vice Principal Carroll shook his head. "Everything is easier said than done. . . ."

"Except for talking," Marlo interjected. "That's about the same."

The children trained their cold, glittering eyes upon her. She swallowed as the lip-gloss girl, Miss Young-blood, and Mr. Babcock exchanged eye rolls.

"Um . . . *whatever*," Mr. Babcock said coldly. "It's just that . . . what good is poetry anyway? All that rhyming mumbo jumbo . . ."

"How I tire of dragging my work down to a reader's l-lowly l-level!" Vice Principal Carroll shouted, rising quickly to his feet. The upholstered love seat fell on its carved, serpentine back. "Miss Peitho! It's sn-snack time!"

The vice principal stormed out of the Audaci-Tea House, leaving several sheets of paper behind in his wake. The children grumbled as the goddess returned carrying a large tray held upright by a neck strap. On the tray were piles of different-colored soaps and a pitcher of deep-red tea.

The goddess poured two glasses of tea and handed

them to the Fausters. Marlo took a sip and grimaced, her face collapsing like a soufflé made of used Kleenex.

"*Tart!*" she gasped. "My tongue feels all tight and shrively!"

Peitho nodded knowingly. "Sassy-Frass tea," she said in her milk-and-honey voice. "For extra-tart tongues."

"What's with the soap?" Marlo asked. "Do we have to wash up before we eat or something?"

Peitho's lips curled like red ribbon on a Christmas present. "Something like that," she said as she held a bar of bright pink soap to her flawless face. "Finally, a soap with a FLAVOR you can SAVOR!" Peitho exclaimed with all of the effervescent perkiness of a glamorous game show presenter. "It's Double-Bubble Soap: the OFFICIAL flavored soap of Wise Acres! Double-Bubble Soap gives you great suds and a treat for your taste buds: plus a DELICIOUS SURPRISE INSIDE! So whether you're in the bath or the shower, you can scrub up and chow down with the yummiest soap around. Double-Bubble Soap: Wash your mouth out with luscious flavor!"

"Um . . . is this some kind of commercial?" Marlo interrupted.

The goddess scowled at Marlo. "It's called *product placement*," she said out of the side of her mouth. "The good people at Chemi-licious Industries generously provide their discontinued products for *free* in exchange for this endorsement."

Milton stared at Peitho with faraway eyes and a soft, gummy smile smeared above his chin like a micro-waved crayon.

The goddess undid the strap around her neck. "My, I'm *so* tired," she said, widening her deep chocolate eyes. "I wish some strong young man would help me serve all the—"

"I'll do it!" Milton chirped as he took Peitho's tray and hooked it around his neck. The goddess blessed Milton with another megawatt smile and pinched his blushing cheek. "And they say chivalry is dead," she cooed. "Though we *all* are, so maybe they're right!" Peitho sashayed away in a wiggling swish of sheer white linen.

"If this soap tastes gross, I can always lick you," Marlo said as they walked over to the first group of chuckling children.

"Why is that?" Milton replied groggily, as if waking up from a dream.

"Because you're a *sucker*."

Two kids—a boy and a girl—with glasses and stringy brown hair crossed their arms and glared at Milton and Marlo.

"Hi!" the girl said coldly. "I'm a human being! What are you?"

Marlo clutched her side. "*Please* . . . I had an appendectomy right before I died. Don't make me laugh or the sutures might split."

The girl sneered and shook her head. "Whatever, new girl . . . Hey, dweeb. I'll have the peanut butter soap with a grape jelly middle."

Milton handed the girl a light-brown piece of soap that oozed purple goop from the center.

"Mashed potato soap with gravy inside," the boy said.

The strap bit into Milton's neck. It felt like he was being hanged, backward, in slow motion. After handing the boy his snack, Milton pulled at the strap with his finger. The boy snickered.

"I'd make fun of you about that, but I fell for it, too," he said in a voice huskier than his apparent years.

"What do you mean?"

The girl snorted. "Peitho is the goddess of persuasion. She gets all of the boys and even some of the girls to do her work for her."

A scowling little boy with a brown stocking cap stormed over. "You're an ugly twerp . . . and I'll have the pizza-flavored soap with mozzarella cheese inside."

Milton handed the boy his soap.

Marlo leaned into her brother. "You can't just take that. . . . You've got to sling it back."

"But I don't want to dignify dumb remarks like that with a response," Milton said as a girl grabbed a bar of corn chip soap with a salsa center.

"You've *got* to," Marlo whispered as the children chomped into their soap. "This place is like prison."

"Prison? What do you know about prison?"

"You've got to immediately single out the toughest prisoner and beat him up."

Marlo grabbed the wrist of a little girl whose face was almost totally obscured by a mop of teased blond hair.

"Hey . . . who's the sassiest kid here?" Marlo asked, scanning the room. Her eyes settled on the serious boy and the girl with the burgundy-streaked bangs. "Is it them?"

"Moses Babcock and Cookie Youngblood?" the girl mumbled, her mouth frothing. "They go for the throat whenever they open their mouths, but they're not the meanest kids here."

"Yeah? Then who is?"

Just then, a stocky badger demon with white bands streaked across its gray-and-black face marched into the Audaci-Tea House, wheeling a girl on a dolly.

"*That's* the sassiest kid in Wise Acres," the girl said, scooping up a bar of spaghetti-flavored soap with a marinara middle. "Moxie Wortschmerz."

The little girl couldn't have been more than eight years old. Her greasy light-brown hair was tied tight with elastic bands sporting little colored balls on the ends. Her dark green eyes bugged out with rage, as if trying to escape her pasty, glowering face. She was wearing what looked like a straightjacket.

"*Her?*" Marlo replied. "What's so mean about that little rug rat?"

Moxie's intense, quivering eyes settled on Marlo. The little girl stuck out her tongue. It was covered with a silver sheath. Marlo gulped and grabbed one of the few remaining bars of soap. She bit into it, distracted by the creepy little girl's stare. Marlo's mouth foamed over with a torrent of sour, bitter salt.

The children began to snort and hoot.

"I *knew* she'd pick that one!" a little boy exclaimed. "Figures Creep Show would go for paste flavor with a booger filling!"

"Yuck," Marlo said as she spat out the bubbling soap bits. "It tastes like . . . I don't know . . . kind of familiar . . ."

She tried to wash out the disgusting flavor with a tart swish of Sassy-Frass tea. "Sort of like medicine . . ."

"I know what kind of medicine it tastes like," Milton said with a smirk.

"What?"

"It probably tastes a lot like *your own* medicine," Milton replied before scanning the room, hoping to unload more of his Double-Bubble burden.

"Soap's on . . . come and get it!"

4 · A MATTER OF PRINCIPALS

PRINCIPAL BEA "ELSA" Bubb, covered in more smears and globs than usual, stepped back from her painting. After screwing up her screwed-up goat eyes at the canvas, she realized that of all the crimes she'd committed throughout eternity, her latest crime against art was heinous enough to send her all the way downstairs in a one-way handbasket.

Principal Bubb was in a funk. And not the kind of funk that requires platform shoes and moving one's booty to the music. The *bad* kind of funk. The kind of funk that makes eternal creatures dredged from the deepest depths of children's nightmares do crazy things, like try their hand (or claw, rather) at painting.

The principal sighed. The sharp, rank stench of her

hastily consumed lunch—baby panda liver, candied Limburger, and extra-clotted cream puréed into a not-so-smoothie—curled her snout-hairs . . . or *would* have had she not curled them herself only this morning.

Having Satan for a boss was one thing. You rather expected to be abused, misused, overworked, and under-appreciated. But working beneath an angel—the holier-than-thouest archangel of them all, Michael, now doing business as the Big Guy Downstairs, aka the Devil—was something else entirely. Michael's insufferable saintli-ness, his effortlessly condescending perfection, his tak-ing every opportunity to saddle up his high horse and then—with an almighty "giddy up"—gallop down the moral high road, leaving everyone else behind in heaps of flaming rectitude . . . it made him somehow more diabolical than the epitome of all evil himself.

"Um . . . Miss Principal, ma'am?" a leathery pink demon with tiny bat wings and an unnerving baby face said uncomfortably, standing on a pedestal in the cor-ner of the principal's Not-So-Secret Lair. "Are you done painting me?"

Cerberus, Principal Bubb's three-headed Pekingese, writhed in the demon's arms, chewing a bone with sav-age delight. Unfortunately for the wincing demon, that bone happened to be his humerus, a situation that didn't exactly tickle the anguished creature's funny bone.

Principal Bubb set down her palette and brush and wiped her filthy claws on her filthy, paint-spattered smock.

"Yes, Cato," she grumbled. "We're through."

Cato walked over to the canvas and studied the gruesome smudges. The painting featured Cato, dead and bloodied, at the center of a grisly crime scene. The principal—rendered in crude blotches that captured her likeness perfectly—was looking over the body, painted next to a medical examiner. The two figures smeared together.

"I seem to have painted myself into a coroner," the principal said. She wiped away a tear of blood from her snot-green eyes.

"Are you all right, O Mistress of Malevolence?" Cato inquired.

"Of course I'm not all right!" she shouted. "The Netherworld is in a shambles, ever since Michael—that pseudo son of Perdition—was put in charge, after that miserable, meddling goody-two-shoes Milton Fauster testified against him at the Trial of the Millennium!" Fire smoldered behind the principal's jaundiced goat eyes. "I want to squish that little squirt till he . . . *squishes and squirts. . . .*"

Principal Bubb grabbed a remote control from her desk and waved it at a bank of old televisions mounted on the wall of her Not-So-Secret Lair. Two orange, spray-tanned faces formed on the surface of the sputtering cathode ray-tube screen.

"I'm Bobo Bagatelle," the unnaturally tanned newswoman chirped.

"And I'm Muck Raker," her male counterpart interjected.

"And you're subjecting yourself to URN—the Underworld Retribution Network—I Can't Believe It's Not News! hour," they announced in perky unison.

Principal Bubb scratched at a particularly scaly patch on her thick, anaconda arms. "I need to take my mind off this train wreck," she murmured.

"And we're here with Vice Principal—excuse me, *Mr.*—Mark Twain!" Bobo continued.

Bea "Elsa" Bubb gasped. "*T-Twain* wreck! *Vice Principal Twain?!* Why isn't he back in Wise Acres, doing his job?"

Muck nodded, his shiny black helmet of hair as dark and stubborn as an oil spill.

"Yes, the recently ousted vice principal of Wise Acres, the circle of Heck for kids who sass back!" the anchorman continued. "So, please, tell us your shocking story and don't spare any hyperbolic, inflammatory detail. . . ."

Ousted? Principal Bubb thought as the warped image of a dapper old man in a white linen suit appeared on her television screen.

"Imagine my surprise when I found myself, just last week, rudely prodded by a band of incorrigible brutes with pitchsporks, and told that my services would no longer be needed in the bad-mouthin' burrow of Wise Acres!" Mr. Twain complained in his Southern drawl.

The man had wild white hair, thick gray eyebrows, and a bushy salt-and-pepper horseshoe of a mustache drooping down over his grumbling lips.

"I was thrown outside like a cantankerous can of old-man garbage!" he continued with a nettled twitch of his mustache. "And Principal Bubb didn't even have the decency to tell me herself *why* she removed me!"

"*Because I didn't!*" Principal Bubb shrieked. "I had to find out about it on the Underworld Retribution Network, along with the rest of the accursed!"

Mark Twain cocked a bushy gray eyebrow.

"Sure, my prickly management style and acid tongue often got me in a heap of trouble, but to yank me outta there without so much as a 'how do you do' . . . and replace me with, of all folks, Lewis Carroll . . ."

The principal shook her hideous head in disbelief.

"Wait . . . Lewis Carroll?! The author of *Alice in Wonderland*?!"

"Yes . . . *Lewis Carroll*," Mr. Twain said with a bemused smirk. "The architect of Wonderland itself. A man a few saucers short of a tea service . . . It's no wonder that truth is stranger than fiction. *Fiction has to make sense.*"

Principal Bubb tried to muster as much composure as a festering, several-thousand-year-old (give or take a century) demonness could.

What is this all about? Who would go around me and do something like this? Why Wise Acres? Why now?

"Principal Bubb has obviously taken that old adage

never the 'twain' shall meet to heart . . . having her demons do her dirty work for her," Mark Twain continued, veins of outrage bulging on his sagging old neck. "The principal, as we all know, is the poster creature for gross incompetence . . . heavy on the *gross*. And now it is quite clear that she is determined to surround herself with fellow incompetents who won't question her unquestionably inept decrees. . . ."

The principal sighed with bitter frustration as Bobo shook her platinum-blond head, forcing her perpetually smiling face to frown with concern.

"Wasn't Mr. Carroll—excuse me, Vice Principal Carroll—the unwilling guest at a minimum-security Bedlam and Breakfast for a spell?" she asked.

Mr. Twain nodded. "Yes, the Placid Pastures Easy-Breezy and Extra-Restful Resort for the Criminally Insane," he explained.

Principal Bubb's jaw fell open like a trapdoor with a rusty hinge.

"Wise Acres' new vice principal was institutionalized?!"

Mark Twain gave a wry chuckle. "The only job that man should be holding is a *nut* job," he continued with a weary shake of his head. "Apparently he has a little problem in the 'distinguishing his own self-conceived fantasies from the world around him' department."

The two newscasters shook their heads with mirth and outrage.

"Sounds like the children deserve better than Lewis

Carroll," Bobo said with a smirk. "And *certainly* better than Bea 'Elsa' Bubb . . ."

"You heard it here first: 'Baby Gate: Upheaval in Principal Bungle's Rumpus Room'!" Muck chortled. "With the principal as the butt of a Netherworld-wide joke! And that's a big butt, Bobo."

"This sort of rash move isn't her usual, for lack of a better word, *style*," Bobo added. "Bubb is known for being an unquestioning line toer and shameless manure shoveler."

"Well, there *is* rather a lot of it down here," Muck interjected with a wicked laugh.

Principal Bubb slashed angrily at the television with her remote as if she were waging an invisible sword fight. The anchorman's smug face fizzled out of existence.

This could only be the work of one creature, the principal fumed. *A creature with majestic wings soaring high above both my head and my authority.*

"Michael!" Principal Bubb barked, her voice exploding throughout her Not-So-Secret Lair like a verbal grenade.

She couldn't just come out and say this whole thing was a mistake. That would make her look like she didn't know what was going on, which she didn't. Better to be viewed as a rash and reckless decision maker than to be perceived as weak, powerless, and ineffectual.

Principal Bubb activated her No-Fee Hi-Fi Faux phone—two electronic, voice-activated thimbles, one on her thumb and one on her pinkie talon—and extended her claw, holding it up to her ear.

"*Michael,*" she hissed into her thumb as the phone dialed the number.

"We are sorry," an obnoxiously calm recorded voice relayed in measured syllables into her ear, "but the party you are trying to reach—THE ARCHANGEL MICHAEL, NOW THE BIG GUY DOWNSTAIRS, RULER OF THE UNDERWORLD, EVERLASTING— is unavailable. . . ."

Principal Bubb slammed her claw down upon her desk, briefly forgetting in her fury that her claw *was* her phone.

"Children deserve better, my hoof! The only thing those whippersnappers deserve is the snap of a whip!"

The Principal of Darkness shoved her throbbing talons beneath her armpit and plopped down in her chair.

In the afterlife—as up on the Surface—image is everything. And it was hard to imagine an image as unimaginably ravaged as her image was now. If Principal Bubb wanted to remain in charge of Heck, she needed to turn this runaway twain, er, *train* around.

"I don't even know where I'd begin," the principal moaned, kneading her face like warm Silly Putty into something that was as far from silly as you could get without accidentally backing into it.

I need a publicity campaign, she thought. *If I can get the*

Powers That Be to believe I am competent and respected, I'll become competent and respected! And if the underworld sees me as a beloved, nurturing caregiver, they will have trouble unseating me.

The principal rose from her chair but had trouble unseating herself.

But who should I hire? Principal Bubb wondered.

Just then, a peculiar yet ingenious idea crossed Principal Bubb's mind like a raccoon loping across the street in the dead of night.

I'll get those tart-tongued brats in Wise Acres to come up with a campaign for me . . . while I still have the power to do so. A campaign for kids by kids!

Bea "Elsa" Bubb, the torment of terrible tots for time immemorial, stewed as she gritted her fangs.

Michael's not back up in Heaven plucking harp strings, the principal fumed. *He's in the Netherworld, where humanity shows just how low it can go. And now it's time to show Michael how low I can go . . . by keeping a very high profile indeed. . . .*

5 · WHEN THE GOING
GETS GUFF

MILTON AND MARLO were shoved along the dusty, rubbish-strewn hallway carved out of dense deposits of old, outdated reference books.

"Move it!" one of the two badger demons growled. "You know what happens to slowpokes here?"

"No . . . what?" Marlo replied as she dragged her feet.

"They are *poked slowly*," the creature replied, emphasizing the words "poked" and "slowly" with twin jabs of his pitchspork.

The digital news tickers lining the peeling paper walls streamed an intensely boring salvo of blather.

Hey. What's ^? DY wn2 hng ot @ d mal? mayB aftr we

cUd hng ot sumwhr Ls? WE . . . Then I was like why are you looking at me like that and then she was like . . .

Milton shook his head.

"With the news ticker, this place is kind of like a shabby Times Square," he commented. "Maybe 'Divided By' Square. Get it? Because—"

"It's the Fritter-Tape Machine," a demon badger snarled, gesturing to the wall with his long striped snout. "It's where wasted words go. Pointless text messages . . . worthless phone calls that impart nothing . . . blogs—*lots* of blogs—meeting minutes that seem like hours . . ."

They stopped in front of a door marked DRESSING-DOWN ROOM. The badger demons shoved Milton and Marlo inside.

The room was a large walk-in closet with a cracked mirror, a couple of folding metal chairs, and a garbage can overflowing with clothes.

"*Brock!* Look what the badgers dragged in!" screeched one of the two decomposing parrot demons perched before the mirror.

The badgers threw Milton and Marlo into the chairs. The parrots fluttered to their shoulders.

"*Brock!* I've seen better hair in a shower drain!"

"*Brock!* My cat coughs up better-looking stuff!"

"What are you two squawking feather dusters

doing?!" Marlo complained, sticking a finger in her ringing ear.

The parrots shot each other a quick sideways glance.

"*Brock!* Teasing your hair, of course!"

Marlo batted her parrot away and bolted to her feet.

She walked over to the overflowing garbage can and picked through the clothes. There were threadbare tweed jackets with elbow pads, scratchy mismatched socks, wingtip shoes, bow ties, and weird, shiny electric shirts with terrible slogans scrolling across them.

Chronic Bed Wetter . . . If Stupidity Were a Crime, I'd Totally Be in That Place Where They Keep All of the Crime People . . . No, I Didn't Fart. That's Just How I Smell . . . What Is Having a Friend Like? . . .

"We're not wearing this junk," Marlo said, crossing her arms defiantly.

"*Brock!* You know that dream where you show up at school naked?"

"Um . . . yeah," Marlo replied tentatively.

The parrots fluttered above Marlo's head, brandishing their cruel talons and slashing at the air around them.

"*Brock!* We could make that dream come true!"

As the Fausters grudgingly changed, Milton noticed

a piece of paper stuck to his shoe. He knelt down and pulled it free. A dried glob of Double-Bubble Soap foam had glued the torn page to his sole.

I must have stepped on this in the Audaci-Tea House, he thought as he read the page. It was an entry from an old encyclopedia.

The Encyclopediatric Whybrary of Wide-Eyed Wonder Series

Volume 19: Maulstick—Mysophobia

Entry: Music of the Spheres (*SEE:* Rosetta Tone)

Pythagoras was a Greek philosopher back in a time even before your parents were born! He was very smart yet he wore curtains. He founded a religious cult based on loving mathematics and despising beans.

Beans, beans the tragic fruit!
Pythagoras feared that when you'd toot
You'd lose your soul, and then you would die.
So be wary of beans if you're some old Greek guy!

Pythagoras and his followers thought that the universe was made up of numbers. Smarty-Pants Pythagoras, though not in possession of pants, also realized that music was made up of mathematical intervals that made a musical tune either pleasant (ooooh!) or unpleasant (ugh!).

The Music of the Spheres was—according to our friend Pythagoras—the musical intervals that described the distance between the planets. By using these ratios, Pythagoras discovered the physical relationship between mass and sound . . . the symphony of the stars that keeps the heavens spinning! It was, he theorized, a specific harmony that called Creation into being and a complementary dissonance that gave the universe its tension, keeping everything "just right!"

We can't hear the tone that makes a symphony of life because we're not God. Even Pythagoras, when he wasn't wearing drapes and clenching his butt for fear of farting to death, couldn't hear it!

So next time you're practicing your violin, be careful: you just might hit upon the Music of the Spheres and accidentally remake Creation!

Milton tucked the page into his new pants. Minutes later, Milton and Marlo emerged from the Dressing-Down Room. They were clad in rumpled tweed jackets, ill-matched socks and shoes, and shirts flashing humiliating phrases.

"We look like complete dorks," Marlo groused,

trying to button her way-too-small coat to hide the blinking "Everybody Likes Me . . . To Go Away" slogan creeping across her chest.

"Worse: you look like *writers*," slurped one of the aardvark demons as it waddled toward them.

"But what's with the demeaning slogans?" Milton asked.

"We find it slows down sassy tongues," the demon explained in a sloppy, wet gurgle. "Now move along. Girls and boys are separated for classes. You're only allowed to trade jibes in the Audaci-Tea House."

Marlo grabbed Milton by the hand. "Remember, whatever happens, we stay together," she whispered, leaning into her brother. "We'll meet up in that tea place between classes and trade intel, okay?"

Milton nodded, just before the aardvark demon lassoed him with its tongue and dragged him away down the hallway.

The classroom was a small lecture hall with a pitched floor, a lectern at the front of the class, and rows of elevated seating. What set the room apart from your ordinary lecture hall was that it was composed entirely of moldering old books, as if it had been carved out of the most overstocked library *ever*. The lectern was a teetering totem pole of textbooks, the benches were rows of stacked novels and manuals, and the desks were piles of notebooks and message pads. Unfortunately, every message pad was filled with notes from past students of Wise Acres, going back—if the Ye Olde English was any indication—thousands of years.

Though the teacher—an old man with a grizzled, unkempt goatee and dark hair swept over his balding head—hadn't yet begun the lesson, Milton felt as if he were barging in on some private party. He edged along the rows of staring, smirking children and found an unoccupied patch of bench. He moved to sit, yet a stern, dark-haired boy with knitted eyebrows scooted to block him.

"This seat is taken," the boy grunted.

"By who?" Milton asked, looking around the class but not seeing anyone else searching for a seat.

"By anybody but *you*," the boy replied, glowering, his gaze daring Milton to do something about it. "You want the seat? Go on. I'd like to see you try. If you have a problem with me, go tell Mr. Dickens."

Charles Dickens . . . the author of Oliver Twist *and* A Christmas Carol? Milton thought, casting a quick glance at the teacher as he arranged his notes on the lectern.

"Hey," Moses Babcock called out from the next row over, beckoning Milton with his finger. "There's a space over here."

Milton climbed down to the next row and sat down.

"Thanks, um . . . Moses, right?"

The boy nodded and held out his hand. His dark, judgmental eyes grazed Milton up and down like fingers on an abacus, trying to solve Milton as if he were an equation that didn't quite add up. Milton shook the boy's hand. The boy's serious, professional manner made Milton feel like he was meeting with a lawyer or the CEO of a Fortune 500 company, not a fellow kid darned to Heck.

Mr. Dickens coughed.

"Good afternoon, young men," the teacher said in a somber, British-inflected tone. *"WISE ACRES. Uncreative Writing with Mr. Dickens.* Our last class—and oh, how tiresome it was!—had us studying literary clichés. If you recall, clichés should be avoided like the plague. . . ."

Milton leaned into Moses. "Why is Charles Dickens, one of the greatest writers of all time, teaching in Heck?" Milton whispered.

Moses shrugged with indifference. "I beg to differ . . . though I never beg. I just differ," the boy replied out of the side of his mouth, scribbling on his pad, taking notes over the notes that some other boy had taken years and years ago. "It is debatable that he is one of the greatest writers of all time, a phrase so open to interpretation as to be meaningless. But from what I have heard, he and the other teachers are here for how they *lived,* not for how they *wrote.* Personally, I much prefer nonfiction. Books loaded with irrefutable facts that you can use against people . . ."

Milton felt a strange sense of camaraderie with Moses. But not the warm and fuzzy kind. More like a pair of handcuffs linking one convict to another. He, like Moses, was a fussy, infuriating fault-finder who needed to prove how smart he was all the time by correcting others. Milton had thought that the other kids would appreciate him pointing out their mistakes. But instead of showering him with appreciation, they usually showered him with loogies for his efforts. The teachers never seemed all that pleased with Milton's helpful corrections either.

A terrible scratching screech shattered Milton's thoughts. Mr. Dickens had scrawled the word "Exposition" on the chalkboard.

"And that is clichés in a nutshell . . . and now on to exposition. It is to the fiction writer as Kryptonite is to Superman," the teacher explained. "It turns a potentially heroic story into a flabby weakling in a leotard. Exposition is where excessive information is foisted upon our hapless reader under the auspices of helping them to better understand a story's plot, characters, or setting. It is the labored telling, not the revelatory *showing.* . . ."

Mr. Dickens assessed the blank faces staring back at him. The teacher glanced down at his class roster.

"You . . . Milton Fauster," Mr. Dickens said. "How

did you get here? What led you to this peculiar fate, sitting here in this den of disquisition?"

"Well, I guess you could say I was the wrong boy in the wrong place at the wrong time," Milton replied.

Mr. Dickens shook his head. "No, that borders on the compelling," he replied. "Your cryptic statement makes us want to learn more. Tell us, instead, using the cruel craft of exposition."

Milton swallowed as the other children's flat, disdainful stares bored into him like drills.

"Well, I was just your average, textbook almost-straight-A student—PE had always dragged down my grade-point average—who became a fatally injured human s'more after the school bully, Damian Ruffino, stuck dynamite up the butt of a gigantic marshmallow bear. After that, everything went downhill . . . all the way down to Heck. Soon after I got here, my sister Marlo and I—along with our new friend Virgil—stole jars of Lost Souls and used them to make a balloon. I was the only one who managed to escape, though. But after evading human sacrifice at the hands of a religious death cult, I got 'popped' back to Heck after hiding in a crate of popcorn kernels. . . ."

Milton prattled on for another twenty minutes, telling his tale of preteen torment in agonizing, almost real-time detail. He was blogging with his mouth. Though Milton knew he had long since lost the attention of his audience, he couldn't stop.

"That was as boring as watching a banana take a nap," a grumpy boy in a brown stocking cap declared after Milton had finally stopped.

Mr. Dickens flipped a willful strand of hair over his balding pate and patted it down onto his scalp.

"Exactly, Mr. Crump!" he said.

The teacher erased the chalkboard and wrote the word "Foreshadowing" in a fluid stroke scrawled with one unbroken squeal of chalk.

"An eraser hurtles through the air, striking an unsuspecting head," Mr. Dickens muttered as he paced behind his gently listing lectern of books. The boys exchanged looks of smirking confusion with one another.

"Foreshadowing is a technique used by writers to arouse a reader's curiosity," the teacher continued, tossing the chalkboard eraser back and forth between his hands. "Like Hansel and Gretel leaving behind a trail of breadcrumbs, foreshadowing is the deft placement of clues to hint at what may befall a character at story's end, so that the event in question—when it arrives—seems somehow inevitable to the reader. . . ."

Mr. Dickens suddenly tossed the eraser at Mr. Crump's furrowed forehead.

"Hey!" the boy exclaimed angrily.

"You should have seen it coming," Mr. Dickens replied, his thick beard twitching with suppressed laughter. "Such is the danger of foreshadowing. . . ."

Foreshadowing, Milton thought as he drew a pair of

wings on a knight that some bored "Wise Acre" had doodled generations ago. *Preparing for what comes next without it looking like you're preparing for what comes next . . .*

Angelo Fallon, the fallen angel Principal Bubb had hired to get rid of Milton—to slit his throat with a razor-feather and capture Milton's last breath as proof—was still out there somewhere. . . .

Milton scanned the scornful faces of the boys surrounding him. They were furiously exchanging insults with one another like stockbrokers trading shares.

But that was back in Precocia, back in the other reality. Maybe here, in Wise Acres, Principal Bubb sent a different angel to "off" me, and he could be right in this classroom. Or Bubb simply hasn't thought of it . . . yet. But if it happened before, it could happen again. At least this time I know that there is a group of fallen angels for hire here in the underworld and that Principal Bubb is despicable enough to recruit one of them to rub me out: completely.

Milton drew a question mark halo above the knight-angel's head.

The question is, what good does this do me? How can I prevent Bubb and some angel assassin from editing me out of my own story?

6 · SPELLiNG DiSASTER

"ROSES ARE RED, orchids are black, why is her chest as flat as her back?" Cookie Youngblood taunted.

"Ugh! Nice perfume . . . did you marinate in it?" chimed in Cookie's blond second-in-command.

The walk from the door to the empty seat at the front of the lecture room felt like an eternity. And considering that Marlo was dead, she knew a thing or two about what eternity felt like. It wasn't that she didn't have a quippy comeback. Far from it. Dozens of withering one-liners were backed up in Marlo's throat like a frantic crowd trying to flee a burning building through a mail slot. That was the problem. There were too many options.

What Marlo needed was something so utterly devastating, so perfect in its absolute, undeniable supremacy that it stifled all hopes of counterattack. What she needed was the snappy-retort equivalent of the atomic bomb.

"I'd slap you, but that would be animal abuse" . . . no, too blunt. *"What did you have for breakfast, Booger-Frosted Loser Flakes?"* . . . no, too kindergarten.

Suddenly, Marlo found herself standing beside an unoccupied pile of old textbooks at the front of the class and was gripped by a terrible realization. *The moment has passed. It's all about timing. A late comeback is worse than no comeback at all.*

Marlo sat down on the shaky pile of ancient textbooks. She had to switch gears. Instead of fighting fire with slightly hotter fire—dousing the girls' flaming defamation with something that burned up all of their oxygen—Marlo had to act like she was *so* cruel and clever as to be miles above their reindeer games. This would get their imaginations working against them, so Marlo wouldn't have to try so hard.

Marlo crossed her arms and leveled her violet eyes at the girls, willing her pupils extra-wide and unfathomable.

"Is that all you've got?" Marlo croaked, her tongue not quite depressed but still a little glum. She punctuated her statement with a sarcastic "couldn't be bothered" stare at the ceiling.

A thin mousy slip of a woman slunk into the lecture hall, carrying a shabby doctor's bag. After quickly regarding the snickering crowd of disrespectful girls, the woman—her brown-gray hair tied into a tight bun—scuttled to the blackboard with all the mad desperation of someone rushing across the deck of a sinking ship for a life preserver. She scratched hastily on the chalkboard with loopy, wide-spaced letters:

RUDE-IMENTARY GRAMMAR

"Who's she?" Marlo muttered. "She's like a walking nervous breakdown in support hose."

"She's like a walking nervous breakdown in support hose," repeated a sour-faced little girl in a mocking tone.

A girl with granny glasses and flat-orange hair that looked like it had been gooped on with tempera paint leaned into Marlo and whispered, "Don't mind Bree Martinet. She can't help obnoxiously repeating everything."

"She can't help obnoxiously repeating everything," Bree both echoed and proved.

The orange-haired girl held out her clammy, pale hand. "Flossie Blackwell."

Marlo gave the girl a limp, cautious handshake in return. She cast a wary gaze at Cookie Youngblood and her friend.

"Cookie Youngblood and Concordia Kolassa," Flossie explained. "Stay out of their way. They'll tear you apart like a toddler unscrewing an Oreo."

"So our teacher—"

"So our teacher—Miss Dickinson—was a terrific poet up on the Surface. One of the best. My faves are 'I Heard a Fly Buzz When I Died,' 'I Felt a Funeral in My Brain,' and 'Heaven Is What I Cannot Reach.'"

"Apparently she couldn't either," Marlo replied. "Reach Heaven, that is."

Flossie shifted in her seat, now knee to knee with Marlo.

"That's the funny thing . . . not funny ha-ha but funny strange," the bright-eyed girl whispered. "Miss Dickinson was agoraphobic when she was alive."

"Someone afraid of being gored by a bull?"

Flossie stared back blankly at Marlo.

"I'm totally kidding," Marlo replied. "So she was afraid to go outside?"

Flossie smiled. "You do good deadpan."

"I've definitely got the 'dead' part down pat," Marlo said, allowing herself a crooked smile.

"So Miss Dickinson was invited upstairs, to Heaven," Flossie continued. "But all of that wide-open-space stuff freaked her out, so she got herself transferred down here to this dark, cramped Heck-hole."

Miss Dickinson cleared her dainty throat. "Yes . . . um . . . good afternoon, young ladies," she said quietly.

"WE CAN'T HEAR YOU," a large Latino girl thundered from the back.

The teacher winced. "Right . . . thank you, Miss Caustilo," Miss Dickinson continued, raising her voice exactly one decibel louder. "Today I thought we'd try something a little different."

The girls in the back row gave the teacher a sarcastic round of slow-clapped applause. They stopped suddenly when burly badger demons pushed in three glass enclosures on wheels, like old-style telephone booths with collapsing doors.

Miss Dickinson noted the confused looks plastered upon the girls' faces. The girls found it difficult to bad-mouth something they didn't fully understand.

"A word is dead when it is said, some say. I say it just begins to live that day . . . so I've decided to have you *experience* the power of grammar, rather than have me rattle on about it. Hopefully this exercise will have you young ladies appreciating the intoxicating allure of a truly *grammarous* life!"

Miss Dickinson smiled nervously amid the awkward silence. She sighed and scratched off USE MORE PUNS from a list of suggestions lying on her lectern.

"So, do we have any volun—"

"I'll do it," Marlo said, taking off her coat and swaggering over to the nearest booth.

While Cookie and Concordia had already marked their turf with their sassy mouths, few could match Marlo for her reckless abandon. Hopefully this would shift the "new girl is incredibly lame" dynamic a few ticks in Marlo's direction.

Cookie Youngblood glared at Marlo as she tugged open the booth's collapsible door.

"Think you can run away, new girl?" Cookie said with a sneer of her lip-glossed lips as she rose from her bench of old books.

Cookie slid into the second booth while a round-faced girl with short brown hair rose to her feet and shuffled down the aisle.

Miss Dickinson allowed herself a smile as the girl entered the third booth.

"Wonderful!" she exclaimed. "Let us commend Misses Marlo Fauster, Cookie Youngblood, and Annabelle Graham—"

"*Banana Hall Merge,*" Annabelle mumbled from inside the booth.

"Hey! She's doing her weird letter scramble thing again . . . freak," observed Pansy Cornett over her granny glasses.

"Those are called *anagrams*, Miss Cornett," the teacher corrected.

A girl rolled her large, expressive eyes, mouthing, "Oh my God."

"And, please, no face-texting in class, Miss Duckworth," the teacher scolded. "Anagrams are a delightful way to keep one's mind sharp. In any case, I am most indebted to the girls' initiative! It is far better to be the hammer than the anvil."

Moxie Wortschmerz vibrated in her white straight-jacket.

"*Oo oyon-eyed, ilk-ivered, eef-ained, atsbane!*" the little girl spat, her silver-sheathed tongue twitching in her mouth like a metal finger on the trigger of a gun.

Miss Dickinson frowned. "Now, now, Miss

Wortschmerz. Saying nothing sometimes says the most."

The teacher pulled out three crowbars from her shabby leather doctor's bag and walked to the booths in tiny, uncertain steps.

"You young ladies have all heard of spelling bees, I trust?" Miss Dickinson said.

"Total *duh*," a heavily made-up girl seated in the back said tartly.

"Well, this is something a little different," Miss Dickinson said with a sly smile as she slid the crowbars between the handles of the booths' doors.

"Um . . . what's with the crowbar?" Marlo said from behind the glass as she tried to open the door. "Isn't that against fire code?"

Miss Dickinson lifted a large jar full of buzzing insects out of her satchel.

Marlo, Cookie, and Annabelle smacked the glass with their palms and yelled.

"*This* is a spelling *wasp*," Miss Dickinson said, her dark bulging eyes gleaming as she connected the jar to three tubes leading out to the booths.

"Wasp?!" Marlo gasped, fogging up the glass. "Are you, like, totally off your rocker, Betty Crocker?!"

"People in glass booths shouldn't cast aspersions," Miss Dickinson replied as she unrolled a sheet of paper. "Especially if the booth in question is filled with stinging insects."

The teacher cleared her throat.

"The rules are simple. You spell a word correctly, and nothing happens. You make a mistake, and you become booth-mates with a wasp. The harder the word, the more wasps are introduced. Are you ready to play?"

"LET US OUT OF HERE, YOU PSYCHO!" Cookie screamed.

"Excellent. First word, Miss Graham: *extract*."

Annabelle's brown almond-shaped eyes settled nervously on the ceiling of her booth.

"Extract. E-X-T-R-A-C-T. Extract."

"Wonderful!" Miss Dickinson said as she walked to the next booth.

"Now you, Miss Youngblood: *wistful*."

Cookie swallowed, then blew a strand of streaked metallic-red hair out of her fearful eyes. "Wasteful?"

"*Wistful* . . . and stop stalling. I know stalling when I see it."

"Wistful. W-I-S-T-F-U-L-L . . . no . . . WAIT! Just one 'L'!"

A faint shadow of disappointment crossed the teacher's plain face. "That was very close, Miss Youngblood."

Miss Dickinson sidled over to Marlo's booth. "Miss Fauster: Spell *antediluvian*."

"Auntie who?" Marlo gasped.

"*Antediluvian*," Miss Dickinson repeated. "It means before the biblical flood. You do know the story of the Great Flood, don't you?"

"Yeah, yeah . . . where Noah and Joan of Arc took all of the twin animals to America to prove that the world was round."

"I'll just get the wasps ready, then," Miss Dickinson said as she secured the corrugated hose to the buzzing jar.

"Antediluvian," Marlo said with exasperation. "A-N-T-I-D-I-L-O-O-"

"WRONG!" the teacher exclaimed in a voice louder and deeper than anyone thought possible. She opened a tiny trapdoor on the roof of Marlo's booth, allowing a wasp to pass through.

"Now back to you, Miss Graham," the teacher said as Marlo yelped and flailed inside her booth. *"Complex."*

"Um . . . *complex*," Annabelle replied warily. "C-O-M-P-L-E-X."

"Correct. Now *you*, Miss Youngblood: *vigilant.*"

Cookie bit her shiny lip. *"Vigilant.* V-I-J-"

"Oww!" Marlo yelped as a wasp stung her on the arm.

"No," Cookie gasped. "V-I-G-I-L-A-N-T. *Vigilant.*"

"Correct," Miss Dickinson said with a frown as she stepped in front of Marlo's booth. "Now you, Miss Fauster: *antidisestablishmentarianism.*"

"What?!" Marlo shrieked. "That is SO unfair! That is the *state fair* of unfair! Pass!"

"You can't pass, Miss Fauster. And, judging from your atrocious spelling skills, I'm assuming that this isn't the *first* class you haven't passed. Now spell the word or feel the sting of learning."

Marlo fogged up the glass with her breath and tried to spell out the word with her finger. "Antidisestablish-whatever. A-N-T-I-D-I-S . . . um . . . E-S . . ." Marlo sighed. "Just send in the wasps," she said with defeat.

Miss Dickinson tipped the wasp jar into the tube. Marlo pressed her hands against the open slot on the ceiling.

She screamed as angry wasps attacked her hands. A swarm darted inside the booth.

"Owww! *Double-dipping diaper monkeys!*"

As Marlo squealed in pain from inside the locked booth, Lucky poked his head out from the pocket of Marlo's coat, left behind on her stack-of-books seat.

A little blond girl screeched. "Teacher! The new girl brought one of those cruelty-free mink stoles with her!"

Miss Dickinson slid the crowbar from the handles of Marlo's booth. Marlo wrenched open the folding doors and spilled out onto the floor. The teacher handed her a tube of white cream.

"Miss Fauster . . . why do you have an animal with you? Heck has a very strict 'no-pets' policy. Even teacher's pets aren't allowed."

Marlo slathered the soothing cream all over her sting-swollen arms and face.

"He's . . . Lucky," she groaned.

"Like a charm?" Miss Dickinson replied.

"Like a *ferret.*"

Miss Dickinson scowled as she tentatively scooped up Lucky in her spindly arms.

"He's my muse," Marlo said, thinking quickly. "You know: to help me write and stuff."

"Really?" the teacher replied dubiously.

"Yeah," Flossie chimed in. "Marlo told me. He's . . . inspiring."

"Then he belongs with the Muses," Miss Dickinson explained as she walked toward the door.

Marlo peeled her sore, smarting self off the ground.

"What do you mean?" she asked as she followed her teacher to the door.

"The Nine Muses—Calliope, Clio, Erato, Euterpe, Melpomene, Polyhymnia, Terpsichore, Thalia, and Urania," the dead spinster poet said. "From Greek myth. They sat at the throne of Zeus and sang of his glory. They fill writers with the inspiration they need to do great work."

"And they're *here*?" Marlo replied.

"Yes and no," Miss Dickinson said. "*Yes*, they are somewhere in Wise Acres, and *no*, the teachers and students don't know where. Our muses are always kept *just* out of reach. So we will never again taste the divine satisfaction of our deepest feelings captured with the perfect turn of phrase . . . and the inspiration that so eludes us is right here, so close and yet so far."

A badger demon appeared from down the hall.

"Snack?" it asked as it settled its dark and shining eyes on Lucky.

"No . . . a *muse*," Miss Dickinson corrected. "Please take it to the Muses in room, oh . . . what is that number?"

The badger grinned a snarl of savage teeth. "Nice try, Miss Dickinson," it replied as it took Lucky—squirming, hissing, and spitting—into its burly, prickly arms. "I'll take this . . . *thing* . . . there."

"He better be okay!" Marlo said as the badger demon loped down the hallway past several cats saddled with leather pouches.

Miss Dickinson set her frail hand on Marlo's shoulder. "Your muse will be fine," she assured her. "He will be more than cared for—*he will be worshipped*."

Marlo watched the strange trio of burdened cats as they padded down the hallway.

"What's with the cats?"

"Furriers with MEOW: the Mail Expressed Overnight Whiskers. They've been making deliveries back and forth ever since Mr. Carroll became vice principal last week." Miss Dickinson shrugged her bony shoulders. "Things keep getting curiouser and curiouser . . . but, alas, forever is composed of puzzling 'nows.'"

And meows, *apparently,* Marlo thought suspiciously as an orange tabby rubbed itself against her leg. *I wonder what's in those pouches.*

7 · PUBLIC RELATIONS ENEMY NUMBER ONE

A TALL, DIGNIFIED man with flowing hair, cropped velvet knee breeches, and a lily for a boutonniere wrote what had to be the longest class name Milton had ever seen.

IN WHICH WE MAKE EACH AND EVERY WORD COUNT: HOW TO MAKE A LIVING IN DEATH EXPLOITING YOUR ACCURSED FLAIR FOR LANGUAGE . . . WITH MR. WILDE

Mr. Wilde straightened a portrait of himself as a young man that was hanging on the wall behind him.

"I read some of your books, *Oscar*," said a thick, surly-looking boy with one long, bushy eyebrow perched across his brow. "And I think they're wonderful—"

"Thank you, Mr. Vittorio," the teacher said with a polite nod.

"*—if you're having trouble falling asleep,*" the boy continued, earning a laugh from his friends.

Mr. Wilde slammed his delicate hand against the lectern. "You mouthy little malt worm!"

The teacher smoothed his hair, gathering himself quickly. The portrait behind him, Milton noted with confusion, looked suddenly older, the hair having gone gray along the temples.

"Mr. Vittorio's 'critique' of my work brings up an important point," Mr. Wilde continued, folding his slender white hands behind his back. "Literature is so subjective that you will never please everyone, or often *anyone.* Most classics become so—classics—long after the author has expired. To put it in a way that you boys can understand: *writing is no way to make a living.*"

The teacher paced before his portrait with long, youthful strides. The once-smooth face of the man in the painting was now lined and furrowed.

"In a time where everyone can express himself, expression ceases to be valuable as an art form," Mr. Wilde explained in his low, languid voice. "Everyone who can send one of your electronic messages fancies himself a writer . . . and most every one of them is *wrong.*"

Milton was having trouble concentrating. The constant hiss of whispering, sideways glances, and snorting explosions of mocking laughter was making him paranoid. Any one of these kids could be another fallen angel, paid by Principal Bubb to give Milton a close shave with a razor-feather. Even if no one in the classroom was presently plotting to off him, Principal Bubb could be, right now, hiring an angelic assassin. . . .

"Through publicity, promotion, and propaganda, however, you can help shape the world for the rich and powerful—exchanging your wicked ways with words for a decent salary," Mr. Wilde continued.

Moses Babcock eyed Milton intensely, as if he were a puzzling new form of bacteria that he was examining under a microscope. Milton wiped away the nervous beads of sweat forming on his upper lip.

I've got to think of some way out of this before I completely lose it.

"In fact, you have been handed an opportunity to reshape public opinion for our very own Principal Bubb."

"Principal Bubb?!" Milton blurted.

The boys stopped their whispering and stared at the new kid with dubious interest.

"Yes, Mr."—the teacher glanced down at his class roster with his gray, heavy-lidded eyes—"*Fauster.* She is looking to remake her image, and since you sassy young men think you're too smart to be taught, my fellow teachers and I have decided to make this a competition, to see if you are all as smart as your mouths. Now you can file those sharp minds against one another, making them even keener."

"A contest?" Moses said, leaning forward in his seat,

but not to the extent that he appeared fully engaged by an authority figure. "What will the prize be . . . *sir*?"

Mr. Wilde curled his delicate lips. "The prize, Mr. Babcock, will be . . . decided at a later date. Let us just say that the top entries for whoever can create the best public relations strategy will receive extra credit, certain privileges, and special . . . *consideration* . . . by Principal Bubb."

Moses Babcock laced his fingers behind his neck and leaned back on his stack-of-books seat. "It seems a shame to make it a formal contest," the boy said, staring admiringly at a cardboard mountain pinned to the wall. "That would just get everybody else's hopes up. If you get right down to it, it's really no contest at all."

The cardboard mountain had several photos of students taped across it, with Moses Babcock's picture at the top. Mr. Wilde rolled his eyes.

"Yes, Mr. Babcock, we all know that you are currently at the top of Mouth Brashmore, our symbol of student achievement. But that doesn't automatically rule out any of your fellow classmates having a fair—"

"I'd like to enter," Milton said.

The class grew as quiet as a ninja's fart.

Mr. Wilde fought back a smile. A grimacing old man stared back from the portrait behind him.

Moses wrested his lips into a smile, though his eyes burned with icy malice.

"No offense, Milton," Moses said, "but I haven't

heard you utter one clever thing since you've been here. I'd be happy, though, to help you."

"I'm good," Milton replied nonchalantly. "And I can name all of the clever things *you've* said, Moses, on the finger of a boxing glove."

There was a brief, thick pause, then suddenly an explosion of laughter. Milton could practically feel the subtle shifts in status rippling throughout the room.

Moses glared at Milton before, again, wrenching his scowl into a practiced smile. "Well played," he said, the words falling out of his mouth like ice from an ice machine. "I look forward to more of your contributions. . . ."

Mr. Wilde strode toward Milton with a swish of his pinstriped trousers and handed him a sheet of paper. "There's nothing wrong with Mr. Babcock that a little reincarnation wouldn't cure," the teacher whispered warmly before handing out instructions to the other dozen or so boys who had raised their hands to enter the contest.

Milton scanned the worksheet.

Public Relations Problem:
Principal Bea "Elsa" Bubb

Situation Analysis: Principal Bubb is, to put it mildly, disliked. To put it mediumly, hated. To put it spicily hot, detested with unquenchable rage and loathing. Worse yet, she's not respected. Her weakness as an authority figure is the sole issue that the demonic and divine can agree upon. This public relations campaign must heighten positive underworld awareness and support of Principal Bubb as a valuable educational resource. Good luck: you'll need it.

Milton wasn't sure why, exactly, he had decided to enter the contest. He supposed it was a knee-jerk reaction to that mean-jerk-reactor Moses, wanting to one-up the smug boy who had been masquerading as an ally. But perhaps most of all, Milton craved the hypnotizing routine of schoolwork. His mind needed a break from worrying about eternal torment, assassination attempts by fallen angels, and how filthy his sheets and pillowcase were likely to be.

Milton tapped his chewed pencil on his stacked-book desk to the sound of frantic scribbling around him.

Remaking the principal's grotesque image into something likable was a daunting, if not impossible task. And Principal Bubb was the *last* creature in all of creation that he wanted to help. But perhaps Milton could come up with something that would both help the principal and make Heck a better place. . . .

Milton stole a glance at Moses, who was busy writing down his strategy. The boy seemed too skinny to be a fallen angel commando and didn't seem to be hiding a flaming halo or a pair of deadly wings feathered with keen blades. But he *did* seem to be the type of kid who would love nothing more than to stab you in the back.

Then it hit Milton. He jotted down his thoughts before common sense evicted them from his head.

Strategy:

What would help heal the rift between down here and up there? Angels! Fallen angels that have been forsaken. Tough angels that can help keep Heck safe for all. This, combined with a kinder, gentler image, will make Principal Bubb a likable yet not-to-be-trifled-with figurehead for juvenile rehabilitation.

D-Press Release Example:

Principal Bubb Makes Netherworld Security a High-Profile Priority

HECK: Principal Bubb has recruited a band of fallen angels to act as Heck's personal security force. This, she says, will help to protect her students and employees from an increasingly dangerous and unstable underworld.

"I have thousands of years of experience but am also sensitive to the winds of change," Principal Bubb says while playfully tousling the hair of one of her beloved students. "I can make Heck a safe, fun, and effective place: thanks to the recruitment of the fallen, whom I have dubbed Heck's Angels. This will free me to fill the underworld with compassion and tolerance."

Tactics:
- Hiring of fallen angels to serve as Principal Bubb's security detail, their involvement overseen by an independent committee to reinforce the principal's regime as thoroughly accountable and trustworthy. Have students assess her performance on a regular basis. Make her own position an electable one, showing her confidence.
- Appearances at high-profile events to increase Principal Bubb's visibility, ideally events where she is associated with security and child development.
- Day of the Darned: a Netherworld-wide child appreciation day, with lavish parades (everybody loves a parade) and a grand prize: allowing one lucky student to graduate "upstairs."
- Articles in popular underworld magazines such as <u>Dead People</u>, <u>Out of Time</u>, <u>Better Crypts and Cemeteries</u>, <u>Reaper's Digest</u>, and <u>Next-of-Kin Circle</u>.

Milton smirked to himself as he handed in his paper to Mr. Wilde.

The principal was obviously desperate if she needed to enlist the help of students to save her ample butt. And his public relations strategy—Milton had to admit with a rare lack of humility—was brilliant. If Bubb was officially aligned with the fallen angels, she wouldn't be able to use them in any sort of illicit, underhanded way. They would be far too visible to do things like, oh, I don't know . . . *covertly murder Milton*. This would open Principal Bubb up to a whole new level of accountability.

Sure, the last thing Milton wanted to do was actually *help* Principal Bubb, but this campaign—if Milton won the contest and the principal actually went for his crazy idea—could solve Milton's "not having his throat aired out by a fallen angel's razor-feather" issue and help *every* kid in Heck by making the place somewhat "less completely awful in every way."

The class bell tolled. Mr. Wilde took his portrait from the wall—the decrepit man in the painting now a withered sack of skin rattling with brittle bones. The teacher shook the painting vigorously like an Etch A Sketch, with the subject—Mr. Wilde—regaining his bloom of youth.

Mr. Wilde wiped his brow with a handkerchief. "That was close . . . you students age me so," he mumbled.

Moses Babcock glared at Milton as he and the other boys handed in their entries. The boy quickly scribbled something onto his palm with a pen, then walked over to Milton.

"Best of luck on your strategy," Moses said, squeezing Milton's hand and vigorously shaking it as if he were pumping water from a well. The boy's eyes simmered with contempt as he let go of Milton's throbbing hand and stormed away.

Maybe he's just intense, Milton thought. *Maybe Moses means well and just comes off cold and confrontational.*

Milton stared at his palm. On it was a word written in fresh ink.

LOSER

Milton sighed.

Or maybe I just made my first enemy here in Wise Acres. . . .

8 · LiViN' (AT) LARGE

DALE E. BASYE grimaced as he pushed away the emptied tin of cat food in disgust.

That Simply Scrumptpuss Fisherman's Stew tasted like it was made with real *fishermen,* he thought, scratching at his patchy beard.

So much had happened in the last few months. Far *too* much. Ever since that creepy kid, Damian Ruffino, had exploded like a big, bully of a zit on the Avalawns golf course outside of his former McMansion in the United Estates of Nevada, Dale had become a fugitive: on the run and on the lam.

Mmmm . . . lamb, Dale thought, patting his growling stomach.

It's not like it was Dale's fault. Not really. Not completely. Damian, that pushy, pimple-faced preteen, had actually tried to blackmail him. . . . Okay, blackmailing him for unabashedly stealing the boy's idea about an h-e-double-hockey-sticks for children—where the souls of the darned toiled for all eternity, or until they turned eighteen, whichever came first—and turning it into a hugely popular video game. But two wrongs don't make a right. Three rights, though, make a left, driving-wise. Dale had learned this because Las Vegas—or *Lost Vague-us,* as he had called it while trying to navigate its confounding cat's cradle of streets—was designed so that most every thoroughfare cunningly led you into the open, pickpocketing arms of a casino. So many roads trying to lead you to ruin. And Dale, it seems, had been speeding to ruin on the expressway.

Damian's gruesome death had—regrettably—happened several yards away from Dale after a lively argument that—unfortunately—occurred in front of a group of nosy witnesses playing through to the next hole and—regrettably, unfortunately, and super-sad-to-say—was captured in its entirety by controversy-hungry anchorwoman Biddy Malone and the KBET: The Only Sure "Bet" in Las Vegas news team. The news crew had been covering the AGHAST (Adults Galled by Heck and Such Things) protest outside of Dale's home after his *Heck: Where the Bad Kids Go* video game had reportedly turned many a teenage mind to mush.

It didn't matter, though, that Dale had had nothing to do with Damian's one-boy meat-splosion. What mattered was that it had happened on TV, and if something happens on TV, then it's true, or at least trueish. And considering that Damian left behind very little to actually autopsy, former-author-turned-video-game-tycoon-turned-convict-to-be Dale E. Basye was just one wrong move away from making the nightly news yet again.

He had been forced to give up everything, to leave his entire life behind him. Or, more to the point, Dale was now forced to live fifty feet behind his old life, having holed up in his former garden shed.

His ostentatious three-story McMansion had been quickly emptied by his wife—not his real wife but his covetous trophy wife, former Uzbek supermodel Goldie Grrr—and the house had been put up for sale.

How Dale longed for his family, his *real* family, the one he had lost when his success had grown faster than his ability to handle it properly. But his prospects for regaining his *former* former life—the life he had spent in Portland, Oregon, as a struggling children's author writing cheeky, groan-inducing books impervious to most every book list imaginable—were as empty as the house he now stared at forlornly through the window of his dingy garden shed.

Suddenly, something stirred inside the mansion. A hawk-nosed man with sandy, feathered hair and a polo shirt tucked into his chinos walked past the second-floor kitchen window.

"Phelps Better?" Dale muttered as he watched the unaccountably aggravating vice president of engineering for Virtual Prayground Technologies, the company that had purchased the exclusive video game rights to *Heck: Where the Bad Kids Go,* strut through Dale's house as if he owned the place.

A blond woman with a surgically tightened face teetered across the front yard on her high heels and, with a ladylike grunt, removed the FOR SALE sign from the expensive, imported dirt.

"Just bought my house?" Dale continued, drinking water that he had collected from his overly ambitious sprinkler system. "But why?"

The beady-eyed man opened the refrigerator and stared at his reflection in the mirror that Dale had installed so that he could see what he looked like when opening the refrigerator. Dale grabbed a pair of binoculars and brought his former kitchen into sharp focus. Phelps grinned at his own image, surely the only creature to ever do so. He took out an emery board from his back pocket and then proceeded to file down two little hornlike nubs sprouting just above his temples.

"His horns," Dale muttered. "They're *real* . . . not the trendy body-mod he claimed he and the other engineers on the *Heck: Where the Bad Kids Go* development team got for 'brand cohesion' or whatever. But something that actually grows out of his freakin' skull."

Phelps pulled out Dale's last can of Rojo Toro—an experimental Mexican energy drink originally used to keep stolen organs fresh on the black market—and slammed the door with his hip. He tapped his Bluetooth headset and took the spiral escalator to the main level.

"Aleister?" he spoke into his headset, strutting out onto the patio looking like a Borg on Casual Friday. "You should answer the phone with your name so that people know who they're talking to. That's a *Better* way of doing it. Get it? Like my last name?"

Phelps brayed like a mule, his eyes disappearing into crinkled slits.

"I'm in it now. Basye's house," he said, mangling Dale's last name like most everyone did, making it sound like some kind of French skin disease. "*My* house now. Bring the team over tonight and we'll go through it, top to bottom, and try to find some clue to his whereabouts."

Phelps tilted back his can of Rojo Toro.

"I'm really worried about the guy—"

Wow, maybe I misread Phelps, Dale thought.

"*—not!*" Phelps cackled, brushing back his feathered, parted-in-the-middle hairstyle that hadn't changed since the mid-1970s. "So we can kill him, of course!"

Dale swallowed, but the horrible cat food aftertaste seemed to claw its way back up his throat.

"He knows too much," Phelps continued. "Not as much as me, though, because I'm *Better* at everything. Get it? My last name? But he knows more than is good for him. If the police catch him, he'll start blabbing and it'll become a 'thing' . . . a thing we can't control. And

I'm all about control," he said as he fished out his iSlab from his chinos and began tapping out a note to himself.

What could I possibly know that could be so important to him?

"He doesn't know that what he knows is important," Phelps said. "That his book . . . the game . . . that it was all *real*."

Real? *But that's impossible. . . .*

"Or as real as that kind of thing can be. But soon everyone will know, and it'll be too late for them and just right for me. I'll show my dad what I'm capable of. And then he'll be proud. Get it? *He'll*. It's a joke, only Better, because *I* said it."

His dad? Why would someone go through all of this trouble to impress their dad?

"And once I get my dad's attention, I'll make him pay for leaving me up here," Phelps Better said as he pulverized his empty can of Rojo Toro in his hand. "Dearly."

At this point, Dale realized that running away from his old life wouldn't be enough to survive. He'd have to run away from life *itself* to truly be free of the mess he'd made of things. A total do-over. Every adult's dream come true. But first he'd have to convince the world, and especially Phelps Better, that he was no longer of this world . . . or die trying.

9 · TEACHERS' PET PEEVES

MILTON SAW HIS sister kneeling just outside of the Teachers' Lounge, pretending to tie her shoe. After a moment's babbling, the room went as silent as a mime's wake. Marlo was peeking through the crack between the slightly open door and the doorjamb. Milton could see a group of forlorn teachers sitting miserably around a crooked table covered with coffee ring stains.

Milton tapped Marlo on the shoulder.

"Eeeek!" she squealed, falling over in a heap.

Milton stood over her. "You've been tying your shoes for five minutes," he said.

A dark-haired woman with bags underneath her eyes scowled from behind the door. "No one likes a Nosy Parker," the woman said while pretending to smoke a piece of chalk. *"And I should know!"* The teacher slammed the door.

"I'm guessing that was Dorothy Parker," Milton said as he helped his sister from the floor.

"What's a Dorothy Parker?" Marlo grunted as she got to her feet.

"She was a critic and humorist back in the twentieth century."

Marlo brushed herself off. "Well, the 'critic' part seems intact but I think she left the whole 'humor' thing back on the Surface."

Milton and Marlo walked down the sparsely populated hallway.

"So . . . why were you eavesdropping?" Milton asked.

"Eavesdropping? *Geez,*" Marlo replied. "Everyone's always telling me to listen to my teachers, and now that I actually *do,* you get on my case about it."

Milton glanced over his shoulder. The hallway was empty.

"What did they say?" Milton asked.

Marlo tugged her tweed coat closed, hoping to hide the "My Clothes Attract Attention . . . Not to Mention Flies" slogan scrolling across her electric shirt.

"When the teachers weren't harping on each *other,* they were harping on Vice Principal Carroll," she relayed. "They say he's as nuts as a bag of nuts rolled in extra-nutty Nutella and then covered in more nuts."

"They said that?"

"I'm paraphrasing. They said he locks himself away in some shed, his Absurditory, so he can come up with more crazy stuff. The teachers were also talking about how miserable they were because they couldn't write anymore, not anything good anyway."

"Why is that?" Milton asked.

"Because they're being kept from their muses . . . and the part of their souls that they poured into their books or something . . . which, um, reminds me. Speaking of muses . . ."

"Where's Lucky?" Milton asked, noticing Marlo's coat didn't have the same, vaguely ferret-shaped lump in the breast pocket.

Marlo relayed her experience with Miss Dickinson.

"She said he'd be okay, and I kind of trust her," Marlo added. "As much as you can trust someone who uses wasps as teachers' aides, that is."

The other Lucky poked his head out of Milton's coat.

"We should probably hide him, though," Marlo said. "It's only a matter of time before they take Lucky Two, too."

They walked across the book-strewn floor (mostly romance novels and serial Westerns). A cat brushed past Milton's leg. And then another. Milton sneezed as the cats padded down the hall and around the bend with something approaching urgency.

"More of those cats," Milton said, wiping his nose. "I wonder where they're going?"

"To Lewis Carroll," Marlo said as she and her brother turned the corner. "That's what Miss Dickinson said.

They're Furriers, carrying messages back and forth for Vice Principal Crazy Pants."

The two cats were joined by another, a jaunty black-and-gray tabby. The cat was wearing a leather pouch tied to its back.

"If we could just see what's in those bags," Marlo said as she trotted up behind the cat and made the fatal mistake of touching it.

Hissssssssssssss-ssssspiiiiiit!

The feline erupted into a mewling storm of claws and teeth.

"Owwww!" Marlo yelped, her forearms cross-hatched with oozing scratch marks. *"Bad kitty!"*

Cookie Youngblood, Concordia Kolassa, and two other girls strutted toward Milton and Marlo.

"Don't blame the cat, New Girl," Cookie said with a sneer. "It was only trying to cover up what it thought was poop—that's what cats do."

The girls laughed as Cookie assessed Marlo from head to toe, attaching snarky comments along the way.

"It's like Papa Smurf ate Smurfette, then threw up on New Girl's head. . . . New Girl's nose looks like a thumb that lost its nail. . . . New Girl's body couldn't decide if it was a boy or a girl, so it just gave up. . . ."

When Cookie finally finished, Marlo smiled and wrapped her pale arms around the girls. "Dearly bedeviled, we are gathered here today to mourn the loss of Cookie Youngblood's mind. This tiny speck of brain is survived by her shapeless stick of a body. Cookie's mind will be sorely missed—but maybe if we keep throwing stuff at it, we'll hit it. . . ."

The girls rolled their eyes as they turned left toward the Audaci-Tea House.

Marlo balled her hands into fists and slammed them into her hips. "Man, that girl bugs me," she seethed.

A Siamese cat darted down the hall. It sniffed at a patch of wall with intense interest, then started scratching furiously. In just a matter of seconds, it had dug a small tunnel through the compressed wall of old encyclopedias.

"Let's see where the itty-bitty kitty committee goes," Marlo said as she followed the cat.

"I don't know," Milton said, his eyes watering and itchy. "My cat allergy . . ."

"Maybe we can find out more about the vice principal's Absurditory. *C'mon!*"

Marlo squeezed herself through the cramped shredded hole with Milton elbowing along close behind. They emerged in a dark, neglected corridor. A few yards away was another iron spiral staircase—smaller and shabbier than the main turret staircase—shooting up through the crumbling floor of ancient, decomposing books. The Siamese cat had a shred of ancient, excavated paper in its jaws.

"C'mere, kitty kit-kat," Marlo cooed as she pussyfooted toward the creature. Suddenly, she lunged at it and snatched the paper from its muzzle. The cat hissed and spat before bounding up the staircase.

"This must be the back entrance or something," Marlo said. A winding trail of dusty paw prints led up to a tiny door at the very top of the staircase.

Marlo and Milton stared quizzically at the yellowed parchment.

In the beginning was the Word, and the Word was . . . *whoops!*

"Whoops?" Marlo murmured as she and her brother squinted at the oddly shimmering handwriting that seemed to writhe and wriggle on the page.

Sorry, I seemed to have dropped my ambrosia. Butter fingers! Anyway, in the beginning—that is, before anything was formed—was the Word. A Word that promulgated My will and My commandments. Hmm . . . that sounds so . . . *bossy*. What I want to convey is that by My Word, I have created all Creation, speaking All Things out of Nothing. And that Word was Me: no second to the Most High, but the supreme eternal Author. Wow . . . that sounds like I'm *awfully* full of Myself!

"Is this like Bible stuff or something?" Marlo asked.

"Sort of," Milton said. "But it's different. Like it was dictated. Maybe this is an early draft of the Bible. It's weird . . . ," Milton said, blinking really fast. From the corner of his eye, the writing appeared different, written in a foreign language. "The original Bible was supposedly in Aramaic, but we can read it. This must be written in a special kind of ink that allows us to—"

"What are you guys doing?" a voice asked, booming in the dim, musty stillness.

Marlo tucked the parchment into the pocket of her nasty tweed coat. A short, narrow-faced boy with a sharp, shrewd gaze peered back at the Fausters.

"Um, hi . . . uh," Milton replied.

"Roget Marx Peters," the boy replied.

"Right. Anyway, we're kind of—"

Roget looked up the stairs.

"Listen, squirt," Marlo said. "This is none of your business."

"Well, I'm *making* it my business, concern, undertaking," Roget replied stonily.

Marlo glared at the boy. "Careful, or I'm going to give you a high five . . . in the face . . . with my shoe. But okay. Just don't tell anyone what we're doing."

"What *are* you doing . . . carrying out . . . undertaking?"

Milton and Marlo padded up the creaking steps.

"It's hard to tell," Marlo said as she reached the top step. "Just following these weird messenger cats to . . ."

Marlo flipped open a plastic flap on the tiny door. Outside, in the uncared-for grounds covered with undergrowth and a taunting tangle of Sassafras and Syca-Yew trees, was a huge shed shaped like a grinning cat head.

". . . the big scary cat shack."

Milton joined his sister at the top of the stairs.

"It's a pet door—"

"Animal portal, creature exit," Roget muttered.

"Leading out to Vice Principal Carroll's Absurditory," Milton finished. "Of course . . . it's like the Cheshire cat from *Alice in Wonderland* . . . I didn't know Wise Acres had a backyard. . . ."

"It's part of the Talk-Back Forty," Roget offered. "An undeveloped, wild, uncultivated part of Wise Acres that stretches nearly all the way out to Wisecrackatoa . . ."

The Siamese cat bounded across the grounds and darted through another pet door, hidden in the Cheshire cat's teeth. Marlo tried to wedge herself through it, but it was too small.

"I'm double-jointed," she grunted. "So maybe I can just dislocate my shoulder . . ."

"And become a permanent fixture of the architecture," Milton said as he helped tug Marlo loose. "We need to think of another way."

Lucky poked his head out of Milton's coat, taking hungry sniffs of air.

"A ferret," Roget mumbled. "Weasel, polecat . . ."

Marlo felt around in her coat pocket. "That gives me an idea," she said.

"Notion, thought, concept . . ."

"Look, I'm going to punch you in the head, skull, noggin if you don't shut up," Marlo said, routing around her pocket. "Good . . . I still got it. . . ."

"*Have* it," Milton and Roget said simultaneously.

Marlo pulled out her half-eaten bar of booger-and-paste-flavored soap.

"Why did you keep that?" Milton said with a grimace.

Marlo shrugged. "The taste of paste takes me back," she said, giving the bar a few licks. "Kindergarten, specifically. Plus I'm resourceful. You never know when something will come in handy. . . ."

Marlo reached for Lucky and set the squirming ferret on her lap. She rubbed the foaming bar of soap all over Lucky's head and tail. Marlo sculpted Lucky's ferret ears into stiff points.

"Um . . . ," Milton said warily. "He's going to scratch your eyes out."

"Nah," Marlo said as she worked up the fur on Lucky's head into a sticky lather. "He loves the attention."

Lucky hissed.

"See? That's ferret-speak for 'Thank you, Marlo. You are both kind and beautiful.'" She rubbed soap on Lucky's tail until it stuck up in the air.

"There!" Marlo exclaimed as she set Lucky in front of the pet door. The supremely irritated ferret was nearly paralyzed with indignation, his ears and tail pointed straight and prickly with dried soap suds.

"It's just like they always say: a ferret makes a lovely cat," she explained.

"Nobody says that," Milton replied. "But he *does* sort of look like a cat. . . ."

Marlo pushed Lucky through the plastic flap.

"Hey! What are you—"

"Go follow the other kitties," Marlo instructed Lucky. "Vice Principal Carroll probably has cans of tuna labeled 'Eat Me' in there."

Lucky sniffed at the air with interest. A cat playfully batted the Absurditory pet door, beckoning the ferret with its twitchy rhythm, like wounded prey. Lucky hunkered down before darting across the grounds toward the big cat-faced shed.

Marlo wiped dried soap scum off her hands.

"Now the vice principal will give Lucky a message, he'll head straight for you—like he always does—and we'll get to read it."

Milton shook his head doubtfully. "I don't know . . . he'd have to be pretty mad to think Lucky is a cat," he murmured.

"Feline, mouser, grimalkin," Roget muttered.

Milton sighed.

"I just hope the vice principal isn't wearing his Looking Glasses when he slips Lucky a message."

10 · BOTCH YOUR LANGUAGE!

"WHAT DO HITTITE, Aramaic, Latin, Phoenician, and San-skrit all have in common?" Miss Parker asked as she paced in front of the class, tugging on a strand of fake pearls dangling from her wrinkled neck.

"They're all incredibly boring?" offered a smug, pudgy girl.

"They were members of the worst basketball team ever?" interjected a girl with dark braids.

"They were the latest dance moves when you were a little girl back in the Middle Ages?" spat a large, olive-skinned girl. The hefty girl leaned back against a stack of moldy, outdated astronomy textbooks printed before Pluto was designated a planet and *definitely* before it was eventually stripped of its planetary status, making the outdated textbooks strangely *in*dated.

Miss Parker sighed, barely able to summon the energy to lift her chalk to the blackboard. Though known for her wit, an eternity spent among the tirelessly impertinent had left Miss Parker feeling at her wit's end.

"As shrewd as Misses Scathelli, Zanotti, and Caustilo are, they are all shockingly wrong in this instance. Hittite, Aramaic, Latin, Phoenician, and Sanskrit are all . . ." Miss Parker scratched on the chalkboard:

DEAD LANGUAGES

Marlo raised her hand.

The teacher glanced down at her roster. "Yes, new girl? Miss . . . *Fauster*? You have something vital to add to the class I have yet to teach?"

Marlo had no idea why she had raised her hand. She was to "raising her hand in class" as Abraham Lincoln was to bungee jumping. But her need to be recognized as some kind of tart, teenage trouncer of all things status quo had apparently hijacked her arm while her brain had defected.

"What use is learning a dead language?" Marlo asked.

Instantly—from Miss Parker's dark, heavy-lidded stare—Marlo could tell that her teacher had heard this question many times before.

"Miss Fauster, if I may for a moment deflect your

question with several of my own?" Miss Parker asked, her eyes gleaming above bags so stuffed with world- and underworld-weariness that they looked like luggage.

"Yes . . . you may," Marlo replied, trying to appear sassy to impress the other girls.

The class subtly leaned forward in their mildewed book benches, anticipating a fight.

"Are you currently one of the living?" Miss Parker asked.

"Um . . . no."

"So that would make you *what*, exactly? Take your time, Miss Fauster, as you've already taken plenty of mine."

"Dead . . . I guess."

"Very good! You are in fact *dead*. As is everyone currently in the underworld. And what do we teach here in Wise Acres, Miss Fauster?"

"Words and stuff."

"Words and stuff," Miss Parker repeated with a smirk. "How eloquently put. Another way of saying that—the *accurate* way—is 'language.' Last question: this one for all of your dignity, if there's any left. Are you game?"

Feeling the heat of her fellow students' stares goading her on, Marlo folded her arms in defiance. "Game? I'm Parcheesi, Candy Land, and Chutes and Ladders all rolled into one."

Miss Parker smiled despite herself. "Touché, Miss Fauster. Now, what have you learned since your arrival here in Wise Acres?"

Marlo shrugged. "Besides that wasps sting and that I'm dead, nothing useful."

"Bingo!" Miss Parker exclaimed, a brief touch of color flushing her chalk-white cheeks. "You are learning dead languages because you are *dead,* you are in *Wise Acres,* and it will be of *no use to you whatsoever!*"

A pretty, auburn-haired girl showed her irritation with a double-barrel-roll of her wide blue-green eyes.

Miss Parker smacked her palms against the lectern. "Don't look at me in that tone of voice, Miss Duckworth!" the teacher exclaimed. "I can't help that I'm forced to, in essence, teach boredom. But there is a cure for boredom, and that's curiosity."

"What's the cure for curiosity?" Marlo asked.

"Thankfully there *is* no cure for curiosity," the teacher replied with a sly wink, Marlo having somehow graduated from tongue-tied-small-fry to wise-guy-ally in the blink of an eye.

Miss Parker thrummed her fingers against her lectern. "The word 'language' is Latin, meaning *tongue,*" she said. "Which is why the first thing I do in the morning is brush my teeth and sharpen my tongue, because language, you see, is a powerful thing. But perhaps you'll only appreciate its worth once it's been frittered away."

The teacher squatted down behind her lectern, rummaging through a large white canvas bag, and emerged with an armful of what looked like snorkels. She passed them out to the girls in the front row, who handed them over their shoulders to the girls behind them. Miss Parker walked over to Moxie Wortschmerz, whom a demon badger had wheeled in and set at the back of the class. The girl wriggled angrily in her straightjacket.

"You are—understandably—excused from this exercise, Miss Wortschmerz," the teacher said.

Moxie furiously clacked her silver-sheathed tongue against the roof of her mouth. Miss Parker returned to her lectern.

"Now, girls, please put on your Sass-Masks."

"Sksam-ssas," mumbled a girl with sleek, side-swept bangs.

"Huh?" Marlo said as she fiddled with her mask.

Flossie leaned into Marlo. "That's Roberta Atrebor," the perky girl explained. "She has to say everything backwards and forwards. It's like how some people have to wash their hands all the time."

"At least that makes sense," Marlo replied as she strapped the mask over her face. "I mean, have you *seen* the kind of things hands touch?"

As soon as Marlo put the Sass-Mask on her face, it tightened just under the jaw.

"Hey! What gives?!" she shouted. In the corner of her goggle mask, a digital readout clicked from 100 to 97.

Miss Parker smiled as the girls complained, struggling to remove the masks that sealed over their faces. "You might want to save your witticisms until I've had a chance to explain what exactly a Sass-Mask *is*," the teacher said, fiddling with her fake pearls. "They're a little experiment of Vice Principal Carroll's. He's developing a subscription-based language, where one would have to *pay* to use it."

"What?!" Marlo gasped inside the stifling mask. "That's crazy . . . a language you have to *pay* for?"

The readout on Marlo's goggle lens now read 87.

"Off the record, I think most of our eccentric new vice principal's ideas are not just plain terrible, they're *fancy* terrible: terrible with raisins in it. But at least with these Sass-Masks, you might learn the value of words."

"What are the numbers in this thing all about?" Winifred Scathelli gasped from inside of her mask. "They keep counting down!"

Miss Parker paced in front of the class in her plain black dress. "If we were to dish out words as if they were currency, like money, and not squander them recklessly as if they didn't mean anything—and what are words if they have no meaning?—then we would all be much better off."

Miss Parker took a handful of brightly striped straws and walked up and down the rows of confused, snorkeled girls, dropping the straws into their air tubes.

"The numbers on your goggles are your allotted words. Think of words as a gift and your Sass-Masks as a prepaid gift card."

"What happens when it gets to zero?" Marlo asked, her goggles blinking 80.

"Why don't we find out?" Miss Parker replied. "First, what do you fine young women think of my dress?"

There was a sudden, muffled explosion of derogatory commentary spewing from the girls' mouths.

"Words can't describe your outfit, so I'll just barf!"

"Your dress makes a statement. Too bad it's 'I have zero taste'!"

"That outfit is so ratty it belongs in the sewer!"

Miss Parker smiled.

"*Excellent*. Now complete this sentence. . . ." She wrote on the chalkboard.

YOUR MOMMA'S SO FAT . . .

". . . her belly button makes an echo!"

". . . she climbed into the Grand Canyon and got stuck!"

". . . when she wears a red dress, all of the kids yell, 'Hey, Kool-Aid!'"

Marlo noticed her goggle readout hovering at 16.

"What-if-I-just-hyphenate-all-of-my-words-so-they-only-count-as-one?" Marlo asked.

"While clever, Miss Fauster, your Sass-Mask knows better."

"Oh," Marlo said, her goggles flashing red. Suddenly, a gush of sticky sweet-and-sour paste filled her mouth. She could hear the girls around her gasping.

Yuck! Marlo screamed out in her mind as her lips were sealed shut. She tried to wrench them free, but the inside of her mouth felt like a balled-up fist wearing a flypaper glove.

"You all sound like Neanderthals with toothaches," Miss Parker snickered. She grabbed a large bottle of fizzy liquid from the canvas sack.

"Finally . . . I can hear myself think," she said as she systematically drizzled the liquid down the girls' snorkels. "The reason you can't talk is because of the Epoxie Stix I put in your masks. It's sort of a candied cement."

Miss Parker poured the liquid down Marlo's breathing tube. The sweet-and-sour paste was washed away by a carbonated wave of astringent citrus.

The class bell tolled. Marlo's Sass-Mask relaxed its grip on her face like a starfish hit with a tranquilizer dart.

"Vice Principal Carroll will soon have all the students wearing these things, I'm afraid," Miss Parker muttered. "And probably the teachers, too, soon after that. Wise Acres will become a quieter place, I'm sure, yet a much more boring one. . . ."

Marlo tossed her mask aside and slowly staggered toward the door, joining the gurgling flow of the other girls, all of them smacking their lips like dogs eating peanut butter.

"Miss Fauster . . . as one Nosy Parker to another, try

to remember the cure for boredom," the baggy-eyed woman said with a smeary, weary smile.

Marlo wiped her mouth with the back of her hand.

"Curiosity," Marlo replied with a croak.

And while the vice principal might be able to shut my mouth, he sure as heck won't shut my mind, she thought as she stumbled into the hall.

11 · MAY i TAKE A MESSAGE?

MARLO AND FLOSSIE sat across from one another in the Audaci-Tea House, a tray of grammar crackers between them, desperately trying to remove the gummy taste from their mouths. Marlo looked down at the little phrases etched into her grammar cracker.

CONRAD AND ELIZA CAN'T HARDLY BELIEVE THEY WON'T BE GETTING PUDDING AFTER SETTING THE FIRE.

Marlo bit into it. A rotten-tooth-mold taste flooded her mouth.

"Yuck!" she said with a grimace. "This is even worse than those Epoxie Stix."

Flossie nibbled carefully along her grammar cracker.

"You've got to be careful to just eat the parts with good grammar," she said, looking up at Marlo through a part in her stiff, orange-red bangs. Marlo glanced back down at her cracker.

AFTER ROTTING IN THE CELLAR FOR WEEKS, MY SISTER BROUGHT UP SOME APPLES.

Hmm . . . that seems weird. Like the sister is rotting, not the apples, thought Marlo.

"YOU'RE MESSING UP ITS HAIR," THE DOG GROOMER TOLD HER ASSISTANT.

That seems okay, Marlo thought as she took a bite. She was rewarded with a gush of warm, nutty sweetness.

"Yum," she said. "Good grammar tastes good."

The goddess Peitho walked by carrying a bowl of fruit. "Sour grapes?" she offered.

Marlo plucked a grape from the bowl and popped it into her mouth. She grimaced at its sharp, pungent taste. Flossie stared at the goddess as she swept away in her flowing white gown.

"Peitho sure is pretty," Flossie said with a soft sigh.

"I wouldn't want to be that pretty anyway," Marlo lied as she munched on her sour grapes. "Too much trouble."

Outside the teahouse, a boy darted down the hall after a fuzzy white blur with a leather pouch lashed to its back.

"Lucky! He's back!" Marlo said as she bolted from her chair.

Milton was panting at the end of the hall, with Lucky—at his feet—chewing at the leather strap tied around his midsection.

"Let's see what the carrier-ferret brought back for us," Marlo said as she caught up with her brother.

Milton nodded, unlatched the pouch's clasp, and pulled out a scroll. He unrolled the parchment on his thigh.

My dear mysterious, anonymous benefactor: a guardian angel if there ever was one!

To think, only a few weeks ago I was tucked away in Bedlam, with nothing to do but tear my hair out and surrender myself to a sad tale not of my making. And now—such Fortune!—a new story with me as the protagonist, in a setting ripe with arcane knowledge! So many pieces to the ultimate puzzle that most everything else has been driven out of my head!

I feel I am so very close to cracking the code: finding the "cheat" as the young people here say. There are just a few stern wrinkles—the kind that plague the faces of so many adults—that are in want of ironing. Some final artifacts are needed to create artifiction.

So, to make a short story long, I remain very truly yours, and look forward to the latest illuminating missive from my benevolent patron,

> *The Late C. L. Dodgson*

P.S. Included is—in my waggish way—a status report on my progress!

Reason's picnic ruined: rant by crawling ranT

Overwhelmed by whimsy's vertigO

Spinning yarn with abandoN

Expressing the inexpressible with thunder divinE

Tales told till true, every ear shall see; every eye shall hear

To have the last word, I have found the very first word

And so I'll spread an affliction of fiction till the afterlife is mine to dream!

Milton studied the message. There was more to it than just a bunch of scattershot phrases. It felt like some kind of puzzle. Like an . . .

"Acrostic," Milton said. "That's what this is."

"A crossed tick? And who is C. L. Dodgson?"

"An *acrostic*. It's a type of word puzzle. And Dodgson was Lewis Carroll's real name. He was really into word puzzles. *Alice in Wonderland* is filled with them. Most of the so-called nonsense parts were actually a kind of clever code—"

"*Anyway.*"

"Anyway, an acrostic is a poem where certain letters form a secret word, usually the first letter of each line." Milton traced the letters with his fingertip. "See? It spells R-O-S-E-T-T-A. *Rosetta.* But this looks like a double acrostic. See the last letters of each line? T-O-N-E. *Tone* . . . hmm . . ."

Milton dug into his pocket and pulled out the encyclopedia page he had found stuck to his shoe.

Entry: Music of the Spheres (*SEE:* Rosetta Tone)

Milton rummaged through Lucky's leather pouch. "Wait, there's something else. . . ."

Milton pulled out a windup metal cricket and a tiny fork. He studied the silver, tri-pronged piece of cutlery.

"It's like a tuning fork," he mumbled.

Marlo snickered and shook her head. "This is great."

"What?"

"You're like my outboard brain," Marlo said. "Why should I waste my time stuffing my head full of junk when I have *you*? So what's with the tuning fork and cricket toy?"

"I don't know," Milton said while Marlo wound up

the odd brass cricket. "Usually tuning forks have two prongs, but this one has three. Most tuning forks are designed to vibrate at a specific pitch. . . ."

Milton tapped the fork against his knee while Marlo released the windup key, causing the cricket to chirp in the most peculiar—

Everything seemed to go white and fuzzy around the edges. Milton's and Marlo's minds went blank. Whether for five seconds, five minutes, or five hours, they couldn't be sure.

"What happened?" Marlo asked.

Milton looked around the hallway, dazed, as if he just woke up from a short yet intensely deep nap.

"I'm . . . I'm not sure," he said. "I must have zoned out or something."

"Yeah, me too. We're probably exhausted from all of this nothing-going-on." Marlo rose to her feet. "Look, this isn't getting us anywhere. All we have for our trouble is a weird fork, a sticky ferret, a metal grasshopper, and a cross-stitched poem—"

"*Acrostic.*"

"Whatever. The point is . . . ," Marlo said before faltering as she noticed two aardvark demons waddling out of the Audaci-Tea House. Each had a silver tray strapped to its back. The demons were headed toward the entrance.

"Interesting," Marlo muttered as she followed them down the hall.

Milton trotted after her. "What are you doing?" he asked.

On one tray was a teapot and a porcelain teacup. On the other was a plate full of tiny white blobs.

"Hey!" Marlo shouted out. "Where are you two going?"

One of the lumbering creatures glanced over its shoulder as it toddled along.

"It's Vice Principal Carroll's teatime," the demon aardvark grunted. "He has the same thing every day: two cups of strong tea and a plate of meringue cookies."

The aardvarks snuffled along the hall until they arrived at the base of the turret staircase.

"Listen, you guys work . . . way too hard," Marlo said, a little out of breath after rushing behind the two surprisingly fast "pig-aroos." "Let me take him his tea."

The two demon guards traded a quick, dark glance before snorting in what must have been laughter but sounded more like a spoon caught in a garbage disposal.

"I don't think so," one of the guards grunted as it made its way toward the first step.

Marlo jumped in between the two creatures.

"Marlo," Milton said, forcing his voice into something that sounded calmer than he felt. "What do you think you're—"

"Hey, you two anteaters or whatever," Marlo said, sensing that there are few things more offensive to an aardvark than being referred to as an anteater. "I wasn't asking. I'm going to take the vice preposterous his tea and there's nothing you can do about it. . . ."

The two aardvark demons—their brown-gray skin flushed red with rage—squared off on either side of Marlo.

"I wish these things had Mute switches on them," one of the guards grunted. "But since they don't, maybe a good tongue lashing will keep her quiet."

Marlo swallowed. "Strawberry shortcake, huckleberry pie . . . ," she chanted, keenly assessing the aardvark demons as they reared to attack. "I'm going to jump till your tongues are—"

The demons shot out their long, sticky tongues. Marlo hopped into the air just as the creatures' tongues slurped and curled beneath her feet, tying themselves into a pink, slobbery knot.

"—*tied*," Marlo said.

She quickly robbed the demons of their silver trays and keys. Marlo bounded up the stairs with a rattle of teacups and plates.

"Marlo!" Milton gasped as the demon aardvarks played a futile game of tug-of-war with their tongues.

Marlo cast her crooked, mischievous smile down at her brother from the top of the stairs.

"Malice in Wonderland is going to crash the Mad Hatter's tea party," she said as she unlocked the drum portal leading outside. "Don't wait up!"

12 · TEA AND PSYCHOPATHY

"HELLO? TEATIME *T-MINUS now,"* Marlo called from the Absurditory's double doors, which were painted to be the grinning Cheshire cat's two front teeth. "Is anybody"—Marlo scanned the bewildering interior—*"completely* off their meds?"

The small cottage was just one big room with all of the usual components: chairs, lamps, sofa, writing desk. . . . Only all of these furnishings were in the wrong place. *Seriously* wrong. A black-and-white checkerboard carpet was tacked to the ceiling along with a chair that hung down like a chandelier, while an *actual* chandelier sprouted up from the burnished wood floor. What Marlo had initially thought were suspended lamps proved to be large, red-and-white mushrooms that—judging from their shredded stalks—some of the more athletic messenger cats were using as scratching posts.

And then there was the stuffed monster raven. It hung above like a big feathered bat, with a wooden tabletop nailed to its back.

Marlo could see a sheaf of papers on the raven writing desk above, held in place with an elastic band. She set her silver tea service tray down beneath the prodigious cap of an upside-down mushroom, tucked her blue hair behind her ears, and jumped up toward the fiberglass mushroom, gripping the rim and pulling herself up onto the gills.

Marlo shimmied up the stalk to the ceiling and reached for the capsized chair. She grabbed its arms, and—her body somehow recalling a summer's worth of preteen gymnastics—executed an upside-down pull-up until she was "sitting" in the chair. Marlo carefully strapped herself into the dangling seat belt, wedging her legs under the chair's red velvet-padded arms to prevent her from falling and breaking her neck.

The blood rushing to her head and her hair hanging down like a stringy blue curtain, Marlo leaned toward the raven desk. Atop the sheaf of papers was an ancient parchment, yellowed and coarsened by time.

Okay . . . let's try this again. In the beginning was the Word and the Word was with God, and the Word was God. And with this one, single, luminous Word, His True Name, He—see, now I'm doing the third-person thing. I think

it works better that way, makes Me appear less conceited . . . You didn't write that last bit, did you? And this part? Hey, cut it out or I will smote you, so help me, Me . . .

There was a sticky note affixed to the side of the ancient document, written in different handwriting than that on the parchment. The same writing as in Lewis Carroll's note . . .

This unspoken Name. It is forbidden to speak, and therefore has yet to be captured by theologians. The oldest reference is "Jehovah," yet His True Name would have to be much older than that, and—more than likely—beyond a human's normal capacity for speech, keeping Creation "Password Protected" . . .

Beneath the document was another page torn from an archaic encyclopedia.

Weisen, Josef (Wīzənt, Jōzəf), 1303–1392, German metallurgist obsessed with the resonant properties of metal. Weisen's work involved the alchemical synthesis of rare metals such as theotonium (Th: the element of godliness) and ahsonium (Ah: the element of surprise) to fashion tools that would harness divine forces. Weisen, after losing his family to the Black Death, went mad and devoted his remaining years to harnessing elemental powers in order to "mock" the God that took his loved ones away. He recruited other "dark" artists to help him increase the spiritual resonance of his rare metals. Weisen's forge had a strict "if you smelt it, you dealt it" policy, meaning that whoever created a tool had to test it themselves. Weisen died shortly after forging a divine hammer, which—purportedly after striking a blow—rattled him and his fellow metallurgists apart to nothing. . . .

Beneath the documents was a map. Marlo smoothed it out. It was hard enough to read, in its fussy Victorian pen strokes, but all the blood in her head had her on the verge of fainting. At the top of the map was written:

The Outer Territories

Wise Acres was at the bottom of the map, delineated as a great, gated mound. In the upper left-hand corner was a tall, sort of trident-shaped building marked THE TOWER OF BABBLE, opposite a dormant volcano marked WISECRACKATOA.

Tower of Babble? We didn't see anything like that when we came here, Marlo thought as her ears buzzed with blood. *We totally would have seen something that big. . . .*

In between Wise Acres and the tower was a stretch of land, populated with hundreds of tiny "Y"s. Across them all, written in mad, florid loops, was a sentence that Marlo found both baffling and unnerving:

Here There Be Grammonsters!

Another sticky note was stuck to the map, with a few of those strange metal cricket toys secured to the desk with tape. Marlo squinted hard to read the precise, infinitesimally small lettering, a labor made extra-challenging as her vision began to go dark around the edges, as if she were looking at the note through the wrong end of a glass telescope.

The Rosetta Tone virus grows at an astonishing clip, gripping onto sympathetic memories to create a startlingly real and infectious delusion: tricking the mind into expelling all reason! The sonicrobial virus—that is to say, a disease composed of sound waves rather than bacteria—effectively converts the human mind into a factory for multiplying fantasy a millionfold. A virulent, phantasmagorical freeforall! The speed of mutation is astounding. When directed and shaped by specially modulated Retuning Forks, the Rosetta Tone wages a high-intensity attack on its host, foisting upon the victim a predetermined reality that unfolds in surprising ways. When the outbreak hits its perfect fever pitch—multiplied and solidified by multiple hosts experiencing the same delusion—all sanity perishes!

Marlo heard voices outside the Absurditory. She quickly unbuckled herself and—clutching the velvet armrests tightly—flipped herself upright and hopped onto the wooden floor.

"What a lovely jabber-walk: the perfect blend of jabbering and walking. And a most productive morning, setting the Retuning Forks about the Territories . . . Oh dear: we are nearly half-past teatime! Imagine, if it were *perpetually* teatime, we would never be late for it!"

Vice Principal Carroll, Marlo thought, her heart racing as she knelt, prone and all too visible, in the middle of the wooden ceiling-floor. *And he's got company. . . .*

Marlo spotted a long cupboard in the corner of the room. She hopped atop the nearest toadstool, opened the cupboard door, and slipped inside just as the vice principal parted the cat-tooth doors.

"Splendid!" Vice Principal Carroll exclaimed as he entered the Absurditory. "Our tea is here!"

The vice principal had a peculiar speech affectation—not quite a stutter, but more of a slight verbal stumble.

Marlo could hear him stop just outside her cupboard.

"Oh goodness! I count eleven meringues! I will have a word with the waitstaff, and I assure you that it shall be a *stern* one."

His footsteps retreated. Marlo breathed a quiet sigh of relief.

"How long do we have before the assembly?" asked a queer, high-pitched girl's voice.

Assembly? Marlo thought, crouched low in the cupboard, pressed against an assortment of cups and saucers.

"Not to worry, my dear Sylvie," Vice Principal Carroll replied. "As I am the vice principal, the assembly shall begin promptly upon our arrival. Would you care for a spot of tea, Bruno?"

"Not unless you have some spot-of-tea-remover," replied a low, gargly sort of voice. "I wouldn't want to soil my nice new clothes."

The vice principal chuckled blithely. "You young sprites are certainly particular about the state of your wardrobe!"

Sprites? Like fairies?

"Well," Sylvie said in her strained squeak of a voice, "an upsy-daisy teatime—while a charming diversion—can be a sloppy affair."

"I shall fetch us additional teacups, then," the vice principal said as his footsteps approached the cupboard. "To better capture our upturned tea tempests . . ."

Marlo gulped her beating heart back down her throat as Vice Principal Carroll grabbed the doorknob.

"Please . . . don't go through the bother," Sylvie exclaimed. "Let us simply have our tea beneath the mushroom, as we shall be running out of time."

"Hopefully not before we run out of conversation," Vice Principal Carroll replied as he walked away from the cupboard.

Phew, Marlo thought. *That was too close for comfort . . . but just close enough for* dis*comfort.*

She could hear the dainty sipping of tea.

"Ah . . . nice and black, just like I like it," the vice principal murmured. "It helps when the tea is steeped in ink!"

"Tell us your new story!" Bruno said with a slurp.

"Yes! Oh do!" Sylvie exclaimed. "And, Bruno, mind your manners!"

Vice Principal Carroll snorted with mirth. "Sillies . . . my next story shan't be *told*—it shall be *lived*! That is rather the point of this whole escapade: to wipe away the limitations of language—obliterate the very *need* for it— and create something fresh and whimsical, something free and unencumbered. And once all of their wagging, wasteful Mother Tongues are tied, I will remake all of creation however I like: to weave the ultimate story, with Lewis Carroll as the master storyteller!"

There was a brief pause, filled with the tinkling of teacups. Marlo's breath sounded like a hurricane to her ears.

"I must be off," Vice Principal Carroll said.

Yeah, Marlo thought. *Way, way off!*

"Would you two care to be my special guests at the assembly?" the vice principal inquired.

"I don't want to go among mad people," Sylvie replied with distaste.

The vice principal laughed.

Marlo had watched more than her fair share of horror movies. She had heard crazed psychopaths, mad scientists, and fiendish creatures laugh their respectively crazed, mad, and fiendish laughs, but Marlo had *never* heard a laugh as unmoored from the sandbags of sanity as Vice Principal Carroll's.

"Oh, you can't help that," the vice principal said as Marlo heard the creak of him rising from his chair. "We're *all* mad here!"

13 · READING BETWEEN THE ASSEMBLY LINES

THE AUDACITORIUM WAS a deafening hall of echoing noise. The large assembly space was completely covered—the floors, the walls, the ceiling—with mildewed ceramic tiles. Marlo felt like she was wading into a thick pool of sound.

There was a round, slowly rotating stage in the middle of the Audacitorium, with the sassy boys and girls of Wise Acres seated around it on stacks of rotting encyclopedias and phone books. The teachers sat in bent, rusted chairs on the stage. Vice Principal Carroll stood at a podium, his back facing Marlo, cradling what appeared to be a child under each arm.

Marlo spotted Milton up by the stage, sitting in typically nerdy "Oh, pick me! Pick me!" fashion near the front. She scampered urgently up to a pile of decomposing books next to him.

"Milton!" she yell-whispered amid the hum of snide chatter.

Milton's eyes went wide at the sight of his sister: her tweed coat shredded, her cheeks scratched and oozing blood.

"What happened to you?"

"Let's just say that I really, really hate mockingbirds and I really, really know how to type my name on those big stone-step letters," she replied, setting herself down beside him. "The front drum door was closed by the time I got out of Carroll's Absurditory and I had to spell my way back inside."

Marlo scooted up close to Milton, sitting cheek to cheek.

"I found some old papers," she said, her breath redolent of flavored soap and sour grapes. "Another Bibley thing, an encyclopedia page about a Weisen hammer, and a map of the land between Wise Acres and some big tower."

Marlo explained what she had found, trying hard to relay the ancient, prehistorical texts word for word, as well as describe the mysterious map charting the region between Wise Acres and the Tower of Babble.

Milton scratched at his tweed-aggravated neck. "Vice Principal Carroll is, while one of the most imaginative writers in history, definitely, a little, um . . . *touched*. In the head. So I would take anything he says or writes with a colossal grain of salt."

"Well, he wasn't alone," Marlo whispered as a little girl named Hadley Upfling, sitting just behind Milton, trained her frizzed-out mop of blond hair toward them in interest. "He was with two sprites, talking about his plan to undo language and create something new so he could tell the ultimate story: one without words. Like . . . a living story."

"Sprites?"

"Well . . . that's what he *said* they were," she replied uncertainly. "I heard them from his cupboard."

Milton glanced up at the slowly rotating stage. "And were these sprites named Sylvie and Bruno?"

"Yes!" Marlo exclaimed. "He invited them to the assembly! Did you see them?"

Milton pointed to the stage. "Yeah, you just missed them. They gave a little performance with the vice principal. . . ."

Vice Principal Carroll sat down on a busted metal chair, smiling vaguely, with two large puppets on his knees: a little boy and girl, wearing dark green tunics.

Marlo's mouth fell open. "But . . . but he was *talking* to them," she murmured. "I mean, they had different voices, talking over each other at the same time. . . ."

Milton shrugged. "He's really good."

Up on stage, Mr. Wilde paraded languidly to the podium.

"Thank you, Mr. Vice Principal, for that stunning display of ventriloquism," he said in a weary, put-upon voice, as if even the act of being bothered was something that he couldn't be bothered with. "You can throw your voice with the force and precision of a baseball pitcher, and—as we all know—a pitcher is worth a thousand words."

The man loosened the red ascot tied tight around his throat.

"We are—for lack of a better term—*fortunate* to have with us today our neighbor from the Tower of Babble, King Nimrod. . . ."

King Nimrod—the tall, power-hungry ex-king who, at one point in his arrogant life, wished to control Heaven itself—nodded from his chair. He bit into a moldy jelly doughnut. The filling squirted out onto his tunic, causing the vain titan to grimace. Nimrod wiped the vile glob off of his clothing and sniffed it: whatever it was, it certainly wasn't jelly.

"Without further ado," Mr. Wilde said, "let us give a rousing round of applause for Vice Principal Carroll, who has what he considers an exciting announcement. . . . And no slow, *sarcastic* clapping. We figured out that trick long ago. . . ."

The children grudgingly gave the vice principal a smattering of applause as he set Sylvie and Bruno down onto the stage, looking something of a rumpled puppet himself, and approached the podium. Vice Principal

Carroll gave a weak, distracted grin, though—with his eyebrows raised up in the middle of his forehead—his face seemed permanently cast in a troubled sadness.

"Ch-children," he said, his slight stammer returning now that he wasn't speaking through twin ventriloquist dummies. "As you know, you have all participated in a little contest at the behest of Principal B-Bubb. But what you *didn't* know is that this contest was actually contained within a larger contest context!"

The audience grumbled in confusion. The vice principal's face grew stern, yet—with effort—he forced his expressive features into a smile of batty benevolence.

"Little ladies and junior gentlemen, I would like to announce—and *am* announcing, at present, a present I will open right now—the very first War of the Words!"

The children whispered the name back and forth to one another, the four words spreading throughout the large, loud room like a contagion.

"What's a War of the Words?!" shouted a third of the audience in unison, bypassing—as usual—the courtesy of a raised hand.

Vice Principal Carroll waved away the disagreeable outburst. "The adventures first . . . explanations take such a dreadful long time," he said. "I will tell you th-this much . . . there will be two teams, waging verbal warfare against one another. And those teams were decided by your teachers as well as Principal Bubb herself."

"*We* decided?" Miss Parker asked from her seat with a look of petulant disdain.

Vice Principal Carroll nodded. "Yes, Miss Parker. From your rankings of the contest entries for the principal's new publicity campaign. Now on to the stupendous, tremendous, kick-you-in-the-endous War of the Words! Let's meet our valiant contestants!"

He glanced down at his note cards.

"T-Team One: Moses Babcock, Clem Weenum, Roberta Atrebor, Winifred Scathelli, Mordacia Caustilo, Ursula Lambarst . . ."

Marlo leaned into Milton. "What do you think this is all about?" she whispered. "Do you think it has anything to do with what I found in the Absurditory?"

Milton shrugged. "It could, but honestly I'm not sure how much stock to put in anything the vice principal says. I mean, his belfry is almost *completely* bats. Maybe what you found was just some story he was working on."

"Pansy Cornett, Sareek Plimpton, Moxie Wortschmerz, Concordia Kolassa, Jesus Descardo, and Rakeem Yashimoto," Vice Principal Carroll concluded.

Mr. Wilde shifted uncomfortably in his uncomfortable seat. "Vice Principal," he asked stiffly. "Could you please tell us more—*or any*—of the specifics of this event of yours?"

The vice principal looked up from his note cards with soft befuddlement. "Well, Mr. Wilde, the promise of crippling v-verbal humiliation has made the War of the Words the *must-hear* event of the afterlife. See, the contest will be b-broadcast live—or as live as death can be—on NPR: Netherworld Punishment Radio. PURE—Paradisiacal Unity Radio Evangelism—will also be covering the event for those listening upstairs. . . ."

Vice Principal Carroll returned to his note cards.

"Now for T-Team T-Two . . . Hadley Upfling, Flossie Blackwell, Mungo Ulyaw, Bree Martinet, Mack Hoover, Lavena Duckworth . . ."

Marlo tugged her brother's earlobe, as if she were ringing a doorbell, hoping to gain entrance to his brain.

"Oww!"

"Maybe this War of the Words thing is a chance for us to escape," Marlo whispered. "If we get picked, we could—I don't know—just sort of disappear in the hubbub."

"I don't know," Milton replied. "If it's going to be broadcast throughout the underworld, it might be hard to just wander off."

"Roget Marx Peters, Ahmed Crump, Cookie Young-blood, Annabelle Graham, Mathis Vittorio, and Lani Zanotti."

"Well, it looks like we weren't picked anyway," Milton said. "Which is probably a good thing, since we don't know what we'd have to do. I mean, war is Heck, after all . . . even if it's just with words."

Vice Principal Carroll clapped his hands. "My . . .

how very exciting!" he chirped. "I'm on tenterhooks, I daresay! Now, a contest isn't much of a contest without reward, not to mention—though I have, just—reward's dark twin, *risk*. And if the War of the Words is to be the underworld's ultimate contest, it must therefore have the ultimate reward: *release*. The instant gratification of instant graduation—namely a golden ticket upstairs. To that lovely oasis above the clouds."

The children gasped so hard that Milton's ears popped. Vice Principal Carroll's lips curled into an inscrutable smile.

"Wow," Milton murmured. "A Get-out-of-Heck-Free card. Too bad we weren't selected. . . ."

The vice principal flipped through his note cards. "And now our t-team captains," Vice Principal Carroll said as he squinted down at the podium.

Marlo furrowed her brow. "Team captains?" she muttered. "What drippy dweebs would be picked as captains in a dumb war of words?"

"T-Team Captain One," the vice principal announced into his microphone. "Milton Fauster."

Milton swallowed as the children trained the full intensity of their hot, hateful glares upon him, with Moses Babcock shooting off an especially lethal discharge of eye daggers.

Marlo snickered. "Figures," she said. "That's what you get for being a brain. Now you gotta 'honor roll' with the punches in some nerd war."

"And T-Team Captain Two, the opposing team," Vice Principal Carroll declared. "Marlo Fauster."

The scant amount of blood occupying Marlo's deathly pale-to-perfection complexion fled to her extremities.

"*Opposing* team?" Marlo said, locking wide, quivering eyes with the equally tremulous eyes of her brother. "Good God-that-has-clearly-forsaken-us . . . I guess they liked my 'Behind the Brimstone' idea for the principal's new image."

"Behind the Brimstone?"

"Yeah, turning Principal Bubb's life into a reality TV show. Because, you know, when you see people act horrible on those shows, it's strangely endearing. Probably because of all the editing and music they use to make reality so real. So, this way, the principal can continue to be awful and disgusting, and viewers won't be able to take their eyes off her, like a slow-motion train wreck."

Milton nodded and raised his hand tentatively.

"Yes, T-Team Captain One?" the vice principal said, sweeping away an errant lock of hair from his face.

"Y-you mentioned the reward for the winners," Milton asked, the vice principal's stammer apparently contagious.

"*Winner*," Vice Principal Carroll corrected. "Only the team captain will enjoy the ultimate reward. There will be consolation prizes, however, for the rest of the winning team. Lovely gift bags loaded with fabulous freebies."

"Then what happens to the loser?" Milton managed,

suddenly shoving the words out of his mouth, like a skydiving instructor pushing a new student out of a plane.

The vice principal smiled, a Cheshire grin that seemed to dim the rest of his body. "As you can perhaps imagine, the risk must be as *depressive* as the reward is *impressive. . . .*"

The answer, before the vice principal even said it, trickled through Milton's head like water through a sieve. The teachers, meanwhile, exchanged furrowed looks of utter disbelief.

"A contest is all about gravity. And, abiding the laws of gravity, if one goes up," Vice Principal Carroll explained, his index finger traveling up to the ceiling before hovering above his forehead, "then it only makes sense that one would go"—his finger plunged southward, hitting the podium with a reverberating thud—"*down.*"

14 · DEAD MAN'S BLUFF

FAKING YOUR OWN *death is murder,* Dale E. Basye thought from his luxury Goodnight Room in the Wizard of Odds casino, the brand-spanking-new children's book–themed gaming complex on the Las Vegas strip. He was wedging handfuls of rotting hamburger into the rib cage of a stolen skeleton while waiting for the Winderella Ball on the roof to end at midnight. Finding the discarded meat had been easy. The Dumpsters outside of the Very Hungry Caterpillar buffet were filled with it. And he had swiped the skeleton from a local chiropractic office. Dale sighed and stared at the mannequin of a quiet old lady whispering "hush," positioned just next to a table set with a comb and a brush and a bowl full of mush.

I feel a little crazy, he thought. *But it's worth it to keep*

Phelps Better and his goons from nabbing me and staging a real brutal death, not just some kind of counterfeit demise. I've just got to kill me first.

That afternoon, Dale had smuggled his pseudo body into the casino in a large suitcase. He had been sure to register at the desk for an ostentatious Goodnight Room luxury suite and to stroll past as many security cameras as possible, all to boldly document his stay. Dale had even made a public scene after losing at the Poker Little Puppy tables.

The key to faking your own death, Dale knew, was to leave no recognizable body behind. Fire and explosives were a natural first choice, but Dale was worried that he might hurt someone in the process (namely himself).

Throwing his bogus body into Lake Mead had occurred to him, but Dale didn't want to wait around gosh knows how long before the body was dredged up. He needed to be freed—immediately . . . *tonight!*— from the tyranny of his messed-up life and the anxiety of Phelps Better's surprisingly well-funded manhunt. Mysterious men with dark suits, sunglasses, and earpieces talking into their cuffs outside of Dale's old haunts . . . it was conspicuously weird even by Las Vegas standards.

Wiping his filthy hands, Dale assessed his gruesome alter ego. It was like some hideous meat puppet that not even Hamburger Helper could help. But it was roughly his size, and after the impact, appearances wouldn't matter, as long as it carried his ID.

Dale dressed the body in his nicest suit, tucked his wallet inside the jacket pocket, cinched a fedora over the body's exposed cranium, and walked it out into the hall.

A waitress dressed as Aslan from the Craps Tables of Narnia eyed Dale and the body suspiciously.

"Dead drunk," Dale replied with a wry grin. "He had a few too many in the Charlie and the Cocktail Factory lounge."

The waitress nodded and—with a halfhearted roar—disappeared down the hall.

Phew . . . that was close, Dale thought as he boarded the elevator and punched the button for the roof-level amusement park. *I feel like I'm in a DVD extra for one of those old* Weekend at Bernie's *movies. . . .*

The elevator door opened onto a scene of garish, neon-lit full-sensory assault. Most every sin was represented here on the Wizard of Odds rooftop: Greed, Envy, Pride, Gluttony, Dopey, Happy, Grumpy . . . though some of those might have been dwarves, Dale thought with confusion as he carefully maneuvered the body past a bank of Little Slot Machines That Could, their incessant chugging chant of "I think I can win, I think I can win" nearly pushing him over the top.

Finally, with the Winderella Ball thinning out, Dale could see his destination. Just beyond the Blackjack and the Beanstalk ride was the colossal candle on the casino cake: the 512-foot-tall Wicked Witch Tornado Ride.

The thrill ride had supremely foolish daredevils strapped into a tiny two-person house and whirled so high up into the air, at ninety-nine miles per hour, that apparently (on a clear day, it is said) you could actually see Kansas. The house then came freefalling down, where it flattened a cackling animatronic witch.

Dale conveyed the body across the rooftop arcade, threading it through the throng of oblivious revelers as if he were swishing his partner to and fro in a ballroom dance competition. He arrived at the back of the yellow-brick line. Dale sighed nervously.

Buzzers sounded from across the rooftop gallery. A crowd of people swarmed around a huge, elephant-shaped Horton Hatches the Nest Egg slot machine.

Dale seized the sudden distraction and made his way to the front of the line. A bored teenage girl dressed as a Munchkin unlatched the entrance gate. He sat down in the cramped, house-shaped compartment as the girl buckled him and the dapper meat skeleton into the ride. She arched her fake orange eyebrow at the body.

"Is he, like, okay?" she asked around her chewing gum. "The Lollipop Guild will get on me if he's sick or something—"

"Is that a monkey with wings?" Dale replied as he pulled a penknife from the inside of his coat.

"Huh?" the girl said as she looked over her shoulder.

Quickly, Dale cut the restraining belt strapping the body to the house. "Oh, nothing," he said as he pocketed the knife. "Just some hairy kid with a weird backpack. My friend? The famous Dale E. Basye? Or should I say *in*famous? He's just tired. Being a fugitive from the law, not to mention a writer . . . it's taxing. That's Dale E. Basye. *B-A-S-Y* . . ."

"Right," the girl said, checking her watch.

"I changed my mind," Dale said, straining against the restraint. "I guess I don't have what makes the muskrat guard his musk."

"Huh?"

"You know . . . *courage*? What the Cowardly Lion wanted in the *Wizard of* . . . never mind. Just let me out, please. But my friend, the famous *Dale E. Basye* here, will stay. . . ."

The Munchkin girl shrugged and unbuckled Dale's safety belt.

Dale wove his way through the crowd back toward the elevators as the ride lurched to life. In a matter of seconds, nine house cars shot hundreds of feet into the air above the tawdry, dazzlingly desperate Las Vegas night. The house formerly occupied by Dale was catapulted to the top of the shuddering 512-foot-tall vortex of metal rails and churning soot.

"Ding-dong," the Munchkin girl announced apathetically as one of the houses plummeted down upon the mechanical witch. "The witch is—"

Suddenly, a body was flung into the night sky from the top of the twister.

"*Dead!*" the girl screamed.

The girl's shriek—which, to her credit, had an appropriately shrill, Munchkin-like quality—caused an outbreak of screeches and gasps throughout the rooftop gallery. The body flew up and over the lip of the Wizard of Odds casino, bathed in emerald lights that cast a sickly green halo in the sky, and upon fulfilling its upward arc, plummeted downward. A rush of gawkers pressed against the railing.

"Looks like he's a-gonna land in the Betting Zoo," a middle-aged man in a cowboy hat drawled.

The crowd of thirty-something people winced in unison.

"*Touchdown,*" a large sunburned man said with a grimace.

A little boy peered over the edge. "Hey, all those animals are giving the poor man kisses."

An elderly woman shook her head in disgust. "Lions, and tigers, and bears . . . *oh my* . . ."

Dale noticed three men in black suits and buzz cuts pierce the edge of the crowd, mumbling into their cuffs.

"Who was that poor man?" a tiny platinum-blond

woman at the base of the ride asked, struggling to maintain her balance atop her high heels.

The Munchkin girl shrugged from the guardrail.

"Some guy . . . a fugitive or writer or something: Daly Bosseye, I think," she replied nervously.

The mysterious, black-suited men shot knowing looks at one another. Dale backed away toward the elevator.

That worked out even better than I expected, he thought as he rounded the corner by a Winnie-the-Pot machine with its obnoxious bouncing Tigger. *The animals will leave nothing behind but my ID and a whole bunch of gruesome vacation photos. . . .*

Dale stepped into the elevator, fighting the flow of gawkers surging to the accident. There was no going back now. He had to get out of Dodge or—more specifically—Las Vegas, Nevada. He needed to find a safe haven in which to install and run Dale E. Basye Version 2.0. He needed to dye his hair, grow a beard, and change his name (he was toying with Dr. Tyberius von Skywalker).

He stole carefully into his room and hastily collected his things in a canvas sack, along with some towels and the remaining contents of the mini-bar. Dale slipped into the service elevator as the sound of sirens swelled, shrill and urgent, in the distance.

Dale emerged from the back of the Wizard of Odds casino into the neon confusion of Las Vegas. A hundred feet away, just beyond a blockade of emergency vehicles, was Phelps Better, scratching at his confounding horn nubs, his horsey face trained suspiciously upon the horrified medics in the frenzied Betting Zoo.

Leaving behind nothing . . . leaving behind everything, Dale reflected sadly as he pulled his cap down low and slunk away, swallowed up by the crowd.

Pretending you're dead is a lifelong commitment, Dale mused as he typed furiously on his laptop in an abandoned hut in the Oregon wilderness. He had bought the chic wood hut on Craigslist from an animal behaviorist, Dr. Chuck Woods, who, after researching the habits of woodchucks, decided to chuck his woodchuck hut when his *Woodchuck* book made good.

Dale's insurance policy money, along with a substantial settlement from the Wizard of Odds casino for criminal negligence, had all gone to his estranged family, so he wouldn't have to worry about them. They would, thankfully, be taken care of. All of Dale's Heck-related monies, however, had been wholly absorbed by Virtual Prayground Technologies and Phelps Better, like some huge paper towel soaking up a spill.

Ever since the greatly exaggerated reports of his death, Dale had felt phenomenally free, his life a blank page. As a writer, Dale used to feel a profound sense of dread and anxious obligation at the prospect of a blank page. But now, every blank page was an opportunity, an opportunity he had seized 1,712 times, if the pages piled up on his desk were any indication.

Unlike his usual writing method (a vexing, excruciating process akin to milking a rabid squirrel), the words now flowed effortlessly from his fingertips. Dale felt as if his latest novel was being conjured more than created.

The Great American novel, Dale mused as he filled up another page with perfect prose. *The career-defining epic that has always seemed just out of reach. But here I am, writing what is not only my best novel by far, but also perhaps the best novel I have ever read, and I've read several!*

Dale had no idea where he was going—the tingle of thrill and discovery traveling up and down his spine like electric eels—yet he knew he was nearly through, probably a page away, as he tied together every plot point with the skill of a surgeon.

Suddenly, Dale was seized by a painful twinge in his hand. His fingers grew numb and stiff as they tripped clumsily across the keyboard.

"Oww," he mumbled as he massaged his cramped, trembling hand. "Maybe I could use a break after a week of almost nonstop typing. . . ."

However, the throbbing muscle ache only seemed to grow worse, creeping past his wrists, climbing up his arms, and nesting painfully in his hunched shoulders. Beads of sweat formed above his brow as his middle-aged body became almost wholly defined by the riot of searing twinges.

Dale rocked back and forth, restless and uncomfortable all over. His breath grew shaky and his teeth ground together with a wince-inducing squeak.

"Oh my," he mumbled, his voice cracking as it became almost impossible for him to swallow. "I fear this may be . . ."

With his quivering index finger, Dale managed to peck out two final words on his manuscript.

THE END

And with that, Dale E. Basye became the first person ever to die from writer's cramp.

15 · THEM'S
FIGHTING WORDS!

"I WON'T FIGHT you!" Milton screamed. He was trembling so hard it felt like he was being shaken. "I won't—" Milton yelped, waking himself up.

Mr. Wilde loomed above him, his hands on Milton's shoulders. "Fight you?" Milton said, his voice slurry with sleep as he propped himself up onto his elbows.

"You were having a dream," the teacher whispered. "Quite a corker from the sound of it."

Milton rubbed his eyes and reached for his broken glasses. "Marlo—my sister—and I were tied together, at the wrist," Milton said. "And she was trying to cut me with a knife, but I wouldn't fight her."

Mr. Wilde gave a rueful smile. "Trying to cut you

down, no doubt . . . *with her words,*" the man replied in his upper-crust British accent. "As she will in your upcoming tourney."

Milton looked around the darkened Boys' Totally Bunks, where all of the boys were sleeping on shelves, arranged according to the Dewey decimal system—the system of classification that libraries use. Some of the boys, though, were missing.

"Why are you here?" Milton asked.

Mr. Wilde sighed. "When Vice Principal Carroll arrived, the teaching staff merely viewed him as a dotty nuisance," the teacher explained. "But now it's clear that he is both seriously deranged and *serious*—at least about this War of the Words business." Mr. Wilde handed Milton his clothes. "Get dressed. We're almost late."

Milton noticed a few of the other boys getting dressed silently while the others slept away.

"Late for what?" Milton said as he slipped on his shirt, which was currently scrolling "My Momma Dresses Me Funny."

Mr. Wilde, quietly imposing at over six feet tall, strutted for the door. "For your first meeting of Spite Club—a criminally extracurricular club dedicated to giving you unenviable contenders a fighting chance in the War of the Words."

★   ★   ★

Twelve children—a blend of boys and girls known collectively as Team One—circled Milton in the Grimnaseum: a fittingly named room liberally decorated with hanging chains and hooks and flooded with black light that made everyone's teeth creepily white. The grumbling children sat on a stack of mats in the corner. Mr. Wilde silenced them with the booming sound of his boot striking the unvarnished floor.

"THIS ISN'T A GAME!" Mr. Wilde shouted. "This is *real* . . . the stakes are *real*. And if you want to survive the War of the Words—and perhaps even somehow win it—you will *zip it*. Understand?"

Moses opened his mouth, but thinking better of it, merely nodded.

Mr. Wilde loosened his red cravat with a hooked finger. "Team Two will receive similar yet unique training from Miss Parker shortly after our meeting tonight. This way, they, too, will have the necessary skills to wage verbal warfare, yet not *identical* skills, as that would raise suspicion and would not serve you well on the battlefield."

Milton raised his hand.

"Yes, Mr. Fauster? Or should I say *Team Captain*?"

Moses Babcock glared at Milton in the ultraviolet pseudo darkness.

Milton swallowed. "I . . . well . . . this will sound dumb . . ."

Several of the children did a wretched job of stifling their snickering.

"But what *is* Spite Club? Is it to help us cheat at the War of the Words?"

"Not cheating, per se," Mr. Wilde replied as he paced in front of what looked like a deflated bouncy house. "At least that wasn't its initial intent. We formed Spite Club shortly after Vice Principal Carroll's arrival. He made sweeping, ridiculous changes to our curriculum, as if he didn't want any of you to actually learn. But now the stakes are even higher, so we have to step things up a bit. You have been inadequately prepared for a debate of this caliber—"

"Debate?" blurted a jowly Hispanic girl before grudgingly raising her hand. "Um . . . *sorry*," she added with great difficulty.

"Yes, the War of the Words is a debate, Miss Lambarst . . . *Ursula*," Mr. Wilde said while languidly tugging off his bright white gloves. "*The debate to end all debates.* And Vice Principal Carroll doesn't seem interested in providing ammunition for this battle of wits, for reasons clear only to him, though I suspect that most everything is rather dodgy when viewed through his skewed looking glass. Now back to Spite Club. Before we begin tonight's session, let us review the rules. Mr. Fauster, our newest member, can you speculate as to what the *first* rule of Spite Club might be?"

Milton bit his lower lip and shrugged. "To have fun and try your best?"

Mr. Wilde scowled as he tucked his gloves inside of his immaculate velvet waistcoat while the children snickered. "That it definitely *not* the first rule . . . or *any* of the rules." The Irish playwright and novelist handed Milton a laminated card. "Don't despair, Mr. Fauster . . . our little covert club only has a few clandestine meetings under its belt."

Milton studied the card in the confounding ultraviolet light.

THE RULES OF SPITE CLUB

1st rule: Talk about Spite Club.

2nd rule: Really, I mean RUB IT IN THEIR FACES!

3rd rule: If someone gets tongue-tied or their argument goes limp, they're tapped out and the debate is over.

4th rule: One debate at a time.

5th rule: Shirts and shoes. And preferably pants. But no slacks.

6th rule: Arguments will go on as long as they have to, if not longer.

7th rule: If this is your first debate at Spite Club, you HAVE to argue. No arguments!

Mr. Wilde inflated the sagging, collapsed structure behind him with an electric pump. The bouncy building slowly filled with air, becoming a large, white twenty-two-foot by twenty-two-foot plastic dome.

"This is the Disputation Dome," Mr. Wilde explained as the structure grew firmer behind him. "In it, you will work out your differences in the most direct way possible. It is, as you may rightly assume, very bouncy. The added 'lift' of helium makes the interior extra springy. You will first go inside as teams—as either Rubbers or Glues—before sparring one-on-one. Inside, you will be wearing these. . . ."

Mr. Wilde held up a small mask, like a surgical mask to cover the mouth, only made of metal with a nozzle at the center and a small cartridge sticking out the side.

"This is your Paint-Brawl mask. It translates your arguments into paint. The more forceful your point or barbed your barb, the more devastating your verbal assault will be. In this way, you will *physically* experience the raw power of each other's words—which arguments stick and which rebuffs merely rebound."

The Disputation Dome was fully inflated. It resembled a massive, puffy igloo, with one small door and several see-through plastic windows along the sides.

Mr. Wilde clapped his elegant, labor-unbothered hands. "So who would like to begin things?" the foppish man asked, scanning the black-lit faces in the room.

Milton knew, as captain—a position he'd neither

asked for nor felt he deserved—that *he* should be the first one to enter the dome. Out of the corner of his eye, he saw Moses Babcock stir, his hand twitching at his side. Instantly, like a quick-drawing cowboy in a Wild West showdown, Milton raised his hand, leaving Moses behind in the dust.

"Excellent reflexes, Mr. Fauster," Mr. Wilde said with a smirk. "You'll lead the Glue team with Clem Weenum and Roberta Atrebor."

Mr. Wilde handed the children their Paint-Brawl masks and three vests. Milton slipped the vest on over his shirt. It was incredibly sticky and, once in place, seemed to grip him tightly like a python.

"Now for the Rubber team. Winifred Scathelli, Mordacia Caustilo . . . and for the leader . . ."

Moses Babcock stepped forward. "I am the most qualified to lead the team," the boy said, staring Milton down peripherally while somehow maintaining eye contact with the teacher.

Plus you really, really want to hurt me, Milton thought as Mr. Wilde handed Moses, Winifred, and Mordacia their Paint-Brawl masks and rubber vests.

The inside of the Disputation Dome was coated with a highly reflective film. It looked like the inside of a colossal bag of Jiffy Pop popcorn.

Mr. Wilde poked his head through the door. "This bout will simply be an exhibition match. A chance for you to get a feel for *real* verbal combat. The topic will be 'advertising for children.' Moses, you will take the 'Pro' position."

Moses Babcock slipped on his Paint-Brawl mask and spun toward Milton. "Advertising gives children the skills they need to be responsible consumers when they grow up!"

A burst of bright purple paint shot out of the boy's mask, hitting Milton in the chest. Milton doubled over in pain. The sting of the paint seeped inside him as he knelt on the floor of the inflatable arena.

"No jumping the *gums*, Mr. Babcock!" the teacher shouted.

"You didn't . . . say it would hurt," Milton managed as he rose from the floor.

"You didn't ask," Mr. Wilde said. "Wasp venom, courtesy of Miss Dickinson. It puts the 'pain' in 'paint.' Rubber versus glue! Five minutes. No one leaves until it's through."

Moses singled Milton out yet again. Milton could see the boy's face crinkle into a grin from behind his mask.

"Banning advertisements is a restriction upon freedom of speech!" the boy shouted, shooting a blotch of paint at Milton's shoulder.

Milton dodged the point, then lobbed one of his own.

"That's not the issue. What advertisers *really* want is the freedom to exploit children. To brainwash them into becoming good little consumers who think happiness can only be purchased!"

The paint shot out of Milton's mouth and hit Moses

squarely in the chest. He was thrown back, yet the point bounced right off him, hitting Clem Weenum. The little boy squealed as he fell.

"This isn't fair!" Milton yelled. "They're wearing rubber vests that deflect the paint!"

Mr. Wilde pressed his head against one of the clear plastic windows. "*They're* rubber. *You're* glue. Whatever you say bounces off of them and sticks to *you*. . . ."

"But—"

"What are you going to do, Milton?" Winifred said. "*Cry?*"

A small blob of paint shot out of her mask and hit Milton in the stomach. The impact didn't hurt much, but the wasp venom stung regardless.

Milton sighed. He had to somehow survive the next few minutes—as well as protect his team—and do it wearing a vest covered with glue.

Roberta trained her mask back at Winifred. "Don't worry, Winifred," she replied. "It's Be Kind to Animals Day, so we won't get angry at you."

Roberta's slur hit Winifred in the ribs.

"Oww!"

Moses stalked toward Milton.

"They're so slow they couldn't even catch their breath!"

Milton jumped. The blob of purple paint whizzed beneath his feet as he hit the ceiling, stuck fast by his glue vest. Milton tried to wriggle himself free.

Clem stepped up to face the Rubber team. "Oh yeah?" he spat. The boy's spray of paint barely made it across the Disputation Dome.

Moses smirked. "That's right—it's team against team," he murmured to Mordacia and Winifred. "So let's start with the runt of the litter."

The Rubber team surrounded the little boy.

"Without ads, most of your favorite shows couldn't afford to be made!" Moses yelled.

"B-but . . . what about public tele—" Clem sputtered.

"Ads don't have some magic power to make you want things!" Mordacia shrieked.

"Yeah," Winifred added. "You can't blame them for bad parenting!"

Clem was doused in purple paint. He screamed in agony, rolling across the floor as the wasp venom seeped into his tiny body.

Milton freed himself from the ceiling and fell to the jouncing floor. The Rubber team closed in for the kill.

"Ads teach kids how to manage their finances," Moses spat, "which is an important skill to have when you're grown up!"

Milton threw himself in front of Clem.

"They show you something cool so you have to save and learn the true value of money!" Moses continued, spewing paint and venom.

"*Aaaarrrgghhh!*" Milton screamed as he absorbed the full brunt of the Rubber team's verbal assault.

The venom burrowed its way through Milton's clothes and into his skin. The poison seemed to gnash at his nerve endings with waves of sharp, burning pain.

Milton looked up at Moses, Mordacia, and Winifred gazing down upon him. Their eyes were sparkling with merry mischief: never before feeling as in their element as they did now, in this coliseum of cruelty filled with sharp-tongued boys and girls learning how to be even *more* so.

Roberta helped Milton to his feet.

"We've got to shoot below the belt!" Roberta said. "*Beneath* their rubber vests."

"I don't play like that," Milton said. He locked eyes with Moses. "But I *could*. And it would devastate him."

Milton could see a lump traveling down Moses's throat.

"And he knows it."

Milton looked down at Clem. The boy's dark brown eyes had rolled back into his head. He was seizing.

"Get him out of here," Milton said. "I'll cover you."

Roberta nodded as she hooked her hands underneath Clem's arms and dragged him across the inflatable floor.

"Oh, *boo-hoo*," Moses taunted. "If we said anything to offend you, it was *purely* intentional!"

"Yeah, he's so weak he can't even hold up his end of a conversation!"

Roberta pulled Clem from the Disputation Dome.

There was so much purple paint flying that Milton couldn't even see the door through the spray.

Moses stalked toward Milton. "It's over, loser," he said with a painful snort of purple paint that slashed at Milton's neck. "But you're probably too dumb to realize that. In fact, you're so dumb you probably can't even spell *IQ*."

Milton spun around as fast as he could. "Advertising aimed at children encourages negative social consequences, such as eating junk food!" he shouted, spewing paint. "It's unethical, because most kids don't have money and have to pester their parents to buy stuff for them, leading to hostility in the home!"

Milton ducked to avoid the paint rebounding off of Moses's chest.

"And children are more susceptible to advertising, as most kids haven't developed the tools to view advertising critically!" Milton shouted. The globs of stinging paint bounced furiously between Moses and the wall, slamming into him as if he were the paddle in a game of paddleball.

"Owwwww!" Moses roared as he was beaten back, clutching his chest.

Milton took a deep breath as he stood before Moses, with Mordacia and Winifred stricken dumb beside him.

"You're just jealous because you know I'm a better leader than you," Milton said, a pure ball of paint spewing from his mouth, hitting Moses square in the heart, piercing his rubber vest and hurling him backward against the wall.

A buzzer went off outside the Disputation Dome. Mr. Wilde unzipped the portal. He surveyed the dripping splotches of purple coating the inside of the bouncy structure. It looked like someone had made a Barney smoothie and forgot to put the top on the blender.

"My, such . . . colorful language," Mr. Wilde said. He walked over to Moses and helped the moaning boy to his feet.

"The truth hurts, doesn't it, Mr. Babcock?"

Milton emerged from the inflatable arena feeling like he had taken a bath in a tub full of thumbtacks and Tabasco sauce. He saw Roberta wiping paint off Clem with a paper towel.

"How did you find the door so quickly?" Milton asked. "There was so much paint flying I couldn't see anything."

"It was easy," the dark-haired girl replied. "When I came inside, I took thirteen steps forward, turned left for another four steps, and then fell back six steps. So I just did it all backwards."

"Right," Milton said with a smirk. *"Easy."*

Mr. Wilde dragged Moses out of the Disputation Dome and set him against a stack of gym mats. The teacher turned to Milton with a dramatic swish of his waistcoat.

"While you played well, Mr. Fauster, two of your

team members left the dome before the end of the competition. So this first bout goes to the Rubber team."

Moses, Winifred, and Mordacia let out a trio of half-hearted "yays" through their swollen, purple-stained lips. The rest of Team One stared at Milton with a quiet, grudging awe.

While Moses may have won the bout, it was clear to Milton—and everyone else in the Grimnaseum—that Milton had won something far more valuable: the trust of his team.

"You can't afford to be so selfless in the War of the Words," Mr. Wilde cautioned, sweeping his dark-brown, shoulder-length hair out of his face. "Nor can you ignore any chance to defeat your opponent with a below-the-belt blow. . . ."

A soft fog seemed to settle over the man's light-gray eyes, normally so bright and quick.

"It's between you and your sister, Mr. Fauster, plain and simple. One of you will win—*big-time*—and one of you will lose in the worst way possible. You must do everything you can to make sure that losing person isn't *you*. Because you can bet your finest china that that is *exactly* what she is doing right now. . . ."

16 · GETTiNG THE HANG OF iT

MARLO YAWNED SO widely that she felt like a human Pez dispenser, dispensing nothing but sour, exhausted confusion. She had been roused from a fitful sleep by Miss Parker to participate in some special club—an *unauthorized* club—to help her and Team Two hone their debating skills. *Apparently a debate,* thought Marlo, *is more than just arguing with rules.*

Miss Parker sat by a stack of foam mats piled in the corner of the Grimnaseum. She crossed her arms, managing to look stern despite balancing upon a sagging Exorcize Ball.

"I was never wildly famous. My name was never writ large on the roster of Those Who Did Things," Miss Parker said, leaning into the children. "Most of the time, I didn't do anything. I used to bite my nails, but I don't even do that anymore . . . especially now that they've stopped growing. But I *do* know the power of words, and I can teach you a few pointers before you do battle at the War of the Words. This will be a match with winners and losers, not whiners and snoozers. The stakes will be both as high as Heaven and as low as . . . *down there*. I can't stress to you enough that this is *serious*. It's not a game."

"So how are you going to teach us, then?" Marlo asked.

"*With games.*"

A little Asian boy named Mungo Ulyaw pointed at the small mountain of white and silver vinyl drooping listlessly in the corner. "What's with the deflated bouncy castle?" he asked.

"It's for Mr. Wilde's group," Miss Parker replied, rubbing the bags under her tired eyes with her fingers. "Team One holds their own Spite Club meetings late at night while we hold ours early in the morning. You will be kept apart from them as much as possible until the debate. Now, from what Mr. Wilde tells me, Team One is a group with some serious language and logic skills. But Mr. Wilde wants to loosen their uptight tongues. You children, though . . . you don't really have that problem. Speaking without thinking is second nature to you. I want to ensure that when you shoot your mouths off, every shot hits its mark."

Miss Parker pivoted atop her Exorcize Ball and reached down for a large, flat box.

"We'll start things off with a leisurely game of Squabble."

The teacher laid out a checkered board on the unvarnished floor and poured four small mounds of wooden tiles on each of its four sides.

"Um . . . you're having us play Scrabble?" asked Mack Hoover, a strong-jawed boy who looked perpetually peeved.

"It's *Squabble*," Miss Parker clarified. "Scrabble with some *sauce*. Now, Mack, I'd like you, Annabelle Graham, Ahmed Crump, and Marlo Fauster to come up here, please. I'll show you how it's done."

The four groggy children dragged their feet across the Grimnaseum floor and sat cross-legged at each corner of the board. They looked over their letters carefully and arranged them to their liking on the slender wooden racks.

"Miss Fauster, you may start," Miss Parker said as she knelt awkwardly on the floor.

Marlo placed four letters vertically on the left-hand edge of the board.

D-O-V-E

"'Dove,'" Miss Parker read aloud. "Unambitious, but what the hay. Now, when you spell a word, you have to defend it. Make a case for what is 'right' about your word, and the next player—going clockwise—will oppose your word by bringing up something *bad* about it. Understand?"

Marlo nodded. "Yeah, I get it . . . okay, um . . . doves are a symbol of peace," she said.

"Good," the teacher said. "Now your turn, Mr. Hoover. Argue against Miss Fauster, then add your word."

The boy squared his tense jaw in contemplation. "Doves are basically pigeons, and I hate pigeons," Mack Hoover explained in a husky, impatient tone. "The way they strut around with their chests sticking out as though they own the place. I hate the way they hang around parks and poop everywhere. They're dirty, mean, attract rats, and still lonely old people insist on feeding them bread crumbs so that we get even *more* pigeons. . . ."

Miss Parker nodded, impressed. Mack Hoover built a word horizontally from the "V."

V-A-I-N

"*Vain*, it means conceited, but . . . um . . . maybe it makes you so obsessed with how you look that you find a cancerous mole or something and get it removed before you die."

"But it also means futile," Annabelle Graham interjected with a shake of her plain, brown tomboyish hair.

"And useless, ineffective, fruitless," added Roget Marx Peters.

"No helping," Miss Parker scolded.

Annabelle put her letters out onto the board in a vertical stack ending on the "N."

G-R-A-I-N

"*Grain* . . . you can also make 'A GRIN' and 'A RING' out of the letters," explained Annabelle. "Grain is good and nourishing—"

"And an allergen," Ahmed Crump added with a scowl, spelling out R-E-D horizontally from the "R."

"Red is the color of blood, which you need to live," the grumpy boy said.

"And it's also the color of a grisly crime scene," Marlo countered while laying her tiles on the board, building up from the "D."

Q-U-I-D

"I think it's some kind of British money. And money is good."

"Or bad sometimes, if you buy bad things with it," Mack Hoover countered. "Plus it's *squid* with its 'S' cut off. And it shouldn't even count because it's British slang."

"Duly noted," Miss Parker said as Mack spelled out "Q-U-A-I-L" horizontally from the "Q."

"Quail are, I don't know, a bird," he explained. "Which I guess you could eat. But they're kind of like pigeons, which are really gross, and filthy—"

"We know your position on pigeons, Mr. Hoover," Miss Parker said. "Plus you just argued against yourself."

"*Thanks,*" Annabelle said brattily as she spelled "L-E-A-F-Y," dangling down vertically from the "L."

"*Leafy* . . . like healthy salad."

"Or like the yard in fall when you have to waste a Saturday raking and not even make minimum wage," Ahmed said as he spelled "F-E-T-I-D" horizontally from the "F."

"Fetid is a, um . . . cheese, I think."

"That's *feta*. Don't be a dork," Marlo said.

Miss Parker frowned. "Good arguers don't resort to name-calling, Miss Fauster."

"I wasn't arguing. I was simply pointing out that I'm right about him being wrong. *Fetid* is like something that really stinks."

"Like Limburger," Ahmed added with a frown. "Which is a cheese."

"Let it go, Ahmed," the teacher said with a smirk.

Marlo laid out two tiles on either side of the "I."

Z-I-T

Marlo stared at the tiles fixedly.

"Go on," Ahmed goaded smugly. "Let's hear your 'Pro-zit' argument."

"Well," Marlo said, rubbing her chin for inspiration, as that was where zits usually reared their ugly heads, like pus-filled prairie dogs peeking out of their burrow, "when you get them, that's because your hormones are going crazy, and that means you're maturing, which is a good thing."

"You can't make zits a good thing!" Ahmed complained. "They are ugly and disgusting!"

"Like pigeons," Mack muttered.

"See? You can argue over just about anything," Miss Parker said, packing the game back into its box. "Now that we've warmed up our wits with zits, we'll move on to stronger stuff: *Hangman*."

The children laughed with disbelief.

"Yeah, I can tell that this is *really* preparing me for some big debate or whatever," Cookie sneered, her sarcasm set to "kill."

Miss Parker crossed the room to a tall structure covered with a tarp, her heels clacking against the floor. The teacher clutched the corner of the large gray sheet.

"I can assure you, *Cookie*," Miss Parker said, stretching out the name until it practically creaked, "that you haven't played Hangman quite like this. . . ."

She tugged the tarp from the structure. The children gasped. There stood a tall wooden gallows: a long horizontal crossbeam supported at both ends by twin wooden beams on which dangled a noose.

Miss Parker's thin lips curled into a mischievous smile that seemed to burn away the years etched across her face.

"So you're going to strangle us?" Hadley Upfling asked from behind her curtain of hair. "That's pretty extreme even by Heck standards."

Miss Parker stepped up onto the wooden platform.

"Whether or not you're strangled is entirely up to *you*," she explained. "Can you decipher and spell common phrases before you run out of guesses? The state of your neck hangs in the balance!"

Ahmed Crump unfolded his arms so that he could make a show of refolding them again.

"This is dumb," he said, glowering from beneath the brim of his brown knit cap. "Why should we do this?"

"You children have an abundance of quips and zingers," Miss Parker replied with a chill, "yet a debate requires something with more substance. Wit has truth in it; wisecracking is simply calisthenics with words. This game will make your words feel *real* to you so that you wield them with more authority. Hopefully creating a 'win or noose' situation will give you the incentive you need to *truly* think about language. . . . So, who would like to go first?"

Miss Parker scanned the small sea of wary faces for at least one island of interest.

Marlo fidgeted on her foam mat. She didn't know the first thing about leading a bunch of mouthy kids in some debate. Then she noticed Cookie's arm twitch at her side. If Cookie raised her hand and did something that no one else wanted to do, she would be special, maybe even a leader. And if she did that, there would be no way that Marlo could ever convince anyone—including herself—that she could be their captain.

"I'll go first," Marlo said as she quickly rose from the mat before she could think better of it. Cookie glared at Marlo from beneath her fringe of red-and-blond streaked bangs.

"Ha!" the girl snorted as Marlo walked up to the gallows. "How dumb. It's cooler to wait and make sure it's safe . . . *right*?"

Marlo stood atop the wooden platform next to Miss Parker and a small whiteboard.

"Now, don't worry—yet don't *not* worry, either—it's all really simple," the teacher said, smiling with surprising warmth considering that she was slipping a noose over Marlo's head. "I'll write a phrase on the whiteboard and you try to guess it in six tries. With every wrong guess, the gallows will click." Miss Parker gestured toward a wooden crank next to the gallows' trapdoor. "And when it gets to six . . . *gllehhkkkkhhh!*" she added, with her tongue hanging out and her head resting on her shoulder. "That's all she wrote. Got it?"

Marlo nodded glumly, the red noose strangely cool against her neck.

"Great. I like your enthusiasm," Miss Parker said as she scrawled two sets of dashes—one set with five, the other with eight—onto the board with a marker. "Now go ahead and guess."

"Um . . . 'M,'" Marlo said. "No! Wait . . . okay, yeah 'M.' For Marlo."

Miss Parker shook her head. The teacher walked

over to the wooden crank and gave it a tug. The crank clicked down one notch and the platform reverberated with a deep shudder.

"That was an 'N' for 'No' . . . or maybe 'Noose,'" Miss Parker said with a grave expression. "Try again."

"N!"

Miss Parker dragged the whiteboard next to the crank and marked an "N" with three terse squeaks of her marker.

_ _ _ _ _ _ N _ _ _ _ _ _

"Um . . . 'F'?"

The teacher shook her head and gave the crank another tug.

Click!

"May I suggest a vowel?" Miss Parker said.

"Oh, right. 'A'!"

Click!

"I meant another vowel besides 'A,'" Miss Parker clarified.

"Oh . . . ," Marlo said.

"'O' it is!" Miss Parker said as she marked the board.

_ _ _ _ _ _ N _ _ O _ _ _

"I meant . . . never mind," Marlo muttered. "Um . . . 'E'!"

_ _ E _ _ _ E N _ _ O _ E _

"Good!" Miss Parker said.

"'I.'"

Click!

"Ai-yi-yi! Maybe we should move on to conso-nant*sssss* . . . ," Miss Parker said, trailing off into a hiss.

"'S'!" Marlo blurted.

_ _ E _ _ EN _ _ OSE _

"You're doing well, Miss Fauster. But let me give you a hint: it's the two most beautiful words in the English language for a writer."

Movie rights? Marlo thought, biting her lower lip in desperation.

"'V'?"

Click!

"Can you see the board, Miss Fauster?" Miss Parker asked.

"Yes, I can see—"

"You can *what*?" the teacher asked with her hand to her ear.

"*See!*" Marlo yelled.

C _ EC _ ENC _ OSE_

"Are you okay, Miss Fauster?"

"Yes, I'm okay!"

"O-what?"

"*K!*"

C _ ECK ENC _ OSE _

"Good!" Miss Parker said with a mischievous grin. "But remember: you have to focus, or else—after the War of the Words, you'll find yourself going straight to—"

"'L'!" Marlo yelped.

C_ECK ENCLOSE_

Writers are always complaining about not having enough money, Marlo thought, a cold sweat dripping down her spine as she stood on the gallows. *Like, what, they need a second butler for their summer homes? They must make so much money. . . . I mean, you always see their books at the library or on those illegal download sites. Every day they're probably getting some nice fat check. . . .*

" 'H'!" Marlo said.

CHECK   ENCLOSE_

Miss Parker glanced nervously at the clock.

"It's almost morning," the teacher said. "Now don't leave us hanging. Indecision and extended pauses at a debate are even worse than saying the wrong thing."

The teacher sighed, shrugging as she prepared to heave the crank for one final tug. Marlo swallowed hard. Her mind was racing like mice on a hot plate.

"Um . . . wait. Uh, Check Enclose . . ." She smacked her forehead. "Duh! 'D'!"

The morning bell tolled. Miss Parker smiled.

—Smissed!

The tired children filed out of the Grimnaseum, yawning and stretching.

The baggy-eyed teacher loosened the cool red noose from Marlo's neck, slipping it over her head like a necklace. All of the fear that had filled Marlo as she stood up on the platform, waiting to be dunked like a lead tea bag on the end of a rope, turned to rage.

"You were going to let me break my neck!" Marlo spat.

Miss Parker gave a mysterious, smudgy smile as she coiled the noose in her hands. The teacher took a big bite of the rope.

"Huh?" Marlo gasped with confusion.

"Yum . . . red licorice," Miss Parker muttered. "Miss Fauster, when you're at a debate, you have to *feel* like every word could be your last. Hopefully, at the War of the Words, you'll remember what it felt like up here on the gallows. Playing to win means playing as if your afterlife depends on it . . . which, for you, *it will*. . . ."

Marlo self-consciously rubbed her neck, still feeling the itch and burn of her noose necklace, as she walked out into the hallway. She headed to the Audaci-Tea House with the aim of shoveling something into her growling stomach to shut it up.

It was so early that barely anyone was in the café. There was only a teacher—an old guy with a scraggly half-beard and thinning hair—and a little olive-skinned girl with wide shoulders, slurping up something from a bowl.

The teacher approached the counter, where a badger demon—wearing a full-body hair net—stood at attention brandishing a rusty ladle.

"Please, sir, can I have some more?" the man asked.

"We're all out of gruel, Mr. Dickens," the badger

demon replied with a smirk. "Guess we're just serving irony today, huh?"

Marlo glanced down at the little girl's bowl.

"Hey . . . what are you eating?" she asked.

The girl's face turned a queasy green. She dropped her spoon to the table.

"Ugh . . . I think I'm going to have an explosive vowel movement!" the girl said as she ran out of the Audaci-Tea House.

"Vowel movement?" Marlo mumbled as she checked the girl's abandoned bowl. It was some kind of foul-smelling broth with letters bobbing at the surface.

"Figures . . . alphabet soup," Marlo muttered.

This gave her an idea.

If they won't let me see Milton before this big battle, Marlo thought as she grabbed a stale grammar cracker from the table, *at least I can leave him a little note.*

She took a spoon and scooped up a handful of letters from the alphabet soup, then arranged them carefully on the cracker.

> BRO
>   EVEN THOUGH ONLY ONE
> OF US CAN WIN WE HAVE GOT
> TO STICK TOGETHER
>   AND THAT IS GOING TO BE
> TOUGH BUT WE CAN DO IT
>   ME

Marlo blew on her dripping creation.

"It's like an edible ransom note," she said, admiring her handiwork as she trotted down the hall toward the Boys' Totally Bunks.

Marlo padded softly down the hall. The sound of strained mewling oozed from around the bend. Marlo hugged the wall and saw a clowder of cats struggling to transport a long, heavy package strapped to their backs. They inched and slunk away toward the rear exit leading out to the Absurditory. The coast now clear, Marlo trotted to the Boys' Totally Bunks and slid inside the empty room.

She paced the abandoned sleep shelves until she found *J810.4f Fauster, M.*

Marlo lifted Milton's pillow and hid the grammar cracker note underneath. Lucky, curled up in a wad of filthy sheets, poked his twitchy nose out from the bedding. Marlo gave the ferret a quick yet spirited scritch between the ears and bounded away.

Lucky stretched and yawned. He coiled around and around, like fuzzy white water going down an invisible drain, before stopping suddenly—a whiff of something vaguely redolent of food snagged his sensitive nose. He followed the trail of scent to Milton's lumpy pillow and burrowed beneath, munching on a selection of consonants and vowels. His belly full of A-B-Cs, Lucky tunneled back under the covers to catch some Zs.

17 · CUTTING REMARKS

PRO

ONLY ONE
OF US CAN WIN
AND THAT IS GOING TO BE

ME

MILTON JUST COULDN'T let go of the odd note Marlo had left for him underneath his pillow yesterday. Even after another night spent arguing in the Disputation Dome, and the long, tedious days of lessons sandwiched on either side like tasteless nutrition-free bread, Milton couldn't believe that his own blunt, self-serving sister could be so blunt and self-serving.

"Whatever happens, we've got to stay together," she had told him just before they arrived in Wise Acres.

Right, Milton thought bitterly, sitting on a stack of foam mats in the Grimnaseum, waiting for his last Spite Club session to end. *That was before the War of the Words. Before Marlo had a chance to graduate upstairs while I take the flaming Slip 'n Slide all the way down.*

Milton sighed as he stared, lost in thought, at the dangling chains and hooks decorating the room.

Marlo is right. We should both do our best to win. Maybe she left that note to goad me into trying my hardest, knowing I might have second thoughts about battling my sister at some big debate broadcast throughout the afterlife. The good *news is that one of us could get out of this place, to a better place, above the clouds. Perhaps the winner could even, somehow, help the loser. But Marlo's note was so harsh. . . . Wise Acres must have gotten to her. . . .*

Two boys—Sareek Plimpton and Jesus Descardo—sparred in the corner, trading insults and slaps with one another.

"Go, Jeezuss!" mocked Concordia Kolassa, her contemptuous face stretched long as if she were sucking a pogo stick. "You can do it! You're the original comeback kid!"

"It's pronounced *Hay-Seuss,*" the Latin American boy replied with the robotic fatigue of someone who has responded to the same tiresome taunt too many times to remember.

Sareek bobbed and weaved around the boy. "You couldn't pour water out of a boot if the instructions were on the sole!" he said, following his taunt with a slap across the cheek.

Mr. Wilde strutted toward a large wooden crate full of sporting goods so old and decrepit that they were practically sporting *bads*. He rummaged through the crate, pulling out two mesh-metal face protectors and two white padded vests.

"Now that our dander is sufficiently 'up,' let us move on," Mr. Wilde said. "We only have a few moments left before Team Two arrives, thus concluding our final meeting of Spite Club."

The teacher walked over to a whiteboard, detailing twelve children's rankings. The names were arranged in a bracket diagram, with the winners of various bouts spreading from either side of the board, until only two names met in the center: Moses and Milton.

"How come Moxie's name isn't up there?" Ursula Lambarst asked, her jaw squared with suspicion.

Mr. Wilde eyed Moxie Wortschmerz, vibrating in the corner on her dolly, with a trace of apprehension.

"I'm afraid that if I unsheathed her tongue, it would be like uncorking the bottle of a violently verbose genie," he explained. "Plus, I find her presence extremely unnerving, as will Team Two. So, for the time being, Moxie shall serve as our—"

The wild-eyed girl clacked her silver-sheathed tongue in fury.

"—mascot."

Mr. Wilde walked over to the middle of the Grimnaseum floor. He dropped the vests and face protectors onto a rectangle of mats.

"Mr. Fauster and Mr. Babcock, please put on your protection," Mr. Wilde said as he went back to the crate and rifled further.

It had *to be Moses,* Milton thought with soft dread as he buckled on his padded vest. *I'm so tired of fighting him all the time. His hatred of me is so . . . exhausting.*

Milton slipped on the mesh metal face protector.

It's like a fencing mask, Milton thought, his breath hot and strangely comforting inside the helmet.

Mr. Wilde returned with two weapons underneath his arms.

"Now, this final exercise will aim to settle a classic dispute," the teacher said. "And that is: which is mightier, the sword"—he tossed Moses a sleek, slender rapier—"or the pen." He tossed Milton an extra-long ballpoint pen.

Milton rolled it in his hands, temporarily immobilized with disbelief, hoping to find some secret attribute that somehow made the pen a weapon. But other than the pen's ability to make lines with ink, it seemed perfectly ordinary and utterly unfair.

"You've *got* to be kidding," Milton groused. He looked over at Moses, who was swiping the air around him, making it scream in wounded anguish.

Mr. Wilde smirked. "I should have introduced your weapon first, Mr. Fauster, to better match the saying," the teacher said as he dusted off his dark velvet waist-coat. "But that would have dampened the moment's dramatic thrust. . . ."

Milton could feel Moses gloating from behind his mask.

"The two of you will duel while making a convincing argument on a subject of my choosing," Mr. Wilde said. "Once your position is made, you will be allowed to swipe your opponent: Mr. Babcock with his sword and Mr. Fauster with his pen."

Great, Milton thought, wilting inside like a corsage the day after prom.

"If Mr. Fauster can sign his first name on Mr. Babcock's chest, he is the victor. If Mr. Babcock runs Mr. Fauster through with his sword, *he* is the victor. The topic is 'cats versus dogs.' Mr. Fauster, you will take the 'Pro dog' position. Now . . . *go!*"

Milton nodded with grim resolve. He held his left arm gracefully behind him for balance and aimed his pen at his opponent's chest.

"Um . . . dogs are often called 'man's best friend' because they exhibit a profound loyalty to their owners."

Milton thrust his pen forward in quick frantic spirals and managed to mark an "M" onto Moses before the boy backed away.

"Cats can be loyal, too," Moses responded. "If offered love, they will respond—"

Moses thrust forward lithe and swift. Milton dodged the attack and parried with his pen, yet Moses was able to connect with a swipe just below Milton's mask.

"Oww!" Milton yelped, touching his bleeding neck.

"Good work, Mr. Babcock," Mr. Wilde commented. "Next time, less parry and more feint."

"There have been many studies showing that people who own dogs lead healthier lives," Milton said. "Dogs require exercise, which benefits both dog and master."

Milton lunged, yet only managed a quick swipe, earning himself an "I."

"Sure, dogs can help with your health or whatever," Moses retorted. "But there are no records of cats killing or severely injuring people. I mean, two words: pit bull . . . *en garde!*"

Moses shuffled toward his foe, knees bent, with the skittering alacrity of an angry crab, slashing Milton's chest.

"Dogs can be taught commands," Milton said, gritting his teeth through the pain. "Can you say the same for cats?"

Milton charged, yet Moses parried with precision. After a flurry of jabbing thrusts, Milton marked Moses with a sloppy "L."

"Cats wash and take care of themselves," Moses said. "They don't get all dirty like dogs."

Moses faked a lunge, then caught Milton off guard, jabbing him in the stomach.

"*Cat box!*" Milton yelled, marking Moses with a quick and furious "T" before the boy could defend himself. Moses swiped his foil wildly with blind rage.

"Research finds that cat owners have lower cholesterol and a reduced risk of heart attacks!"

Moses and Milton were locked together, pen to sword.

"Sources!" Milton spat back.

"Pending!"

"The same claims," Milton grunted, "could be made for *all* pet owners!"

Milton smudged Moses's padded vest with a sloppy "O."

Mr. Wilde, showing a rare burst of unrestrained emotion, clapped his hands.

"Touché, Mr. Fauster!"

Moses was furious. "Cats look after themselves!" he seethed. "Not like codependent canines! The Egyptians worshipped them!"

Moses cuffed Milton in the ear with the hilt of his sword. Milton staggered back to the wall.

"Studies show that dogs can sense illnesses in humans!" Milton roared back, slashing at Moses's sword. "Dogs offer companionship to those who suffer serious health problems!"

Soon, Moses was backed against the Grimnaseum wall, pinned without any means of escape.

"I mean," Milton panted, "have you ever heard of a seeing-eye *cat*?!"

Milton knocked the boy's sword out of his hands. It landed on the floor with a thunderous clatter.

"Excellent job, Mr. Fauster!" Mr. Wilde congratulated him. "Now finish him off."

Milton, panting, stared at the defenseless boy, crumpled against the wall. Milton shook his head. "He's not armed," he said, tossing his pen to the floor. "It wouldn't be fair. We'll call it a draw."

Milton took off his mesh face protector, pinned it beneath his arm, and extended his hand to his rival.

"Good match," he said.

Moses stepped forward and offered his hand. After a few congratulatory pumps, the boy lifted his hand, balled it into a fist, and brought it down hard on the back of Milton's head.

Mr. Wilde stalked forward.

"That's quite enough, Mr. Babcock!" the teacher scolded. "There is nothing as unseemly as a sore loser!"

Moses gave Milton a swift kick in the stomach. He took off his face protector.

"I may be a loser," Moses said with a wicked leer, "but *I'm* not the one who's sore."

Moses dropped his helmet to the floor and swaggered away.

Mr. Wilde helped Milton to his feet.

"Nice form, Mr. Fauster," the teacher said. "But you could use a few pointers."

Milton rubbed his bruised and tenderized chest.

"I think Moses gave me plenty."

Mr. Wilde gave Milton a sour grin. "The public is wonderfully tolerant. It forgives everything except genius."

The teacher's smile faded quickly. Like a letter that had been ghostwritten in invisible ink.

"If you want to survive the War of the Words, Mr. Fauster, you will have to work on your killer instinct," he said gravely, "or risk being killed and made *extinct* at the hands—or mouth, rather—of your sister. . . ."

18 · WHERE ANGELS DARE TO TREAD

LIMBO—HECK'S WAITING (and waiting) room for wicked wastrels—was abuzz. Reporters swarmed like flies on hot "scoop," waiting for Principal Bea "Elsa" Bubb's latest, most controversial employees to arrive through the sugar-spiked, barbed licorice–choked gates.

The principal stole a look at her reflection in the "PULL IN CASE OF WATER" box in the howlway.

"It's showtime," Principal Bubb muttered. "Bea is *back*. For good. For bad. For always . . ."

The principal, wearing a dress slit to her garter-snake garters, strutted through the Foul Playground, a waste-land of broken Barbies, shattered Sit'n Spins, jumbled jump ropes, handicapped hula hoops, and G.I. Joes that had long since gone AWOL from anything remotely resembling fun. Boogeypeople (hideous demons dressed as slightly less hideous demons) held the reporters and photographers at bay, waving their mossy green arms and staring down interlopers with their big glowing Cyclops eyes.

Cerberus, Principal Bubb's three-headed lapdog, savaged a squeaky unicorn toy outside of a Clubfoot House—a ramshackle play structure that listed to one side. The creature swiftly severed the chew toy's proud horn before turning two of its hideous heads toward the principal as she approached.

Principal Bubb waved to the assembled reporters as she made her way to Limbo's KinderScare facility for a photo opp.

Just beyond a big, sputtering neon sign blinking KINDERSCARE: WHERE LITTLE KIDS GET BIG NIGHTMARES was a dingy room decorated with grimy handprints and goopy snot smears. A haggard goatlike nanny demon stood over a group of petrified toddlers feigning sleep in their frosted gingerbread coffins.

"Why, hello, wee ones of Limbo!" the principal roared, her booming voice causing a fresh peal of terrified shrieks.

"Um . . . Principal Bubb," the teacher bleated. "I was just putting the children down for their nap. . . ."

"No worries," the principal said as several photographers followed her inside. "I'll put them down—*you children are hideous*. See? That's a joke. I put them down."

A bug-eyed demon photographer from *Eternity Today* magazine trained its camera upon the principal.

"I kid," Principal Bubb said, primping for the photographer. "I love children . . . especially with béarnaise sauce."

An excited mob formed outside the gates. Principal Bubb left the KinderScare facility and clacked through the throng of "me!-me!-media" jackals.

The Gates of Heck opened with a gush of sulfurous steam. Out strode nine creatures—tall, proud beings radiating equal parts majesty and menace—with halos of sizzling flame hovering over their heads.

An angel wearing an eye patch led his commando team of fallen angels into Limbo's unwelcoming Unwelcome Area. Four lizards in gold lamé suits slithered into a spotlight, crawling across toy musical instruments. The lead lizard shot a heavy-lidded gaze over his Ray-Bans, and crooned into his tiny microphone while his backing band played a smoky jazz ditty.

> *"If you've lived a life so bad, that you drove your*
> *parents and teachers mad . . ."*

The one-eyed angel glared at the lizard, his eye like a dark sun trained through a magnifying glass on an unsuspecting anthill. Principal Bubb swiped her foreclaw below her chins.

"Take five, lizards."

The principal turned to the tall angel, his long raven's wings tucked tight to his proud back.

"Principal Bubb," she said, holding out her claw. "Your new boss."

Flashbulbs exploded as the photographers and reporters got over the stupefying shock of nine hulking celestial outlaws standing before them.

The dark angel smirked from beneath his upside-down horseshoe of a mustache. After an awkward beat, he shook hands with the principal.

"Azkeel," he said in a snide, smoky voice.

Principal Bubb puzzled over Azkeel's face.

"Have we met before?" she asked.

"*Please,* Principal," Azkeel replied. "Flirting with me is flirting with disaster. . . ."

"No, it's just that you seem so—"

"Mr. Azkeel!" a woman wearing white tailored business vestments cried. "Mary Claire Divine with *Gabriel's Horn: Your Daily Blast of Good News.* Could you introduce your fellow fallen angels?"

Azkeel gestured to the four once-heavenly creatures to his right.

"Of course. This is Malaku," Azkeel said, holding out his arm.

A fierce, sculpted angel, shirtless with a shaved head and spikes jutting out from his wrists, sneered. His eyes burned with malice.

"Diabolus."

A silver-haired woman with bright green eyes, claws, and faint leopard spots covering her neck, arms, and legs smirked.

"Zagan."

A barrel-chested man with a nose ring, pierced lip, and six links of chain hanging down from his neck like a tie acknowledged the reporters with a jaded gaze.

"Rahab."

An Asian man with blond hair and earrings, dressed head to toe in black leather, smiled at the crowd.

Azkeel turned to his left. "This is Marchosias."

A teenage girl with large black wings and flaming red hair nodded shyly to the crowd. She had the greenish-gold eyes of a wolf, and when she smiled, a finger of flame leapt from her mouth, licking her black lips.

"Lahash."

A burly creature wearing a cast-iron hood and a vest sprouting silver blades at the shoulders, spread its splendid red wings.

"Belphegor."

A woman with translucent hair and dressed in a tight, chain-mail bodysuit slid her large silver sunglasses down her slender nose, assessing the crowd with her pitch-black eyes.

"And Molloch."

The female reporters in attendance gasped despite themselves at the dark-skinned boy's beauty. Molloch's brilliant blue eyes flared like sapphires.

"He's gorgeous," whispered Mary Claire Divine.

"Now, Miss Divine," Molloch sneered, his razor-blade-feathered wings glinting from over his broad shoulders. "Don't bother trying to get on my good side. I don't have one."

Principal Bubb's taped-on smile began to lose its stick. All eyes were on Azkeel and his cast-out comrades. *She* was the reason the fallen angels were all here, the most daring hiring coup of all time.

The principal stepped in front of Azkeel. "Now here's the scoop on the brilliant decision making that led to—" she began before a demon reporter cut her off.

"Willard Glick, *Brimstone Beacon: The Nastiest News, Served Un-Easy with a Side of Beacon*," the creature barked. "Mr. Azkeel, why did you decide to become an employee of Heck?"

The dark angel stepped around the principal's gluteus way-maximus and resumed his place at the front of the pack.

"Excellent question," Azkeel replied with a cold smile. "If I may speak for my fellow fallen, we have always felt an affinity for the horned and wrathful, the hoofed and spiteful, the tailed and tyrannical . . . our brothers and sisters similarly forsaken by the Big Guy Upstairs. And when Principal Blubb here—"

"*Bubb*," the principal seethed.

"—reached out to us with its offer—"

"*Her.*"

"—to protect the netherworld's children, our most precious resource, we jumped at the opportunity. Or swooped, actually. Plus," Azkeel added with a cruel, thin-lipped smile, "the money was good."

The principal, quivering with attention withdrawal, stepped in front of Azkeel, extending her arms wide. The drooping flesh draping her arms made her look like a gigantic flying squirrel.

"Behold: *Heck's Angels!*" Principal Bubb exclaimed, glaring at her loyal-when-threatened lackeys.

Most of her demon staff broke out in less-than-spontaneous applause.

"Now if you'll excuse us," the principal said as she ushered Azkeel and the other eight fallen angels out of the Unwelcome Area toward the howlway. "We have important matters to discuss. . . ."

"I think that went well," Principal Bubb reflected as she and the fallen angels entered her Not-So-Secret Lair.

Azkeel turned swiftly on the heel of his boots. "Listen, Principal," he said, puzzling briefly over Bea "Elsa" Bubb's mismatched mudslide of a face, "we're not here as part of your personal publicity blitz. We're here to further our own interests."

"Which *are*?" Principal Bubb spat back.

"Which are of no interest to you at this time," the dark angel said.

An angry quiet settled in the principal's high-tech lair of security screens and blinking computers.

Molloch swept the room with his piercing blue eyes. "Nice digs," he said in his dark, smooth voice. "I could do wonders with a place like this. A foosball table, a pinball machine, a medieval rack . . ."

"That would make for a lovely decoration," Marchosias said with a soft puff of fire.

"Right," Molloch replied with a sly grin. *Decoration.*"

Azkeel sat in the principal's chair, putting his boots up on her massive mahogany desk. He reached inside his leather vest.

"Let's get down to business," he said, smoothing out a blueprint on the principal's desk. "Our first official act as Heck's Angels—a name we find offensive but grudgingly acknowledge as 'catchy'—is, as you know, to provide security for the upcoming War of the Words. We have obtained a diagram of the venue—the Tower of Babble—which was no easy feat. The technological schematics, I was told, are only available on a need-to-know basis."

"Who told you?"

"You don't need to know," the fallen angel continued. "The point is that Vice Principal Carroll is making quite a statement by getting King Nimrod to host the War of the Words there, after that whole kerfuffle with the original Tower of *Babel*. It's like he's thumbing his nose at The Big Guy Upstairs Himself. That guy is either lionhearted or harebrained. But, of course, you know all of this, having sent the vice principal to Wise Acres yourself. . . ."

Right, Principal Bubb stewed. *My decision completely.*

Azkeel leaned back, his hands clasped behind his neck. "In fact, that was one of the reasons why we accepted your offer," he said. "You must be something of a maverick, swimming upstream from all of the procedural bilge water that's been clogging up the afterlife like a gas station toilet. Making bold decisions, working around those who stand in your way. And hiring us . . . wow, however did you come up with *that* one?"

The principal shrugged her calcified shoulder humps like two elderly camels hitting a speed bump in the desert.

"It just sort of . . . *came to me,*" Principal Bubb explained.

Azkeel folded his majestic wings behind him, each perfect pinion meshing perfectly with the other. The effect was somehow both graceful and threatening.

"You may have employed us, but that doesn't mean we take orders from you," he said, tucking his finger beneath his eye patch for a quick scratch. "Our arrangement is one of mutually advantageous coexistence. We, your Heck's Angels, will scratch your back. . . ." Azkeel's eye grazed the principal's lumpy back with distaste. "Figuratively, of course," he said, rising from the chair. "And you scratch *ours.* Just between the wings."

The fallen angels strode toward the door with military precision.

"Sorry to crash your little all-ages purgatorial dance party and run," Azkeel said, his strong hand gripping the door's iron handle. "But we've got some planning to do. But not to worry: we'll let you know what we're up to. We are your dutiful employees, after all. And it's our duty to protect and to serve: whatever serves *us* . . ."

What have I gotten myself into? the principal thought miserably.

19 · HAViNG THE LAST LAP

MARLO KICKED HER feet off the edge of a pile of foam mats. She was irritated that Milton had made no move to respond to her alphabet soup note. It was like an olive branch, and she was a dove—or a filthy pigeon, if you were Mack Hoover—extending a message of peace. But no. Milton's *lack* of a message must be a message in itself: he had no intention of working together with Marlo, and it was every tongue for itself at the War of the Words.

The goddess Peitho stood with Miss Parker in the Exorcize Area of the Grimnaseum, a dreary corner crowded with barbed trestles and bitter medicine balls.

"Persuasion is another tool in an arguer's arsenal," the stunning, shapely goddess said, her voice coiling sweetly in the air like incense.

"But persuading isn't arguing," Cookie Youngblood argued.

"That's a great point, Cookie," Peitho said with a smile that made you forget who you were, or what you were wanting in the first place, like how you can open the refrigerator and suddenly have no idea what you're hungry for. "Thank you so much for bringing that up, Cookie: that persuading isn't arguing."

Cookie grinned, placated and pleased with herself, though she wasn't quite sure why.

"Persuasion is a like a velvet hammer," the goddess continued, her chocolate brown hair piled up on top of her head like a hot-fudge sundae. "It delivers a soft blow, dazing your opponent. It's different than mere flattery—simply buttering someone up with creamy talk. Persuasion has an end game. It's an art. It's bending people to your will in gentle, invisible steps. . . ."

Peitho stepped up to Cookie and brushed her finger against the girl's cheek, which reddened softly under the goddess's touch.

"It's like with this sweet girl here . . . Cookie or whatever," Peitho purred. "She had an argument that I quickly defused through acknowledgment, repeating what she said to insinuate that I was actually listening, giving the illusion of gratitude in exchange for her worthless opinion, and then using her own name liberally, as there is nothing sweeter to a person's ears than the sound of their own name."

Cookie's smile drooped like a mustache. "Hey . . . wait a second—"

"But, Miss Peitho, persuasion is *easy* for someone like you," Marlo offered. "I mean, you're the goddess Peitho and so beautiful and perfect and always say just the right thing. Like how you're here this morning, Peitho, helping us, which is so sweet, by teaching us the art of persuasion. But what do *I* know? I'm just a grubby dead girl with a tongue like a hunk of spoiled luncheon meat, not a goddess like *you*, Peitho. I should probably just go back to my bunk and get some sleep, huh?"

The goddess beamed. "Why, thank you, dear! And of *course* you can go back to your bunk and get some—" Peitho's brain skidded to a stop. Storm clouds of outrage darkened her sunny disposition. "Why, you—"

"It's Marlo. *Marlo Fauster.* That's my name, and you can repeat it back to me all you want, but it won't work: I am persuasion resistant. No one can get me to do something I don't want to do, unless I *want* to do something I don't want to do. . . ."

Most of the other children—save for Cookie Youngblood, who was still smarting from her sweet-talking defeat—smirked back with admiration.

"Thank you, Peitho," Miss Parker said, stifling a guilty smile. "I think you've shown us—whether you intended to or not—that pride can easily short-circuit most anyone's logic."

The goddess left the room in a furious swirl of robes and a less-than-ladylike harrumph.

Miss Parker turned to Marlo. She shook her head with gentle surprise.

"I must admit, at first I wasn't quite sure what to make of you, Miss Fauster," she said. "You seemed fresh yet not the sharpest tongue in the knife drawer. But now I see that perhaps your cleverness lies in your ability to not appear so. Someone who wears out her opponent through sheer tenacity."

The girls began muttering to themselves. The teacher pulled out a whistle and gave it a piercing toot.

"Time is running out . . . for all of you!" Miss Parker barked. "We only have a few minutes to go over the finer points of Linguastics before you begin your pilgrimage to the Tower of Babble."

The teacher took two slender tubes of what looked like sugar and slowly emptied them onto the ground as she strolled the perimeter of the Grimnaseum.

"As bats use sonar and salmon use scents, we use *words* as our language," she explained. "Oftentimes, I feel that man invented language solely to satisfy his deep need to complain. Without it, though, we would not be able to say *exactly* what we mean to."

The teacher wended her way through the Grimnaseum, occasionally stopping to make intricate sugar swirls on the floor.

"Language is how we carve up the world around us . . . how we organize it into concepts. And carving up the world keenly takes both a sharp vocabulary and a sharp tongue."

"Tongue?" repeated Hadley from behind her hair.

"Yes, though our words have wings, they often fly not where they should. The key is a strong, agile tongue, achieved through rigorous Linguastics, or—in layman's terms—tongue exercises."

"Tongue exercises!" Marlo and Cookie gasped in unison. "That's stupid!"

The two girls glared at each other, shocked and disgusted that the same words had flown off their tongues at the same time. Miss Parker blew her whistle.

"All I heard was *blah blah blah* . . . I want to do a hundred laps . . . *blah blah blah* . . . Now go to it, you two!" the teacher ordered.

Cookie and Marlo rose grudgingly from their foam mats and started to jog. Miss Parker tooted her whistle like a peevish teakettle.

"Not with your feet!" she exclaimed, pointing to the lines of sugar spilled onto the ground. *"With your tongues!"*

"You can't possibly be—" Marlo began before being silenced by Miss Parker's whistle.

"Without a strong tongue, your arguments will fall flat, and we've only got a few minutes to lick you into shape. So go! Tongues to mats!"

Marlo sighed and began following the trail of sugar with the tip of her tongue. Despite a nagging undercurrent of "sour, filthy foam rubber mat," the sugar tasted good, as Marlo's tongue had been tormented with tartness ever since she arrived in Wise Acres. After only a few minutes of tracing the tangled path—especially the spirals—Marlo's tongue began to ache. Some of the other children snickered as Cookie and Marlo crawled across the floor on their hands and knees. Miss Parker blew her whistle.

"You four!" she said, swiping her accusing finger at Mungo Ulyaw, Bree Martinet, Mathis Vittorio, and Lani Zanotti. "Drop and give me fifty tongue push-ups. *Now!*"

The four children lay facedown on the floor and, grunting, tried desperately to raise themselves off the mats with their mouths.

Marlo's mouth was a dried-out cave harboring pure agony. She was a few painful laps ahead of Cookie, whose complaints were both unintelligible yet loud and clear behind her. The morning bell tolled. Marlo, a few yards from the end of the winding sugar course, rolled on her back, her swollen tongue lolling out the side of her mouth. Miss Parker sighed and rubbed her baggy eyes as the children gasped and moaned on the mats.

"Yet, with the tips of your tongues in tip-top shape, you'll always be able to dish it out, no matter what is served. Now best of lick—*luck*—to you all. . . . You'll need it."

Milton and the rest of his team fidgeted inside the "Talk-Back Forty" of Wise Acres, just within the dreary rear gates—lashed with sticks and stones—that creaked open in the breeze. A peculiar nervous, electrifying dread had taken up residence in Milton's muscles, making him feel as if he had contracted the flu at his own surprise party.

Marlo and Team Two were waiting a dozen yards away. Milton and his sister cast confused sideways glances at one another. Were they allies? Were they enemies? Neither of them knew for sure.

A pulsing symphony of noise sounded from beyond the gates. It throbbed softly yet insistently like a million chirrups. The swelling tone masked an eerie scream of wind in the distance.

Lucky squirmed inside Milton's coat, awake and restless. Milton sighed. He'd have to let his pet ferret stretch and frisk a bit. There was no stopping Lucky once he was awake, which was seldom. Milton turned his back to the other children and carefully set Lucky onto the shredded paper ground. A torn index card fell from Milton's pocket.

hewhaY

What does it mean? he thought as he picked up the card. The writing, he now realized after intercepting the vice principal's crazy cat-conveyed notes, was unmistakably

Lewis Carroll's. *The Y at the end is capitalized, meaning that the word itself is a name, only written in reverse, which would make it . . . Yahweh. That name is kind of familiar. . . .* Milton tucked the note back into his pocket. *Maybe I can figure it out on the way to the Tower of Babble. . . .*

Milton's mind kept going fuzzy. The ceaseless chirping seemed to worry apart his thoughts just as they threatened to congeal into something meaning-ful. The effect wasn't sedating, exactly, more like . . . mesmerizing: flowing across Milton's consciousness like the tide.

A white Volkswagen Rabbit convertible pulled up just outside the gates and came to an abrupt stop. The car had hood-mounted loudspeakers, a satellite dish in the back, and a large aluminum trailer hitched to the rear. There were even what looked like tiny screens, surveilling murky landscapes from dozens of angles, flickering across his windshield. The driver's-side door—emblazoned with WAR OF THE WORDS WELCOME WAGEN in bright purple letters—flung open and out tumbled Vice Principal Carroll. His Victorian waistcoat ruffled in the wind as he checked his pocket watch with haste.

"Oh my ears and whiskers! How late it's getting!" he grumbled.

The trailer rattled and shook like a tremendous rat-trap housing an enormous and enraged rodent of unusual size. A muffled roar—like a maddened bull, spitting and yowling in hideous confusion—issued forth.

"Snnnaaahhhhrrrrrrk!!"

"That . . . sound," Milton said to the small group of teachers assembled to supervise the children. "What was it?"

"That sound was the snark!" Vice Principal Carroll called out as he strode purposefully across the grounds to his Absurditory. "And today you children will be engaging in a snark hunt!"

"You want us to go hunt something called a snark?" Ursula Lambarst asked, pretending to chew gum so that she appeared more confident than she felt.

"Oh, goodness no," the vice principal replied, securing a large top hat to his head with an elastic band tucked beneath his chin. "The snark will be hunting *you*. . . ."

The creature within the trailer let loose a growl, sounding like a clap of incarcerated thunder. Milton gulped. Vice Principal Carroll carried two leather briefcases. He set them down before the children.

They look so familiar, Milton thought as the man dawdled over to his Cheshire cat cottage.

"I knew I forgot something," the vice principal muttered as he darted inside his Absurditory. "I fear I'd forget my very head if it weren't resting comfortably on m-my shoulders!"

As Vice Principal Carroll disappeared through his surreal shed's two front teeth, Lucky sniffed around Milton's feet before slowly following an invisible trail of scent to the nearest briefcase.

"*Lucky!*" Milton yell-whispered, but his command was lost in the unnerving howl of the whistling wind. Lucky snuffled at the open leather satchel.

"Got them!" the vice principal exclaimed as he emerged from the Cheshire cat's grinning mouth, holding two pairs of handcuffs. Milton eyed his pet nervously.

Lucky . . . c'mon!

Lucky, smelling something in the briefcase, spilled inside.

"Vice Principal Carroll," Moses Babcock said, his eyes darting from Milton to Lucky to the vice principal. "Milton has a—"

Clem Weenum elbowed Moses in the ribs, silencing him.

"B-big responsibility as team captain," the vice principal said, stopping in front of the briefcases and snapping them shut.

"No, he has a pet," Moses continued.

"Tattletale!" Clem shouted.

"Vice Principal Carroll," Cookie exclaimed. "Clem just called Moses a tattletale!"

"Moses means a pet *peeve*," Milton said. "About tattletales."

Milton looked over at his sister. She smiled briefly, but then a terrible grimace overtook her face.

It's like she can't even stand the sight of me, Milton thought, frowning.

Owww . . . my tongue, Marlo thought, her mouth a throbbing traffic jam of aches and pains. *And Milton . . . it's like he's disgusted by the very sight of me!*

Vice Principal Carroll shook his head as he gave Milton one of the briefcases, then handcuffed it to his wrist.

"You imaginative ch-children!" he declared. "You will make for such diverting radio!"

The vice principal walked over to Marlo.

"Now here are your n-note cards for the debate," he said as he quickly handcuffed the second briefcase to her wrist. "Take good care of them. . . ."

Vice Principal Carroll ambled down the overgrown slope to the back gates of Wise Acres. He pushed the gates open wide with a screaming squeal of iron. Marlo twitched at the sight of open land. Her body yearned for escape, for making a run for it, but the squads of badger and aardvark demons eyed the children with steely purpose. There would be no unsanctioned field trips today.

"B-behold the Outer Terristories," Vice Principal Carroll said with a haunted awe. "A place where language comes *alive.*"

The Outer Terristories, Marlo thought with a shiver as the wind whipped into a chorus of screeching whistles and chirping swells. From the map in the vice principal's Absurditory. That must mean that everything—all of that crazy stuff about a sonic disease and reshaping

Creation—is *true,* including that part about—Marlo swallowed—*Here There Be Grammonsters!*

The vice principal grinned mysteriously, his lips a pale pink caterpillar crawling above his chin.

"The War of the Words effectively b-begins n-now," he said. "Finding the venue—the Tower of Babble—will be half the b-battle."

Milton raised his hand. "Then what's the other half?" he asked nervously.

Vice Principal Carroll stared off into the horizon.

"The *real* battle . . ."

MIDDLEWORD

Language is like a rickety bridge stretched out between what we think and what we actually say. Whether our thoughts cross successfully depends less upon a sturdy vocabulary (or how many weighty words the bridge of our mouth can support), but how, exactly, the person waiting for us on the other side interprets those words. Speaking your mind doesn't guarantee that your words will fall on deft ears.

The problem lies (or is it lays?) with words themselves. Words are to "precision" as Dr. Seuss is to "qualified medical care" (unless, of course, you've pulled your green eggs and hamstrings). At first blush, you might think that words convey meaning, but perhaps it's meaning that conveys words. Unlike numbers, words seldom add up. Take $2 + 4 = 6$. Simple, straightforward, and irrefutable. But now try two plus four. Two what, exactly? Two submarines full of weasels? Four hornets' nests? The only thing that could add up to is trouble.

Even blue plus yellow is a sticky scenario. If you're talking paint on a painting, they could very well make green. If you're talking bluebirds and yellow canaries in a blender, then you'll probably end up with red . . . not to mention five to ten years in prison. In that way, words are rather like colors, where one person's green is another person's chartreuse, lime, olive drab, or even (gasp) teal.

Words themselves are merely signposts pointing toward meaning. Words can mean many things: especially mean words. Do we really mean the mean things we say, or do our mean words really mean more than we meant to mean? Sometimes inflection and intent are the only things separating Praise-a-dise from Diss-topia.

Sure, actions may speak louder than words, but if your "action" is the surgical chewing out of the principal during the school assembly while accepting the office of class president, then those words can explode louder than any bomb.

The tongue is a most fascinating weapon in that it slays without drawing blood, leaving behind a wound that festers and pesters and never truly heals. . . .

20 · THE BEAST OF TiMES, THE WORST OF TiMES

"WAIT!" MR. WILDE called out as the children staggered from the gate to begin their pilgrimage through the Outer Terristories. The teacher was joined by Mr. Dickens, Miss Parker, and a middle-aged man the children had never seen before.

"Vice Principal Carroll has agreed to allow you escorts," the foppish man said as he buttoned up his waistcoat in the chilling breeze. "Namely, *us*."

Marlo squinted at the uneasy middle-aged man at Mr. Wilde's side. "Who's that guy?"

Mr. Wilde eyed the man with a sideways glance, as if the new adult wasn't worth the full weight of his gaze.

"A new teacher . . . a Mr. Dale E. *Basye*," the playwright

and novelist said, mangling the freshly dead writer's last name.

"It's *Basye* . . . like 'bay' and 'sea' squished together."

"Are you sure?" Miss Parker said with a smirk. "It's certainly not spelled that way."

"Yes, I'm sure!"

"Mr. *Bay-sea* is a . . . 'writer,'" Mr. Wilde said, using the most sarcastic air quotes that Marlo had ever seen. "Still warm."

"How do you mean?" Winifred Scathelli asked.

Mr. Dickens leaned into the smug, jowly girl. "Still warm with the Surface," he muttered. "Hasn't fully accepted his present circumstances. In a moment, he will more than likely comment on all of this being some crazy, crazy dream. . . ."

"What a crazy, crazy dream." Mr. Basye snickered to himself as he massaged his throbbing wrist. "I must have passed out from the writer's cramp. I dreamt I was in someplace called Hack: Where the Bad Writers Go, but they turned me away."

"Because you were too good a writer?" Pansy Cornett asked.

"Heavens no! Because of the grisly drop-deadlines. Anyway, so after Hack, I was sent here to *Heck* as a substitute teacher. . . ."

A riot of chirps washed over a long stone fence in the distance, like waves breaking over a reef. The surge of sound was the audio equivalent of a night sky crowded with twinkling stars. The chirping sent Milton into a mild trance. He stole a glance at his sister, hoping to latch on to something real, like a visual lifesaver to prevent his muddled mind from washing away. Marlo's dark violet eyes were impenetrable as she stared up at the sky.

Milton sighed.

This is ridiculous. Marlo may be evil incarnate, but she's still my sister.

Milton walked over to Marlo while the usually unflappable Mr. Wilde seemed to flap slightly around the edges.

"We'd best be going," the teacher said warily, grabbing Milton by the shoulder.

"But—"

"We'll be approaching the Tower of Babble in two teams—our Spite Club teams," Mr. Wilde said as he corralled his thirteen charges together. "Mr. Dickens will join our group, while Mr. Bazzie—"

"*Basye.* Like 'bay' and 'sea'—"

"—will join Miss Parker's group."

Miss Parker glared at the insufferable substitute teacher before leveling her gaze at Mr. Wilde. "Really, Oscar: you shouldn't have. . . ."

"Oscar?" Mr. Basye said as he walked next to Miss Parker. "As in *Oscar Wilde*? Ha! This dream keeps getting better and better! Imagine me, Dale E. Basye, alongside such literary greats as Oscar Wilde, Charles Dickens, and whoever you are. . . ."

Miss Parker clenched her jaw. "Yes," she seethed. "Imagine *that*. . . ."

Milton looked over his shoulder at his sister. Marlo was nearly indiscernible amid the purple-orange haze. But Milton had this weird feeling that whenever he wasn't looking at her, she was looking at him and that they were just out of sync with one another.

What else is new? he thought as Marlo disappeared over a rolling hill of windswept paper.

"What's that?" Sareek Plimpton asked.

"What's that?" Clem Weenum parroted back.

A stone barrier became visible in the thinning haze. It gained clarity with every step that Milton took and seemed to stretch out for miles on either side of him and his team.

"Welcome to the War of the Words!" Vice Principal Carroll announced from his roving white Rabbit beyond the barrier. "In a grammarena they bravely go, at the tippy-toppy of our show! Team One is at the very brink . . . of exactly what, I shudder to think! Let them wake from their little nap before they meet what's in the gap!"

Milton pointed to a small breach in the fence. "There's a gap in the wall," he said.

"I guess we're supposed to pass through," Mordacia Caustilo said.

Concordia Kolassa shot the heavy-set girl a wounding glance. "Some of us with more difficulty than others."

As the teachers and children approached the gap, they could see something moving inside it. But it wasn't merely one creature. It was a morphing *succession* of creatures.

"Oh my!" Vice Principal Carroll declared. "A hawk, a tarantula, a snake, a boar, a scorpion, a—"

"What—" Milton started before a sight rendered him instantly mute.

"Wolf!"

It was just like the creature that he and Marlo had seen outside the gates of Wise Acres: that fearsome, brutish beast of matted fur and slavering jaws.

"How are we supposed to get past it?" Pansy Cornett said in a tiny, ragged voice.

Milton noticed that the stationary parade of disagreeable creatures was always in the same order: from hawk, to tarantula, to cobra, to boar, to scorpion, to massive wolf. The only thing that the creatures had in common is that they were all chained to a post, trapping them in the gap in the fence.

Vice Principal Carroll gave a breathless, blow-by-blow account of the scene, a narration that grew more detailed as Milton and his team approached. It was almost as if the vice principal was describing the action a split second before it actually *happened*.

"It's a sequence," Milton said over the mind-numbing commentary. "If we each rush past when it's a scorpion—the smallest of the animals—we should be okay. We just jump over it."

Moses sighed, shaking his head.

"Great idea, Team Captain," Moses said in a way that made it vividly clear that he neither found the idea great nor Milton worthy of his team captain status. "The next creature is that werewolf thing. The worst of all of them."

Milton studied the shaggy wolf-beast just before it shrank down into a hawk.

"Not a werewolf but . . . a *What*-Wolf!" Milton muttered. "A wolf that can become different creatures."

Moses spun his finger around his temple in tight "this guy is crazy" circles.

On the other side of the gap, through clots of ashy reddish-purple murk, Milton could see a strange, silvery forest.

Mr. Dickens stepped forward. "Mr. Fauster is right," he said as he eyed the gap intently. "We'll just have to Jack-be-nimble our way through. . . ."

With surprising athleticism, Mr. Dickens bounded through the gap and leapt over the scorpion. The What-Wolf turned as it materialized and roared at the English novelist before sprouting feathers and shrinking back into a hawk. The shape-shifting creature strained at its various chains, but the links held fast.

Mr. Dickens dusted off his gray suit. "My, what an artful dodge *that* was!" he chuckled, smoothing out his tousled beard. "What are you waiting for? The ghost of Christmas past?!"

One by one, Mr. Wilde and the children jumped through the break in the fence, vaulting over the furious scorpion that tried to jab each valiant vaulter with its stinger.

Moses bounded through, leaving Milton the sole team member behind.

"C'mon, Team Captain," Moses taunted, several yards from the fearsome What-Wolf. "Or are you afraid everyone will see the big wet spot on your pants?"

The creature's succession of forms hastened into a nightmarish blur.

Milton had to time his jump perfectly. *Hawk, tarantula, snake, boar . . .*

He leapt into the air just as Moses kicked a stone toward Milton. Milton tripped and fell into the gap.

. . . scorpion . . .

21 · AT THE END OF
THEiR TROPE

MILTON GRABBED THE stone and, just as the scorpion began to swell and grow hair, smashed the poisonous arachnid flat.

He sprang from the ground to find his team. After a few hundred yards, Milton joined the teachers and children as they stood outside the rim of a gleaming forest. The light reflecting off the trees was blinding. Milton shielded his eyes from the glare.

Each tree was clad in a reflective bark, with silvery, highly burnished leaves that bounced light from one to the other like a game of optic hot potato. The effect was intensely disorienting.

"Thick, beneath yon arching trees, where silver-crested ripples screech!" Vice Principal Carroll prattled.

"Word paintings melt into the breeze, bearing fruited figures of your speech. . . ."

Milton could see Moses's silhouette hanging away from the others.

"Thanks for tripping me, jerk!" Milton spat at him as he joined the group.

Moses turned, a neat smirk slashed across his smug face. "You're being paranoid, Team Captain," he replied. "I was only trying to help you."

"Help me? How? By tripping me?"

"No, by trying to smoosh the scorpion for you," Moses said loudly so that everyone could hear as he stepped over a small mound of upturned dirt. "It's not my fault you're clumsy. Don't make a *mountain out of a molehill*. . . ."

The ground began to quake and swell. The mirrored trees shuddered, sending a shower of glitter into the air. The forest floor bulged and distended, knocking the teachers and children onto the ground as the earth churned beneath them, the forest becoming a steep mountain peak. Milton clutched one of the trees. The bark was so reflective that he could see the terror in his eyes. He also noticed dozens of tiny tuning forks sprouting from the ground, like the kind that he and Marlo had found in Lucky's messenger bag. Staring at them was like watching candles flicker. It was oddly hypnotic.

"What is this place?" Pansy Cornett whined as she

set Moxie Wortschmerz, lashed to her rolling dolly, against one of the trees.

Wisps of gray clouds clotted into a dark, conspiring mass overhead.

An Afro-Asian boy named Rakeem Yashimoto stared up at the clouds. "Looks like it's gonna rain cats and dogs," he said, pulling up his lapel.

A clap of thunder boomed. The mountain began to slowly flatten. Small, fuzzy blobs cascaded down from the sky, hitting the ground with squeals, screeches, mewls, and yaps. The animals shook off the shock of impact and bounded around the children in coursing streams of fur.

Milton ducked beneath a canopy of mirrored leaves for shelter. He held the briefcase handcuffed to his wrist up over his head.

"What's going on?" Winifred Scathelli gasped as a frightened Rottweiler fell onto a hissing Abyssinian. The two animals fought viciously a few feet from her.

A cascade of canines and free-falling felines tumbled down, coating the floor of the forest until the children and teachers were hip-deep in squirming, scratching animals.

"I can't . . . *even move,*" Roberta Atrebor complained. "All these mutts and kitties . . ."

"Not mutts . . . and kitties," Milton muttered as the animals piled up on all sides, pressing into him, making it hard to breathe. "But . . ." His eyes sparked with insight. "This place . . . it isn't a forest. It's a *Metaphorest*."

"Of course," Mr. Wilde said as he attempted to wriggle free from a squirming mound of precipitated pets. "How . . . droll."

"Ugh," Jesus Descardo grunted above the choir of yaps and yowls. "What do you mean by *Metaphorest*?"

"Because it's raining cats and dogs," Milton said. *"For real*. And before that, Moses made a mountain from a molehill."

Moses wrenched himself free from a fuzzy, writhing heap. "Don't pin the blame on me," he said before yelping in pain.

Another clap of thunder boomed. The shower of plummeting pets abruptly ceased. Milton could see that Moses had a note pinned to his forehead reading "blame." He winced as he plucked the pin from his bleeding flesh. The boy, furious, crumpled up the note and stormed toward Mr. Wilde as the cats and dogs began to slowly dissolve away to nothing.

Moses grabbed Mr. Wilde by the collar. "You're a teacher," he said, trying his best to get into the tall teacher's face. "You guys *have* to know what's going on here—"

"Moses, watch your—" Milton interjected.

"So spill the beans!" Moses shouted.

Instantly, Mr. Wilde doubled over in pain. He fell

to the ground coughing. Out of his sputtering mouth came a cascade of beans: pinto beans, navy beans, lima beans, green beans, and even jelly beans. Mr. Dickens ran to the convulsing teacher and patted him on the back.

"It's okay, Oscar," the old man said kindly as Mr. Wilde vomited gallon after gallon of beans. "We always suspected that you were full of . . . well, you know . . ."

Ursula looked around her fearfully. The large, intimidating girl now seemed like a trembling Latino mouse.

"We've got to get out of here," she murmured.

Mr. Wilde heaved and retched, adding another stomachful of beans to the lake of legumes around him.

"Is he gonna kick the bucket?" Ursula asked, her brown eyes wide with alarm.

"Careful what you—" Milton said just as a large bucket materialized several yards away from them.

Jesus Descardo snickered as he stepped toward it. "This is stupid," he said with a shake of his head. "*Loco.* This is all just some kind of trick. . . ."

"Jesus, don't do it!" Milton said as the boy stopped in front of the bucket.

"Or what?" Jesus said as he went to give the pail a kick. "Just watch. Nothing will—"

Just as the boy's foot touched the bucket, Jesus Descardo's body instantly froze, flattened, and turned into a pile of black and white words.

Jesus Descardo's
Head Head Head
Head Head Head
Neck

A	Torso Torso Torso	A
R	Torso Torso Torso	R
M	Torso Torso Torso	M
S	Torso Torso Torso	S

L   **L**
E   **E**
G   **G**
S   **S**
Feet   **Feet**

Vice Principal Carroll instantly squawked his commentary.

"If a player's overcome with dread, his fear like
chains and fetters,
he'll believe that he is truly dead, and dissolve to
words and letters."

"What happened?!" Concordia screamed. The children surrounded what used to be Jesus Descardo.

"I don't know," Mordacia Caustilo said spookily. "But I don't think that this Jesus is coming back for Easter. . . ."

Mr. Wilde finally stopped retching beans and, wiping his mouth with a hanky, rose shakily to his feet.

"We must be going," he whispered. "Mr. Fauster is right. This is a Metaphorest. A place where metaphors—*figures of speech*—come to life."

Milton noticed a tiny, crushed mechanical toy under his foot. He stooped down and picked through the brass gears and components.

Those odd windup crickets, he thought as he rolled tiny springs between his finger pads. *That's what all that brain-fogging chirping is. . . .*

The floor of the Metaphorest was covered with hopping mechanical insects rubbing their crystal wings together. They leapt over clusters of tiny, vibrating tuning forks sprouting from the shredded-paper soil.

Winifred sniffed back tears. "I'm scared," she said, trembling.

Mr. Dickens put his arm around Winifred to soothe her.

A terrible roar rattled the trees, causing a fresh cascade of cold glitter.

"Snnnaaahhhhrrrrrk!!"

Vice Principal Carroll's omnipresent commentary echoed throughout the Metaphorest.

"Hark! What's this? Such bitter tea!
The snark? Oh dear! They'd better flee!"

Mr. Wilde swallowed. "Let's hit the road," he muttered.

The teachers and children immediately fell to their knees and pummeled the ground with their fists.

"Nice one . . . Oscar," Mr. Dickens said as he hobbled and hammered forward.

The snarling roar grew closer and closer.

Milton's hands went numb as he crawled along, pounding the floor of the Metaphorest.

This place is what we make it . . . by what we say, he thought. *So . . .*

"We'd better . . . ," Milton said, tears streaming down his face from the pain, "hop to it!"

Milton sprang to his feet, as did his fellow team members, and bounced across the Metaphorest. The briefcase handcuffed to his wrist swung back and forth like a pendulum. He could hear the sound of mirrored trees shattering in the distance as the snark lumbered closer.

"Good job, Mr. Fauster," Mr. Wilde said, vaulting past the reflective trees. "Now I suggest that we all keep our . . . what I mean to say is, zip up our . . . my goodness, this is more difficult than I ever imagined."

Trees snapped and shattered. Milton could hear the creature panting.

"Each metaphor we make," Milton grunted, "replaces the last."

The creature drew closer. The children could feel its heavy footfalls as it tromped across the Metaphorest.

"It's going to get us!" Pansy gasped with terror. "Maybe we should split up!"

Milton and the others fell to the ground. An incredible pain blossomed from within Milton, dead center, as if he were being torn in half. The children and teachers wailed in anguish.

We're splitting in half! Milton thought, hugging himself as if to hold his body together. *I've got to think of another metaphor . . . a counter-metaphor.* The pain was excruciating. In just a few agonizing moments, Milton would end up like Jesus Descardo . . . or worse.

"We've got to . . . pull ourselves together!" he groaned.

The teachers and children gasped with relief, bunching together in a sweating, panting bunch. Immediately, Milton could feel himself "healing" inside, his guts mending and becoming blessedly whole.

"Now . . . we just have to . . . find our way . . . out of here," Pansy panted.

Milton scanned the seemingly endless rows of mirror trees crowding the Metaphorest.

"I hate metaphors, *na mean*?" Rakeem complained, scratching his puffy bleached hair.

Moses nodded. "So indirect," he added carefully. "They just waste time."

"Shakespeare used them a lot," Milton added. "He didn't invent them, but he popularized their use."

Milton had an idea. He rose to his feet.

Mr. Wilde eyed him nervously. "Be careful, Mr. Fauster—"

"All the world's a stage!" Milton shouted. "And all the men and women merely players! They have their exits and their entrances!"

The trees transformed into stage props: tall branches covered in foil, perched atop stands. The forest floor was now a large wooden platform.

"Snnnaaahhhhrrrrrk!!"

The creature was close. Milton could hear its legs clopping nearer across the plank flooring.

Milton saw the edge of the expansive stage a dozen yards away.

"Quick!" he yelled. "This way!"

Milton, the teachers, and the other children hobbled forward. Drawing upon all of his strength, Milton leapt off the edge of the stage, landing on the shredded-paper ground.

Mr. Wilde and Mr. Dickens hopped off the stage— the author of *Great Expectations* and *A Christmas Carol* tugging Moxie's dolly behind him—followed by the other children, leaving only Pansy and Sareek.

"Phew!" the small, pinched-faced girl gasped, only several feet away from the edge of the stage. She held tight to Sareek's hand as they neared the edge of the stage with relief. "I thought we were all dead ducks!"

"Yeah: *dead as doornails!*"

Pansy and Sareek screamed before losing all of their color and turning into flattened stacks of words, just as Jesus had.

The children gaped in shock. Pansy and Sareek were now nothing more than dry, emotionless *descriptions*.

"Are they—" Roberta Atrebor started, before a savage roar blasted from the stage. There, scratching at the wooden platform with its nine hooves capping nine spindly legs, was one of the most disgusting creatures Milton had ever laid eyes on, which was really saying something considering the nightmarish menagerie of monsters he had had the misfortune of hobnobbing with down in Heck.

"That thing is so gross," Concordia gasped, her long mouth flapping open like a pet door, "that it makes everything I *thought* was gross before almost beautiful. . . ."

The beast had a wide, dripping wet snout that glistened like an open sore. Its skin was scaly like a snake's, and it had a shark's fin protruding from its back. The snark threw back its monstrous head and drew in a deep breath through its flared, gouge-like nostrils, as if it were inhaling the children's fear. Most puzzling of all, it also had a large silver hammer lashed to the back of its neck.

"We best be moving," Mr. Wilde said, backing away from the edge of the stage. "We can't help them now. . . . Let's go. . . ."

Vice Principal Carroll wouldn't create something that would actually annihilate *us,* Milton thought dismally as the creature sniffed at the twin piles of words that had been, only seconds ago, Pansy and Sareek.

The beast trained its hateful glare on Milton, its eyes puffed into wicked slits, like wounds that refused to heal properly.

Would he?

22 · SCOFFER UNDER
THE BRiDGE

MARLO CRUNCHED ACROSS the shredded-paper hill toward a thick grove of trees. She rubbed her aching wrist around the handcuff cutting into her skin. The teachers and children reached the summit, their combined footfalls forming a mind-numbing march. This, with the rhythmic chirping of little metal crickets, rubbing their crystal wings together, was like a roll of Mentos dropped into the carbonated fizz of Marlo's thoughts. Her brain felt sticky and senseless, bursting with foam.

"Well, *Team Captain*," Cookie Youngblood said in a way that leeched the designation of any respect whatsoever. "Do you even know where we are?"

Marlo stopped and assessed the gnarled tangle of spindly trees that leered back at her like a smiling hobo. "Yeah, I know *exactly* where we are," she declared, her white fists pressed into her sides.

"Where?"

"We're lost."

Cookie shook her head and snorted.

"Ladies and gentlemen, I give you our great and fearless leader, *Marlo Fauster*," the girl said, her red-and-blond-streaked bangs doing the hula along her forehead.

Marlo Fauster? Dale E. Basye thought as he tromped alongside Miss Parker in silence.

"I never said my name was Google," Marlo said. The other children stared at her. "You know, because I think I know everything. I don't. But I know as much as you. Which means that I actually know *more* than you, since you all think you know it all but don't and don't know it . . ."

Dale E. Basye stared at the sassy, blue-haired girl, a girl who—until now—he had felt was merely a figment of his imagination. His literary creation. Well . . . that wasn't *exactly* true. He had, um, *appropriated* the source material from that horrible boy, Damian Ruffino. But he—*Dale E. Basye*—was the one who had brought the story of a dead boy and his sister to life. But this whole experience was too weird and strangely real to be just a dream.

"Why don't you bookmark me so you can read me later?" Marlo said, staring at the man who had, unknowingly, been staring at her for a long minute.

"Oh, um . . . sorry," Mr. Basye replied. "It's just that . . . did you say you were Marlo Fauster?"

"I didn't. Cookie did. But yeah . . . so what's it to you?"

"And you have a brother named Milton, I suppose."

"Again, *yeah*. And again, *what's it to you?*"

Dale E. Basye scratched his head. "Well, this is rather odd. See . . . I'm an author."

Miss Parker folded her arms like a cranky old woman on a cruise collapsing a deck chair.

"Oh really? What have you *authored*?"

Dale E. Basye arched his eyebrow. "Well, I got my first break with *The Breathtaking, Wind-Breaking Fartisimo Family*," he said, tooting his own horn.

Miss Parker smirked, her baggy eyes crinkling into mischievous slits.

"Sounds like a book not to be tossed aside lightly, Mr. Basye, but instead thrown with great force."

"Well . . . I *really* made my name with a book called . . . er . . . *Heck: Where the Bad Kids Go*. . . ."

Miss Parker and the children stared back at him with thick stupefaction.

"You've *got* to be kidding," Miss Parker replied icily.

"No, I'm not," Dale E. Basye replied. "Usually when

I'm kidding, people laugh . . . or get mad . . . or sue me for reckless endangerment. Anyway, the book didn't really sell, but the concept was turned into a video game: the biggest video game *ever*."

A flock of goose pimples swam across Marlo's forearms.

"Yeah . . . I remember something about that," she said, recalling her experience as a shadow-ghost back in Generica, where she got sucked into a creeptastic video game—*Heck: Where the Bad Kids Go*—and thrust back into the underworld.

"Really?" Dale E. Basye said, eyeing Marlo curiously. "Well, it was a big deal before it turned into an even *bigger* deal: apparently turning teens into apathetic, monosyllabic zombies. As if anyone would even *notice*. The point is, I came up with this place. This dream. And I'm dreaming *you*, Marlo Fauster. . . ."

Marlo walked up to the man and hit him on the arm.

"Oww!" Dale yelped. "You little psychopath!"

"What's wrong?" Marlo said. "I mean, I'm your creation or whatever, so you must have made that up too . . . and *this* . . ."

She kicked him in the shin. Miss Parker stifled a giggle. Dale E. Basye hopped around on one foot, shouting at the sky.

"Why am I here?! I'm just an opportunist with an overactive imagination!"

"Shush!" Hadley said from behind her curtain of blond hair. "I hear something."

A peculiar clopping noise traveled steadily just beyond the grove of trees. It sounded like a team of horses.

"Snnnaaahhhhrrrrrk!!"

A wet, furious growl filled the grove. It was the sound of a huge, vicious beast hoping to sonically paralyze its next kill. Marlo noticed dozens of the tiny, three-pronged tuning forks—or *Re*tuning Forks as Vice Principal Carroll had referred to them—sticking out of the ground, vibrating, producing a hypnotic hum.

"Those crickets and the tiny forks," Marlo murmured, slipping slowly into a trance, "they kind of make my mind go blank."

Cookie laughed. "Your mind's *always* blank . . . I mean, looking into your eyes is like staring at a window display for a department store that's gone out of business."

Marlo stared groggily at Cookie's shimmering, lip-glossed lips.

"*What* department store?" she replied before shaking herself awake. Another low, reverberating growl filled the grove.

Marlo couldn't locate where the growl was coming from. It sounded like it was growling on all sides, as if she were deep inside the creature and could hear it rumbling all around her. The growl was oddly familiar.

"Where—" Marlo began before something clicked in her mind. *"Wolf?"*

The growl sounded exactly like that of the big, bad disappearing wolf that she and Milton had seen on their way to Wise Acres. Marlo and the other children traveled around the grove, but no matter where they walked, the growl got neither closer nor farther away.

"Maybe we're surrounded," Bree Martinet said, biting her nails.

"It doesn't sound like different wolves, though," Marlo said, puzzled. "It's the *same* growl, only coming from . . . everywhere at once."

It's like Vice Principal Carroll's ventriloquism, Marlo thought with a cold shiver of dread trickling down her spine. *One of those wolves must be able to throw its voice. But why? It must be how it hunts. It can growl and freak you out, make you stupid-drunk with fear juice, but you don't know if you're escaping it or walking right into its—*

Marlo saw a set of slavering jaws peeking out of one of the trees.

"Is that tree . . . panting?" Ahmed Crump said weakly.

"Panting . . . huffing . . . puffing," Roget murmured.

"Unless that's a halitosis tree," Marlo said, beads of cold sweat forming on her forehead, "I think we found another wolf . . . or it found us. Hurry!"

The teachers and children ran as fast as they could out of the grove.

"AHROOOOOOO WOO WOOOahhhhh!" howled the wolf-beast from behind.

They dashed across a small field of shredded paper. An orchestra of mechanical crickets droned beside clusters of silver tuning prongs, vibrating like nervous metal flowers.

"Whoa!" Marlo said, as if addressing a team of invisible horses as she skidded to a stop. She found herself on the precipice of an expansive gorge—a great cleft in the ground hissing with a jeering gale of wind. The two sides of the gorge were connected by a rickety wooden bridge that swayed dangerously in the howling wind. A pair of seriously bent trees framed the entrance to the bridge, bowing toward another pair of similarly stooped trees on the other side.

Lani Zanotti, her dark hair pulled tight from her face in cruel braids, rolled her eyes. *"Right.* Like I'm going to cross this crazy bridge."

"Yeah . . . *really first-class construction* there," Bree Martinet said, jutting out her lower lip so she looked like a spoiled guppy princess.

"How are we supposed to get across?" Cookie asked, her nostrils flared wide.

Marlo bowed, holding her arms out before her in exaggerated supplication. "Oh, *Lady Fartface* . . . your bejeweled unicorn-drawn carriage awaits. . . ."

Cookie glared at Marlo before forcing her sour grimace into a fake smile.

"*Ooh,* that's—what is that word?—oh yeah, '*hilarious,*'" Cookie said, making air quotes with her fingers around the word "hilarious."

Marlo straightened as a sharp, merciless flurry of wind whipped down the vast ravine. She held on tightly to the tree to keep from being blown over the edge.

"*AHROOOOOOO WOO WOOOahhhhh!*"

Mathis Vittorio looked over his broad shoulder. His dark eyebrows knitted together into one long caterpillar of bushy hair.

"I'm not waiting around to be eaten or mauled or whatever," he said in his thick, perpetually put-upon voice.

"Me neither," Mungo Ulyaw said, his brown bowl cut blowing in the wind at Mathis's side.

The two boys ran across the unsteady bridge, gripping the rope rails as they navigated the creaking floor of irregular planks. An explosion of wind, traveling at about half the speed of sound, detonated throughout the chasm, sending a surge of raw force at Mathis and Mungo, slamming into them from behind like invisible hammers, until—

"*Nooooo!*" Miss Parker screamed.

Mathis and Mungo were pitched forward, swept off the bridge, and cast into the gorge below. The two boys, just as they struck the shredded-paper bottom, seemed to transform, turning into two masses of kid-shaped words.

Mathis Vittorio's
Head Head Head
Head Head Head
Neck
A Torso Torso Torso A
R Torso Torso Torso R
M Torso Torso Torso M
S Torso Torso Torso S
    L   L
    E   E
    G   G
    S   S
  Feet   Feet

Mungo Ulyaw's
Head Head Head
Head Head Head
Neck
A Torso Torso Torso A
R Torso Torso·Torso R
M Torso Torso Torso M
S Torso Torso Torso S
    L   L
    E   E
    G   G
    S   S
  Feet   Feet

"What happened to them?!" Marlo screamed over the lip of the chasm.

Miss Parker and Dale E. Basye peered fearfully over the edge.

"I . . . don't know," Miss Parker muttered in quiet horror, her face round and distorted, as if reflected in the back of a spoon.

Vice Principal Carroll's amplified voice boomed from beyond the grove.

*"Your friends, Team Two, are on the bench, beyond
    the aid of bandage.
They've both been pitched into the trench, translated
    into language."*

Miss Parker clapped her hands over her ears. "That insufferable man! Doesn't he ever stop? His running commentary is like one long tiresomely tireless monologue!"

Miss Parker is right, Marlo thought as she stared into the chasm. *Vice Principal Crackpot has been talking ever since we started this War of the Words business. Describing everything we do right as we do it, if not just before. . . .*

Marlo puzzled over the hooked trees bracketing the bridge. They reminded her of Cookie's mocking fingers earlier.

"Oh . . . I get it," she said. "This chasm. It's a *Sar*-Chasm."

"*Right* . . . like *you'd* know," Cookie began before stopping short. "Really?"

"Listen, I have a black belt in sarcasm. *I know this*. The trees are quotation marks, like your sarcastic air quotes."

"So we have to be really sarcastic or something to get across?" Cookie replied. "Yeah . . . like *that* makes sense. I don't see how that's going to help us from being swept away like Mathis and Mungo."

Marlo clutched the trunk of the sloped tree as another savage gust blasted through the gulch. "You know when some character in a book says something sarcastic, how the words are all bent over in Italian?"

"I think you mean *italics*," Miss Parker corrected.

"Unless the characters are sarcastic Italians," Dale E. Basye interjected.

"*Italics*. Right, those," Marlo replied. "So maybe that's what we have to do to cross this Sar-Chasm thing. To keep from being blown away."

The teachers and children played a game of optic catch with their eyeballs.

Mack Hoover shook his head. "Of all the stup—"

"*AHROOOOOOO WOO WOOOahhhhh!*"

"—endously smart ideas I've heard, that's the smartest," Mack said, his voice craggy with fear. "Let's go."

Cookie extended her arm grandly toward the bridge. "Team captains first," she said. "You know, those who know enough to know that they don't know anything."

Marlo sighed.

Sometimes I wish I had a junk folder for my brain, to send all of the spammy stuff I say that always seems to get forwarded back to me. . . .

Marlo grabbed the wooden posts at the end of the bridge. The briefcase handcuffed to her wrist quivered in the breeze.

"Yeah, right, like this will work," Marlo grumbled as she leaned forward at a ten-degree angle until the buffeting wind blasting her back seemed to glide right up off her. She carefully placed one foot in front of the other onto the crooked, sparsely placed planks, which was harder than expected when tilted forward. She gripped the ropes tightly as the wind sent her blue hair streaming up into the air like a fountain.

"Really safe," Cookie mumbled as she stepped onto the bridge, carefully leaning forward until the wind that so desperately wanted to shove her off the bridge flowed up and over her shoulders.

"I've never had so much fun in my life," Mack Hoover said as he trod cautiously behind Cookie.

"Totally not scary at all," Bree Martinet groused as her dense curly hair danced on top of her head like an Ewok after vanquishing an Imperial Army.

One by one the children made the slow, maddening trek across the Sar-Chasm.

"Did you know that italic type was invented in the fourteenth century as a space-saving device?" Dale E. Basye said as Miss Parker readied herself for her crossing.

"*That's really interesting,*" Miss Parker said as she leaned forward, the wind blasting her face. "I could listen to you prattle on about the history of typefaces all day. . . ."

Marlo neared the other side of the Sar-Chasm. The rope bridge shuddered as the wind screamed across its slats and ropes.

"Darn, and I was *so* enjoying myself," she muttered as she carefully placed her foot onto the next warped plank.

"*Snnnaaahhhhrrrrk!!*"

Marlo looked behind her. Pacing on the other side of the Sar-Chasm was the ugliest, most pants-dampening monster Marlo had ever seen. The creature was nine feet tall as it reared up on its back four legs, brandishing another set of legs (two on each side with one up front) with frustrated menace. For reasons as yet unclear, it also had a tremendous silver hammer tethered to its head. The monster glared at Marlo with its puffed slit eyes.

Marlo stumbled as her mind went limp. Her leg dangled between the last two planks. The wind assailed her back, lifting her up and over.

"*Right,* like I'm going to let some dumb wind be the thing that blows me away here in Heck," Marlo said as she gripped the rope railing tight and—remembering yet another move from her brief yet surprisingly useful stint in gymnastics class—tilted forward into the wind. Suddenly she was released from its gusty grip, and she slid onto the other side of the Sar-Chasm.

Something seemed to skitter away from her. Like a big red eye.

"An eye?" Marlo groaned. "I'm probably just seeing things. . . ."

"Snnnaaahhhhrrrrk!!"

The children rushed off the shaky rope bridge that swayed violently back and forth like a jump rope in the hands of two transparent Titans.

"That thing," Marlo said. "It's—"

"Barf-inducing," Cookie interrupted.

"Unfading crib," Annabelle Graham muttered.

"No . . . I mean, *yes*—it's way hurl—but it's like it's hunting us," Marlo explained. "And didn't the vice principal say something about a—"

"Snark," Miss Parker interjected.

"A snark?!" Hadley exclaimed as she stepped off the bridge, her hair swept free of her usually concealed and now openly fearful face.

"A fictional animal species that Vice Principal Carroll created in his nonsense poem 'The Hunting of the Snark' . . . though apparently not so fictional after all. It might be a sort of portmanteau word—a word blending sound and meanings—of 'snake' and 'shark' perhaps, or maybe the sound it makes, a mash-up of 'snarl' and 'bark.' . . . In any case, I doubt something so inelegant and off-putting could make it across this bridge, though Mr. Basye was able to."

The snark set two of its nine hooves delicately onto a

wobbly plank, leaning forward as it mounted the bridge. Vice Principal Carroll's commentary squawked above the wind.

> *"Oh yes! Miss Parker hit the mark. The puzzle*
> *   ceases stumping.*
> *The beast before them is a snark. Let's hear its*
> *   happy hunting!"*

The snark waggled its huge paddlelike ears at the sound of its master.

"Um . . . how can we stop it?" Lani Zanotti asked, clutching her braids for comfort.

Miss Parker gulped as the hideous beast shrewdly navigated the perplexing puzzle of planks.

"I believe Mr. Carroll wrote something about 'charming it with smiles and soap'—"

"*Snnnaaahhhhrrrrk!!*" the monster roared, sending buckets of noxious green spit spraying into the wind.

"But don't quote me," Miss Parker said. "Not that many *do* anymore . . ."

Marlo saw, in the distance, a thick patch of jungle.

"I say let's play a game of hide-and-*sick,* you ugly hammerhead snark," Marlo taunted. "And you're 'it' . . . a big, steaming pile of it. Ollie ollie oxen *freak!*"

Marlo tucked the briefcase under her arm and ran.

23 · REGARD A MERE MAD RAGER

"SNNNAAAHHHHRRRRRK!!" THE CREATURE bellowed, a cloud of swampy green mist spraying out of its long, black-and-green-mottled muzzle.

"It's coming for us!" Winifred squealed, unhinged with panic. The snark's two long, spatula-shaped ears flapped out the back of its misshapen skull with annoyance at the girl's piercing voice. The hideous beast bounded off the edge of the Metaphorest stage.

"*Run!!*" Milton yelled.

The children dashed madly across the shredded yellow paper ground. Milton resented the weight of the briefcase locked to his wrist, but he quickly learned how to swing it like a pendulum, which helped him stay a few strides ahead of his team.

Clem Weenum and Roberta Atrebor tripped behind him. Moses leapt over the two children while Milton stopped and helped them to their feet.

Across the confetti-strewn tundra, Milton noticed a narrow, winding path surrounded by a thick fence of golden-brown reed stalks. The brushlike tips of the dense barricade fluttered in the breeze.

"That twisty trail over there!" Milton panted. "The path is too narrow for the monster. . . . C'mon, *hurry!*"

Milton led his team in single file a few hundred yards up the steep muddy path. The snark skidded to a stop at the mouth of the marshy trail. It nipped uneasily at the unyielding reed stalks.

Rakeem trotted behind Milton, patting down his bleached-blond Afro.

"I just don't get it," Milton panted. "Jesus, Pansy, Sareek . . . they were all too smart . . . to have their smart comments do them in like that. They should have known better . . . we *all* should have."

Rakeem looked up at the ashy orange-red sky. "It's Wisecrackatoa," the boy huffed, giving his braces a quick swipe with his tongue. "A volcano that belches up sassified ash. It fills the whole place with a kind of . . . ambient antagonism. It makes it extra hard for smart alecks like us . . . to hold our tongues. . . ."

Milton sniffed the air. It smelled of hard-boiled eggs and burning paper. "How do you know all this?" he asked.

Rakeem shrugged. "When your school is actually *made* of textbooks, you learn a lot," he explained. "Even when you're trying hard *not* to, *na mean?*"

The trail ended abruptly. In the distance, roughly a parking lot away, set on the slope of a small hill, was a stone coliseum—a ruin—with columns encircling its crumbling marble exterior.

A tsunami of sound washed over the teachers and children. Milton's head was abuzz with cricket chirps. The befuddling swell, accompanied by the hum of vibrating tuning forks, created a stupefying, thought-melting symphony. And through it all, as if conducting the symphony with his tongue, was the voice of Vice Principal Carroll.

"Are we not drawn onward to a new era?
An era, midst its dim arena
Elapses pale!
Party booby trap?
No! I save on final perusal a sure plan if no evasion.
Now, sir, a war is won!"

Mr. Wilde shook his head. "It sounds as if the vice principal may be a couplet short of a sonnet," the teacher murmured.

Milton rubbed his sore, handcuffed wrist and sighed. He wasn't sure what to do. It was like he and his team were trapped in some kind of *mind* field, full of dangers dredged from someone's imagination. He needed time to think. . . .

"*Snnnaaahhhhrrrrk!!*" roared the beast, a thousand yards behind them.

But Milton didn't *have* time. And the vice principal's words were like a restless mob in his head, shoving his brain back and forth between his ears, making meaningful thought next to impossible.

Roberta tucked her sleek dark bangs behind her ears in concentration.

" 'An era, midst its dim arena' . . . 'Party booby trap,' " she muttered before shaking her head. "We need to pass through that building up ahead. It's important . . . at least to me."

"What makes you say that?" asked Milton.

The girl shrugged. "Female intuition," Roberta said, smiling mysteriously. "It's like the GPS of a girl's soul. . . ."

After a brisk hike, Milton and the rest of Team One arrived at the coliseum. The large domed arena of crumbling stone was adorned with lavish yet ludicrous pieces of art.

Roberta puzzled over the sculptures. "Gold log? Kayak? Bird rib, a car, a man, a maraca?"

Clem Weenum—who, though the smallest, had gotten saddled with the task of pushing Moxie along on her dolly—scowled at the nonsensical sculptures.

"What's all of this junk?" he said. "It's like a garage sale at a funny farm . . . and definitely not the funny 'ha-ha' type. Is that a car?"

Roberta nodded. "A Toyota."

The children tentatively passed through an archway and stood before a heavy stone door engraved with a snake eating its own tail. The door suddenly whooshed open, releasing a frenzied din of scraping stone and machinery. The children and teachers were sucked into the spacious arena as if by a vacuum. The heavy stone door slid closed behind them, sealing them in.

Milton warily scanned the deafening amphitheater. The floor was a series of revolving, concentric stone circles—six of them, spinning furiously in opposite directions—with a small, motionless circle of gray stone at the center. The whirring stone bands were engraved, like the door outside, with snakes consuming their own tails, end over end. Each of the rotating snake slabs sat slightly atop the other to create a small, gyrating mountain.

"It's like a big roulette wheel," Winifred said with shock.

"Yeah, in a casino for giants," Mordacia said.

Milton stepped up to the edge of the spinning marble floor. It *was* rather like a maxi-sized roulette wheel with something to prove. Yet instead of segments with numbers, the serpent bands sported phrases that whizzed by so fast that they were difficult to read.

On the opposite side of the coliseum—roughly 100 yards away—was an exit portal. It was open.

Winifred pointed to the portal with her quivering arm. "It's spinning too fast . . . but if we squeezed past this big wheel somehow," she said tremulously, "we could get out the other side."

The walls of the dome pinched in at the middle, leaving no room to edge past the spinning serpent stones.

"I don't think so," Milton said over the grinding whir. "I think the only way out is to somehow stop the wheels from spinning."

"Snnnaaahhhhrrrrk!!"

The beast scratched at the heavy stone door with several sets of claws.

"Man, that thing has irritable *growl* syndrome," Ursula Lambarst said as she stepped fearfully away from the door.

"M-maybe it'll go away," Concordia mumbled while nervously petting the blond ponytail draped over her shoulder.

The snark threw its sizable bulk against the door.

"Snnnaaahhhhrrrrk!!"

Ursula scowled. "It's either going to break in or get a clue and come in through the back," she said. "It's only a matter of time before—"

Suddenly, a colony of screeching bats descended

from the darkened domed roof. Winifred screamed as she tried to—ironically—bat the flying rodents away. The bats had oddly shaped bladelike wings and came at the children and teachers with fluttering thrusts, as if trying to stab them.

Ursula stomped forward. "Waiting here is *una estupidez*," she muttered, tying up her brown curly hair in a scrunchie. "I'm going to try to walk across. Maybe I can figure out what the roulette wheel means . . . *¡Vamos!*"

She pushed Milton aside.

"Stop her!" Roberta cried.

Milton tried to grab the back of the large, bulky girl's coat, but she just barreled ahead with blind, graceless force like a runaway garbage truck.

"No!" Milton yelled as Ursula stepped onto a revolving slab.

Zorch!!

A savage bolt of pure blue-white energy shot from one of the segments, reading OF CABBAGES AND KINGS. Ursula was pierced through the middle like an electric shish kebab.

The flat pile of letters swayed back and forth, as if written on a large, invisible sheet of paper, before fluttering to the floor. Concordia gasped, her wide grayblue eyes glittering with shock and tears. The arena was filled with the pungent smell of ozone, like the smell of a summer thunderstorm or an industrial-strength tanning booth.

Roberta looked up toward the ceiling. "I saw something," she muttered as the stabbing bats swooped in clouds of screeching menace. "Up there. When the lightning flashed . . ." She noticed a corroded metal ladder that was bolted to the side of the dome. Roberta climbed up on to it. "Don't anybody move!" she called down.

Moses cowered as bats darted across his back and tore his tweed coat. "Tell that to these stabbing bats!"

Milton sighed as he looked out across the spinning snakes that hissed with furious, mechanical motion.

"One of us should go first," Moses said from behind Milton. "I elect our brave team captain. All in favor, say absolutely nothing."

Obviously this was some kind of maze, and—if Milton assumed correctly—there was a *right* way to cross it, with the reward being passage, and a *wrong* way, with the punishment being . . .

Milton took off one of his shoes and tossed it at a gyrating snake of stone.

Zorch!!

A bolt of lightning shot out of the marble, striking the ceiling with a sputtering sizzle. Milton sighed.

So—once again—it's Carroll's way or the highway. We've got to play by his ridiculous rules, or get zorched trying. . . .

"Watch it!" Roberta called out from above. The ladder crept up the side of the concave ceiling. Roberta was now nearly upside down as she clung to the ladder. The ladder was crusted with bat guano. Roberta wiped off her hand. "Yuck, bats . . . *stab-bats*. That's a palindrome. So is everything here—"

She hooked her legs on a rung and called down to her team.

"This whole place . . . it's a Palindrome!" Roberta yelled over the whir of wheels and screeching of stab-bats. "Where a word or phrase reads the same forward and backward. Outside . . . all of those weird things . . . Gold log. Kayak. Bird rib. A car, a man, a maraca . . . even 'a Toyota' . . . all palindromes."

A lightbulb went off in Milton's head. Luckily, he was no longer in the Metaphorest or he might have keeled over from his stroke of genius. Milton looked up at Roberta. "What's your last name again?" he asked.

"Atrebor," she replied. "Why?"

"Your name," Milton said. *"It's a palindrome."*

"Yeah. So?"

"So, I think you're the one who is meant to figure this one out."

Moses laughed bitterly and shook his head.

"Way to delegate," the boy cackled. "Oh . . . and *delegate* is a word that means 'to have people do things you don't want to do.'"

Roberta stared at the snake stones spinning beneath her.

"Milton!" she called out. "The disks . . . each one is

a line in a poem. Some are palindromes, some aren't. But the way out of here is to make a palindrome poem. A *meop emordnilap*, I guess. So step on the first palindrome!"

Milton tried to make sense of the blur of words. Then, around the bend, he saw the phrase STEP ON NO PETS coming at him.

"Step on no pets?!" he called up.

"Yeah!"

Milton hunkered down, clutched his briefcase, and prepared to hop on to the phrase. Then, just as he was about to leap, Roberta shrieked.

"No! Not that one . . . *'In words, drown I'?!*"

"Are you sure?!" Milton said, trembling.

"Yes! Do it!"

Milton saw the phrase coming at him. He jumped, his whole body balled up like a fist. Suddenly, the first spinning disk screeched to an abrupt halt. Milton pried his eyelids apart to see if he had been "zorched."

"In words, drown I?" Milton muttered as sweat trickled down his forehead and onto his glasses. The first disk was motionless and silent, yet the others kept gyrating, as fast as ever.

"Sorry," Roberta said, her face flushed red from hanging upside down. " 'Step on no pets' is a palindrome, but it was only written on the disk once. 'In words, drown I?' was on the disk *twice*. So it both begins and ends the poem, palindromically speaking: beginning right inside the entrance, where you were, and ending right at the exit, where we want to be. If we solve them all—"

"If?!" Winifred exclaimed.

"*When*," Roberta corrected, "it will make a path leading straight to the door. Now I just have to find the next line. . . ."

A screeching flock of stab-bats slashed at the air like a dark, homicidal cloud.

Roberta squinted at the peculiar phrases whizzing beneath her, etched upon the second stone serpent.

. . . OOZY RAT IN A SANITARY ZOO . . . I DID, DID I . . . NO, SIR, PANIC IS A BASIC IN A PRISON . . . DRAT SUCH MUSTARD . . .

Roberta scrutinized the spinning disk for a few seconds before smiling.

" '*No, sir, panic is a basic in a prison*'!"

Milton nodded, and just before the phrase whizzed past him, he leapt into the air, landing on the segment of stone. The stone snake stopped with a lurch. Milton lay flat on the cool stone and grabbed on to the etched letters, nearly rolling into the wrong phrase and "zorch-ing" himself into a pile of Milton-shaped words.

Mr. Wilde, who had been holding his breath for nearly a full minute, exhaled with relief.

"Miss Atrebor seems to know what she is doing," he said quietly as to not break the girl's intense concentration.

Roberta swung upside down from the ceiling like a ruddy, girl-shaped chandelier.

" 'Revered now, I live on. O did I do no evil, I wonder, ever?' . . . 'Egad! A base tone denotes a bad age' . . . 'Cats meow, meow the cats,' " Roberta murmured before yelling suddenly. " 'Egad! A base tone denotes a bad age!' "

Milton fought to focus on the blur of words. His eyes hooked onto the phrase as it sped near him. He jumped. The stone serpent screeched to a stop.

Mr. Wilde and Mr. Dickens cautiously walked out to Milton using the newly formed path.

"You're halfway there," Mr. Dickens said, putting his hand on Milton's shoulder. "Let us take over for you . . . we, as your teachers, should have done that from the start."

Milton shook his head as he rose from the stone. "I'm good."

A colony of stab-bats swept past like a collection of black leather knives.

Mr. Wilde stepped up to the edge of the next speeding snake. "If a thing is worth doing, it is worth doing halfway and then quitting," the teacher said. "No shame in that, young man."

Roberta, sweating and her neck stiff from hanging, shouted from the ceiling. " 'Bombard a drab mob!' "

Milton, after a moment's hesitation, spotted the phrase and bounded up toward the next snake just as the correct palindrome approached. The stone disk seized, coming to a complete stop.

"Next one is . . . easy," Roberta gasped from above.

Her olive skin was now a deep purple as she struggled to hold on to consciousness. *"Air an aria!"*

Milton caught sight of the phrase as it sped around the bend. He hopped onto the segment and stopped the stone snake cold. Milton looked up at Roberta, grinning.

"Just one more, Roberta!" he shouted. "The path is almost done. You're doing great!"

Roberta struggled to hang on to the ladder. Her arm was turning blue.

"I . . . can barely see," she replied. "My eyes feel like they're going to pop out of my head. . . ."

The colony of stab-bats swept upon Milton, slashing at his face and arms.

"Snnnaaahhhhrrrrk!!"

The snark kicked two of its hooves through the stone door. Shards of rock danced across the Palindrome. It stuck its wet, hideous snout through the hole.

"Roberta! It's now or never!" Milton cried.

Roberta wiped tears away from her throbbing eyes.

. . . LIVED ON DECAF; FACED NO DEVIL . . . SATAN, OSCIL-LATE MY METALLIC SONATAS! . . . STEVEN, I LEFT AN OILY LION AT THE FELINE VETS . . . NO SIR! A PAPAYA WAR IS ON! . . .

"It's going so . . . fast," she murmured. "I can barely . . . *'Satan, oscillate my metallic sonatas!'"*

Milton stood at the edge of the last spinning snake. Being the shortest in length, it rotated the fastest. Milton's eye snagged the word "Satan" and threw himself to the stone before he could think better of it. The self-consuming snake disk stopped abruptly, just as the snark kicked open the door and wedged itself into the arena.

"We did it!" Milton yelled as he stepped onto the center disk, which simply had one phrase etched upon it: SWAP GOD FOR A JANITOR; ROT IN A JAR OF DOG PAWS.

Moses ran past him for the back door, the path now completed. The teachers led the frantic children across the stepped walkway of palindromes. Milton ducked as the stab-bats swept over him.

"Wait!" he called out. *"Roberta!"*

Mr. Wilde ushered the children through the exit archway before rushing back to Milton at the center of the Palindrome. Just then, Roberta lost both conscious-ness and her hold on the ladder and plummeted down from the ceiling. Mr. Wilde skittered beneath her and—with a brutal "oomph"—swept Roberta up into his long arms.

"In words, drown I," the olive-skinned girl muttered before her eyes rolled back into her head.

Mr. Wilde bounded for the exit with Roberta.

A surge of stab-bats flew past Milton. He held the briefcase up to his face. Everything was a shiny black dance of confusion and pain as Milton tumbled to the floor.

"Snnnaaahhhhrrrrk!!"

A mass of stab-bats converged upon the snark. Milton

darted across the palindrome path as squeaks and snarks exploded behind him.

He emerged from the arena into a darkened thicket. A big red eye seemed to blink at him before darting away.

"My, what big teeth you have . . . ," Mr. Dickens muttered fearfully a few dozen yards away from Milton in the murk. Suddenly, Milton heard a tremendous gulp.

A wolf howled in the darkness. The deep, forceful yowl strangled all traces of bravery from Milton's body. His eyes slowly adjusted to the light.

"H-hello?" he stuttered nervously.

Milton could barely make out the children and teachers wandering the edge of the thicket in a wary daze. They were surrounded by a dense barricade of dead trees laced with glistening white webs.

The children and teachers appeared intact, though Milton noticed something odd about Mr. Dickens. He looked taller . . . strangely swollen and twitching spasmodically.

Probably from fear, Milton thought as he looked around him for the wolf. Out of the corner of his eye, he saw *something* . . . something fierce and savage, right where Mr. Dickens was . . . but when he turned, the teacher was still just a twitching, swollen old man.

"Mr. Dickens?" Milton asked, stepping closer.

My, what big ears you have . . . , he thought. *My, what big eyes you have* . . .

Milton's blood turned to ice water. Whiskers sprouted from the teacher's face. Thick fur grew up and over his collar. Muscles bulged against the fabric of the man's suit until every seam was split.

"Who—" Milton murmured, his throat suddenly coated in sandpaper.

Every trace of Mr. Dickens was gone, replaced by a snarling, seven-foot-tall beast.

"*Wolf!*"

The wolf roared in Milton's face. Its breath was like a raging funeral pyre full of searing heat, the smell thick, sharp, and nauseatingly sweet. With its mouth stretched wide, Milton could see a thatch of black and gray hair at the bottom of the wolf's capacious throat.

"*Help,*" a weak voice gurgled from the beast's gullet.

The thought of Mr. Dickens, curled up, pathetic and wet, inside of the wolf, instantly turned Milton's fear into fury. A scream had been readying in Milton's throat, but by the time it burst forth past his lips, it had become a savage, terrifying roar every bit the equal of the wolf's.

"*Aaaaaaarrrwwwwwllllll!!!!*" Milton bellowed, his face flushed purple with exasperated wrath.

The wolf staggered back on its haunches in shock. Its roar hung in the air with its sonic tail tucked between its legs. Suddenly, its eyes bulging out at the little glowering purple-faced boy perched defiantly atop his tiptoes, the wolf gasped in gape-mouthed terror. In one wet, shuddering retching plop, the wolf spat out Mr. Dickens.

The teacher, covered in bile and semi-digested rodents, lay shivering on the ground. The wolf charged away and disappeared into the brush.

Winifred rushed past Milton and knelt by the teacher's side.

"What did you do?" she asked Milton as she helped the shaken, slimy old man to his feet.

Milton shrugged. "I must have scared the Dickens out of it."

24 · JOKES FALLING iN NOTHiNG FLAT

MARLO BARRELED THROUGH the jungle, shoving aside the spindly trees like rival shoppers at a Going out of Business! Everything Must Go! Sale (though, as a kleptomaniac, Marlo rarely paid full price—or *any* price—while shopping). She could hear some of the other children and teachers panting behind her. A smothered growl reverberated throughout the jungle, so close and low that Marlo could feel it in her bones. She stopped suddenly. Marlo glanced fearfully from vine to vine but could see no trace of an animal. The downy hairs on her arms went stiff. Her body, somehow, could sense that she was being hunted. But by what?

Marlo held the briefcase in front of her with both hands, like a shield. A hollow, slashing rhythm pounded up through the soles of her feet. A howl—stifled as if by a suffocating pillow of dirt—bayed below.

"How—" Marlo muttered with confusion.

The ground shuddered beneath her feet. Cookie, Lani, and perhaps Dale E. Basye—Marlo couldn't be sure—let rent piercing, girlish screams. The floor of the clearing opened up in a lacerating gash of mud and dirt. Lani Zanotti fell into the ground as the dirt floor collapsed beneath her. A brawny, hairy arm snatched her by the leg.

"Wolf!" Marlo screamed as she scrambled forward, hoping to snatch Lani by the wrist.

The snarling How-Wolf dragged Lani kicking and screaming into the open ground until, abruptly, with a deep, painful silence, the girl went limp. Marlo peered down fearfully into the freshly dug tunnel. Lani was nothing more than a two-dimensional heap of words, a label affixed to an empty, girl-shaped jar, its former contents having evaporated into nothing.

Marlo's arms and face were slashed by branches, but the palpitating fear numbing her body pushed back the pain. She heard snapping twigs behind her, poking through the frantic chug of her own panting.

Is that the How-Wolf? Marlo thought, her mind racing as fast as her body. *The thing that got Lani?*

Marlo burst through a snarl of bright green trees.

"Aaaaarrrgghhh!!" she cried as she shot past the rim of the jungle and into an enormous crater. Marlo

tumbled down the craggy edge of the pit, grunting and gagging on grit until she landed painfully at the bottom. She slammed the back of her head on a small boulder.

Dale E. Basye and Mack Hoover were there, too, dazed and bemused as they rubbed their stinging knees and elbows. Cookie toppled down into the pit on top of Marlo.

"What happened?" Cookie moaned.

"I'd explain it to you," Marlo grunted, "but I'm all out of puppets and crayons. Now get off me!"

Miss Parker and the rest of Team Two came tumbling down into the crater.

A thick brown cloud, like a huge pool of spilled chocolate milkshake, coagulated above.

"This can't be good," Hadley mumbled, her blue eyes peering out through a gap in her hair.

The clouds above seemed to rattle, as if a group of Greek gods were getting ready to roll a gargantuan game of Yahtzee. Suddenly, a small boulder fell from the sky.

"Watch out!" Miss Parker screamed as the rock plummeted down upon Ahmed.

Dale E. Basye and Roget ran to the boulder and, with a heave, rolled it off Ahmed . . . but it was too late. He, like the others before him, had been drained of life and reduced to a flat pile of words describing his head, torso, arms, and legs in the simplest of terms.

"Amen . . . *Ahmed*," Dale E. Basye muttered sadly.

Hadley snuffled behind her hair. Flossie put her arm around the weeping girl as the children and teachers stared at the flattened boy-shaped collection of words. Dale E. Basye noticed writing etched onto the side of the boulder.

He knelt down and read the engraving. " *'Two antennas got married. The ceremony wasn't much but the reception was excellent.' "*

Marlo groaned. Her hands balled into furious fists, she stomped the ground with frustration. "What is that?! Some kind of stupid joke?!"

Miss Parker swallowed. "Even worse," she said, her voice flat with unleavened dread. *"A pun."*

Marlo glared at the churning mud-brown cloud above. "Puns," she said with disgust. "I thought they were bad enough on the Surface, when I was alive. But the underworld is *lousy* with them . . . probably 'cause they're the lowest form of humor, right?"

Dale E. Basye bristled at the notion of puns pervading the underworld, more specifically, *his* underworld of Heck. He sort of had a love-hate relationship with punning: he loved it and his critics hated it.

Another boulder spat down from the sky like a leaden loogie.

"Watch out!" Miss Parker yelled. The boulder fell only a few feet away from Flossie. She read the engraving on the side.

" 'Two Eskimos sitting in a kayak were chilly, but when they lit a fire in the craft, it sank, proving once again that you can't have your kayak and heat it, too. . . .' "

The children groaned.

"It's like someone is *pun*-ishing us," Bree muttered.

Vice Principal Carroll's voice pierced the drone of cricket chirps and humming tuning forks.

"In modern-day word-fare, some jibes strike as unfunny.
At least—in the pit—you shan't find them unpunny!"

"That's it!" Marlo exclaimed. "This place is a Punishment Pit!"

Two more boulders dropped from the sky. Hadley narrowly dodged one as it impacted—it was so close to her that she was pelted hard with grit.

" *'Did you hear about the optometrist who fell into a lens grinder and made a spectacle of himself?'* " she said, reading the side of one boulder.

Mack read the other. " *'Did you hear about the butcher who backed into his meat grinder and got a little behind in his work?'* "

A great, reverberating rattle—like stone thunder—boomed from above.

"Heads up, everybody!" Marlo yelled. "They're dropping fast and flurrious now!"

A half-dozen boulders dropped from the thick, seething cloud.

"I give my dead batteries away free of charge."

"I forgot how to throw a boomerang but then it came back to me."

"What's the definition of a will? (Come on, it's a dead giveaway!)"

"Watch out!" Cookie screamed as a hailstorm of boulders rained down upon them. Marlo tried to scrabble up the side of the crater, but it was too steep and the dirt too crumbly. The briefcase handcuffed to her wrist slapped her on the forehead. Marlo struggled to free her wrist.

"Stupid . . . thing," she grumbled before giving up. Three boulders dropped into the pit, shaking the crater and starting tiny avalanches of dirt and rock.

"We can't climb out," Flossie said as she rolled back down the side of the pit, unable to get a firm purchase on the grit wall.

Another boulder fell right next to Marlo, rolling across her foot.

"Oww!"

"A vulture boards an airplane, carrying two dead squirrels. The stewardess looks at him and says, 'I'm sorry, only one carrion allowed per passenger.'"

Hadley groaned as two boulders fell on either side of her.

"How do you tickle a rich girl? Say 'Gucci Gucci Gucci!'"

"I bet my butcher a hundred bucks that he couldn't reach the meat off the top shelf. He refused, saying that the steaks were too high."

Bree tried to scramble up out of the pit but fell flat on her back in a cloud of upturned dust.

"What do we do?!" she cried hopelessly.

Mack Hoover shrugged. "I'll probably just wait for all of you to be flattened, then climb on top of you," the boy replied matter-of-factly.

Marlo shot Mack a look so withering that, had he been a flower, he would have instantly lost all of his petals.

"That's awful!" she shrieked as a fresh volley of punishment rained down from above. "Hey, what do Mack and a vacuum cleaner have in common? They're both Hoovers that *suck*!"

The boy began to slowly lift from the ground, up and out of the pit, until he was deposited—safe and sound—ten feet from the edge. Marlo's dark violet eyes ignited with sudden understanding.

"That's it!" Marlo shrieked as another boulder fell down from the cloud, smashing one of its quarry kin into pebbles. "We have to make puns out of each other—then we can float out of the pit just like Mack!"

A fresh peal of thunder boomed overhead. A cloudburst of boulders erupted.

"Aaaaaarrrrrnnnnnggghhh!" Flossie groaned as she struggled to free herself from between two heavy pun-stones. The chocolate-brown storm cloud darkened directly over her, ready to birth another deadly litter of boulder babies. Marlo bit her lip in concentration.

"Um . . . why do dentists love Miss Blackwell so much? Because she *Flossies* after every meal," Marlo yelled.

Flossie slowly rose from the boulder-strewn floor of the pit.

"My leg!" she screamed. "I can't feel it!"

Dale E. Basye rolled away the stone that had been pinning her down. Dangling beneath the girl, replacing her left leg, was a flat pillar of words.

Flossie
Blackwell's
L
E
G
Foot

Flossie floated safely to the top of the Pun-ishment Pit as the dark brown cloud rattled like phlegm in an old man's chest. She leaned against the exposed roots of a tree, whimpering, as she caressed her literalized leg.

Marlo zigzagged across the rocky floor of the pit as she dodged another volley of falling boulders. She locked eyes on Hadley.

"Okay . . . uh . . . Why was the diner so angry when

Hadley lost her finger making his French fries? Because he was, er . . . *fed-Up*fling!"

Hadley levitated slowly in the air, *maddeningly* slow, wobbling back and forth, as if Fate itself were weighing the merits of Marlo's terrible pun. Marlo ran beneath Hadley and tried to shove her to safety.

"Sorry," Marlo apologized as her briefcase smacked the girl in the head. "I Hadley my doubts about that one."

Hadley finally landed a few feet away from Flossie by the edge of the crater.

Dale E. Basye noticed Bree Martinet, her thick curly hair dusted with dirt, quivering beside a boulder.

"Why was the indecisive director so upset after Bree auditioned for Hamlet?" he yelled against the rumble of rock above. "He didn't know whether to Bree, or not to Bree!"

Bree was hoisted up by invisible arms and deposited just beyond the edge of the pit.

Marlo stumbled toward Lavena Duckworth, who, though silent, managed to vividly convey her terror with her amazingly expressive face.

"What's a Duckworth?" Marlo gasped as a falling boulder sent up a cloud of choking grit. "Depends on the market value!"

Lavena was whisked away to safety. Dale E. Basye dodged a pair of rolling boulders and fell on his hands and knees in a pocket of sharp gravel. Annabelle Graham was hiding beneath a trio of semi-pulverized stones.

Dirty sweat ran down the hollow of her neck in muddy trickles.

"Um . . . let's see," Dale E. Basye murmured, never one for working under pressure. "Why did Mr. and Mrs. Graham name their daughter Anna*belle*? Because she takes a *toll* on everyone around her. Get it? Like a bell."

The plain, stocky girl slowly rose from the ground in jerky fits and starts. Marlo rolled her eyes at Mr. Basye.

"Bra-freakin'-vo!" she said, clapping slowly.

"Hey," Dale E. Basye replied brusquely. "It was better than *fed-Up*fling!"

Marlo shook her head and crawled along the ground through a pile of fallen boulders. Roget Marx Peters was balled up in a makeshift igloo.

"Why is Roget such a terrible long-distance runner?" Marlo said. "Because he always Peters out!"

Roget was pulled out of the stone shelter and heaved up into the air, where he landed next to Mack Hoover.

Dale E. Basye saw Miss Parker trying to scale a stack of fractured rock. The cocoa-colored cloud looming above the oblivious teacher deepened in color until it was a bubbling pool of black coffee. The seething cloud unleashed another mass of boulders. Dale E. Basye yelled at the sky through cupped hands.

"Why did Dorothy fail her driver's test? She was a terrible Parker!"

The woman was yanked up into the air and cast to

the side of the pit. The stack of rock that she had stood on only seconds before was pounded into cobblestones and gravel. The cloud rumbled like a giant blender full of marbles. Miss Parker crawled to the side of the Punishment Pit on her elbows.

"Why were Mr. Basye's parents so sad upon first laying eyes on their son?" she yelled. "Because they'd have to see his face on a 'Dale E.' basis!"

The man was snatched into the air and thrown alongside Miss Parker.

"Thank you," he gasped. "I was nearly *punnelled.* . . ."

In the pit, Marlo and Cookie—each zigzagging through the rain of tumbling rocks—ran smack into each other.

"Oooofff!" they gasped, falling to the ground as the brooding cloud above swelled and thickened. "Watch where you're—"

A boulder landed in between them with a massive, ground-quaking thud.

"*A tribe of cannibals caught and ate a saint sent to them as a missionary. Moments later, the cannibals became violently sick, since—as they say—you can't keep a good man down.*"

Cookie and Marlo groaned.

"Okay, Cookie," Marlo said, her face stinging with upturned grit. "Let's pun each other out of here, on the count of three. . . ."

"How do I know you'll do it?" Cookie asked suspiciously.

"Well, because if I *don't*, we'll both be down here alone, flattened by falling joke-rocks," Marlo explained. "*That's* how you'll know . . . okay?"

Cookie nodded grudgingly. "Okay . . ."

"Now one, two . . . *three!*"

Marlo and Cookie shouted over each other against the thunder of cascading boulders.

"What's Transylvania's favorite snack food for kids?! *Cookie Youngblood!*"

"Where was Marlo sent to live after her parents died? In a *Fauster* home!"

The two girls seized each other by the hand and floated out of the Pun-ishment Pit. They collapsed in a heap by the other children. Marlo and Cookie noticed their clasped hands and quickly pulled away. Their hands resembled gophers darting down their respective holes at the screech of a hawk. The churning cloud of jostling rock evaporated back to nothing.

Miss Parker groaned as she hobbled over to Flossie, who was rocking back and forth, staring miserably at her leg.

"Does it hurt?" she asked.

"No," the girl replied wretchedly. "Not exactly. It just feels so . . . *flat*. Not like my leg, but like someone *talking* about my leg . . ."

Miss Parker helped the girl to her foot.

"Let's go while you at least have a leg to stand on. . . ."

25 · DERANGED AND REARRANGED

TEAM TWO—WHAT WAS left of them, anyway—straggled through a sparsely treed wood. Marlo and the others tromped across the patchy shredded-paper grove in silence, still a little pun-shy after nearly calling it "quips" in the Pun-ishment Pit. The woods ended suddenly at a peculiar, shimmering shanty. The oversized shack looked as if it had been assembled with thick, twinkling smoke. Outside of the hovel was a large rag, with pieces of ham and tuna resting on top of it.

"Um . . . *that's* random," Marlo said against the pervasive metallic chirping and subsonic hum.

Annabelle squinted down at the rag, screwed up her face with concentration, then glanced up at the billowing bungalow.

"Anagram Hut," the girl declared as she wiped away a clot of dried sweat and dirt from the corner of her eye.

"Huh?" Mack said between clenched jaws.

"Rag, ham, tuna . . . you scramble the letters and get 'Anagram Hut,'" Annabelle replied, as if it were as glaringly obvious as a pimple on the tip of your nose.

Miss Parker studied the girl. "Annabelle Graham . . . *Anagram.*"

"Of course," Marlo interjected. *"You* should go first. Your amazing, rearranging word-brain will be able to lead us through."

Annabelle nodded and opened the door. It was strangely heavy, considering that it appeared to be made of smoke. Miss Parker, Dale E. Basye, and the children entered the hut. After they passed through the entrance, the doorway slid frantically along the wall and up onto the ceiling, until it disappeared altogether. The children felt around for the entrance but it was gone. The walls were impenetrable. Not smoke at all.

The Anagram Hut was furnished with an assortment of puzzling objects, such as a belt lying in the middle of the room.

Marlo approached it. Then something invisible slammed against her shins.

"Oww!" she yelped. "There's something here. . . ."

Annabelle squatted on the ground like a police detective investigating a crime scene. "A belt. *Table.* 'A belt' is an anagram for 'table.'"

Next to the belt was a palm plant. Annabelle stood up to examine it.

"Hmm . . . palm," she muttered. "Oh, duh. *Lamp.*"

Lavena rolled her eyes at Cookie and twirled her finger by her temple. Marlo scowled at the two girls.

"Hey, I don't see you two Einsteins solving your way out of this place . . . and I've *met* Einstein. So I know."

Lavena mouthed "whatever" as Annabelle continued her sweep of the hut. Next to the belt, on the floor, was a hairy case.

"Hairy case . . . *easy chair,*" she muttered. Hiding beside the hairy case/easy chair were two tiny creatures—like small ogres—slamming into each other repeatedly before falling to the floor with clumsy ineptitude.

"Oafs . . . *sofa.*"

Above them—floating near the ceiling—was a small car, running in neutral, with, of all things, a chicken on top of it.

Annabelle gazed up in wonder. "Car . . . idle . . . hen . . . oh, right: *chandelier.*"

Next to the far wall was another small car, with a tiny pointy-eared creature inside eating what looked like a pie. A long wire draped with dangling pieces of food led away from the car.

"Hmm . . . food wire. *Firewood.* So this must be . . ."

Mack Hoover stepped toward the food.

"Man . . . the closer I get to the stuff, the angrier I get!" he said, gritting his teeth.

Annabelle rubbed her chin. "Hmm . . . hate. *Heat*. So this car with the elf and pie . . . car elf pie . . . fireplace! Of course! Everything in here is like a normal room, only all of the letters are jumbled, making them something else!"

Dale E. Basye shook his head with rumpled wonderment.

"Wow . . . that's incredible," he said. "How did you develop this skill? It's like bottled beans. Un*canny*."

Miss Parker elbowed Dale E. Basye, hard, with an elbow as sharp as her tongue.

"It's kind of like dyslexia, I guess," Annabelle replied, wiping beads of sweat away from her permanently sweaty upper lip. "Only I can control it."

"Shhhh," Marlo hissed. "I hear something. Over there . . ."

Marlo and Annabelle crept by the wall. Marlo could hear a steady "wow" noise that grew louder and louder.

Dale E. Basye covered his ears. "That din . . . it's almost unbearable," he grumbled.

"Wow . . . din . . . *window*," Annabelle muttered.

Annabelle tried to grip the wall and open the window, but nothing would budge. A small cat floated in the air next to the source of the noise, clutched by invisible hands.

"Cat . . . held . . . *latched*. Darn . . ."

Hadley stepped in front of the sofa/oafs and onto a plush throw rug.

"*Ooh*," she purred as her fingers stroked the cashmere pilings. "This is so cozy . . . I just want to curl up and—"

The small, shaggy blond girl began to grow in fitful spurts.

"Die!" Hadley screamed. "I'm dying!"

Annabelle squinted at the once-scrawny little girl as she shook her blond hair back and forth in agony.

"You're not dying," Annabelle muttered. "You're growing. And it hurts. . . ."

Hadley was soon the size of a baby elephant.

"Grow . . . hurt," Annabelle pondered. "*Throw rug!* That's it! Get off the rug!"

Hadley heaved herself off the decorative carpet. The pale, quivering girl instantly began to shrink down from a size 57 back to her usual barely size 1 proportions.

Bree Martinet 'studied something puzzling by the wall opposite where the door had once been.

"Hey, what's this?" she asked as she poked at seven strips of fabric hanging from the wall.

Annabelle chewed the words over in her mind. Marlo stepped toward Bree, cautioning the pouty, long-haired girl.

"You'd better stay away from them until Annabelle can—"

"Why?" Bree asked, before suddenly—

The Bree-shaped pile of words fluttered onto the floor. Miss Parker stifled a gasp.

Annabelle sighed as she stared at the seven drab strips.

"Seven strips . . . *Vipers' nests* . . . ," she whispered sadly.

"Then there's stuff here much more dangerous than furniture, apparently," Marlo said, her voice shaky as she watched what was once Bree Martinet fluttering on the floor.

Suddenly, across the Anagram Hut, a can of soda pop, surrounded by bits of assorted snacks, appeared. The can floated closer and closer to the children. A number was written along the side of the can: *3.14159*.

"Hmm . . . this one is tough," Annabelle muttered, biting her lip. "Cola . . . food . . . and a long number . . ."

"The number," Dale E. Basye offered. "It's pi."

"As in chocolate cream?" Marlo asked.

"As in *the numerical value of the ratio of the circumference of a circle to its diameter,*" Dale E. Basye clarified.

"Oh . . . right," Marlo replied. "That's what I meant. I mean, a chocolate cream pie is shaped like a circle."

Annabelle shushed them so she could concentrate. You could practically hear the letters shuffling in her head as the can came at them, faster and faster.

"Okay . . . then that means, cola . . . food . . . pi . . . um . . ."

Mack Hoover pushed past her. "This is stupid," he

said irritably. "It's coming right for us! Maybe I can just smack it away—"

"Wait!" Annabelle cried out as Mack swatted at the can.

"It burns!" Mack yelped.

"Your hand," Miss Parker murmured.

```
        F   F   F
        I   I   I
    p   N   N   N   T
    i   G   G   G   H
    n   E   E   E   U
    k   R   R   R   M
    y   S   S   S   B
        W   R   I   S   T
```

"What was that?!" Mack Hoover gasped as he stared at the jumble of letters that was now his hand.

"Cola . . . food . . . pi . . . *a pool of acid*," Annabelle explained. "Now, please, there's not a lot of things that I'm good at, but I *am* good at this. . . ."

Marlo knelt down before a corncob, covered with worms that spelled out the word "mom."

"What do you make of this, Graham the Word Cracker?" Marlo asked.

Annabelle looked over Marlo's shoulder. "Cob . . . worms . . . wait: The worms have little hooks in them. So they're bait. Cob, bait, mom . . ." Annabelle swallowed.

"All right, guys, we're in big trouble," she said, slowly backing away from the corncob.

"Why?" Miss Parker asked with concern.

"I think Marlo is kneeling in front of an atomic bomb," Annabelle squeaked.

Marlo turned, somehow even *more* deathly pale. She backed carefully away from the corncob.

"What do we do?" Flossie whined, hobbling to Marlo's side on her good leg.

Marlo sniffed the air. Something odd tickled her nose. A rich aroma that her nostrils couldn't quite place.

"There's a strange smell here," she said.

"There's *always* a strange smell wherever you are," Cookie retorted, hugging herself to keep from shaking apart.

"*It's not me.* It's not a stinky smell, so much as a—"

Marlo smiled. Her pleased grin looked like the sun rising over a craggy mountain peak.

"I got this!" she said, feeling in front of her. "You're not the only wordsmith around here, Annabelle. It's an *odor*. Otherwise known in the Anagram Hut as a—"

"*Door!*" Marlo and Annabelle exclaimed in delighted unison as Marlo pulled open the invisible door, exposing a portal leading back outside. The teachers and children raced outside before the odor dissipated, and their door closed forever.

"Great job, Annabelle!" Marlo said as the group followed a dusty path winding away from the Anagram

Hut. The path was studded with hundreds of tiny tuning prongs and chirping brass crickets.

"Thanks," Annabelle said shyly as they hiked up the ever-steepening path. "Everyone always told me I was crazy for the anagram thing."

"Yeah," Marlo replied. "Me too. Not for word stuff, but for most everything else . . ."

The dusty trail led up to a stone archway, a sort of long tunnel dug out of the stone.

Marlo stopped and squinted up at the archway. "Looks like the coast is—"

A deep roar, like a trio of howls twisted into a rope of sound, blasted through the archway.

"—totally the opposite of clear."

A humongous reptile emerged from the curved stone passage above. The children screamed as the hideous lizard stretched open its jaws, revealing three rows of monstrous, misshapen teeth.

The enormous creature was like a dinosaur, only covered with thousands of flapping book pages for scales. Its terrible size and shape seemed in a constant state of flux, altering in subtle ways, making it hard to define. Its gnashing beak swapped various shades of red with its seething, pinwheel eyes. Its serpentlike neck twisted and curled, then contorted and coiled. Its cudgel-tipped tail thrashed at the ground before, a moment later, merely lashing at it. The beast's talons were at one point keen and cruel, the next sharp and brutal: the same, only *different*.

"What is it?" Flossie croaked.

"It's some kind of dinosaur," Dale E. Basye managed once he regained control of his incapacitated tongue.

"No . . . not quite," Roget murmured. The boy strode a few yards along the path, just before the trail began its precipitous climb up the rock face. The children were frozen behind him in utter horror. Something glinted just ahead. Roget bounded toward the object and plucked it from the ground. The blurry object—some kind of weapon—shape-shifted restlessly in the boy's hands.

"I've got this one," Roget said with quiet confidence. The children stared, dumbfounded, at the small boy with the shrewd, narrow face as he walked up to the morphing monster.

Roget peered up at the beast and looked the savage creature straight in the . . .

"Eye, orb, peeper, optical organ," the boy muttered.

Instantly, the creature's face became more distinct, more *defined*.

Roget smiled, gripped the hilt of the blurry object in his hands, then—with a flourish—brandished his gleaming . . .

"Sword, saber, scimitar, blade . . ."

The weapon gained keen, deadly clarity in Roget's hands. He stepped forward. Roget tromped along the trail leading up to the treacherous . . .

"Precipice, cliff, crag, rock face . . . ," Roget muttered,

the ground becoming more solid beneath his feet with every step.

Soon, he found the—

"Den, lair, cave, burrow . . ."

—of the great beast.

Roget drew in a deep, steadying breath. Summoning every ounce of—

"Strength, might, muscle, vigor . . ."

—he could muster, Roget dug his feet into the ground, drew his arms back up over his head, and—

"Lobbed, threw, pitched, flung . . ."

—his mighty weapon into the air. It sailed forward with deadly speed and accuracy. It pierced the snarling creature's—

"Chest, torso, breast, upper body . . ."

The beast thrashed, shifting shape after furious shape until, in an instant, the mighty—

"Thesaurus, lexicon, synonym finder, equivalence location tool . . ."

—was dead.

The once-fearsome beast fell from the top of the rocky escarpment and lay twitching in its final death throes several yards away from the children.

After a moment of stunned silence, Dale E. Basye shuddered. "A Thesaurus?" he muttered with disbelief.

Marlo snickered. "Wow, that thing is *synonym* toast," she quipped. "Let's hear it for Roget!"

The children and teachers gave the boy a stupefied

round of applause. The surviving members of Team Two cautiously wended their way around the dead Thesaurus and trekked up the steep trail and through the musky archway. They emerged, greeted by a cacophonous symphony of burbling nonsense. Marlo clapped her ears as the sound rattled both her bones and her nerves.

"What's that horrible sound?!" she complained. "And where's it coming from?!"

From up ahead, Marlo could hear the familiar, nearly ceaseless and senseless commentary of Vice Principal Carroll, squawking through his loudspeaker.

"O frabjous day! Huzzah! Huzzear!
You've conquered every scrabble!
Yet, I fear, your coasts aren't clear,
Near the Tower of Babble!"

26 · QUEASY AS A-B-C

MILTON AND HIS team milled outside of what looked like a giant concrete igloo, painted in faded, peeling red, blue, and yellow. It looked like it was built with massive blocks—twenty-six, by Milton's count—with a long, horseshoe-shaped opening jutting out the front. Each of the cubes, like the alphabet blocks of a baby giant, had a single letter on it, barely legible, as if painted years ago and nearly wiped away by generations of strong wind, which didn't make sense to Milton, as Vice Principal Carroll apparently had created all of this—this massive entrance exam to the War of the Words—in only the last few weeks.

Marlo and the straggling remains of Team Two joined the others outside of the building. Milton couldn't help but smile when he saw his sister. He was filled with a cool gush of relief at the sight of her. Marlo grinned from ear to ear as she saw her brother, bedraggled yet not rendered a heap of flattened words. Wonderfully alive—well, *intact* at least—geeky, twerpy, and thoroughly *Milton*. The brother she couldn't live without even if she tried.

Yet something kept their feet pinned to the cricket-infested shredded-paper ground.

Is she smiling because I'm okay and that she knows she can bully me in the debate? Milton thought, the slow insidious grip of paranoia seizing him around the brain stem. His smile faded until it was as vaporous and transient as a homeless ghost.

Was he smiling because he knows he's super smart and good with wordy stuff and can beat me in the debate? Marlo thought as her grin snapped like a rubber band across the bottom of her face.

Seconds ago they had wanted to rush into each other's arms. Now they were hip-deep in uncertainty.

"What would you have us do now, Team Captain?" Mr. Wilde asked.

"*Snnnaaahhhhrrrrk!!*"

Milton saw his sister trying not to look at him, but she was staring at him in that creepy way of hers out of the corner of her eye.

Milton sighed. "Well, the snark sounds like it's on the prowl, and this place is crawling with wolf-beasts, so we'd probably better go inside this big Playskool igloo and just get it over with," he said with frustration. He marched reluctantly toward the opening.

The teachers and children passed through the long archway and into the spacious, domed chamber. It was a sweltering, tomblike cave inside. Milton strained to see in the smoky darkness. His nostrils were assailed with the strong asphalt-and-motor-oil smell of hot tar. Milton heard an incessant bubbling, like someone had forgotten a swimming pool full of stew on a burner.

Spotlights streamed down from overhead, punching optic nerves like fists. Marlo's eyes clenched closed in pain. It was like when her mom would rip down her triple-ply tinfoil blinds on Monday mornings, only magnified.

Each spotlight was trained upon a wide platter of stone, twenty-six of which were strung together over a gurgling pool of steaming tar in a sort of bridge. The stepping plates had a letter of the alphabet engraved upon them and were painted bright red. The bridge began with the letter "A" and ended with, unsurprisingly, the letter "Z."

Vice Principal Carroll's voice drifted into the building. Somehow he could comment on everything happening *as* it was happening.

> *"To survive the Abecedarium, you'll be asked*
> *to use your cranium.*
> *Tell a story with each letter—just one word,*
> *no less or better!*
> *And in order alphabetical to avoid a nasty spectacle!"*

A chorus of scrapes sliced through the gurgle of boiling tar. The entryway was now barricaded with thick candy-cane bars.

"Everything here is meant to push us along," Milton said. "The longer we stay here, the more of us we lose."

Milton could feel the heat of Dale E. Basye's stare.

"Can I help you with something?" Milton asked.

The man eased out of his stupor.

"You must be . . . Milton Fauster," he said softly.

"Yes, I am."

Dale E. Basye swallowed. "Well, it's nice to write you . . . I mean *meet* you . . . I think. I'm not really sure," he said, his voice rolling slowly away like a pebble down a steep hill.

Milton looked at Marlo for guidance.

"It's a long story . . . ," Marlo replied. "*His* story, apparently. I'll tell you all about it later. . . ."

Marlo stopped abruptly, unsure whether there would even *be* a later, much less one shared between her and her brother.

"*Aaaaarrrrrgggghhhh!!*"

A shriek exploded across the Abecedarium. It was snuffed out with blunt, horrific abruptness. Something fluttered to the ground along the murky edge of a spotlight. A tall, skinny stack of words beginning with the name "Concordia Kolassa."

Cookie Youngblood screamed. Long spikes jabbed

up randomly through the floor, with no rhyme yet deadly reason. One of the sharp, jutting spears pierced Flossie's word-foot. She looked down and smirked.

"Guess there's an advantage to having a short story for a leg," the girl mumbled, brushing her orange hair out of her eyes as she frantically scanned the floor.

The long spikes thrust through the ground with haphazard savagery. Milton noticed that none of them seemed to puncture through the steps of the alphabet bridge.

"We're supposed to get on the bridge," Milton called out. "C'mon! Everybody, get on a letter. We have to write a twenty-six-word story or die trying!"

"But there's only twenty of us, idiot!" Moses spat back. "We can't possibly—"

"Then some of us will have to double up!" Miss Parker shouted.

The children clambered onto the narrow bridge of lettered plates poised high above a pit of bubbling, searing-hot tar. Milton wheeled Moxie onto the bright red "A" just as a spear shot up through the ground and tore the cuff of his tweed pants.

The children and teachers scrambled to claim an empty platter. No one wanted to stand toward the end of the bridge, by X-Y-Z, so Milton edged his way along the row and occupied the red "X." Marlo joined him, reluctantly, on the open "W" step.

After everyone was safely on the bridge, the chain of lettered plates clicked.

"What's going—" Cookie gasped.

Each lettered plate began to tilt—click by click—with the intent of gradually tipping everyone into the gurgling tar below.

"It's moving!" Winifred cried.

"We're supposed to make a story," Milton yelled, "or we'll be hurled into the boiling tar!"

The children stared at Moxie, quivering on her dolly.

"Um . . . ," Mordacia Caustilo said from her "M" platter. "How is she—"

"*A!*" Moxie roared, her silver-sheathed tongue sticking out of her wide-open mouth.

"*Bear!*" Clem shouted.

"*Came!*" Moses exclaimed.

"*Down!*" Roberta yelled.

Lavena Duckworth opened her mouth, but—due to years of silent yet sassily expressive face-texting—no sound came out. The girl's face muscles twitched spasmodically. Suddenly, the platter pitched her into the tar. The girl became nothing more than a Lavena-shaped collection of words the instant she struck the surface. The "E" platter clicked back into place as the entire bridge tilted forward.

Mr. Dickens straddled both the red "E" and "F" steps.

"*Everest . . . From . . . ,*" he croaked.

"Great!" Flossie yelled, before straining to perform a straddle-split to reach the "H" platter. *"Heights!"*

"Indeed, Just!" Mr. Wilde exclaimed, the long-legged man occupying both red letters.

"Knowing . . . Life . . . !" Dale E. Basye declared as he stretched his less-long legs onto both the "K" and "L" platters as if this were an alphabetic game of Twister.

"Meant!" Mordacia yelled.

"New!" Cookie shouted.

"Opportunity!" Hadley said, poking the air in front of her to denote a period.

"Packing!" Rakeem exclaimed.

"Quickly!" Roget added.

"Ready!" Annabelle shouted.

"Set!" Mack roared.

"Um . . . Go?" Winifred murmured. The pouty-faced girl was instantly pitched into the bubbling tar beneath.

Mack strained to reach the "T" platter with his left foot.

"To!" he yelled.

"Undertake . . . Valleys," Miss Parker grunted with each of her feet placed on both of the bright red letters.

Marlo panicked. It felt like every time she had ever been called upon in class—piled one on top of the other—the teacher somehow knowing the exact point that Marlo had begun to space out.

The "W" platter clicked beneath her hard leather shoes.

"*Whee!!*" Marlo exclaimed, using air quotes to show that she meant this to be an exclamation.

That left Milton to somehow come up with an "X" word. The bridge of platters twitched impatiently, now tilting forward at a near forty-five-degree angle.

Marlo had used an exclamation captured with quotation marks, which meant that Milton should follow that exclamation with a name, for attribution's sake.

"*Xavier!*" Milton shouted, crossing his fingers into an "X" to show his fellow Spite Clubbers how the name was spelled. His relief was fleeting, however, as he glanced hopelessly at the remaining two letters, utterly unoccupied, beside him. The bridge clicked another degree. The children squealed. Milton threw himself onto the "Y" platter.

"*Yelled!*" Milton gasped as he flailed desperately for the bright red "Z." The alpha-bridge clicked. The remaining children and teachers fought to regain their balance. Milton grunted as he strained forward. A large bubble of tar burst beneath him, spraying his face with scalding-hot drops of burning black. The bridge clicked.

Marlo used her brother's back as her own personal bridge and raced to the "Z."

"*Zestfully!*" she cried.

The tar drained out of the pool below. The twenty-six

platters straightened, much to the relief of everyone, then rearranged with a series of clicks and pops into a set of steps. Marlo hunkered down on her knees as the "Z" platter lowered, becoming the last step of the stairway. A concrete door slid open, leading out to an underground hallway that sloped back up to the outside.

Moses departed the red "C" and stormed down the stairs.

"Nice job, Team Captain," he seethed. "You got three of us 'word-ered' in there!"

"What was he supposed to do?!" Marlo spat back at him automatically, genetically programmed to defend the brother that only *she* was allowed to torment.

"I wasn't talking to you," Moses said, shoving the others out of his way.

Milton, stepping out of the tunnel back onto the crinkly paper floor of the Outer Terristories, turned to address his accuser.

"I did the best thing I could think of at the time," Milton replied. "What would *you* have done?"

Moses paused. "I . . . I would have had everyone figure out what they were going to say *before* we walked out on a bridge suspended over boiling tar, for one thing!"

"And get Shake-*speared* in that A-B-C place?" Marlo replied.

Milton turned to his sister. "Thanks, but I can fight my own battles."

Marlo stared into her brother's hazel eyes. They

seemed sharper, harder . . . not a pair of squishy milk duds like they used to. Marlo straightened her ugly tweed coat.

"Yes . . . I'm sure you can. I'm sure you *will* . . . ," she said with a dismissive sniff as she turned to walk away.

"*AHROOOOOOO WOO WOOOahhhhh!*"

Just thirty yards away, a great, shaggy wolf bayed at the smudgy soft-purple sky.

It locked its crazy eyes on Milton and Marlo.

"*Run!*" Milton yelled as he and his sister darted away from the beast. The wolf bounded after them, taking huge, hungry strides that gobbled up the distance between it and its prey. Milton looked back over his shoulder. There was something different about this wolf's eyes. Its ink-black pupils were shaped like hooks. *Like question marks.*

Milton had first encountered a sort of What-Wolf, then a Who-Wolf, and now a—

"Why," Milton gasped as he and Marlo ran, "*Wolf!*"

"Of course . . . it's a stupid wolf . . . and why? . . . because it *can*," Marlo panted beside him. "They're all over this place . . . *Here There Be Grammonsters* . . . remember? I met up with another one. . . ."

"How did it . . . try to get you?"

"It dug through the ground. I have no idea how."

"That's it!" Milton wheezed. "Who, What, Where, When, How, and Why . . . the basic questions that reporters and investigators have to answer. I ran into a

What-Wolf, a Where-Wolf, and a Who-Wolf. You must have run into a . . ."

"How-Wolf," Marlo replied, looking over her shoulder. "So what is this one? And why is it . . . chasing just us?"

Milton's handcuff sawed into his tender wrist as the briefcase swayed back and forth. The pain itself seemed to sap the energy from his legs. He heaved the briefcase onto his shoulder as if it were a leather boom box. A high-pitched whine emanated from inside the satchel.

"The briefcases!" Milton cried. "Listen to yours . . ."

Marlo swung her briefcase up onto her shoulder. She, too, could hear a high-pitched whine.

"With their big wolf ears," Marlo puffed. "It must drive 'em nuts."

"That's why they're chasing us!" Milton replied. "So all we have to do is get rid of them . . ."

"We're wearing . . . handcuffs . . . *Blind-Stein*," Marlo gasped, a stitch sewn tightly in her side. "And I'm not giving that thing any . . . finger food."

Milton looked back at the wolf—which was so close he could smell its hot, swampy breath. It was almost upon them.

ZOT!!

Milton and Marlo skidded to a stop.

"*AHROOOOOOO WOO WOOOahhhhh!*"

Another wolf-beast roared viciously in front of them.

Its pupils ticked along the rims of its yellow eyes like a clock.

"That's the same wolf we saw when we first came to Wise Acres!" Milton exclaimed. "It must be a *When*-Wolf."

The two shaggy creatures spun around to face each other, growling and pacing. Milton and Marlo collapsed to the ground, hugging each other under the delusion that they could form an impenetrable, wolf-resistant Fauster ball.

The Why-Wolf glared at Milton's and Marlo's briefcases. Its long, pointy ears twitched in torment at the persistent, shrieking squeal. It reared back on its massive, muscular hind legs and charged toward the quivering mound of Fausters.

27 · RUN OFF AT THE MOUTH

IN MID-LUNGE, THE When-Wolf swiped at the Why-Wolf and sliced a deep wound in its side. The beast howled in agony.

The Why-Wolf let loose an anguished howl as the When-Wolf thrust its furious muzzle into the creature's side, ripping out a bloody mouthful of guts and tissue. The Why-Wolf fell lifeless to the ground, heaving one last hot, humid breath.

The When-Wolf panted over its victim, its shaggy gray fur matted with blood. Its long ears twitched, tilting toward the source of their suffering.

Marlo peeked fearfully through her fingers. She gasped.

The When-Wolf spun its head toward Marlo and lunged at her with its razor-sharp claws.

"Nooo!!" she shrieked, cowering before the seven-foot-tall beast.

Milton sprang from the ground between the wolf and his sister. He swung his briefcase soundly at the creature's head. The wolf snapped and tore at it with its vicious jaws. Milton saw a flash of white fuzz through a jagged tear in the satchel.

Lucky! Milton thought with desperation. *I forgot he was in there!*

The When-Wolf, enraged by the startling blow to its head, rested its crazed, restless eyes on Milton.

"AHROOOOOOO WOO WOOOahhhhh!"

It lashed at the briefcase and loosed its painful, high-pitched screech with one ferocious swipe. The handle, now free from the satchel's torn leather housing, dangled from Milton's wrist. The When-Wolf clutched the half-mauled briefcase in its claws, cradling it back and forth quizzically. The pupils along its wide yellow eyes ticked to "midnight."

ZOT!!

The creature was gone. Milton and Marlo panted together on the ground, staring at the pair of massive wolf tracks just a few feet away from them, slowly pooling with spilled Why-Wolf blood.

"Lucky!" Milton gasped, staring pathetically at the briefcase-handle bracelet and the shreds of leather fluttering across the shredded-paper ground. "I . . . couldn't save him! I forgot he was in the briefcase, and then like an idiot bashed the wolf with—"

Marlo wrapped her arm around Milton's shoulder.

"You saved me," Marlo said with awe. "It was like . . . *instinctual,* even though you—"

She uncoiled her arm from Milton's neck and stared at him, hard.

"Why didn't you reply to the note I left you?!"

Milton lifted his heavy gaze from the remnants of the savaged briefcase.

"What was there to possibly say?!" he replied, looking her square in the eye, still trembling from the wolf encounter. "'Only one of us can win, and that's going to be me. . . .'"

"That's not what I wrote," Marlo said with a soft shake of her head. "I wrote that, even though only one of us can win, we have to stick together, and though it's going to be tough, we can do it . . . which was all really hard to write with alphabet soup letters."

Milton scrunched up his face. "Was Lucky awake when you left the note?"

"Yeah, I think he . . . Hey, do you think that fuzzy pig made some edible edits of my note?"

Milton snorted. "He *totally* did . . . and to think, all this time, I thought my own sister was out to get me— more than usual, that is. . . ."

Marlo crushed Milton with an embrace of relief and

gratitude. Milton smiled before sighing sadly as he noted the mauled briefcase.

"Lucky—"

Marlo pushed her brother back, smiling in his face.

"Is fine! Remember? The When-Wolf we met before . . . the one with the other Lucky. He was the *same* Lucky, only from a different time! The When-Wolf is now with us, back there . . . back then. Didn't all that time in the Time Pools teach you anything?"

"You're right!" Milton said, a slow smile spreading across his face. "Of course . . . so there were two Luckys for a while, until now, when he returned back . . . and the other Lucky—the *real* Lucky—is back in Wise Acres, I guess. So that briefcase the wolf left . . . it was the one I was going to be carrying all along."

A gust of wind blew away a small, gore-stained pile of torn index cards. One card, half-submerged in Why-Wolf blood, stubbornly refused the wind's coaxing. Milton plucked it out of the pool, grimacing. He studied its puzzling words and pictures.

STAND

SDRAWKCAB & WORD WORD
WORD WORD

"What do you think it means?" Marlo asked, looking over her brother's shoulder.

Milton shrugged. "It's hard to tell with Vice Principal Carroll. It could mean nothing. It could mean *everything*. . . ."

He tucked the card into his coat and looked out at the horizon. The screeching, burbling wind was louder than ever. Milton squinted at something through his glasses. The children and teachers were gathered before some sort of promontory, staring at . . .

Milton took off his glasses and wiped the lenses with his sleeve.

No, it can't be. Must be dirt . . .

"Um . . . are those, *people*?" Marlo said, her keen kleptomaniac's vision confirming Milton's discovery. "Hovering in the air?"

Milton and Marlo joined the others at the headland. There, about a quarter-mile away, was a sort of towering, shivering trident, nearly invisible, more like a gigantic vibrating smudge that pierced the clouds. Its silhouette resembled Vice Principal Carroll's tiny tuning forks littering the Outer Territories. What really struck Milton—apart from the building being virtually invisible and larger than any he had ever seen, or even imagined—was that it was filled with people who just seemed to float in the air. They scurried about like ants in a ginormous ant farm.

"I often felt that God, in creating Man, somewhat

overestimated his ability," Mr. Wilde said as he gazed upon the structure in wonder. "But this could be one of those rare instances when I've been proven wrong."

Milton could see Vice Principal Carroll's white Rabbit driving in the distance. It flickered between the sparse grove of trees edging the bleak, spare clearing.

"There's no need to be so dour.
You've arrived—yes!—at the Tower!"

Clem Weenum rubbed his eyes, desperately craving a nap.

"But . . . I don't understand," the little boy said with a yawn. "How are all those people floating up in the sky?"

Moses snorted. "*Duh*, Juice Box. It's obviously built using some kind of reinforced glass. . . ."

Vice Principal Carroll's voice squawked through his hood-mounted loudspeakers.

"Glass, I fear, would be unsound.
This tower, here, is made of sound!
Every language—quibbling, grousing—
makes a sturdy sort of housing.
The tongues they overlap and weave
a tension that you won't believe.
The Tower stands as monument
to the power of argument."

Dale E. Basye gazed up at the structure. He winced as he pulled a neck muscle.

"So how do we get there?" he asked, rubbing the base of his head.

"Now that you are nearly done,
You'll run the Run-On Sentence Run!
Three of you, I here anoint,
Will go to Punctuation Point.
Milton, Marlo, and you, Dale,
Shall do your best, the point, to scale.
Only two of you will make the Tower.
The third? Before the snark shall cower!
So make your statement: don't be slow.
Now get ye ready set and go!"

The children and teachers had collected behind Dale E. Basye, who, uncharacteristically, found himself at the front of the class. The freshly dead author gazed off in the distance at Punctuation Point.

The cliff forked off into three distinct paths. The path on the left was straight, direct, and studded with large round stones, ending abruptly at a massive boulder resting at the edge. The center path—marred with splotches of mud and murk—meandered in uncertain twists, sloping steadily down before coming up sharply in an odd, uncertain curl at the edge of the cliff. The loop was a story tall and incomplete, like an extra-suicidal skateboard ramp anchored by another boulder. The path on the right climbed gradually up to a sharp, declarative point where a tall stone obelisk awaited, perched emphatically atop another boulder. Beyond the cliff was a thick mote of white nothingness surrounding the shimmering, shrieking Tower of Babble.

Hadley Upfling crossed her arms stubbornly. "Well, what if they just don't go?" she asked. "What's the vice principal going to do about—"

"*Snnnaaahhhhrrrrk!!*"

The nine-legged beast roared, spewing a spray of toxic green snot from its moist, snub-nosed snout. It galloped straight toward Hadley and Clem, who—being the smallest—had straggled behind the rest of the group. The snark held its hideous head low as it charged at the two children.

Hadley and Clem screamed as the snark trampled them into two, flat piles of words.

"*Snnnaaahhhhrrrrk!!*"

The children and teachers scattered like skittish confetti in a really terrible parade. The snark set its slitted eyes upon Dale E. Basye and pawed the ground with its foreleg. The middle-aged man swallowed.

"Looks like it's game time," he muttered as he glanced hectically over his shoulder at the three paths.

The vice principal's voice squawked as he relayed the event to the radio audience.

"You best be getting on your mark,
before you're savaged by the—"

Marlo clapped her hands to her ears.

"Doesn't he ever stop?!" she shrieked, her nerves frazzled and frayed.

The snark jerked and lunged at the running, ragtag remnants of Teams One and Two. Frustrated, it dug its hooves into the ground. The beast caught sight of Milton, Marlo, and Dale E. Basye at the base of Punctuation Point. Clouds of green steam and spray gushed from its snout.

Milton held on to his arms to keep them from trembling.

"We've got to try," he said as he gently urged Marlo forward. "It's our only way out. I'll take the left, you go center. . . ."

Marlo nodded and wiped her eyes. "Lucky no one can see me cry on the radio," she said.

Milton made his way up the slope to the far path. The path was straight, steep, and studded with large rocks, spaced apart at regular intervals.

Milton ran. And jumped. He ran across the hard ground of compressed paper. Hopping. Over. Rocks. It was hard for him to think beyond each smooth round stone. Just when a thought, a sentence, formed in his head, Milton leapt. And when he landed, he started all over again. Running. Jumping. Getting closer and closer to the end of the cliff.

This course, Milton thought, *is a sentence. A bunch of them. And they end just up ahead. With a big fat period.*

Marlo darted up to the winding center path. The more she ran, the more confused she became. Each footfall raised not only clouds of paper dust, but also clouds of doubt.

Is this even really running? Marlo thought as she jogged along the circuitous trail. *Am I even getting anywhere? What's with all of this mud? Is it to make it easier for the snark to get me? Would it even need help getting me?*

As Marlo made her way toward the question mark–shaped summit, the ground grew murkier beneath her feet.

What's all this—

She slipped in a small, curved patch of mud and fell to the ground, suddenly unconscious. Milton saw his sister, curled up and motionless on her path, and bounded away from his course of short sentences. Milton arrived at Marlo's side, hooked his hands beneath her arms, and brought her to her feet. Marlo's eyes fluttered, like butterflies trying to steal hard-boiled eggs at a picnic.

"Thanks?" she murmured. "I must have slipped into a comma?"

The snark galloped toward them along the flattened paper-lands.

"Snnnaaahhhhrrrrk!!"

With a deep inhale, Dale E. Basye bounded up the slope to the long, sharp point. He dodged the various round stones and puddles dotting the landscape.

Dale E. Basye was running! Fast! He felt strong! Sure, terrified and confused—like at a family reunion—but remarkably alive, considering the fact that he could very well be dead! Each step felt bold and sure! Positively declarative! He felt as if he were rushing toward some emphatic conclusion!

Milton grabbed his sister by the hand. Up ahead, their paths ran parallel to each other, the ground broken up into a series of uniform grooves.

"We have to dash!" Milton shouted.

Milton and Marlo—running side by side—leapt over each dash—the dashes breaking up the path every so often—with the snark—huffing and snarling behind them—gaining with every hoof-fall—of which it had nine, outnumbering the Fausters' frantic feet by five—until the beast was practically upon them—its fetid breath blasting their backs—with Milton and Marlo giving one last surge of speed . . .

The snark cantered to a stop. It stared at three dots on the ground, blocking the trail.

"What is that?" Marlo asked, trying to catch her breath as she looked behind her.

"An ellipsis," Milton replied. "The three dots. They

symbolize an omission of words, or when your thoughts just sort of . . ."

". . . trail off?"

"Yeah."

The snark stared at the ellipsis . . . gently swaying with numbing doubt. The snark shuddered, shook its head fitfully, and rose suddenly to its nine feet. It furiously stomped the ellipsis until the ground was pockmarked beyond comprehension.

"Snnnaaahhhhrrrrk!!"

The snark settled its glare on Milton and Marlo. Milton swallowed. He noticed a pair of thin, curved shield-like curls of metal lying on the ground nearby.

"Grab a parenthesis!" he shouted to Marlo.

Milton and Marlo snatched up the parentheses just as the scaly-skinned beast careened toward them. The large metal hammer lashed to the back of its neck glittered. The snark charged (with Milton and Marlo hiding inside the two curved brackets) but the beast couldn't get at them. The creature quickly recovered and came at them again, gaining momentum with every hoof-fall. Yet when it rushed at the pair of parentheses (Milton and Marlo protected within), its hammer blow merely glanced off. The snark stomped in frustrated circles.

Milton and Marlo slowly backed away, huddled together, halfway up Punctuation Point. Marlo stepped on a large pair of dots in the ground.

"Ouch: my colon?" she yelped. She dropped her parenthesis shield and clutched her lower abdomen in agony.

"Another punctuation mark," Milton wheezed. "It's used to . . . separate two clauses. Too bad you didn't step on a semicolon; then it would just . . . half hurt."

The fallen parenthesis disappeared in the mud.

"Snnnaaahhhhrrrrk!!"

The snark sniffed the air, leveled its hammerhead toward them, and charged.

"We can't protect ourselves with just one parenthesis . . . can we?" Marlo grunted. "Or . . . outrun it?"

Milton shook his head. "I don't think so."

"Then you should run?" Marlo said, supremely irritated that every statement she made curled up at the end like a question.

"I won't leave you here. End of statement."

Dale E. Basye ran toward the end of his path, toward Exclamation Point, for all he was worth, which—given the inflation of age—wasn't much. He looked over his shoulder at Milton and Marlo.

Dale E. Basye swallowed as the hideous snark galloped toward the two children in 9/8 time.

"No!" the man yelled. He ran to help them, but as soon as he strayed from his path, he was besieged by a swarm of tiny marks.

"Hyphens?"

With his bluish-green-gray eyes, Dale E. Basye saw

the hideous bird-lizard-bull-horse creature stagger toward the pale-faced blue-haired girl and her four-eyed brown-haired beanpole of a brother. The middle-aged man tried to shuffle his size-ten feet to help the down-on-their-luck preteens out of their not-to-be-believed situation, but the poorly-developed sentence was so ludicrously-burdened with over-hyphenated words that the late-author found it next-to-impossible to move, despite his highly-motivated state. With a mighty shiver, he shook off the hyphenating-hive of word-linking marks and rushed to Milton and Marlo's aide.

The trotting snark was only a few dozen yards away. Thinking either fast or not at all, Dale E. Basye ran at the snark and, with a heroic leap, bounded onto its back.

"Man, this thing gives ugly a bad name," Dale E. Basye muttered as he fought to stay on. He clutched the large metal hammer and hung on for dear afterlife.

"*Giddy-up!*" he yelled as he kicked the beast in its sides with his heels.

The snark charged blindly toward the tip of Exclamation Point, blindly in that Dale E. Basye had his arms wrapped around the creature's eyes. Dale stared at the tall, rigid obelisk, resting defiantly atop a rounded boulder, up ahead.

"An Exclamation Point!" he exclaimed as the snark charged up the steep slope. "What a way to end a sentence! So, now where were we? Oh yeah . . ."

Straddling a stampeding monster toward a

precarious precipice guarding an invisible tower of sound, Dale E. Basye felt like a character in one of his own crazy stories.

Maybe it didn't matter if this was all in his mind or if he was, indeed, *dead*—swept under the rug of the afterlife in some kiddie version of h-e-double-hockey-sticks—but, instead, maybe it mattered that he was *finally* doing something for others, somehow saving the day in a place that never saw the sun, running off the edge of a cliff with a run-on sentence crowding his feverish mind. . . .

The snark tried to stop as it galloped full speed, but its nine-legged velocity was unstoppable!

With that, Dale E. Basye—astride the galloping snark—soared off Exclamation Point, his afterlife sentence complete, falling into the velvet arms of a vaporous, infinite whiteness. It was as if he, the subject of his own sentence, had trailed off the margins of a colossal sheet of paper. The snark hurtled through the air, screeching as it twisted in arcs of flailing surprise, until the silver hammer lashed to the creature's head slammed into the base of the Tower of Babble.

The sky-high cathedral of sound vibrated with the brutal impact. Milton and Marlo panted at the edge of Exclamation Point.

"What's going—" Marlo began until shock waves shook the Outer Territories.

Milton's mind . . .

. . . started . . .

. . . sinking.

Everything around them began to lose its grip on everything else, going soft and slack along the edges.

Soon everything went w h i t e. Absolutely . . .

W   H   I   T   E.

28 · A RAW DEAL

PRINCIPAL BUBB TEETERED atop a chair as she tacked a tacky poster onto the wall of her Not-So-Secret Lair. The poster depicted a gazelle straggling behind its herd as the creatures fled the dogged advance of a fierce wolf.

INDIVIDUALITY: STANDING OUT IS THE QUICKEST WAY TO BECOME SOMEONE ELSE'S DINNER

As the principal strained desperately to balance her tremendous bulk upon the pitiable chair, everything suddenly . . .

. . . went . . .

w   h   i   t   e.

After a . . .

. . . moment the . . .

. . . principal came to . . .

. . . on the floor . . .

What was that *all about?* she thought, her mind feeling scrubbed raw like a freshly dressed wound. Principal Bubb glanced at her clock that read 13:13—the same time it always read—yet the principal had the nagging feeling that time had somehow passed, as much as time could here in Limbo.

The principal clawed her way back to her feet, clutching her desk to support her wobbly legs.

It must be the stress, Bea "Elsa" Bubb thought, rubbing her horn nubs.

A hermit crab–like demon stuck its eyestalks through a crack in her door.

"Mmmm . . . ma'am," it mumbled shyly. "I . . . um . . . there is something to see you, Madam Principal."

"Some*thing?*" she replied as she clacked to her imposing desk. "Don't you mean some*one?*"

The demon guard waggled one if its eyestalks out the door while keeping the other trained on Principal Bubb. "I . . . um . . . I'm not completely sure," it replied meekly.

"*Fine.* Send *whatever* in," she ordered as she sat in her chair, the sitting device squealing in structural pain beneath her inelegant bulk. "But I have to be going. . . ."

The hermit-crab demon skittered away. Through the door passed a lumbering quilt of wounded meat held together with scabs and spite. The principal winced at the sight of it. There was something familiar about the creature, right around the area where its face should have been.

"Um . . . yes?" Principal Bubb hissed with disgust. "May I, er, help you? Though you seem well past that . . ."

The five-foot, ten-inch hodgepodge of weeping sores seemed to nod.

"Principal," it gurgled weakly in a voice knotted with strain. "It's me . . . it's . . ."

Principal Bubb peered deeply into the creature's dark, cruel eyes thrown haphazardly onto its head by Fate's sinister game of roulette.

"Damian Ruffino?" she gasped.

Damian Ruffino was one of the worst children that Principal Bubb had ever encountered in her timeless tenure as Heck's principal of darkness. He made being bad look so easy. Yet while Damian had been a maestro of malevolence, now he was just a mess of meat.

"What on Earth happened? I assume that's where this happened . . . *on Earth.*"

Damian scratched at a rough, crusty patch that seemed to serve as his neck.

"I . . . long story," he replied with a thick rattle of phlegm. "I've come . . . to have a word with you . . . about a deal. . . ." He continued with difficulty. "A deal that we made . . ."

"A deal? Whatever do you mean?"

"You said . . . if I helped you capture . . . Milton

Fauster . . . and deliver you . . . loads of corrupted . . . easily manipulated souls . . . you would make me . . . make me . . ."

Principal Bubb screwed up her seriously screwed up face.

"Well . . . you didn't *exactly* deliver Milton Fauster to me, nor did you—"

"I had to dress up like a girl to find out about the Grabbit's plan in Rapacia, and I nearly pierced Milton's heart with a scepter; then I helped flush him out of Blimpo when his dumb ferret died. . . . I took over a death cult up on the Surface and got new recruits. . . . I tried to make Heck sound cool by getting a book published; then it turned into a really popular video game. . . ."

"So what do you want?" the principal hissed.

"What I want most is for . . . everyone else to be . . . miserable," Damian managed. "But I suppose I would be . . . satisfied with my own . . . my own . . . Circle. . . ."

Damian's pained voice drowned in a pool of pus and self-pity. The hermit-crab demon tapped on the door with its claws.

"Yes?!" the principal snapped like an arthritic twig.

"Um . . . *Heck-o* . . . Madam Principal, ma'am," it replied in a soft, unassuming wheeze.

"WHAT DO YOU WANT?!"

The creature skittered back in alarm. "I . . . it's . . . you see, time for . . . the War of the Words."

The principal sighed. She snatched her sneezing baby panda–skin clutch bag.

"All right, Mr. Ruffino," the principal said as she clacked out of her Not-So-Secret Lair. "Speaking of words, I am a demonness of mine. As good as my word, I mean to say," she said, crossing her talons behind the small—or least-large—of her back. "So we have a deal. Shake?"

Principal Bubb offered her claw. Damian moved to extend his arm but pulled it back just before contact, instead smoothing down his hair.

Bea "Elsa" Bubb rolled her eyes.

Once a reprehensible jerk, always *a reprehensible jerk. At least the boy's consistent . . .*

"We'll talk later and sort out the details," Principal Bubb continued. "I'll have a team of plastic surgeons—we have so many down here—try to put you back together again, Humpty Dumpty. I could never understand that rhyme. Why someone would employ a king's horses to perform delicate surgery, on a large sentient egg, no less, is beyond me. . . ."

A bad feeling started hatching among the nest of bad feelings already occupying the principal's loathsome body.

"Now I must have a word with some mutual *fiends* of ours," Principal Bubb said before pausing for a full-body flesh crawl, "Milton Fauster and his impertinent sister . . . the *last* word, if I have anything to say about it."

"Tell them . . . hi," Damian gurgled with utter contempt from the doorway. He attempted a smile, exposing a mouthful of jagged yellow teeth. "From their ol' . . . pal . . ."

Damian hobbled away from the principal's lair, escorted by the crab demon, for rehabilitation. Soon he'd have no one to answer to, he reflected. And *he'd* be the one giving all the orders. . . .

29 · LiKE A TONGUE
OF BRiCKS

A TALL, IMPERIOUS brute of a man loomed over Milton and Marlo as they regained consciousness, stroking his long, plaited beard. Milton recognized the man from the assembly back in Wise Acres.

The man grabbed Milton and Marlo by the wrists and tugged them to their feet. Standing behind him were Vice Principal Carroll, Miss Parker, Mr. Wilde, and Mr. Dickens, along with the surviving Spite Club members. The two teams looked wasted and pale, like a police lineup of haggard ghosts.

Milton noticed that the walls surrounding them were made from some odd, thin leaded glass. So was the floor. And the ceiling. Milton could see people all around him: slightly warped figures walking above, beside, and below. He knelt down and touched the floor. It was solid beneath his hand but trembling like a stereo speaker blasting music on full volume. But Milton couldn't hear anything beyond a persistent, muffled yammering.

"This is the Tower of Babble?" Milton asked incredulously. "A building held together with sound?"

"Not just sound," the regal man boasted. "But an endless, burbling stream of bickering, squabbling, and contention! Now I command you to accompany me on a tour!"

Marlo folded her arms in defiance. "Who died and made *you* king?" she replied.

The arrogant man folded his arms as well, resulting in a folded arms race. "That would have been my father," the man said. "But *I'm* king now. King Nimrod: Tyrannical Ruler, Master Architect, and Certified Notary Public."

Milton tested the floor with his foot. It felt like walking across a taut, transparent-plastic trampoline. A little demon waddled forward. It was basically a large, unblinking red eye—almost cute—with tiny, rounded arm and leg stubs, a potbelly, and two black, cablelike ears snaking out from the top of its head.

"It's one of those eyeball things!" Marlo exclaimed as the short, two-foot-tall creature gazed upon her, registering her every move.

"Yeah," Milton murmured. "I thought I saw one, too."

Vice Principal Carroll stepped from behind King Nimrod.

"One of m-many Orb-Servers we had recruited especially for the event," the vice principal explained as another unblinking demon waddled into the room and bumped clumsily into its counterpart. "An eye-*witless* news team. Unflinchingly capturing your every move."

The pair of demons stared unnervingly at Milton, like a giant's bloodshot eyes.

"So that's how you were able to report on us?" Milton asked. "To give a running commentary on everything that was happening?"

"I wasn't making comments," Vice Principal Carroll said, smiling, though his eyes still had a strangely troubled cast about them. "I was making *content*! I was telling the story into existence just as it happened! The Orb-Servers merely broadcast your reactions to me so I could incorporate them into the tale: in real time."

Milton's mind was like an over-inflated balloon: *totally blown.*

"But that's impossible. . . ."

"Why, sometimes I've believed as many as six impossible things before breakfast!" the vice principal replied. "See, Mr. Fauster, the Outer Terristories were awash in a specific tone that made you all highly suggestible. I fed this state with a story to guide you, while you all filled in the details. And—between your clever performances and my vivid narration—the radio audience was rapt!"

Marlo's skin prickled purple with rage. "So all of that—all those horrible *grammonsters* we faced . . . all of those nerdy-wordy puzzles . . . all those kids who turned into piles of letters—was just some story?!"

Three tall, skinny demons filed into the humming room. They wore bright yellow jumpers and pink eraser top hats, and had—Milton realized with a gulp—rusted zippers for mouths. Each brandished a long, red wand that matched its beady red eyes.

"N-now, don't be upset, Miss Fauster," the vice principal said as he sat down on a large, weathered steamer trunk in the corner, primly crossing his fidgeting legs. "Your ratings were through the roof! You, in particular, received nearly a gajillion votes! The most of any—"

"A *gajillion*?" Milton puzzled. "That's not even a real—"

"It's that attitude that's costing you votes, Mr. Fauster," Vice Principal Carroll replied. "Try to loosen up a bit."

Marlo smirked. "Wow . . . a whole *gajillion*!"

As Marlo scanned the faces of her fellow team members, she was suddenly struck by their diminished ranks. A lump formed in her throat.

"The rest of my team . . . are they, you know . . . ?" she managed.

"Come," Vice Principal Carroll said as he straightened his white bow tie. "I'll explain m-most everything as we make our way downstairs . . . many, many stairs. Flight after flight of fancy!"

The children and teachers traveled along a coiling, moving sidewalk of pure sound. It was like being conveyed down a frozen river traveling in sluggish spirals inside of an ice palace. The Tower of Babble was as exquisite as it was unlikely. Milton saw distorted figures scurrying to and fro like a colony of ants.

Lewis Carroll gazed past the blurry figures and shadows around him into some private world. "The Outer Terristories was to show you . . . *to show everyone* . . . the destructive power of words," the odd, pasty-faced man mumbled. "A labyrinth of language that we jointly created as you went along. I seeded the landscape with mechanicrickets to create the tone and Retuning Forks to collect and focus the vibrations to create a mass hallucination, with my story feeding every moment."

"So none of it was even real?" Cookie said with her jaw dropped open like a freshly caught fish.

Vice Principal Carroll's face—thin, tense lips fidgeting, as if the man were constantly telling a story to himself—twitched with uncertainty.

"Contrariwise, if it was so, it might be, and if it were so, it would be, but as it isn't, it ain't. That's logic."

"That's *insanity,*" Marlo countered. "Plus you didn't answer my question. About the others."

The vice principal seemed to stiffen at the utterance of the word "insanity," like some sea creature that had washed up on the shore and was prodded with a stick.

"You w-were all dreaming, in a w-way," he stammered. "Imagine that, everyone dreaming everyone, at the same time, the s-same dream! Such p-power! Such f-force!"

Vice Principal Carroll shrugged and smiled.

"The others. The stricken striplings stripped of all embellishment. Their demise, I suppose, depends upon how deeply they believed they would be undone," he said matter-of-factly. "I honestly haven't a clue!"

Annabelle gasped. "Flossie's leg! It's coming back!"

Flossie looked down at her leg. The words were indeed fading.

"It's sort of prickly," the girl said with cautious delight. "And like it's filling up inside."

"With what?" Marlo asked.

Flossie shrugged. "Leg stuff."

Mack Hoover extended his hand. "Me too!" he exclaimed, stretching out his half-hand/half-really-boring-poem.

"Your hand is filled with leg stuff?" Mordacia asked.

"No, my hand! It's coming back!" Mack said.

The memory of the events leading to the whiteout slowly uncrumpled in Milton's mind, like something written on binder paper that had been balled up and thrown in the wastebasket.

"What about Mr. Basye?" he asked. "I remember him and the snark slamming into the Tower of Babble. Why did everything go all white?"

Vice Principal Carroll grew twitchier than usual. "Mr. Basye expired in a run-on death sentence," the man replied evasively. "It was as if he thought that all of this was in his mind . . . as if *he* was the storyteller, not I. And when he disappeared, so did everything—briefly—in the immediate vicinity. Luckily I was able to salvage my prized Weisen hammer—"

That weird hammer, Marlo thought. *The one I read about in the Absurditory . . .*

"But what was once all white is now perfectly *all right.*"

Vice Principal Carroll clapped his hands and glanced down the shimmering corridor of sound. "But enough of my achievements. Please, King Nimrod. Captivate us with the particulars of *your* greatest achievement!"

King Nimrod grew taller in his emerald-festooned cloak and crimson robe embroidered with gold, as if his flattered vanity had added a few extra columns of vertebrae to his haughty spine.

"It would be my pleasure," the man purred. "The Tower of Babble"—King Nimrod extended his muscled arms outward grandly—"is quite simply the greatest building ever constructed. . . ."

"Brag much?" Marlo whispered to Flossie.

"My attempt to build the greatest city while alive—Babel—didn't go so well, as you may have heard. It all started back with Noah."

"Noah?" Milton replied, remembering the kindly, ancient man he had met in the Furafter. "How could *he* have anything to do with this?"

King Nimrod's hands balled into fists. "The Big Guy Upstairs told Noah to help spread mankind out—horizontally—and fill up the earth. I got it into my brilliant mind that our Creator was intimidated by human possibility or—more specifically, *my* possibility. So I built my throne *upward*. I, King Nimrod, would have a throne to rival the mightiest God in heaven! If the Big Guy Upstairs were to send down another flood, my subjects and I would be safe above the waters."

"How did *that* work out for you, Nimrod?" Miss Parker asked with a wink to Mr. Wilde.

"*King* Nimrod!" he roared before taking a quick breath to regain his composure. "But yes, *ma'am*, my first tower was undermined by Him Truly, after he sent his angels down to confuse the tongues of my construction crew so that one could not understand the language of another. . . ."

The eyes of the king glittered with his own perceived glory.

"It was then I vowed to use language against the Almighty Himself! Unlike brick and mortar, quarreling, squabbling . . . these are *endlessly* renewable resources! See for yourself."

The king gestured to a servant—a lovely, dark-haired woman. She knelt before what looked like an ear embedded in the wall and whispered into it.

"What's she doing?" Cookie asked.

"She's spreading discord," King Nimrod replied. "Like a bee spreading pollen from flower to flower, my servants here pollinate each of our millions of mouthpieces."

"Mouthpieces?" Mack replied. "But those are ears."

"Yes, and those are connected to jabbering mouths on the outside of the tower, each with its own sharp, waggling tongue arguing ceaselessly in its own unique language. By whispering antagonistic remarks into the earpieces, we maintain the argument that keeps this place standing."

King Nimrod gazed with white-hot pride at his handiwork.

"I've constructed the tallest structure ever conceived, one that pierces the very fabric of heaven!"

"H-Heaven!" Milton sputtered.

"Yes, the tip of the center steeple," King Nimrod said, grinning behind his thick plaited beard, "the uppermost spire of my throne tower—just below the Tomiary—crosses the lower reaches of Cloud One by exactly one centimeter. So, technically, the Tower of Babble reaches Heaven!"

Milton shook his head in disbelief. King Nimrod was like a spoiled child marveling at his stack of blocks, thinking that he could attain Heaven by physically touching it, rather than receiving it as a reward for a virtuous life. He looked up. The smudgy orange-purple sky of Wise Acres seeped into the tower through the smeary, sonic walls.

Somewhere up there is Heaven, Milton thought as he and the others were scooted along the humming corridor of sound. *Where either Marlo or I could actually end up, depending on who wins . . .*

30 · FOR THE SAKE
OF ARGUMENT

THE MOVING SIDEWALK brought the group slowly closer to
a throbbing pulse of noise coming from below. It was a
booming blend of music and the commotion of a thousand conversations.

"We're here," King Nimrod said as he strode forward.

The sonic sidewalk deposited them at the mouth of a
spacious concourse, alive with noise and activity. It was
like a great, glittering ice chamber, carved from arctic
arguments, supported by glittering beams of sound.

Music poured forth from speakers set upon a tremendous ring, like the kind used for boxing and wrestling. An electric banner reading THE WAR OF THE
WORDS was attached to a long, slender beam above a

huge metal gong. Dancers, dressed as letters of the alphabet, gyrated and high-kicked on the ring to the thumping music.

Surrounding the ring were throngs of people, chattering blithely beneath huge billboard-sized viewing screens. On each was a grid split into twenty-six boxes.

"That's . . . *us!*" Marlo gasped.

Every Spite Club member's face occupied one of the boxes, with those lost in the Outer Terristories dimmed, to show that they were no longer in competition. Beneath each face was a rolling ticker of numbers.

Of votes, Milton thought, judging from the long stream of restless numbers. The top half was devoted to Team One, with Milton in the upper left-hand corner. The bottom had Team Two, with Marlo up front. Her box seemed brighter than the rest, her numbers slightly higher than Milton's.

With its shimmering shapes and cat's cradle of sonic spires, this place—at the convergence of the three towers that gave the Tower of Babble its trident shape—was a perfect example of geometric precision. *It looks like a crystal palace,* Milton thought, *which makes sense, since crystals adhere to the rigid rules of mathematics, as do sound waves.*

Two podiums stood at either side of the ring: stark, black, and somehow foreboding. The ring itself looked like the scene of a crime that had yet to be committed. A sophisticated network of lights, cables, and sound equipment was suspended from scaffolding above. Dozens of Vice Principal Carroll's bumbling, red-eyed Orb-Servers milled along the periphery, capturing the event from a variety of angles.

The dancers reorganized themselves until they spelled out a name. The unfortunate dancer dressed as an "O" had to do double duty, running around the name in circles to the beat.

"You've *got* to be kidding me," Milton said.

VAN GLORIOUS

Applause broke out like a raging epidemic of noise. Onto the stage stalked a tall, gangly young man with long blond hair, expensive sunglasses, pouty lips, and stubble that never seemed to quite become a beard.

"Van Glorious!" Cookie gushed, thoroughly smitten. "Action hero, rapper, clothing line, cologne . . ."

"Pain in the butt," Milton added.

Marlo nudged her brother with her pointy elbow. "Hey, the guy helped us in the Furafter, right?" she said. "Helped us prevent a religious ratings war up on the Surface."

"Right, but *you* didn't have to put up with him," Milton replied. "He has an ego like an especially needy black hole."

A loud, thumping rap beat boomed as Van postured on the stage, singing into his headset.

"We've got a War of the Words. We've got a War of
      the Words.
Kids pecking at each other like a flock of birds.
We've got a War of the Words. We've got a War of
      the Words.
Keepin' arguments fresh: not shakin', not slurred.

Here's Team One.
Their diction is great.
Have you heard these kids? They can enunciate!

Milton's got brains.
Moses? Well versed.
Roberta's gotta tongue that she can put in reverse.

Rakeem has got esteem.
Mordacia, she can shout.
That Moxie girl? She kinda freaks me out. . . ."

One of the Orb-Servers waddled up to Moxie for
a reaction shot. The girl clicked her silver tongue and
struggled to free herself from her straightjacket while
Van climbed up on the scaffolding.

"Do you like sass?
Then here's Team Two.
That Marlo's got sauce: should we share a fondue?"

Marlo smiled as the handsome star blew her a kiss. A pair of laser lips alighted from Van's face, darted across the audience, and fluttered onto Marlo's lips. Milton shook his head.

"That was meant for me, you know," Milton said, recalling the time he and his sister had switched bodies, and Milton had ended up as Van's unofficial assistant/attendant during his blockbuster run as Teenage Jesus.

"That Flossie is shrewd.
Big Mack can dismay.
Wanna synonym, boy? Then your man is Roget!

They got a tough cookie.
And that Cookie can spell.
No one's better with the letters than that girl
    Annabelle.

But now I gotta go.
We're runnin' out of time.
Didya know that some words you just can't rhyme?
Like orange."

The music stopped abruptly and the stage went dark. The crowd shrieked and applauded. Rakeem shook his head.

"Vanilla's mic is rusty," he grumbled. "I've heard better rhymes in Dr. Seuss's waiting room."

King Nimrod and Vice Principal Carroll walked through the crowd and were helped into the ring. The king outstretched his massive arms.

"Welcome to the Tower of Babble!" he boomed. "I am honored to be this event's magnanimously magnificent host, in this bustling bastion of language!"

Vice Principal Carroll leaned into the microphone of the other podium. "Thank you, good K-King Nimrod!" the vice principal said with his soft, clumsy voice. "Before we continue, I'd like to explain our little whiteout. That was not, as the rumors persist, a technical difficulty. It was, instead, an ingeniously inventive advertisement from one of our sponsors, Pearly White Toothpaste: Go From Yellow to *Hello*! For a Rapturous Smile, Open the Gates of Your Mouth Wide with Pearly White!"

Milton turned to Marlo. "Didn't Vice Principal Carroll say that the snark smacking the tower only affected things in the immediate vicinity?"

Marlo shrugged. "Search me . . . actually, don't, or I'll punch you in the throat."

A pair of the king's heavily muscled guards pitched the children one by one up into the ring. The vice principal cleared his throat and stared down at a small stack of index cards.

"As we've heard with our valiant contenders today," Vice Principal Carroll said, "language itself can indeed b-bite back. In fact, there were many moments when I feared our contentious crew had lost its way. Yet, if you don't know where you are going, any road will get you there. And so here they are!"

He extended his arms toward the children hovering by the ropes, kindling a blazing roar from the audience.

"And now, ladies, gentlemen, lovely muses . . ."

Vice Principal Carroll nodded to the left side of the auditorium where nine breathtakingly gorgeous women wearing flowing white gowns were lounging on luxurious fainting couches. One woman, Milton noticed, seemed to be stroking a white fuzzy animal.

"Lucky?" Milton muttered. "No, it can't—"

". . . angels, demons, and everything in between," the vice principal continued. "In the beginning was the Word, and the Word was"—Vice Principal Carroll dropped his index card—"whoops!"

Milton swallowed as the man bent over to retrieve his fallen card.

"Remember that early draft of the Bible we found in the back of Wise Acres?" he muttered to his sister. "And all that Bibley stuff you found in his Absurditory? About the true name of God being the way . . ."

Yahweh.

"Yahweh," Milton mumbled, pulling out one of the index cards he had in his pocket. "It says *hewhaY,* which is 'Yahweh' backward. That's it."

"That's what?" Marlo asked.

"The original Hebrew name of God used in the Bible," Milton answered. *"Yahweh."*

"No way."

"*Yes* way!" Milton said. "But how would just saying it change reality at all?"

Marlo stared at Milton with her wide violet eyes.

"What if he really did it? What if that crackpot cracked the code of all Creation?"

Milton studied the eccentric man behind the podium, grinning mysteriously, like a cat that just lapped up the last of the cream. The vice principal seemed to disappear behind his Cheshire grin.

"Then the Terristories wasn't just a show . . . it was to *show* what he could do!" Milton said as Vice Principal Carroll leaned into his microphone.

"I bring you the second act of our three-act play on words . . . *The War of the Words!*"

31 · DEBATE FOR DE-TRAP

THE CROWD OF deceased all-too mortals, demons, and various angelic beings roared. Their bulging eyes glittered like stars in the inky blackness surrounding the spotlit ring. They waved signs over their cheering and jeering heads, such as USE YOUR OUTSIDE VOICES! DISH OUT THE BEEFS and CHILDREN SHOULD SEETHE AND BE HEARD!

An old man sat by the side of the ring at a table set with more rusty old microphones than a rusty old microphone showroom.

"I'm Howard Cosell," said the man in a staccato, nasal tone, his salt-and-pepper hair seemingly molded directly to his head. "And welcome to the *maim* event: where whip-smart whippersnappers will butt heads and lash tongues to see who is the king of sting, the queen of mean, and the undisputed ruler of refutation."

Milton, Marlo, and the other children were backstage,

being dressed and groomed before they headed out to lock horns and wage verbal war with one another. A bald, round man in a bright pink leisure suit—Mr. Dior, on loan from his uglification and school-picture-taking duties in Limbo—fussed over the boys and girls, smoothing their hair, going a little nutso with the gel, and fitting them with padded, tailored black suits.

"What's with all of the padding?" Cookie complained as she examined herself in the mirror, sashaying back and forth. "What is this, the eighties?"

"Eet is your No-Flak Suit," the man said elegantly in his smooth French accent. "To help minimize zhe damage from zhe flak you will be hurling at zhe one and other."

Milton spent several minutes wrestling with his purple tie before realizing that it was a clip-on. He buckled his belt and marveled at the crease in his pants. A shriveled, shrewlike demon went about the dressing room, picking the children's doffed clothes off the ground (and picking through the pockets, Milton noted, helping itself to spare change, gum, lip balm, and the occasional scrunchie).

Those index cards, Milton thought as he grabbed his torn tweed pants from the floor just before the demon servant swept them away. He yanked out the cards and stared at the pictogram.

Two dogs facing each other, Milton thought. *That doesn't make any sense. The word "Stand" over an eye . . .*

Stand-Top-Eye? That's stupid. I just don't under— That's it! "Eye under stand." I understand! And the weird word . . . hey, that's the word backwards *only backwards! And "word" written four times. Four words. Forwards!*

" '*I understand, backwards and forwards,*' " Milton said aloud as Marlo looked over his shoulder, munching on a bonbon mot. "That's what the note says. I just don't get the two dogs."

"They're the same dog, only one is in reverse," Marlo offered, glancing up nervously at the monitor. "So dog and . . . *God*?"

"No . . . God's true name—*Yahweh,* remember?"

Marlo tapped her foot nervously on the green carpet. "I should have paid more attention in Sunday school. . . ."

"Or gone in the first place . . ."

"So this is about what I saw in the Absurditory, you think? About Creation being password protected with God's true name?"

Milton shrugged. He scratched his itchy, overgelled hair. "Yes . . . I think. I'm not sure. Maybe it has to be spoken both forward and backward to unlock Creation. That could be why my card had it written backwards."

Marlo shook her head dubiously. "I don't buy it. It doesn't make any sense. . . ."

Applause drifted into the dressing room from the auditorium. The nervous children looked up warily at the monitor on the wall.

Howard Cosell leaned into his microphone. "Coming

to you from the too-beautiful-to-believe Tower of Babble, a sonic temple where sound arguments spar until one is rendered senseless. It's time for our very first bout."

The announcer squinted down at the card in his hand.

"*Mordacia Caustilo and Cookie Youngblood . . . and, for Miss Youngblood's sake, I hope Mordacia's tongue isn't a cookie cutter!*"

Mordacia and Cookie shuddered in their chairs. Cookie's face, in particular, contorted into a rictus of nervous dread. Miss Parker gave Cookie a quick hug as a trio of long-legged, impossibly perfect supermodels opened the door.

"Faith, Hope, and Charity?" Marlo murmured. "Wow . . . as if we couldn't feel any worse walking out there, now we have to do it alongside three supermodels whose combined dress sizes add up to zero!"

Faith, Hope, and Charity were dressed in matching one-piece satin bathing suits, purple fishnet stockings, and boots, with thick librarian glasses perched atop their perfect noses.

"You'll be fine, dear," Miss Parker whispered to Cookie. "Oh . . . here." She pulled out a tiny pencil sharpener. "Now stick your tongue out."

Cookie grudgingly obeyed and Miss Parker gave the tip of the girl's tongue a few quick turns.

"There! Nice and sharp!" Miss Parker said.

"You're on," Charity said, radiating sympathy with her dark, generous eyes.

The supermodels urged Cookie and Mordacia out of the dressing room and out toward the stage.

"She's large and in charge!" Howard Cosell announced. "She's Mordacia Caustilo, from the Principality of Andorra, the sixth smallest nation in Europe! But don't let her country's size fool you . . . Mordacia's got one big mouth on her! Cause of death? Irony alert: Mordacia died at a birthday party after a deadly game of Twister. Give it up for Mordacia Caustilo!"

The audience broke out into fresh peals of applause as they stepped into the ring. Up on the display grid, numbers exploded like popcorn in a microwave beneath Cookie's and Mordacia's pictures as the viewers at home cast their votes.

"And, facing Miss Caustilo is Cookie Youngblood!" the announcer continued. "Cookie was an army brat born in Oklahoma, where the only thing drier than the climate is the population's sense of humor. Cookie got her name from her late mother, who wanted her daughter to be 'one tough cookie.'"

Faith, Hope, and Charity steered Cookie and Mordacia to their podiums. The supermodels knelt daintily to the floor, picking up large ROUND ONE placards, then strutted the perimeter of the ring holding them high above their heads as the audience hooted and hollered.

"How did Cookie expire? She was trapped in a

malfunctioning photo booth and 'flashed' to death. Let's hear it for Cookie Youngblood!"

Two hulking demons—thick, heavily muscled creatures with bald heads screwed tight between their broad shoulders—climbed into the ring, wearing tight, gleaming, silver bodysuits. They stalked toward Cookie and Mordacia, each crouching beside a podium before zipping their suits completely over their contorted, seething faces. The suits crawled with clouds of silvery static before settling into the digital likenesses of two girls: Cookie and Mordacia.

"What's with these guys?" Cookie asked as the demon crouching beside her glared back at Cookie with her own accusing face.

"Your Alter-Cater," the announcer replied, his sharp Brooklyn accent slashing like a razor. "To add more punch to your points. And now your topic: *Beauty Contests.*"

"*Beauty contests?!* Are you *kidding* me?!" Cookie and Mordacia gasped, the first and last time they would ever agree on anything.

"Miss Youngblood, you'll be 'Pro' while Miss Caustilo, you'll be taking the 'Con' position," the announcer explained. "Now go!"

Cookie gripped the side of the podium and scrunched up her eyes, hoping to summon her first argument. After collecting her thoughts, she leaned into the microphone.

"People like watching beautiful people," Cookie

explained. "And a lot of girls really enjoy being in beauty contests or they wouldn't. *Be in them,* that is. Nobody is forcing them. Beauty is like art, so a beauty contest is . . . like a big art show. Right?"

Cookie's Alter-Cater rushed across the ring at its counterpart, grabbing it by the face with its massive hand. The crowd applauded as Cookie's numbers ticked up on the massive display screen.

Mordacia's head seemed to sink into her shoulders. She drew in a deep breath.

"Beauty contests promote an ideal of female beauty that hardly *any* girl can attain," she declared, "which creates tremendous pressure, making girls go on crash diets, get plastic surgery, or simply feel gross about themselves."

Mordacia's Alter-Cater broke free from its attacker's face-grip.

"Women in beauty contests are judged strictly by their looks," Mordacia continued, finding her rhythm. "I know, I know: *the talent competition.* But c'mon: no one ugly ever wins no matter how high they twirl their baton or whatever. Men don't have *handsome* pageants. It's demeaning."

Mordacia's Alter-Cater shoved its opponent across the ring where it hit the corner post with a massive clang. The audience applauded. Cookie squared her jaw as Mordacia's votes surpassed hers on the screen.

"Men are judged by their physical prowess all the

time," Cookie said, pursing her lip-glossed lips. "It's called *sports*."

The crowd giggled at her remark, earning her more votes. Cookie's Alter-Cater threw itself backward against its opponent, seizing Mordacia's Alter-Cater by the face with its muscled butt cheeks.

"*Oooh* . . . a Bavarian Butt-Clench!" Howard Cosell commented. "That's gotta hurt!"

Cookie sneered as she watched her argument gain the upper cheek.

"And just like some guy can get a prize for having muscles, why not a woman for her grace and style?" Cookie added.

Mordacia barreled through Cookie's applause.

"By reinforcing beauty over brains, beauty pageants ensure that women will never be taken seriously!"

Mordacia's Alter-Cater broke free and pounded its opponent in the back of the neck with its fists laced together.

"You can't be serious! Beauty contests give women a chance to be noticed. Lots of famous actresses got their starts that way . . . and the winners help publicize charities and other things they care about it," Cookie responded. "Besides, *you're just jealous*."

Cookie's Alter-Cater hoisted its opponent up into the air, then slammed it soundly to the ground.

A buzzer sounded.

"Thank you, ladies," Howard Cosell said. "Your time

is up. And—judging from the votes—it seems that *your* time, Miss Caustilo, is *extra* up!"

Mordacia's votes tallied up to nearly 19 million, while Cookie's hovered at roughly 200 million.

Faith, Hope, and Charity escorted the girls backstage to the sound of catcalls and applause.

Mordacia fought back tears as she fell into her leather chair. Cookie swaggered past her and snatched a bottled water from an ice bucket.

"Hey, nice job, Cookie," Marlo said.

Cookie swiveled on the heels of her shiny black shoes. "Yeah, it was. You'd better not screw it up."

The crowd cheered as the Alter-Caters crouched beside the podiums. Their suits crawled with silver static.

"And now for our next bout," Howard Cosell called out from his ringside table. "Moses Babcock versus Flossie Blackwell! Moses, I supposes, hailed from Nyack, New York, where he held the record for Cause of Most Teacher Nervous Breakdowns. Mr. Babcock has a rare *Peanuts* allergy and was critically injured after exposure to an *A Charlie Brown Christmas* marathon. Let's give a lukewarm War of the Words welcome to Moses Babcock!"

The crowd cheered and jeered. Milton turned to Moses as he straightened his purple tie.

"Good—" Milton managed before Moses stormed off, parting the red curtains as he made his way to the stage.

"—luck."

Marlo grabbed Flossie's hand. "You'll be great," Marlo said with a nervous smile. "Hey, and your leg is almost all better."

Flossie nodded. "Mr. Dior was able to cover a lot of the letters up with shoe polish. Well . . . here goes nothing . . ."

Flossie walked down the red-carpeted path to the ring.

"The only thing more flamboyant than Miss Blackwell's fire-engine red hair is her five-alarm fault-finding," Howard Cosell declared. "Hailing from Ottawa, Canada, Miss Blackwell is a true nitpicker's nitpicker. Her father writes IKEA instruction manuals and her mother is a fact-checker for *Sophistic's Choice* magazine. Miss Blackwell died of a chronic tongue cramp after launching a filibuster in her school cafeteria, protesting the vague accounting of ingredients in the Meatloaf Surprise. Put your hands together for Flossie Blackwell!"

The Alter-Caters pressed a button on their silver belt buckles. Suddenly, the raging static resolved into crisp, full-body images of Moses and Flossie.

"Okay, then, kiddos. Here's your topic: *Is there a Santa Claus?* Miss Blackwell, you're 'Pro.' Mr. Babcock, you take the 'Con' position."

Flossie swallowed. Backstage, Marlo crossed her fingers so hard that her middle and index fingers practically switched knuckles.

"Simply put, there *is* a Santa Claus," Flossie said with an open, toothy smile. "I mean, millions of children worldwide wake up on Christmas morning and—boom—toys and candy. And no one *else* takes the credit for all of that generosity, and surely they would, right? Plus, the proof is in the cookies: little bites taken out . . . milk half drunk. C'mon. The evidence is irrefutable."

Flossie's Alter-Cater stomped out confidently to the center of the ring, extending its hand to its opponent. Moses shook his head, a smug smirk taking residence above his chin.

"Flossie, you are deluded—as were your parents when they named you . . ."

The remark earned wicked laughter from the demon portion of the audience, resulting in an upsurge of votes. Moses's Alter-Cater clopped its opponent on the side of the head.

"To begin with, look at the physics," Moses asserted. "No one can fly around the world, visiting every child: *in one night*. How can a sleigh even *fly*? How can Santa get into apartments that don't have chimneys? How would he even fit through the largest chimney, for that matter? Plus *no one* ever sees him delivering presents. Even Big Foot and the Loch Ness monster had grainy pictures taken of them."

Moses's Alter-Cater seized its opponent by the thighs, lifted it up into the air, and threw it—hard—down on the canvas. A profound silence followed as votes came pouring in for Moses.

After her tongue went for a quick swirl in her dry mouth, Flossie retorted. "I submit, as evidence, a newspaper item, published in the *New York Sun* in 1897, stating in no uncertain terms that—and I quote from memory—'Yes, Virginia, there *is* a Santa Claus. He exists as certainly as love and generosity and devotion exist, and you know that they abound and give to your life its highest beauty and joy.' *End quote*."

Flossie's Alter-Cater flipped back up to its feet and charged its opponent, its head slamming into the other Alter-Cater's stomach. Moses shot Flossie a look so dirty that the girl wanted to rub hand sanitizer all over her face.

"Okay, then how about this," Moses countered. "*Santa discriminates on the basis of income.* How come all the rich kids get the best presents while the poor kids barely get anything? Plus, parents use him like some kind of bully, forcing their kids to be good in exchange for the prospect of gifts."

Moses's Alter-Cater fell to the mat and swung its legs fiercely beneath those of its opponent. Flossie's Alter-Cater, however, simply leapt into the air to avoid the kick.

"I was under the impression that this debate was about the existence of Santa Claus, not a judgment of his character," Flossie replied. "Santa Claus, also doing business as Father Christmas, is a popular, enduring symbol of generosity and helping those in need, beloved by billions all over the world!"

Flossie's Alter-Cater threw itself back against the ropes and sprang at its opponent, knocking it to the ground.

"This popularity is driven by multinational companies, eager to create new markets for their toys as potential gifts!" Moses spat back. "It's globalization, not goodwill. Plus there's something kinda creepy about an old guy breaking into your house once a year."

The Alter-Cater hopped out of the ring and grabbed a fold-up chair. It crept through the ropes and snuck behind Flossie's Alter-Cater as it bowed to the audience.

"As you said yourself, Moses: Santa Claus is good for the economy," Flossie replied with a nervous grin. "From gifts to decorations, holiday food, cards, and wrapping paper, there are millions of hard-working people who depend on the belief in Santa Claus."

Moses's Alter-Cater held the chair over its head and rushed at its opponent from behind.

"But it's a sham!" Moses shrieked, losing his cool. "We shouldn't be outsourcing our generosity. We should be giving for giving's sake!"

Flossie's Alter-Cater dodged its opponent's blow, with the bulky demon falling facedown on the mat. The buzzer sounded as Moses was soundly beaten. The crowd cheered. Flossie's fans ecstatically waved NOTHING

IS COMING UP MOSES and FLOSSIE'S POSSE! signs as the children were escorted from the stage.

"Next, we have Round Three: Rakeem Yashimoto versus Roget Marx Peters," Howard Cosell announced in his insistent voice, like some obnoxious, nap-deprived toddler poking you in the ear. "Born in Yemen, Rakeem Yashimoto was something of a nomad, having moved so much due to his parents' careers. His father is the editor of *Calligraphy Today*—the only magazine where every issue is written by hand—and his mother is MC Soo Shimi, Japan's Number *Ichi* rap star. So, between a writer and a rapper, Rakeem's got some *serious* linguistic chops. . . ."

Backstage, Milton and Marlo stared desperately at the monitor as Rakeem and Roget sulked to the stage.

"This is all just a distraction . . . I know it. We just have to figure out what the vice principal is trying to distract everybody *from*."

Vice Principal Carroll walked into the backstage waiting room, dressed in Victorian finery, from the tips of his shiny black leather boots to the top of his enormous velvet, red-and-gold top hat. He smiled mysteriously as he chatted with the children who were staring at themselves in the dressing room mirror with wide-eyed dread.

"Speak of the demented," Marlo muttered.

Milton watched as the vice principal slowly approached. Behind him, the eccentric man pulled a large silver hammer—the same hammer that had been lashed to the snark—in a little red wagon.

"The guy is a few Bradys short of a bunch," Marlo said.

In the ring, Rakeem and Roget debated the topic of curfews for children.

"See, youth crime is starting to climb," Rakeem said, his braces flashing like tiny switchblades in his mouth. "Got kids makin' trouble—soon they're doin' time."

Roget gripped the sides of his podium and shook his head, peering sharply back at Rakeem.

"I strongly disagree, take issue with, challenge, and oppose curfews for children. Curfews don't reduce crime, as most juvenile law-breaking, delinquency, and wrongdoing takes place right after school."

Vice Principal Carroll walked up to the Fausters and gave a gentle tip of his tall, flamboyant hat.

"What's with the hammer?" Marlo asked, pushing out her lower lip.

"Just a few details to hammer out for the big finale," Vice Principal Carroll said as he stared at the monitor on the wall.

The two Alter-Caters circled one another in the ring.

"What is often considered crime today was considered normal, customary, ordinary, and conventional in the past," Roget declared. "Like playing in the streets and wandering around the neighborhood. We need to be wary, cautious, careful, and circumspect, drawing the line between actual crime and the things we just don't like."

Roget's Alter-Cater lunged at its opponent. Rakeem's burly demon doppelgänger dodged the attack.

"You got kids on the streets, bumpin' out to the beats, gangs are hangin' then they're bangin' and there ain't no peace," Rakeem maintained. "Curfews keep 'em out of trouble, solve crime on the double, and if you disagree, you must be livin' in a bubble!"

Rakeem's Alter-Cater seized Roget's in a deadly headlock. The audience applauded. Rakeem's vote tally shot well past that of his challenger. Faith, Hope, and Charity escorted the two children out of the ring.

"It's like a f-fairy tale, isn't it?" the vice principal murmured with a far-off gaze. "A fairy tale full of monsters, conflict, and children who must *Grimm* and bear it to survive."

Milton noticed words embroidered on the back of the vice principal's fancy hat.

MAD HATTER SLAPDASH HABERDASHERIES (UN)LTD.

I still think he's keeping something under his hat, Milton thought with a sense of dark, foreboding curiosity as applause spilled in from the ring. *And I wouldn't be surprised if he pulled a rabbit out of it. A big white rabbit . . .*

32 · MEETING THEIR MATCHES

"SHE'S MALIGNANT, INDIGNANT, and strapped tight to equipment . . . it's Moxie Wortschmerz!"

The crowd roared at the furious, quivering little girl lashed to a dolly.

"Your topic, boy and gargoyle, is 'Are Video Games Too Violent?'" Howard Cosell announced. "Mr. Hoover, you'll be taking the Pro 'yes, they are bad' stance while you, Miss Worcestershire Sauce, will be arguing against."

Mack Hoover took a confident swig of water, swished it around in his mouth, and set the bottle back on the podium with a mighty thump.

"Are video games too violent?" he asked as his Alter-Cater swaggered to the center of the ring. "If we have to ask, the answer is a resounding *yes*. There is tons of research proving that video games damage young minds and cause aggression. And as the games become more realistic, the brain has a harder time distinguishing reality from fantasy."

Mack passed the topic over to Moxie. The little girl—her dark green eyes bulging with fury, her silver-sheathed tongue flapping viciously in her mouth like a beached piranha—looked daggers at Mack. Her Alter-Cater stood motionless by her side, muscled arms folded, its digital Moxie-face glaring.

Mack swallowed. "I . . . um . . . the sole purpose of these games is to heartlessly k-kill others," he faltered. "D-doing so for hours on end is bound to . . . to lead to a more violent s-society. . . ."

Mack's Alter-Cater strutted back and forth at the center of the ring, attempting to goad its opponent to battle. Meanwhile, Mack, who had started out so confidently, was sweating bullets.

"V-video games are an outlet . . . helping kids to blow off steam," he said, casting wary glances at Moxie, who was grinning like a jack-o'-lantern. "It's important to . . . to release these n-natural instincts. If we didn't and . . . k-kept it all stuffed inside, we'd all just . . . b-blow up."

Mack's hulking Alter-Cater looked back at Mack for guidance. The boy hung his head and pounded the podium with his fist. "I can't take it anymore!" he shrieked. "She's freaking me out!"

Moxie and her Alter-Cater smiled, quivering like twin rattlesnakes about to strike.

"You win!" Mack yelled as he stormed out of the ring.

Howard Cosell shook his head with disbelief.

"Just when I think I've seen everything, 'everything' gets one weird thing bigger," he said as Charity wheeled Moxie across the mat on her dolly. The angelic super-model smiled and waved as she teetered out of the ring in her seven-inch-heeled boots.

"Now on to Round Five: Annabelle Graham versus Roberta Atrebor! Annabelle Graham was a latchkey kid from Burnsville, Minnesota. With little money for books and no neighborhood library, Annabelle learned how to switch letters around in her head and made dozens of new stories from her worn copy of *Bridge to Terabithia*. Cause of death? Chronic TMJ from an industrial-strength jawbreaker. Let's hear it for Annabelle Graham!"

Annabelle and Roberta dragged themselves out to the stage, where only one would return a winner.

"Born in Milano, Italy, Roberta Atrebor can out-argue anybody, anytime! In fact, when she visited the Grand Canyon, her own echo conceded in a debate. Miss Atrebor died in the Thai-Tanic: a theme restaurant that crashes into an ice-cream-berg every hour. Unfortunately for Roberta and forty-seven other diners, the last meal was entirely too realistic for their tastes. Wave your hands in the air as if you cared for Roberta Atrebor!"

As the audience cheered—Heck-bent for linguistic leather—two burly badger demons trudged into the dressing room: one carrying a small steamer trunk, the other pushing a lavish throne on a dolly.

"Outstanding, underlings!" the vice principal exclaimed. "Take those out to the ring just before Mr. and Miss Fauster are due for their epic argument!"

Milton nudged his sister with his elbow.

"Let's grab a bite before the debate," he said, staring at Vice Principal Carroll, just a few feet away.

Marlo rubbed her queasy belly. "Yuck . . . just the thought of food is making a chunder-storm in my stomach."

"C'mon," Milton urged, leading his sister to the snack table in the far corner of the room. He leaned into Marlo.

"Remember those weird mechanical crickets and tuning forks out in the Outer Territories?"

Marlo nodded. "Yeah . . . their noise made me sort of woozy all over. Like I disappeared a bit. And everything seemed to get more real around me."

"Exactly! Maybe that's what he's trying to do, except *everywhere*. The tone must be the same pitch as the Music of the Spheres—like in that old encyclopedia page I found. Perhaps Vice Principal Carroll needs God's true name as the password to jimmy the lock of Creation and reshape everything in his image."

Marlo shook her head.

"But the whole 'Yahweh' thing . . . I don't buy that

as God's password. It's too obvious. It's like Grandma Fauster's *Generica Online* account password: Fauster123. I mean, *c'mon*. It took me two seconds to crack that and send out that fake holiday newsletter."

"Well, what do *you* think it is, then?"

Marlo rubbed her chin and glanced up at the monitor, where Annabelle and Roberta were duking it out, debating over the topic of school uniforms.

"Uniforms help to create a sense of camaraderie, a sense of belonging, a sense of community," Roberta suggested from behind her podium.

Her Alter-Cater stretched itself out on the ropes, limbering up for its assault.

"Uniforms suppress individualism," Annabelle countered, "and requiring them in school encourages teachers and staff to treat all students the same: not recognizing them for who they really are."

Annabelle's Alter-Cater stood before its opponent chewing gum with quiet menace. It blew a bubble that, with a few surly puffs, blew up in Annabelle's Alter-Cater's face.

"But they make everyone equal," Roberta interjected. "That way, if a kid can't afford the trendiest clothes or the latest sneakers, she won't be made fun of."

Roberta's Alter-Cater responded with a powerful right hook that left its opponent hunched over, clutching its side.

Annabelle snorted.

"Hey, both you and I know, *Roberta*," she said, throwing the girl's name back at her like it was a wad of dirty gym clothes, "as well as every kid in Heck, I might add, that no matter what you wear, kids will always find *some* way of making fun of you. It's as plain as the nose on your face."

Marlo furrowed her brow. "As plain as the nose on my face," she muttered. "It was right there all along. . . ."

She turned to Milton. "That first draft of the Bible we found. God said it right there . . . *In the beginning was the Word, and the Word was . . .* whoops!"

"Whoops?" Milton replied.

"Yeah! Just think: right after you say the word 'whoops,' something surprising happens that usually changes everything! And Chief Crazy Pants—"

"Crazy Pants?"

"*Vice Principal Carroll* doesn't have that page . . . he doesn't know the real password!"

Roberta and Annabelle returned from their bout: Roberta strutting just a little taller, the apparent winner, with Annabelle sulking in behind her.

"It's brutal out there," Annabelle murmured as she grabbed a bottle of water from an ice bucket on the snack table. Her black No-Flak jacket was so damp that it practically dripped with desperation and perspiration. "Just seeing how many votes you're getting or not getting—in real-time—it's totally unnerving. Made me feel like a total loser."

Marlo patted the girl's slouching back but stopped suddenly when she felt how damp it was.

"Um . . . it's okay," Marlo said, wiping her palm on her black padded pants. "Hey, 'total loser' is an anagram for 'stellar too,' you know . . . just going out there and doing your best, showing all those stupid people that you can talk smart and hold your own is amazing."

Annabelle smiled and wiped the sweat from her upper lip.

"*Stellar too* . . . yeah, you're right!"

Vice Principal Carroll waddled toward Milton and Marlo. "Before you t-two go on, here is a little something to ingratiate you both to various audiences: a guaranteed vote booster!"

The vice principal handed Milton and Marlo two index cards. "I initially put them in your briefcases, but your briefcases seem to have suffered some wear and tear. . . ."

Milton's card read *Yahweh*.

"It's a good-luck word in Heaven," the vice principal said.

"How come mine says Hewhay, then?" Marlo said with a smirk. "Is it because you're planning to—"

Milton elbowed his sister silent.

"*Hewhay* is an expression of exuberance in the underworld," Vice Principal Carroll replied, not meeting Marlo's eyes. "It's rather like 'boy howdy'! Now, when I hit the gong—signaling the end of the tournament—you both say the words at the same time, to acknowledge both of our audiences. Now g-good luck!"

The vice principal extended his hand out to Milton. Milton shook it warily and noticed that the vice principal had the word "bazillion" written on his palm with black Sharpie.

"Remember, just b-begin at the beginning and go on till you come to the end; then s-stop. That always worked for me. And, above all, be yourselves. . . ."

Mr. Wilde snickered to Mr. Dickens, both loitering nearby.

"And *this* coming from a man whose real name was Charles Lutwidge Dodgson."

The vice principal gave Marlo's hand a quick, slack shake.

"Hmm . . . clammy," he commented as he wiped his hands off on his gray corduroys. "No need to be nervous, dear. Sylvie, Bruno, and I will be in the front row, cheering you on! You'd be amazed at how far our voices can carry!"

Vice Principal Carroll shuffled away as Faith, Hope, and Charity entered the dressing room.

"You're both on now," Hope said to Milton and Marlo with a wide, genuine smile that spread across her face like honey on bread.

Miss Parker softly gripped Marlo's hand as the Fausters made their way to the door.

"Just trust yourself," she said. "And be a kid. Try to have fun."

Marlo snickered bitterly as cold dread filled her insides.

"But we're not kids. Not here. Kids can lose sometimes and nobody cares. But some kid today is going to lose *everything*."

Mr. Wilde whispered in Milton's ear.

"Your sister will attempt to fluster you. Be sure to listen carefully to what she means, rather than what she says. And, above all, don't take anything she says personally. Out there, there are no enemies, only war. . . ."

33 · BRAWL iN THE FAMiLY

"NOW THE MOMENT you've all been waiting for," Howard Cosell announced, "our final bout, where you'll hear discourse and *dat*course, delivered by Team Captains Marlo Fauster and Milton Fauster . . . a catty Cain and more-than-Abel sibling rivalry, playing out before your very ears—dead and well said. Don't even think of moving that radio dial. . . ."

Milton and Marlo parted the ropes and entered the ring. Wild applause washed over them like a tidal wave of sound. At the center, on the mat, was a plush, wing-backed throne, the vice principal's silver hammer, the steamer trunk, and a gong. Milton looked up at the tower. The gong and hammer were at the very center, right beneath the middle prong of the tower, with the left and right prongs jutting out to the side, just like a gigantic . . .

"Tuning fork!" he gasped.

"Same to you, *Rumpel-Milt-Skin,*" Marlo said as terror seized her by the throat and stomach.

"No, this whole place. The Tower of Babble. It's a humongous tuning fork! At least that's how Vice Principal Carroll is going to use it: like a huge transmitter! That's why everything went blank when the snark's hammer smashed into the tower. It sent out a reverberating tone—the Music of the Spheres. Now all the vice principal needs is the password to Creation to remake everything. Not just a shared illusion this time, like in the Outer Territories, but to actually *change the code behind reality!*"

Howard Cosell leaned into his bank of microphones.

"And though we can't contain the excitement here at the Tower of Babble," he said with his brash, nasal yammer, "we *can* contain our caustic combatants. . . ."

A team of demons erected four walls of steel mesh, enclosing the ring on all sides. The effect was like a wicked metal flower blossoming in reverse, turning the ring into a steel cage.

Marlo stared anxiously at the silver bars around her. Despite a life (and afterlife) of flirting with crime, she had always been uneasy with the notion of "being behind bars." Perhaps this was what made her such a good thief: she *had* to be, to keep from getting caught.

Milton noticed the steamer trunk beside the throne.

It was unlatched. Poking from beneath the lid was the tiny porcelain hand of a ventriloquist's dummy.

Sylvie and Bruno, Milton thought, as the Alter-Caters crouched beside the podiums, waiting.

"He's going to wait until there are a bazillion viewers watching," Milton whispered to his sister, "and then throw his voice farther than anyone ever has before. To tell the story that tells Creation . . ."

Milton and Marlo simultaneously realized that they were still holding hands. They dropped them with a swift urgency usually reserved for snake handlers.

"Do what you have to do to keep the argument going," Milton said.

Marlo snorted, though her violet eyes were damp, twinkling with all of the lights around her.

"I've never, *ever* had a problem with that," she said with a smile.

"What was I thinking?" Milton replied, grinning through tears. He dried his eyes, wiped his nose, and pulled himself together as the eyes of the afterlife scrutinized his every move.

"We'll be as boring as possible, to keep the votes way under a bazillion," Milton whispered as they walked toward their podiums. "That seems to be—"

"No," Marlo said with a shake of her head. "The opposite of that. We're going to give them blood. Get our votes way high, if not higher. Then, at the end, we both go 'whoops.' Actually, you go 'whoops,' and I'll go, um . . . 'spoohw' . . ."

"I don't understand," Milton replied.

"*That's* a first," Marlo said as the crowd hooted and hollered. "If it's the right password, then we'll be the ones telling the story, and if it's wrong—if it really is Yahweh or whatever—then the vice principal will have to be the one to say it, and we'll just try to hold him off as long as we can."

Milton had to admit, his sister actually made sense.

"Okay . . . um . . . *will do, mildew,*" he said while awkwardly fist-bumping her.

"That's not how you . . . never mind," Marlo said with a smirk.

Milton started to walk away but instead gave Marlo a quick, tight embrace before assuming his podium. The crowd cheered, waving HOW MARLO CAN YOU GO?! ONE IN A MILTON! and BETTER ARTICULATE THAN ARTICU-EARLY! signs.

"Two sharp siblings, each *Faustering* grudges against the other," Howard Cosell said dryly. "Milton, the youngest—a socially awkward straight-A student who never threw caution to the wind, preferring to place it gently at the bottom of his sock drawer, and Marlo— the bluebird of sassiness—a sticky-fingered, impulse-challenged felon with a gift card for gab. Cause of death? They were both killed in an exploding marshmallow bear accident."

Milton gripped the edges of his podium tightly, his white knuckles blanching even whiter.

"Now on to our topic," Howard Cosell continued. "Are you ready?"

Marlo cleared her throat. "Being ready is a personal choice, and one that—"

"No, that's not the topic. Your topic is"—the announcer shook his head as he read the words—"'Is There an Afterlife?'"

The crowd gasped.

"Miss Fauster, you'll be taking the 'Pro' stance while, Mr. Fauster, you have the 'Con' position, as well as my sincerest condolences."

Milton's and Marlo's faces went sour, like astronauts who had broken wind in their spacesuits.

"There must be some mistake," Milton said into his microphone.

"That's what Mom said the day you were born," Marlo replied, much to the wicked delight of the audience.

Milton glanced at the scoreboard. Milton and Marlo were both nearly a billion votes away from a bazillion, with Marlo—somehow, due to her unaccountable popularity—ahead by several hundred million.

"I'll begin by laying out three essential Pro-Afterlife arguments," Marlo asserted. "One, we're all here now. Two, I mean, *duh.* And three, please refer to points one and two."

Her Alter-Cater—the hissing-and-spitting image of

Marlo—rushed at its opponent, grabbed Milton's Alter-Cater by the waist, then flipped it onto its back.

"Oooh . . . a Running Powerslam!" Howard Cosell exclaimed.

The audience applauded as all eyes and various sensory organs trained upon Milton for his response. Milton reached for the one thing that always gave him a sense of security in an uncertain world: the emotionless certitude of science.

"Adopting a . . . strictly scientific viewpoint," Milton said, his words falling away from him in a clumsy tumble. "There is no hard evidence that a soul even exists. And by soul I mean some form of consciousness that survives after death. And without a soul, you can't have an afterlife. You can't have . . . *this.*"

Milton paused, daunted by the prospect of proving that everyone listening didn't really *exist.*

"Or what we think this is," he continued, hoping to pull Marlo's argument out from beneath her. "It's just something proposed by religion to pacify us, a way to cope with the fact that death is inevitable for every living thing. I mean, if there's supposedly an afterlife, why isn't there a, um . . . *before*-life?"

Milton's Alter-Cater rose from the mat and circled its opponent, suddenly grabbing its arm and twisting it behind Marlo's Alter-Cater's back. The audience murmured as they grappled with the puzzling nuances of Milton's argument.

"Milton," Marlo replied. "Would you consider yourself a religious person?"

Milton's mind went hot.

What is Marlo doing?

"I . . . I always believed that there had to be *something* . . . but I didn't think that humanity could even comprehend something as big as death, much less describe what it was like in every detail."

"I counter that you *do* have a religion, and that religion is *science*," Marlo said with icy-cool poise.

Marlo's Alter-Cater broke free from its armlock and lifted Milton's Alter-Cater into the air and off its feet. It threw its counterpart down to the mat and stood confidently over it, daring it to move.

The audience went wild. Marlo's votes spiked like the EKG of someone shocked back to life after a heart attack. Milton couldn't believe it: Marlo was *really* debating, not just spewing abuse back at him like usual.

"Life—and death—are full of mystery," Milton continued. "Science helps us make sense of it all. It turns what was once superstition into facts. And it seems to me that the world could be even *better* if we spent less time fighting over some supposed 'bonus round' we get after death and spent more time appreciating how precious and fleeting our lives truly are."

Milton's Alter-Cater kicked away its opponent's legs from beneath it. It landed on its butt with a thunderous thump. There was a smattering of applause and even some sniffing back of tears. Milton's numbers went up, but he still lagged well behind his sister, who obviously made for better radio.

"Okay, then, *Dr.* Fauster," Marlo said after giving her opponent a round of sarcastically slow applause, "we agree to disagree."

"What?"

"Science is how you choose to see things, with everything that doesn't fit your rigidical 'oooh-oooh, pick me teacher, I know the answer!' equation or whatever just getting tossed away because your brain thinks it's so smart. But look what's telling you that! *Your brain!*"

"I really don't know what you're talking—"

"Stop interrupting," Marlo interrupted. "So if there's no afterlife—no *all of this*—how come people see ghosts and have near-death experiences: kind of like what you're having here onstage right now?"

Marlo's Alter-Cater hopped to its feet, grabbed its opponent's massive arm, and threw the wrestler at the ropes, where it bounced onto its back and writhed in pain on the mat. The audience roared.

"And when we die and our soul leaves our bodies, don't we lose a few grams or something?" Marlo added. "Personally, any weight loss is good by me. Am I right, girls?!"

Marlo's Alter-Cater kicked at its opponent. Her votes shot up like a rocket.

"How do you and your science religion account for that?"

Milton shook his head as his argument rose, dazed, from the mat.

"Wow, where to begin," Milton replied. "People see ghosts like how we look at the stars and think we see a big dipper or a bear. It's just human nature to try to make sense of the senseless—"

"Like how the audience is trying to make sense of your argument."

Milton summoned all of his time-tested Marlo patience and simply ignored her, talking through the laughter.

"And that study, where the body loses twenty-one grams when it dies—supposedly the weight of the human soul—was conducted before modern scientific equipment."

"But you can't prove it's not our souls leaving our bodies for another place, can you?"

"No more than you can prove—logically—that there is an afterlife! That this isn't all some shared delusion . . . a dream!"

"I don't have to," Marlo replied. "I just have to prove that you can't prove that I can't prove it doesn't not exist!"

The two Alter-Caters spun together like a Tilt-A-Whirl, locked in contentious combat.

Vice Principal Carroll emerged from the backstage dressing room and began his long journey through the audience. Milton and Marlo had to get their numbers up quickly before the vice principal could grab the reins to reality.

Marlo caught her brother staring at the board.

"Just because you don't have scientific evidence doesn't mean it doesn't exist," she continued. "In the olden days, even before disco, they thought germs were magic. Now we know they're just really gross."

"But if all of our consciousness takes place in the brain, and our brain doesn't go anywhere when we die, what happens?" Milton countered. "There's no capacity to experience *anything*. . . ."

"Because it's *after*life," Marlo replied. "Again, *we're all here* and *duh*! My opponent has no proof that an afterlife cannot exist."

"Nor have you proved that one *must* exist," Milton countered between gritted teeth. "It doesn't make sense . . . not that *you'd* know anything about that."

Marlo squared her jaw. "What's *that* supposed to mean?"

"I mean that logic has never been your strong suit."

"And being strong has never been your *anything* suit," Marlo replied. "No one likes a bookwormy smarty-pants!"

"Our parents seemed to like that *someone* in the family wasn't always causing them trouble."

The room went cold. Even the two Alter-Caters broke their clench to stare at the two children. Marlo leveled her most lethal gaze at Milton.

"Seriously? You went there?" Marlo replied. "Fine . . . gloves off. Do you have any idea what it's like living in the shadow of someone whose shadow is smaller than yours? So, fine, *I acted out.*"

"*Acted out?* We practically had to have your mail forwarded to detention hall."

"At least I led an interesting life," Marlo replied. "The most interesting thing *you* ever did was die."

Milton grew hot with rage. "I wouldn't even *be* here if it wasn't for you!" he spat.

Marlo smiled. "Here, huh? And where would that be? *Exactly?*"

Milton's Alter-Cater was cornered, its opponent blocking all passage. Marlo had somehow won. She looked up at the numbers. Hers had just crossed a bazillion votes, with Milton only a few hundred behind.

Vice Principal Carroll finally arrived at the ring, excited as he counted the votes. His excitement grew to dismay as he clutched the cage walls, barring him entrance to the ring.

"You know," Marlo said carefully, "you could be right about all of this. It could just be some kind of dream. Maybe we're all in a coma . . . or just *one* of us is, and the rest of us are figments in that coma-person's imagination."

Marlo's Alter-Cater backed inexplicably away from the corner. The audience members viewed each other with suspicion.

"What are you doing?" Milton asked, baffled. "You were winning . . . you're crazy."

Marlo smirked, about ready to lob the worst retort one can in a debate.

"I know you are but what am I?" she said, punctuating her loss by sticking out her tongue.

Milton's votes shot up, passing Marlo's by only a few dozen. Vice Principal Carroll shook the bars.

"Let me in!" he cried.

Howard Cosell shook his head. "Not until the match is over, Vice Principal," he replied in his clipped, nasal voice.

Marlo wiped tears from her eyes. "You know what to do, Lesser Fauster," she said, stepping away from the podium.

Milton nodded and dashed to the center of the ring. He picked up the heavy silver hammer and struck the mighty gong.

The Fausters shrieked in unison.

"Whoops!"

"spoohW!"

The Tower of Babble wobbled and swayed like a drunken hula dancer. Reality seemed to pry itself apart, revealing the brilliant white light underneath.

Soon everything...

...w e n t...

...w h i t e.

Absolutely...

W   H   I   T   E.

34 · THE EMPEROR'S NEW PROSE

Milton's mind

seemed to be a little

blank in the middle, while

Marlo couldn't quite recall

why she was lying on

the mat.

THEY ROSE SLOWLY off the ground and got onto their knees, gaping at the audience members in quiet shock. They were like thousands of smudgy, semi-realized wraiths . . . sketches hastily penciled on gleaming white paper, waiting to be inked in and colored.

"What happened?" Marlo asked as her brain began to slowly fill back with coherent thought.

Milton fumbled for his glasses—thankfully, a cool new pair he had been given before the debate—and set them on his nose, yet the clarity of vision did nothing to make any sense of what had happened.

"I guess we did something," Milton mumbled.

"*I guess we did something,*" Marlo repeated as she found one of her shoes and slipped it on. "Thank you, Honor Roll."

"I mean . . . we did it. I'm just not quite sure what 'it' is. We obviously cracked the code, in that things are all . . . different. So I think we stopped Vice Principal Carroll—"

Milton noticed that the vice principal was no longer by the cage, gripping the cold steel bars.

"Wherever he is . . ."

Milton and Marlo walked to the edge of the ring.

"We must have been protected here, at the center of it all," Milton said. "Like the eye of a storm."

"Yeah, point-blank-out range," Marlo added.

The audience slowly became more distinct, their edges sharper, their shading darker.

"We'd better skedaddle," Marlo said as she jumped onto the cage wall and clambered to the top. "Before the Etch A Sketch of Creation we shook up fills back in with nasty things that want to hurt us."

Outside the ring, Milton could see that everything—from the people to the seats and walls—was labeled with faint words, describing the object beneath in the simplest terms imaginable, with the whole arena smudged as if hastily erased.

"This does, in a weird way, make things a lot easier," Milton said as they heaved open the door and headed outside. "Everything is so clear. No room for misinterpretation."

Marlo shook her head as they crunched across the shredded-paper ground.

"You are like the Duke of Dorks," she said.

Milton shifted from foot to foot with emotional unease. "Look, about what happened in there . . ."

"It's okay," Marlo replied curtly before sighing. "Actually, it was the exact *opposite* of okay. Let's just stuff it at the bottom of our 'Things of Which We Shall Not Speak' box."

Milton looked down at his shiny black shoes. "I took things farther than I should have," he said softly. "Which was lame."

"Shut up."

"No, I mean it."

"So do I: *shut up*," Marlo said, pointing to something

hiding behind a group of Syca-Yews, slowly filling back with color as was everything else in the vicinity. "I hear something. . . ."

Milton and Marlo trotted over to the blob of white concealed by the trees. It was Vice Principal Carroll's white Rabbit hatchback.

"Suh-weet!" Marlo said with excitement. "We can just drive out of here!"

She sighed.

"There aren't any keys. And I don't have a coat hanger handy. . . ."

"The engine sounds like it's on, though," Milton said. "I can hear it purring. . . ."

Milton ran around to the front of the car and flipped up the hood.

"Oh my gosh," he muttered.

"What is it?" Marlo asked as she walked around the car. "The catalytic convertor?"

"Well . . . *sort* of."

In the space normally reserved for an engine were four angry cats, hissing and spitting. What made this even more interesting was that the cats were rotating on four metal crankshafts and had buttered toast strapped to their fuzzy backs.

"Um . . . that's random," Marlo said.

Milton scratched his head.

"It's actually sort of crazy-brilliant."

"How?"

"Well, you know how cats always land on their feet and how toast always lands butter-side down?"

"Um . . . yeah. So?"

"So with the bread on their backs, the cats will never fall on the ground . . . they'll just keep rotating," Milton explained. "And with the cats attached to the engine, it creates a practically infinite energy source!"

"Sort of a perpetual *meow*-tion machine?" Marlo offered with a smirk.

ZOT!!

Forty feet away, the When-Wolf vigorously kicked at the ground with its hind legs. It stood straight in the air to its full, frightening height, clutching half a briefcase in its claws. It scanned the Syca-Yew grove with its ticking yellow eyes as it tried to get its bearings.

"*AHROOOOOOO WOO WOOOahhhhh!*" the beast bayed as it bounded toward them on all fours.

Milton and Marlo ran into the car and slammed the doors.

The When-Wolf, its fur matted with Why-Wolf blood, scratched at the car with its claws. Marlo trembled as she scanned the inside of the car.

"Where is that 'make the car go' thingy . . . Oh, here it is!"

Marlo shifted the car into Drive—the gears grinding with hisses and growls—and it lurched forward. The car swerved through the obstacle course of sketchy, pale trees.

"*AHROOOOOOO WOO WOOOahhhhh!*"

The white Rabbit hatchback pitched violently forward and crashed into an exposed Syca-Yew root. The When-Wolf skidded to a halt, sending up a cloud of shredded paper. It roared, exposing every one of its daggerlike fangs as it stalked closer.

Milton and Marlo huddled together in a ball as the cat engine hissed.

Just as the When-Wolf reared back, it began to flicker, as if standing astride two different points of time at once. The creature whimpered.

"That's what it did before," Milton muttered. "Right before a large—"

A large shadow engulfed the When-Wolf. As the beast flickered on and off, it lost the briefcase it had been clutching. Something huge snapped the Syca-Yew branches from above. The When-Wolf covered its head and cowered. With one swift savage movement, a monstrously large Cheshire cat snatched the wolf with its mouth. Only it wasn't a mouth, exactly. It was the door of a small shed.

Marlo's mouth went slack.

"*The Absurditory,*" she murmured in shock as she gazed upward through the cracked windshield. "It . . . grew a body."

Milton went numb as his brain argued with his eyes. The gargantuan blue-and-orange-striped monster lifted its boxy head as it choked down the wolf through its door-mouth.

"Looks like the wolf didn't blow the house down," Marlo muttered. "The house gulped the *wolf* down."

The Absurditory turned and stared at Milton and Marlo with its blank window eyes. The mewling dwelling's wide, smiling mouth creaked open.

And, with a monstrous swoop, Milton and Marlo were gobbled up by a house.

"Well, well . . . look what the cat dragged in," Vice Principal Carroll said, his face flushed and his hair sticking up.

Milton and Marlo wriggled against their restraints.

"More tea?" he said. The vice principal took Milton's porcelain cup and held it upside down over the table, tilting his teapot to the ceiling. Piping hot tea sloshed upward. Milton looked over at his sister, whose blue hair waved at him in stiff, sweat-matted strands.

Bound to the chair, Marlo scanned the capsized sitting room warily.

"Where's the wolf?"

The vice principal's thin, quivering lips cracked into a smile, like someone snapping a pencil in two.

"He made for rather tiresome company," the man explained, brushing his ascot from his chin.

Milton could feel the Absurditory stalking across the Outer Terristories.

"What happened back there?" Milton asked. "In

the Tower of Babble? How come we didn't remake Creation?"

Vice Principal Carroll smirked and took off his purple velvet top hat, secured to his head with an elastic band. Beneath it was a red-and-white-striped beanie with a small satellite dish spinning on top of it.

"You two weren't wearing your thinking caps. Or *m-my* Thinking Cap, specifically. It amplifies my imagination and broadcasts it out for all to *be*."

"Sort of tele*pathetic*," Marlo replied as she tried to slyly free herself from her hand restraints.

The vice principal tilted his head back and laughed. An awful, strangled sort of sound, like a punctured squeaky toy at the bottom of a bathtub.

"That unsinkable, unthinkable attitude of yours!" he replied. "That's why the audience lapped you both up like cream. And, even though you b-beat me to the punch—while giving me the t-true password, I might add—you planted the seeds of doubt and confusion that I will soon reap."

"Doubt and confusion?" Marlo asked doubtfully. "I'm confused."

"Debating about the afterlife," Vice Principal Carroll clarified. "I knew Mr. Fauster, given the f-formidable task of discounting the listening public's very existence, would bring with him shrewd arguments. The words, all the right ones, would flow from him, while you, Miss

Fauster, would bring that must-listen *sizzle*. There are now enough angels and demons, moved by your arguments, pinching themselves to confirm that they are indeed *real*! This questioning will make it all the easier for me to uproot reality."

Milton spied a fancy, handwritten note sticking out of a leather messenger bag that hung from the vice principal's armrest.

I hope-th these artifacts will be-th of some use to thou.
—Your Guardian Angel

The vice principal rubbed the pad of his index finger on the rim of his teacup. It produced a gentle musical tone, like a note from a glass harmonica.

"From the very beginning, a magical significance was attached to human language."

Milton, his pulse pounding in his head, wrested his right hand free from his bonds. He jerked up suddenly but caught himself with his heel, wedging it beneath the small couch tightly to keep him hanging as he tried to work his left hand free.

"Yet words themselves ceased to hold godlike power . . . until now," Vice Principal Carroll continued. "I have d-discovered that there is nothing separating the word from the thing, from the idea and the actuality."

"You're crazy," Milton said as he freed his left hand, pressing himself between his sister and the armrest.

"DON'T EVER CALL ME TH-THAT!" Vice Principal Carroll shrieked as the tea set fell up to the floor, smashing into a hundred shards of fine-white porcelain. The Absurditory seemed to slow down.

"He meant crazy *cool*," Marlo said, crossing the deep moat of silence after a few long seconds. "Tell us more."

Milton, his foot wrapped around the leg of the couch to keep from falling, worked his fingers on Marlo's bonds.

Vice Principal Carroll, his hand trembling, took a delicate sip of tea.

"F-forgive me," he replied with subdued rage, like a mongoose under sedation. "It takes all the running I can do, to keep in the same place. And if you want to get somewhere else, you must run at least twice as f-fast as that. . . . I'm sure you understand."

"Completely," Marlo replied as she and Milton sought to free themselves.

Beads of sweat on the vice principal's lip slowly traveled up his face.

"A word can mean so many different things that it, in fact, means less than nothing," Vice Principal Carroll said with quiet scorn, as if he were addressing the memory of everyone who had ever doubted him. "So the question is, who is to be master: the storyteller or the words he uses? During my . . . *convalescence,* I decided that, to tell my ultimate story, I needed a way to b-bypass language altogether and instead tell a story with pure thought. To press the reset button on Creation with *me* as the creator. The master storyteller, with every person becoming a character, living the tale I spin."

The Absurditory stopped. Milton could feel the shed lowering to the ground, landing with a soft thud.

"But that's unfair," Milton said as Marlo worked her left hand free.

"To whom?"

"To everyone who happens to *not* be Lewis Carroll," Milton replied.

"But who wouldn't want to exist in my imagination?" Vice Principal Carroll said as a slight tremor took over his left eye. "I could do markedly better than the current Creator, with all of his drab earth tones and physical laws slowing the story down."

"But what you're proposing isn't a story," Milton countered. "A story is like . . . a dance."

"Like the lobster quadrille?"

"No, a *real* dance. Between the storyteller and his readers. A *true* story needs a reader's imagination to survive. What *you* want to do is just dictate a story for everyone else to live. That doesn't make you a storyteller. It just makes you, well . . . *a dictator.*"

Marlo elbowed her brother, letting him know that she was free.

"Thanks for the tea," Marlo said. "But we really must be going!"

Marlo and Milton dropped up from the couch and landed on the cap of a fiberglass mushroom. They hopped down to the ceiling and threw open the door.

Outside stood the tall, skinny, zipper-mouthed demons in their bright yellow jumpers and pink eraser top hats. They glared at the Fausters with beady red eyes.

"Deaditors!" Vice Principal Carroll said as he unbuckled himself from his chair and—with a stunning backward flip—landed on the ceiling. *"Zip them!"*

One of the Deaditor demons waved its red highlight-marker staff across Milton's and Marlo's faces, clamping the Fausters' mouths shut with twin zippers.

Vice Principal Carroll smoothed his hair back into an elegant Victorian bob and straightened his paisley ascot.

"We can't have you two running off at the mouth now," he said with a smirk. "You'll miss the third and final act. The act that gets even higher ratings than the debate itself."

Milton ~~squirmed and tried to shout but he~~ couldn't do anything. It was as if his every thought and action were being edited down to its bare essence~~, allowing no room for sloppy, rebellious expression~~.

The Deaditors tied Milton's and Marlo's hands behind their backs with extra-strength typewriter ribbon.

"Especially since the audience has so much invested in the two of you! The ears of the afterlife will be glued to their radios to hear the winners and losers decided, and—in what will surely be the most listened-to event ever—to hear the loser receive her punishment."

Her? Marlo gulped.

Vice Principal Carroll shrugged. "I may even end it all with a story," he chuckled blithely. "One so immersive that everyone will lose themselves in it completely! And it will be my best yet. Why?"

He tapped his red-and-white beanie.

"Because I'll be wearing my Thinking Cap!"

35 · BY BOOK OR BY CROOK

MILTON PACED IN front of the radio receiver, locked in a cell at the top of the right tower, where he, the teachers, and all the children except for Marlo were being held.

"So, once again, your votes have been tallied, and congratulations, *M-Milton Fauster!*" Vice Principal Carroll exclaimed through the speaker. "A hairbreadth of a victory, but a victory nonetheless! Looks like you're g-going straight to the t-top, Milton! The same, however, can't be said for his sister. Though an audience darling, Marlo Fauster lost fair and square. Be sure to tune in for her tragic and p-poetic p-punishment before she is sent down below. You won't want to miss it! Again, apologies to our viewers who misunderstood our commercial for Blank of an Eye, the new headache relief medicine that wipes away pain, leaving your mind as clean as a blank state . . . I mean a blank *slate*.

Those minutes of nothing were to show you its startling effects. . . ."

Milton switched off the radio and stormed over to the door. He grabbed the shimmering handle of sculpted sound and pulled as hard as he could. Through the blur of the door he could see two Deaditor demons on watch.

"Even if we could open it, we still couldn't get past those demons," Flossie said miserably.

"They're called Deaditors," Milton replied. "They can 'edit' you with those red pen wands of theirs."

Flossie stared at a pile of broken bric-a-brac.

"That weird writer guy, Dale E. Basye . . . I overheard him talking to Marlo about how he 'wrote' all of this. What if he's right?"

"What do you mean?" Annabelle asked, her face shiny with perspiration.

"What if this is all just a terrible story?" the orange-haired girl said, her face blurry with contemplation.

Mack shook his head. "If it was, they'd probably just edit this part out," he replied as he scratched his clipped blond hair. "No action. Just a lot of talking."

Milton sighed with frustration. "We can't just let the vice principal do this," he said. "It's not fair. Us trapped here, helpless, with Marlo—probably trapped in some other tower—waiting to be sent to . . . *you know where.*"

"But we knew it would have to end this way," Mr. Wilde said. "With one of you winning and the other losing . . ."

Moses snorted. "Who cares? Our team *won*! That's all that matters."

Milton walked over to the window. The wind howled beyond, with the Outer Terristories miles below. A raging inferno on the horizon was set to "simmer," the underworld's version of sunset.

"But Vice Principal Carroll is going to turn us all into characters in some mad story of his," he murmured sadly.

Mr. Wilde shook his head as he sat upon one of the many relics crowding the dusty cell.

"I sincerely doubt that the vice principal has discovered how to press creation between the covers of a living book. The Outer Terristories was nothing more than the ultimate parlor trick. Something akin to mass hypnosis."

Miss Parker fingered her pearls like they were prayer beads.

"I, for one, will *never* be a character in someone else's book," she said. "How demeaning."

"I think you've all been without your inspiration for so long that you can't even *imagine* something unless you see it with your own eyes," Milton muttered dismally.

Across from Milton was the center tower, its tip obscured by thick cloud cover, the demarcation line between Heck and the lowest reaches of Cloud One. Milton turned to face the others.

"What did King Nimrod say was in that center tower?"

Roberta twirled a strand of her dark, slick hair with her finger.

"His throne room," she replied. "And something about a Tomiary . . ."

"What would a Tomiary be?" Milton asked the teachers.

Miss Parker rubbed her tired eyes. "It sounds like a mash-up of 'tome,' that is to say a book, and an 'aviary,' an enclosure for keeping birds."

Milton walked over to a pile of dusty artifacts.

"Any idea what this junk is?" he asked as he found an old painting. It was an old portrait of Jesus, surrounded on either side by twelve disciples. They were all eating bagels and sipping orange juice.

Mr. Wilde looked over Milton's shoulder. "The Last Brunch, I assume," the man speculated.

Miss Parker joined them. "King Nimrod must use this spire to store his less-than-priceless religious relics," she said as she knelt to the ground. "Looks like he's something of a hoarder."

Milton picked up a small green pipe. On the side, in florid gold script, was the name GABRIEL.

"Not Gabriel's sacred horn, exactly," Mr. Dickens said as he knelt beside the relics with mild interest. "The horn that was to announce the resurrection at the Last Judgment. But more of a—"

"Kazoo," Milton said. He blew into it. Immediately the room seemed to be filled with a soft sense of peace. Milton tucked it into his black No-Flak pants.

He uncovered a short folding ladder with flat steps and a small platform.

Miss Parker and Mr. Wilde shared a quizzical look.

"Jacob's ladder?" they asked.

"More of a stepladder, by the looks of it," Mr. Dickens observed.

"What's Jacob's ladder?" Cookie asked, her mouth moving as if she were chewing gum.

"It's from the Bible," Milton replied. "A ladder that was believed to reach all the way up to . . ."

A thought crossed Milton's mind, not even taking the time to look both ways.

He dragged Jacob's stepladder to the tall window. Immediately, it began to extend, reaching up and out to the top of the center spire like a vine reaching up for the sun.

"I think I have an idea," Milton said with a mischievous grin.

Jacob's stepladder strained across the yawning, two-hundred-foot-wide gap separating the Tower of Babble's right steeple from its taller center spire. The end of the ladder settled on a windowsill in what Milton assumed was the Tomiary.

Milton hopped onto the ladder and, on all fours, slowly made his way out, leading a ragtag search-and-rescue party to save his sister. He looked over his shoulder at the teachers and children crowding the window—all of them nervous and scared, except for Moses, who seemed almost excited, as if he couldn't wait to see Milton tumble down however many miles, landing with a soul-squashing splat.

The noise of wind and waggling, warring tongues clapped Milton by the ears. He couldn't breathe, as it felt like the whole world was breathing up all of the air around him. Jacob's stepladder—an ever-extending platform of ancient wood and crystal—seemed like a boundless runway to heaven. As Milton crawled fixedly toward the window ahead, nothing else seemed to matter. He had to find his sister, whatever the cost.

Milton was now halfway across. He glanced down and was instantly punished with a nauseating bout of vertigo. Joining him on the ladder were the teachers, Flossie, Roberta, Roget, and Annabelle. Milton thought it was interesting how many of Marlo's team wanted to be part of her rescue party. She must have been more of a leader than anyone had ever given her credit for.

Milton crept, hand over hand, knee over knee, nearer to the window. His coat flapped behind him like a super-hero's cape. He climbed into the window quickly, fell onto the floor, and gasped.

The Tomiary was exactly what Miss Parker had

speculated: a cloistered sanctuary for books. *Millions* of them . . . with no two alike. The circular steeple stretched up for a quarter of a mile, easy, capped with a ceiling of stained glass. The light pouring through the roof . . . Milton had never seen anything like it. It streamed in like a melted sun, golden beams dripping like globs of radiant honey. The light filtered through the stained glass and splashed heartbreakingly beautiful color across level after level of books. It was the perfect place . . . or *would* have been had Marlo been here.

She's got to be in the far tower, Milton thought as Miss Parker climbed off the ladder and into the Tomiary.

"Oh my goodness!" she exclaimed in surprise, with tears instantly forming in her dark eyes.

Mr. Dickens rested his hand on the woman's shoulder. "'*A clean, well-lighted place,*'" he murmured in awe as he took in the airy, whimsical space. "Hemingway, I believe. A refuge from the danger and clamor of the world outside."

Milton noted the winding, ornamental gallery, with each story supported by delicate columns.

"A treasury of wisdom and inspiration," a soft yet clarion-clear voice explained.

An exquisite woman—a goddess, by her stunning, rarified presence—rose from a red velvet couch and approached the visitors. Milton recognized the dark-haired woman from the War of the Words. She extended her delicate white hand.

"My name is Calliope," she said in a voice that gripped him with oblique, penetrating truthfulness. "The muse of epic poetry. Over there are my eight sisters. Clio, the muse of history. . ."

A woman with golden curls fluttered her fingers without looking up from her book.

"Erato, the muse of love poetry . . ."

A young woman with short, spiky dark hair sighed wistfully, her hand on her flushed cheek.

"Euterpe, the muse of music . . ."

A woman with strawberry-blond hair plucked her lute with abandon.

"Melpomene, the muse of tragedy . . ."

A brunette woman with olive skin sobbed loudly into her perfect hands.

"Polymnia, the muse of sacred poetry . . ."

A dark-skinned woman read reverently from a small book cradled between her praying hands.

"Terpsichore, the muse of dance . . ."

A spry little girl twirled upon her bare feet in tight pirouettes.

"Thalia, the muse of comedy . . ."

A woman with almond eyes and golden skin was bent over, laughing, in her plush chair.

"And Urania, the muse of astronomy," Calliope concluded as she gestured to a serious young woman with a tiara frosted with stars, stooped before a long, brass telescope trained outside the far window.

Milton was boggled by this sweeping, monumental church devoted to artistry, sealed away and imprisoned at the top of King Nimrod's egotistical tower. On a couch across the room was an assortment of odd knickknacks: horseshoes, rabbit's feet, four-leafed clovers, and various lucky—

"Lucky!" Milton exclaimed as he ran across the luxurious scarlet area rug to his pet ferret. Lucky rose from his velvet pillow like a spoiled prince coated in just-brushed fur, arched his back, and yawned. He regarded his master with gleaming pink eyes. Milton scooped Lucky up into his arms.

"He's my pet . . . or I'm *his* pet. It's confusing," Milton explained as he nuzzled the fat, sleepy ferret.

Calliope gave Milton an easy, dazzling smile.

"He is your muse, I take it?"

Milton nodded. "Something like that," he replied. "He makes me happy and gives me a weird sense that everything will be okay."

Mr. Wilde and the other teachers toured the elegant and oddly imposing library. Seemingly random collections of books began to stir, like bats in a belfry waking at sunset.

Calliope beckoned the visitors to sit down.

"What brings you here?" she asked with her clear, melodic voice.

"My sister is going to be punished for losing the War of the Words," Milton explained.

"That's awful!" Melpomene sobbed.

"*Awfully* funny!" Thalia snorted, before drying her glittering eyes. "I mean . . . in a darkly comic way, of course . . ."

Milton rubbed Lucky's fur, every stroke helping to calm his hectic mind.

"And Vice Principal Carroll is going to use the event to take control."

"Take control of what?" Calliope asked softly.

"*Of everything!* He's gotten the hack to Creation and, with his Thinking Cap, is going to use the Tower of Babble as a massive transmitter, and—"

Milton could tell from the wide, disbelieving eyes of the muses that they were mentally filing his story under Fiction.

"I know it sounds crazy," he continued. "But the vice principal told me all of this himself."

Calliope brushed Milton's hair. He felt warm and tingly inside, like a hot water bottle filled with boiling ginger ale. He felt like anything was possible.

"We muses know more than anyone that if something can be conceived, it can be realized," Calliope said. "Once an idea is conjured, it is only a matter of time before it is physically brought to fruition."

"French-fry-and-malted-milk-shake ice cream!" Flossie blurted.

The others stared at her quizzically. The girl shrugged.

"Just thought I'd put it out there," she said.

Mr. Dickens eyed the rustling groups of books above with a newfound curiosity.

"Excuse me, but what in *Shakespeare* are those books up there?" he asked. Calliope smiled to herself, a knowing smile that was somehow both warm and inscrutable. She looked at Miss Parker, who had a wide twinkle taped across the bottom of her face.

"Then it's true!" Miss Parker yelped with girlish glee.

"What is true?" Milton asked.

"*This,*" Miss Parker replied, shutting her eyes and drawing a deep breath. A silvery-purple glow surrounded the woman. A group of books filed away in the "P" section shouldered themselves away from the shelves. Once free, they dove down from the top of the Tomiary and fluttered to Miss Parker, darting around her in swooping arcs of delight, like baby birds reunited with their mother.

Mr. Dickens gaped in slack-jawed wonder. Even the normally "too-cool-for-prep-school" Mr. Wilde was entranced and transported, like a young boy watching his first fireworks.

"True artists fill their works with pieces of their souls," Calliope explained. "In the afterlife, these soul-pieces actually reside *outside* of an artist, living in their work. Those original incarnations of pure inspiration . . ."

Mr. Wilde closed his eyes and summoned his works from the shelves—*The Picture of Dorian Gray,*

The Importance of Being Earnest, and others. The volumes frisked and nipped at each other playfully as they skimmed the air around him.

"The feeling is astonishing," Mr. Wilde murmured. "It's like . . . dancing in the rain to the music in my heart."

"Or getting married in a bouncy castle," Miss Parker replied with a childlike grin.

Mr. Dickens closed his eyes. His books—time-tested classics such as *Oliver Twist, A Christmas Carol, David Copperfield,* and *Great Expectations*—nudged themselves free from their roost, waddling to the edge of the shelf like baby penguins before gliding down in playful exuberance.

"It's been so long," Mr. Dickens said, grinning from beneath his unkempt beard. "I had forgotten what it feels like to be inspired. It is like an electric feeling, describing what we really have no words for at all."

Euterpe set her lute down by the edge of her velvet fainting couch and eyed Milton with interest. "Is that . . . a kazoo?" she asked, flipping back her strawberry-blond curls as she glided toward him.

Milton nodded, pulling Gabriel's kazoo from his pocket. "Yeah," he replied. "I found it in— OWW!"

One of Mr. Wilde's volumes clipped the side of Milton's head. The Tomiary was beginning to resemble a tornado in a library, with books zooming in dangerous, liberated circuits around the gallery shelves. The works of Mr. Dickens seemed to lag somewhat behind the output of his fellow teachers.

"While my far-flung soul bits are gratefully emancipated from this secret prison of literary inspiration," the man observed, "they seem to be a touch sluggish."

Calliope smiled, ducking down to avoid impact with *The Portable Dorothy Parker* collection.

"I'm afraid that the more successful an artist's work is, the bigger the press runs. Meaning, the more soul bits that are scattered and diluted. Authors of legal thrillers, for instance, can scarcely move their books at all, much less make them fly."

Euterpe twirled the kazoo thoughtfully in her hands. *"Ahh . . .* Gabriel's kazoo," she murmured. "It was the archangel's way of focusing and amplifying angelic intent, before he took up the horn. Do you mind?"

"Knock yourself out," Milton replied.

The muse put the kazoo to her generous lips and hummed. Immediately, Milton felt at ease and gently buoyant. Euterpe gave the instrument back to Milton.

"What did you do?" he asked as he tucked Gabriel's kazoo back in his pocket.

"I merely hummed the word 'hope,'" she replied before smiling and walking away.

Hope, Milton thought, as if waking from a dream. *I came here for a reason.*

"I've got to rescue my sister," Milton said urgently as

he dashed to the far window. "They're probably keeping her in the left steeple, since we were trapped in the right."

"Too late," Urania commented, her brass telescope pointing down just beyond the base of the tower. "Look."

Milton squinted into the eyepiece. After adjusting the focus to humor his poor vision, a disturbing scene came into crisp view. Marlo—her mouth zipped, her hands tied—was being shoved outside by a team of Deaditors. They were leading her to a metal pole sticking up out of a mound of earth.

"Maybe there's still—" Milton started before a discouraging sight plucked the words from his tongue. On the periphery, marching toward the Tower of Babble, was a team of fallen angels, led by Principal Bubb. Milton's plan to avoid angelic assassination had succeeded on one level—his head was still attached to his shoulders, not severed by a razor-feather—yet it seemed to have failed miserably on another as the team of celestial soldiers converged below.

Milton crumpled inside.

"I'm too late," he said as hot tears sliced down his cheeks. "Marlo threw the debate for me, and I just got caught up in trying to prove her wrong. Now there's nothing I can do. . . ."

Calliope set her soft, subtly encouraging hand upon Milton's upper back. Her touch kept his misery at bay, though he could still hear it howling in the distance.

"There are two words that will open many doors for you," Calliope said.

"'Pull' and 'push'?" Milton replied.

"No: *I'm sorry.*"

Milton turned and peered again through Urania's telescope, this time training it upon the left steeple. The cell was identical to the one he had just fled, only unguarded now that Marlo had been dragged away. Milton studied the waggling tongues, positioned roughly a yard apart, spewing the eternal rancor that held the Tower of Babble together.

"I'm sorry," Milton whispered, feeling the words on his lips, making them seem more real as he took Gabriel's kazoo from his pocket. He smirked to himself as he turned.

"You know what this place needs?" Milton asked nobody in particular amid the ruckus of flapping pages. "Some peace . . . and *riot.*"

36 · A TORTURE'S WORTH
A THOUSAND WORDS

MARLO WAS LED outside to a long metal pole poking out from a mound of shredded-paper pulp. She had been scrubbed raw with salt and gravel and forced to pad outside barefoot wearing a frilly white petticoat. The last time she had worn all white was at the Generica Middle School's Opposite Day dance, where the boys didn't ask girls to not-dance, not accompanied by any music.

Marlo's mind was hot with fury and questions, but her principal modes of expression—her mouth and hands—were now either zipped shut or bound tight. She sighed as the Deaditor demons prodded her forward with their hot-red highlighter wands.

I won't let these ~~meddling, muddling~~ demons edit who I am ~~down to nothing~~, Marlo thought with difficulty as decomposing demon creatures lashed her to an iron pole.

Vice Principal Carroll—wearing his tall fusty top hat, a Victorian overcoat despite the heat, and a light dusting of personal eccentricity—gamboled toward her, as if Marlo's impending punishment were a game of croquet.

"Good evening, M-Miss Fauster," the man said in a voice that reminded Marlo of a corkscrew: making its point in a persistent yet meandering way. "My, aren't we a delightful froth of petticoats today? Rather like a meringue with moldy blueberries on top!"

Marlo struggled vainly against her bonds. The metal pole felt both cold and hot against her raw back.

Vice Principal Carroll flipped open his pocket watch.

"It is nearly t-time. The hurrier I go, the behinder I seem to get. . . ."

Principal Bubb and her team of fallen angels clustered around Vice Principal Carroll. The deranged man bowed and tipped his top hat to the principal, revealing his Thinking Cap beneath. Luckily for the vice principal, his behavior was so consistently inconsistent that such displays of eccentricity went mostly unnoticed.

"Principal B-Bubb!" he exclaimed as he took her claw and, lips quivering with repulsion, kissed it. "How good of you—if that term is in any way applicable—to arrive," he added, picking a strand of coarse bitter fur from his tongue.

Principal Bubb gauged the man quizzically with her yellow goat eyes.

"Traffic was murder . . . and a host of other sins, both mortal and venial," she replied, wiping the back of her claw on her red leather dress.

Vice Principal Carroll gazed with wonder at the team of nine fallen angels.

"We shan't be having any trouble with Heck's Angels about! I have a guardian angel of my own, you know: one that no one else can see!"

Principal Bubb rolled her eyes. "Of course you do."

Marlo noticed one of the angels in particular: a breathtakingly beautiful boy with gleaming, black-metallic skin, piercing blue eyes, and wings feathered with razors.

Angelo, Marlo thought, staring wide-eyed at the boy. ~~*From Precocia. The boy hired to assassinate Milton.*~~ *I wonder if he—*

The boy, Molloch, gazed briefly at Marlo before continuing his sweep of the area.

Nope, Marlo thought with mixed emotions. *He looked right through me . . . like most every cute boy. . . .*

Principal Bubb scowled at Marlo. "So what, exactly, are we doing here?" she asked. "What will happen to the Fauster girl?"

Vice Principal Carroll clapped. "Sentence first; verdict afterward, as they say!"

"No one says that. Pretend that I am a dim-witted cretin and explain things to me simply."

"I have faith that my powers of pretend can easily accommodate your request, Principal. What we are preparing for—the crowning jewel of the War of the Words—is Miss Fauster's punishment before she is dispatched down below."

"About that," Principal Bubb replied. "As much as I despise the girl—and I really, truly, madly, deeply *do*—I'm troubled by the complete disregard of underworld policy here. Introducing minors to h-e-double-hockey-sticks is a bad idea even for a realm *known* for its bad ideas. The girl, like every student in Heck, should make her less-than-merry way through the system, undergo her Soul Aptitude Test, then graduate either above, below, or the other various outcomes."

"Michael, the reigning Prince of Darkness, approved it himself," Vice Principal Carroll replied.

"Of course he did," Bea "Elsa" Bubb muttered with extreme distaste.

"And for a competition of this sort, the stakes must be high. The greater the risk, the greater the reward—"

"Regarding this 'reward,'" Principal Bubb interjected, "I have an even *bigger* problem with that tiresome twerp Milton Fauster jumping the procedural turnstile and landing a coveted spot upstairs. As much as I'd like him out of my pelt, rewarding a notorious troublemaker such as *him* sends the wrong message. Worse yet, it gives the rotten ragamuffins *hope*."

"Again, Principal, it has already been cleared."

"By whom?"

"Satan, if you must know."

"Satan?!"

"Yes, he arranged for the 'prize,' apparently," Vice Principal Carroll said before casting a nervous glance down at his pocket watch. "But if you'll excuse me, we really must be m-moving on. Van Glorious is nearly finished with his halftime performance, and I have to kindle the f-fire, so to speak, that will become the most blazingly popular event in afterlife radio history! Perhaps the last radio event *ever,* as the ultimate storytelling device is about to make its auspicious debut. . . ."

Blazing? Marlo fretted. *Is he going to set me on fire like they did with ~~Noah's wife,~~ Joan of Arc? ~~Or like how island people used to sacrifice young Virginians by throwing them into volcanoes?~~*

The vice principal left Bea "Elsa" Bubb to stew in her own abominable juices as he walked around the mound and pulled a tuning fork from his pocket. His blue eyes glittered with awe as they rested upon the tall metal pole.

"A Rod of Irony," he explained as he paused behind Marlo. "A fitting form of retort-ure for a mouthy young girl."

Marlo began to shiver uncontrollably.

"Now, now," he whispered softly.

"We are but older children, dear,
Who fret to find our bedtime near.
But you shall be the last sight to see,
At least those not conceived by me. . . ."

Principal Bubb hobbled up the mound on her polished hooves.

"Where is the other Fauster child?" she asked suspiciously as she scanned the shimmering Tower of Babble. "I like the troublesome burrs under my saddle to be where I can see them."

Vice Principal Carroll rubbed his sallow chin. "Not to worry, Principal! Mr. Fauster is locked away, tight and tidy at the tippy-top, where he will pose no trouble at all. . . ."

Milton climbed off the last rung of Jacob's stepladder and hopped back into the cell of the right-hand tower.

"Oh, the brave knight returns empty-handed, I see," Moses said, his sarcasm set to "11."

"Shut up, Babcock," Mordacia said, slugging Moses on the bicep before turning to Milton. "What happened?"

Milton trotted to the door. "It's hard to explain," he said, eyeing the blurry forms of guards stationed on the other side of the sonic wall. "But I might have figured a way out of here. . . ."

Milton took out Gabriel's kazoo and trained it upon the nearest ear sticking out of the sonic wall.

"I'm sorry," Milton hummed into the ear, the kazoo focusing and intensifying the sentiment behind the words. He could hear the jabbering mouth on the other side of the wall suddenly stop its incessant arguing, as if biting its tongue. It began murmuring softly before—with a twitch of its ear—falling to the ground, leaving behind a large hole in the wall.

The children were astonished. Moses snapped out of it and folded his arms.

"We wouldn't be able to get past the guards," he declared flatly. "And it would take forever to undo every one of those ear—"

Before Moses could finish, two more mouthpieces fell to the floor, removing part of the door and a portion of floor. Milton smiled.

"It's spreading," he said with satisfaction as he walked over to the window. "If the vice principal can release some sort of language virus, so can *I*. This will undo the Tower of Babble exponentially. So we've got to hurry."

"Why should our team escape?" Moses spat. *"We won.* We're going to get *prizes.* And you'll get to go to Heaven just for being along for the ride."

"First, we have no idea what Vice Principal Carroll has in store for any of us," Milton replied sternly. "Second, all we know for sure is that he's planning some punishment for Marlo. *Down there, right now.* Last, he's just using us as a way of focusing the attention of the afterlife so he can remake Creation in his own image."

Moses shook his head with fuming disgust. "To counter—"

"There's no time for a rebuttal," Milton interrupted. "Turning everything into an argument wastes time, limits our thinking, and forces us to distort facts to get our way. Not to prove a point, but just *win* . . . treating important issues like some kind of game. But here, if one of us loses . . . we all lose. I know this is a hard concept for Wise Acres, but we've got to stop sniping each other and start *helping* each other."

Milton turned to Rakeem.

"Rakeem . . . maybe you could use Moxie there as a sort of battering ram. Once the door is undone, just charge. The others can follow behind. I think the Deaditors will have enough problems of their own. . . ."

"Why is she all pink like that?" Principal Bubb asked as Vice Principal Carroll tapped the tuning fork in his palm. "She looks like a girl-shaped eraser."

"Miss Fauster was exfoliated so that her skin would be extra thin," he replied.

"To what end? So that she looks presentable on radio? Not like some sassy, pasty, iron-deficient ghost?"

"Not iron-deficient, Principal . . . but *irony*-deficient!" the man said, his blue eyes glassy with demented delight.

"The Rod of Irony that Miss Fauster is currently tied to . . . it's a truly remarkable creation, in that it literally attracts remarks."

The man paced in circles around the pole, while Marlo struggled to free herself from her typewriter ribbon restraints.

"You see, Principal Bubb, every word we say has a specific energetic signature. And every *nasty* thing we say has a uniquely specific *nastiness* to it. . . ."

Vice Principal Carroll held up the silver tuning fork, with the initials "MF" etched upon its base.

"During the debate, I captured Miss Fauster's sharpest, most caustic jibes and ripostes, then fabricated this special Retuning Fork," he continued, twirling the fork in his fingers. "And, with a simple tap—"

Vice Principal Carroll gently struck the Rod of Irony with the Retuning Fork. The pole was slowly overwhelmed with bad vibrations until it wobbled and waggled.

"—every hurtful word that Marlo Fauster has ever uttered is now called back to her."

Principal Bubb arched her scraggly centipede of an eyebrow. "You can't be serious," she replied. "That's absurd."

"I take my absurdity very seriously . . . sometimes with sugar and cream. Imagine, every mean-spirited remark you've ever made flung back at you like a verbal boomerang!"

Principal Bubb shuddered. "It's almost unspeakable," she replied.

Two stagecoaches converged one hundred yards away. One was gleaming red—marked INFERNO2GO—and pulled by snarling, decomposing Night Mares that gave off a smoldering scarlet glow as if illuminated from the inside. The other stagecoach—the Trans-Empyrean Express—gently floated to the ground, pulled by a team of immaculate winged Pegasus.

A clap of thunder boomed from overhead. The magenta clouds above swirled and darkened. Marlo swallowed as the Rod of Irony shivered behind her, pressing against her back like a nervous outboard spine.

So that's my punishment, she thought, glancing warily up at the sky. *Getting burned by every bad thing I've ever said . . . haunted and taunted by my own words . . .*

Milton scrambled across Jacob's stepladder for the fourth and final time.

"*Shoo! Shoo!*" Calliope called as she evacuated the Tomiary of its prized collections. She and her fellow muses—upon seeing Mr. Wilde, Mr. Dickens, and Miss Parker reuniting with their inspiration—agreed to release the flocks of soul-fattened books so that they might again inspire their masters, not waste away in some ivory tower. Lucky twitched inside Milton's No-Flak jacket.

"We're almost at our last stop: the left spire," Milton soothed. "No more windy ladder rides, I promise . . ."

Milton hopped off into the empty cell. He noticed a strand of blue hair resting on the floor of sound.

I was right: Marlo was here, Milton thought as he scanned the cell for any activity. *Phew . . . no guards is good guards.* Milton removed Gabriel's kazoo from his pocket and knelt before the first earpiece he saw.

"I'm sorry," he hummed. The ear pricked at the pure, resonant sound. As the jabbering mouth outside calmed, the ear-mouthpiece fell to the floor. Then another. Then another. Soon, wind was pouring into the cell as the walls and ceilings disappeared.

"Good—" Milton said before the floor beneath his left leg vanished.

"—grief!"

Milton scrambled out of the cell and down the stairs, the Tower of Babble dematerializing behind him, undoing itself faster and faster with each coil of stairway.

He leapt upon the moving sidewalk of sound that spiraled down the base of the tower. Behind him, the left tower had all but disappeared. King Nimrod's servants clogged the sidewalk.

Through the thinning blur of wall, Milton could see that the Tomiary—still loaded with all-too-solid books and art objects—was lowering like an elevator, as his infectious "I'm Sorry" virus spread, undoing the tower tongue by tongue.

He sprinted along the sidewalk, through the shimmering halls, barely outrunning the contagious apology that spread from lip to ear, loosening grudges, unfastening hatred, and soothing the tension that kept the Tower of Babble standing.

"Milton!" Roberta cried as she and the other children—led by Moxie, pushed along by Rakeem—escaped the vanishing left tower. They joined Milton where the moving sidewalks converged in loops and knots like a Los Angeles freeway.

"It's working!" Roberta gasped.

Milton's sides ached. He felt like he was on the crest of a wave, one that could never break or be rolled back. But at least he wasn't alone.

"Well, *Captain*," Moses said with a salute that was only mildly sarcastic. "Where to now?"

Milton looked around him, catching his breath.

"I don't know . . . this whole place is being yanked away, like when Lucy pulls the football away from Charlie Brown. . . ."

Moses scratched his arm. "Please . . . I'm allergic."

"Oh . . . right," Milton replied. "Well, I guess we should just go—"

Milton could hear dance music drifting up from the auditorium below.

"*Down*. As fast as we can. Before Marlo gets what's coming to her . . ."

37 · ADDiNG iNSULT TO iRONY

A DARK, BLACK–AND–WHITE storm cloud settled over Marlo. She looked up, its raw force reflected in her wide violet eyes. The cloud churned and seethed with *words*. Millions of them. The cloud whirled faster and faster until it was a concentrated cone focused directly above the Rod of Irony.

"We'd best seek cover," Vice Principal Carroll said to Principal Bubb as they backed away from the pole. "I'll fetch the Orb-Servers. They'll broadcast the event: me at my creative zenith!"

Principal Bubb gazed up at the shimmering tower. She slipped her spectacles up her snout.

"I thought that the Tower of Babble was shaped like a big fork," she commented.

"It is," Vice Principal Carroll replied as they scrambled off the mound.

"Not anymore . . ."

The vice principal's jaw dropped open. The tower had lost its colossal prongs. It was now merely a quarter-of-a-mile tall and resembled a gigantic rook snatched from God's chessboard.

"N-n-n-no," Vice Principal Carroll stammered. "I . . . n-n-need it . . . its reach and frequency . . . I've g-got to act quickly . . . while there's still t-time. . . ."

A mass of ear-mouths rained down from the sky, landing with a sickening plop by Principal Bubb's hooves.

"I'm . . . sorry," apologized one of the disembodied mouths. The principal grimaced with disgust. She stamped out the murmuring lips with her hoof as if they were a talking cigarette butt.

I know who'll be sorry, Principal Bubb thought, grinding her fangs. *This has to be the work of that miserable twerp Milton Fauster. This has his fussy signature scrawled all over it. . . .*

Crowds of people began pouring out of the Tower of Babble like blood gushing from a fresh wound. A team of servants shuttled King Nimrod out of the slowly dissolving building. The king was sobbing into his hands. Vice Principal Carroll rushed up to him.

"Where is the media?" he asked with frantic desperation. "I need to conclude the War of the Words while there's still time!"

King Nimrod shook his head, inundated in and incapacitated by failure.

"Inside," the broken man muttered. "They must think that the destruction of the great Tower of Babble is more important than a little girl getting her comeuppance."

Milton and the other children rushed through the crowd. Milton stopped short as he saw his sister struggling to free herself from the pole two hundred yards away. A large funnel cloud spun over her head.

"Are those . . . *words*?" he asked.

Vice Principal Carroll rushed past him toward the collapsing tower.

"Words are like b-boomerangs," he replied. "They always come back . . . every one of them."

Principal Bubb spotted Milton and the ragtag survivors of Spite Club. She pointed her angry, trembling claw.

"Heck's Angels . . . *grab those children!*" she roared.

The fallen angels circled around the children and teachers, cinching slowly like a noose.

Marlo's too far, Milton thought feverishly. *We need a diversion. . . .*

His eyes settled on Moxie Wortschmerz. The little girl was writhing and vibrating with pent-up rage: so many terrible, terrible words wanting out. Milton grabbed the handles of Moxie's hand truck and pushed her out into the fray, as far and as fast as he could.

"Sorry, Moxie," he panted. "Desperate times . . .

desperate measures . . . at least you'll be able to get everything off your chest."

Heck's Angels formed an impenetrable gauntlet around Marlo. Milton skidded to a stop forty feet from the surly barricade. One of the angels looked fatally familiar. A boy with burnished black skin and piercing blue eyes.

Angelo . . . or whoever he really is, Milton thought. *He doesn't seem to recognize me . . . not that it matters much now.*

Milton reached around Moxie's head and plucked the silver sheath from her waggling tongue as if he were removing the pin from a grenade. He ran, covering his ears, then dove to the ground. Moxie's eyebrows furrowed. Her dark green eyes bulged. Her turned-up nose flared with indignation, sucking up air. Her tiny lips puckered and pursed before opening like the petals of a carnivorous flower. The little girl trembled and hissed like an angry teakettle full of boiling nitroglycerine, before flushing deep red and stretching her mouth wide.

The stream of stinging, caustic curses spewing out of Moxie's mouth was the most brutal string of explosive expletives that Milton had ever heard. They effortlessly tumbled out of the little girl's mouth—shocking swear words in dozens of languages—and spread across the grounds like verbal mustard gas. Even the Deaditors and demon guards blushed at Moxie's abrasive firestorm of uncorked profanity. The girl grinned maliciously, finally obscene and heard.

Vice Principal Carroll ushered a small flock of Orb-Servers out of the tower, like a mother duck corralling her ducklings across a busy street.

The Orb-Servers skidded to a stop as their large red lenses locked on Moxie. Some of the creatures shut their eye-bodies and plugged their ears, censoring the feed, while the others made the mistake of looking to one another for guidance. But when they locked eye-bodies, they created an infinity loop—a camera broadcasting a camera broadcasting a camera—that immobilized them.

The fallen angels drew their swords and leaned into the howling gale of abuse. Milton scanned the scene frantically. There was no way he could make it to Marlo in time.

Suddenly, a squadron of flapping books soared over the children's heads.

"Huh?" Milton gasped before turning back to the shrinking tower, now just a massive, glimmering steeple missing its three lofty prongs.

The Tomiary traveled slowly down the disintegrating skyscraper like a multistory elevator. Milton could see Miss Parker, Mr. Dickens, and Mr. Wilde leaning out the window. Behind them, the muses watched the scene below. And the muses were not amused.

The flying books gathered in the sky, their pages

screaming as they whipped through the air. They clotted together in a sort of gravity-defying archive before dropping down with deadly velocity.

Heck's Angels stood below, novel-gazing, until the mass of books swarmed upon them, hurtling faster and faster, rushing at them with a ruthless rustle. The fallen angels broke formation as they beat back the angry books with their swords.

The funnel cloud seething above Marlo dropped down from the sky. The Deaditors fled.

Sticks and stones may break my bones, Marlo thought, her eyes squeezed shut and tears streaming down her face. *But words will never hurt me . . . even mine. . . .*

The countless words and phrases—Les-Is-Moron, Doodle-Fisted Lard Bomb, Short Bus, Little Miss Waste-of-Space, Brainiac, Sir Loser-Lot, Li'l Bro Pipsqueak, Bleached-Blond Toilet Brush, Mr. Substitute Creature—swirled around her in a malevolent, taunting tornado.

Every wisecrack and not-so-wisecrack that she had ever EZ-baked in her mean-spirited head now besieged her. The words slammed into Marlo, burrowed into her thin skin, and writhed. And scratched. And burned. The pain was blinding. It hurt so much that Marlo's nerve endings couldn't even process it all. It felt like she was being whipped from inside. Like her soul had been wrenched from her body and stamped into the dirt by an angry mob wearing golf cleats.

I . . . deserve this, Marlo thought, skating on the edge of consciousness. *I put all of this pain into the world. With my words.*

Marlo felt as if she were having an ice cream headache all over her body.

Hurting people I didn't even hate. Just because I could. With my anger. That scorching, head-banging, stomach-churning, all-consuming anger. The only way I could get it out was to vent it at others . . . and now it's payback time. . . .

Her heart empty, her soul depleted, her will defeated, Marlo slid down the Rod of Irony and slumped over like a soggy rag doll.

"No!" Milton screamed as he dashed across the chaotic battlefield of swooping books and fierce, sword-wielding angels to Marlo. He hurried behind the pole and untied her pink hands.

"Marlo!" he yelped desperately as he unzipped his sister's mouth. She was like a husk . . . a living shell. He looked into her heavy-lidded eyes, but there was no one home. Marlo was empty.

"I'll fix this," Milton sniffed, whispering into his sister's ear. "I promise."

Marlo seemed to nod as grunts, screams, and the sounds of flapping pages filled the air behind Milton.

Squadrons of books ducked and weaved above, swooping down viciously upon the fallen angels. The winged mercenaries slashed away with their swords.

Meanwhile, the teachers sent their beloved books into battle.

"We're really reading them the riot act now, aren't we?" Miss Parker quipped, her eyes closed in concentration, her face decades younger than it had been only moments ago.

Mr. Dickens grinned. He, too, resembled his younger self, at the peak of his powers, as he wielded *David Copperfield* at the chiseled jaw of Zagan, pummeling the barrel-chested creature with passionate prose.

The teenage angel Marchosias, bleeding from paper cuts, swung her flaming sword at *The Picture of Dorian Gray*, removing half a chapter.

Mr. Wilde groaned. "Everyone's a critic!" he said with a grimace.

In the distance, Milton could see Vice Principal Carroll backing away in horror. He was tugging behind him his gong and hammer.

"This is not how it's supposed to b-be at all!" he muttered as he stepped deeper in the rim of the Territories. "My imagination was to weave the ultimate story . . . and now everything is unraveling."

The vice principal tossed aside his top hat. The spinning satellite dish of his Thinking Cap glinted, like the wink of a mad man, with each frantic revolution. He slammed the hammer into the gong.

"*Whoops! spoohW!*" Vice Principal Carroll shouted,

his supple ventriloquist's voice rolling the words off his tongue both backward and forward simultaneously. Everything grew muzzy. Blurry. Simple. As if all personal responsibility was now in the hands of another. Yet, as swiftly as the Rosetta Tone gripped the minds of those in the immediate vicinity, its resonance passed and faded, like ripples in a pond.

As Moxie's storm of curses petered out, several Orb-Servers blinked their glassy eye-bodies and waddled toward the vice principal.

"Humanity is trapped behind the bars of a verbal prison," Vice Principal Carroll sobbed, surrendering to a complete meltdown.

Bars began to grow around him as he fell to the ground, the gently rolling hill of shredded paper twinkling with tuning forks.

"*Whoops! spoohW!*" the vice principal bellowed, sending out another fleeting blast of tampered creation.

"Such clumsy forceps, words are! If we could only see the world the way a *cat* sees it . . . quietly, without words . . ."

A litter of cats appeared, scattered around him, mewling and padding about in circles.

A rogue flock of books swirled uncertainly in the sky, breaking apart from the mass migration of novels, freed, searching for their masters. The small library—pages flickering, covers flapping—dove downward.

"Language is an oral contract not worth the paper

it's written on! A high-pressure whether-or-not system, raining down drivel!"

A clap of thunder pealed from above, announcing a sudden downpour.

"I would have remade the world in my imagination! And spun a story with more plots than a graveyard!"

As the valley began to sprout tombstones, the flock of books descended upon the vice principal: *Alice's Adventures in Wonderland . . . Sylvie and Bruno . . . The Hunting of the Snark. . . .*

Vice Principal Carroll peeked through his trembling fingers in wide-eyed amazement. A soft, silver-purple glow radiated around him like a small, touring production of the northern lights. His face pinched in the allusion of a smile.

"What's this?" the man muttered in wonder. "My babies? Can it be true?"

One of the books—*Through the Looking-Glass*— fluttered by coyly. Vice Principal Carroll stuck out his arm, with the book fluttering down, alighting on his wrist. He grinned.

"You were always my favorite. For you house my greatest work: *Jabberwocky*. . . ."

Vice Principal Carroll rose slowly from the ground. All of his books, his original inspiration, roosted upon him until he resembled a shaggy creature composed of gently flapping pages and whimsy. The vice principal recited:

" 'Twas brillig, and the slithy toves
Did gyre and gimble in the wabe:
All mimsy were the borogoves,
And the mome raths outgrabe . . ."

An oddly brilliant light enshrouded him, as did slimy tendrils slithered in pools of melted crayon. Exotic vegetation sprang up from the ground—fuzzy, feathery plants the color of bruises. Fiery moths swarmed, tearing at the ground with their legs.

"Beware the Jabberwock, my son!"

A hideous dragon materialized in the air. It burbled and whiffled from behind the vice principal. It flapped its black leathery wings and extended long, sharp talons as it stared at the man, its eyes pure flame.

"The jaws that bite, the claws that catch!"

The creature seized the man viciously around the waist and, with one choking gulp, swallowed him whole. Instantly, the Jabberwock vanished, along with all of Vice Principal Carroll's imaginings, leaving only the bleak hill of shredded paper, rustling in the wind.

The Tomiary landed gently on the ground as the

center steeple that had once supported it vanished into nothing.

The De-Press Corpse slowly emerged from the not-so-towering Tower of Babble. Irv Chudley, a demon reporter from the *Underworld Sintinel,* turned to his photographer.

"Whoa . . . we don't get many of *those* to the gallon. Did you get that?"

The bug-eyed creature behind the camera nodded.

The flying books drifted above in a bunch, so high that they became mere specks in the darkening sky. They hung in the heavens, just below Heaven, balancing on air currents with scarcely a flap of their covers.

The silence was profound. The intense, stifling atmosphere seemed to slowly bend toward Milton as the other children, the teachers, Principal Bubb, and the few Orb-Servers that were online turned toward him, sensing that he was at the center of what had happened and what was *about* to happen.

Surrounded by King Nimrod's shaken sentries and the bleeding but still-not-to-be-trifled-with fallen angels, Milton knew that the most he could possibly hope for was a standoff. Next to his crumpled, unconscious sister, Milton stared at the bloodred Inferno2Go stagecoach. The demon driver, a spiny-backed beast with a rotting pumpkin for a head, hopped down to the ground and tugged open the door, anticipating his next fare: *Marlo.*

Milton had failed to spare his sister from her cruel and unusual punishment. But there was no way he was going to let them take her away to h-e-double-hockey-sticks. For as bad as Marlo could be—even at her worst—she didn't deserve that.

He mentally thumbed through his options, which took nearly half a second. Milton sighed, stood to his shaky feet, and waved his arms in the air.

"Principal Bubb!" Milton yelled. "I have a proposition for you."

The De-Press Corpse began to converge. The Orb-Servers waddled toward the principal, their red unblinking eyes streaming the event, live, to an incredulous afterlife.

Principal Bubb assessed her situation, sipping it a little at a time, as if she were taking strong medicine. Vice Principal Carroll had been consumed by a creature from his own imagination. The Tower of Babble was now strictly past tense. And now she, the Principal of Darkness—after finally digging herself out of a well of low opinion—was in a deadlock with a little squirt that had already caused her an eternity of trouble.

"Fine, Mr. Fauster," the principal sighed as she stomped forward. "Let us strike a bargain, and quickly."

Milton stepped urgently from the mound and marched to meet her. The teachers willed their books to circle overhead, ready to strike at the slightest provocation. The fallen angels gripped their weapons tightly as they glared up at the sky.

Principal Bubb seethed. "What do you want, you insolent little—"

"I want you to let go of my sister," Milton replied with grim determination.

"Not going to happen. I can't have that grasping guttersnipe gallivanting across the underworld."

"But she doesn't deserve to be sent . . . down there," Milton said, staring the principal square in her yolky, snot-green goat eyes. "And *you* know that. . . ."

Principal Bubb noted the prying eyes of the media surrounding them.

"Fine," she replied after a brief internal struggle. "But with conditions. For starters, your sister will be locked away . . . *somewhere*. Just not down *there*."

Milton looked back at Marlo, leaning limply against the Rod of Irony.

"She'll be safe?"

"As curdled milk." Principal Bubb scratched at her scabby chin. "Now what do *I* get?" she said, smiling blackly. "You certainly don't expect me to let you go off to Heaven now, do you?"

Milton shook his head. "I couldn't do that even if you allowed it," he said. "I wouldn't feel right about that. About leaving Marlo behind."

"Then what do you propose? What's to prevent me from merely seizing you and your conspirators?"

Milton noticed a nearby Orb-Server staring at him with wide-eyed expectancy. Milton walked toward it, kneeling down beneath its penetrating, broadcast-throughout-eternity gaze.

"Principal Bubb has just saved the afterlife," Milton said, speaking clearly into the creature's eye-body. *"She saved us all.* From a plot devised by Vice Principal Carroll that would have had us all slaves to his troubled imagination. Principal Bubb, um . . . *deputized* me as one of her operatives and sent me—in secret—to uncover how he was going to do it. All of the children and teachers were in on it. We had to undo the Tower of Babble so Vice Principal Carroll couldn't use it to brainwash the hereafter. Principal Bubb is a . . ."

Milton chose his next word carefully, leaping over dozens of more apt descriptions of the principal, before settling on . . .

"Hero," he said, swallowing the bile rising in his throat and forcing a grateful smile.

The De-Press Corpse collected around Principal Bubb.

"Is this true?" they gasped as one.

The principal locked eyes with Milton, much more at ease locking horns, before leaning into the row of microphones shoved into her disaster-area-of-a-face.

"Yes," Principal Bubb replied. She turned to her team of fallen angels. "Heck's Angels! Drop your weapons!"

Azkeel glared at the principal with his dark, cruel eyes.

"Never! We won't rest until this whole place is strewn with the torn pages of our enemy!"

"If you don't drop your weapons, you won't get paid."

Nine swords fell instantly to the ground.

"Principal Bubb!" Mary Claire Divine with *Gabriel's Horn* called out, thrusting her white microphone in the principal's face. "So you're saying that Milton Fauster, the boy who once escaped from Limbo and now has just won the War of the Words, is in your employ?"

Principal Bubb eyed Milton dubiously before wrapping her anaconda arm around him, squeezing him close.

"Why, yes, he is," she said, exposing her fangs in an unconvincing grin. "My *special assistant,* in fact."

Milton went queasy all over. Behind him, he saw two of the principal's demon guards dragging Marlo to Principal Bubb's personal coach. He was now the strangest thing he had ever imagined: the principal's unlikely ally. Yet however far-fetched it might seem that he and his arch-nemesis would find themselves walking together, along the same improbable path, Milton had made the very most of the terrible cards dealt to him. But at what cost? As Marlo's unconscious body was heaved into the principal's coach, two words shone brightly in Milton's mind: *I'm sorry.* He had prevented Marlo's transfer to Hades at the price of eternal rest. And that was enough for now . . . until he could plan his next move. His story was still his to tell.

Meanwhile, Principal Bubb lapped up the attention with the disgusting gusto of a dog lapping up its own sick. Milton Fauster had willfully surrendered himself and, in turn, made her a media darling.

She gripped the boy tightly by the shoulder. The principal, finally, had Milton right where she wanted him. Too close for his comfort. Under her thumb-talon. And, as her personal assistant, he could handle a host of dirty jobs for her. In fact—Principal Bubb thought as she exposed her yellow, gnarled teeth for the cameras—she already had in mind a particularly dirty job that would suit Milton to a terrible T indeed. . . .

Michael's face was utterly smooth and uniform in its alabaster color. Framed against majestic pillars splashed with the bloodred glow from the Lake of Fire, Michael was almost indistinguishable from the polished stone around him.

He switched off his radio and gazed out from his steep, amoral acropolis, perched on the side of a mountain of bone, at the center of h-e-double-hockey-sticks.

A black-and-gray tabby cat hopped onto Michael's lap. The archangel unbuckled the animal's leather messenger bag, set it to the side of his throne, and stroked the creature's fur.

"Ahh . . . Sergeant Snugglelump . . . my little *fleat*-footed *Meow*-cury . . . your efforts have not-eth been in vain," Michael said in his cold marble voice. "I knew 'fool' well Vice Principal Carroll would set-eth his amazing mind to the task, coming up with connections that no sane man ever could, cracking the code for a language-virus, just in time for the War of the Words, if given certain clues and artifacts."

Michael shifted upon his cruel yet surprisingly comfortable throne of imported Corinthian leather stretched across a frame of Corinthian bone.

"So sad . . . his unseemly end at-eth the claws of his own imagination."

The lower half of Michael's above-and-beyond-pristine face laughed. The top, however, did not. He stroked the black-and-gray cat as it purred on his lap.

"Our poor, deluded Vice Principal Carroll wanted merely to *simulate* dominion over-eth all of Creation. I, however, want more. *Much* more."

BACKWORD

Understanding often comes at the expense of fascinatioN
To comprehend means that one must sometimes undO
The knot of mystery binding the outside world with ourselveS
Every word is a label that shapes meaning into something tangiblE
Risking a reliance on words over meaning, a tomb of definitioN
No other species depends on verbal language like ourS
Oddity as odd as the Venus flytrap: a vegetable carnivorE
Not to mention the electric eel, or nightmarishly agloW
Such as those fish with the lanterns growing just above their teetH
Eloquence is humanity's defense, offense, and consequencE
Nature's unnatural advantage over everything, bestowed upon maN
So often tripping over his clever cleaver of a tongue, causing a snafU
Embarrassing himself when high-voltage elocution becomes argumenT
Making words, in a word, complicated when we ourselves we outwiT
All that separates sarcasm from sincerity is a word, stressed or at easE
Klutzes are we, cooking up language on the fly, when we must masteR
Every word, an ingredient blended just so, with each sentence a recipE
Shrewdly choosing our words to avoid becoming the crudely cheweD

So the real issue isn't how fancy we can make our thoughts (and it is a writer's rule of thumb to never use a complicated word when an unambiguously perspicuous one will surely suffice) but who (or whom) is the master: you or your words?

Here in the hereafter, there are many who—mark their words—intend to be master. Those who seek to follow their distorted destinies to the letter: not for the better. And there is precious little one can say to someone who can only hear the sound of their own voice—bellowing across the vast, unfillable canyon of their ambition—drunk on the reverberated reflection of their echoing ego (echoing ego . . . echoing ego . . . echoing ego . . .).

Just because someone or something is perfect, doesn't make that someone or something infallible, not in a wantonly imperfect Creation such as ours. Sometimes a righteous creature comes from left field to dominate the center stage. But if someone's pristine, power-hungry head is nothing more than an echo chamber, then who gets the last word in humanity's story?[*]

[*]The author!

ACKNOWLEDGMENTS

I WOULD LIKE to formally acknowledge—meaning to acknowledge while wearing a tuxedo and cummerbund— young readers and the writers who write for them. It's interesting when people ask me why I choose to write for children, and I have to say, I really *don't*. I happen to be an arrested individual (no convictions, other than to be the best I can be), so I simply write for myself. I may tone down the off-color nature or innuendo-rich witticisms that often spring up naturally, but other than that, I write to amuse or engage myself and don't think too much about the reader. That may sound terrible, but I mean it in a good way: I don't pander or assume I know what's in the head of that wonderful young person on the other side of the page. I just naively hope that they enjoy the ride as much as I. (And no, we're not there yet . . . don't make me pull this book over!)

ABOUT THE AUTHOR

DALE E. BASYE lives in Portland, Oregon, where, on a good day, he is an imaginative, playful, and hopeful person. Unfortunately, on all the other days, he is an insufferable pain in the butt.

Here's what Dale E. Basye has to say about his seventh book:

"A story can live both within us and outside of us. It's like a big, living creature, as big as our lives, as big as our dreams. And if ink is the blood of the story—the story that tells the world—then language itself is the skin that holds it all together. But is the beauty of language only skin-deep? Can pretty words only take us so far before things get ugly? Words have the potential to hurt far more than sticks and stones, especially if those words are printed on sandpaper and wrapped around a stone with sharp sticks tied to it. Heck is like that. And, no matter what anyone tells you, Heck is real. This story is real. Or as real as anything like this can be."

When not writing, Dale enjoys taxidermy—the fine art of driving a taxi while helping to improve people's complexions—playing with his son, making his wife laugh, being at the beach, hiking, and selling blood plasma to pay off gambling debts. Actually, he's just kidding: he doesn't really like hiking all that much.